Last Exit to
FERAL
LITTLE TOWN. UNDERGROUND.

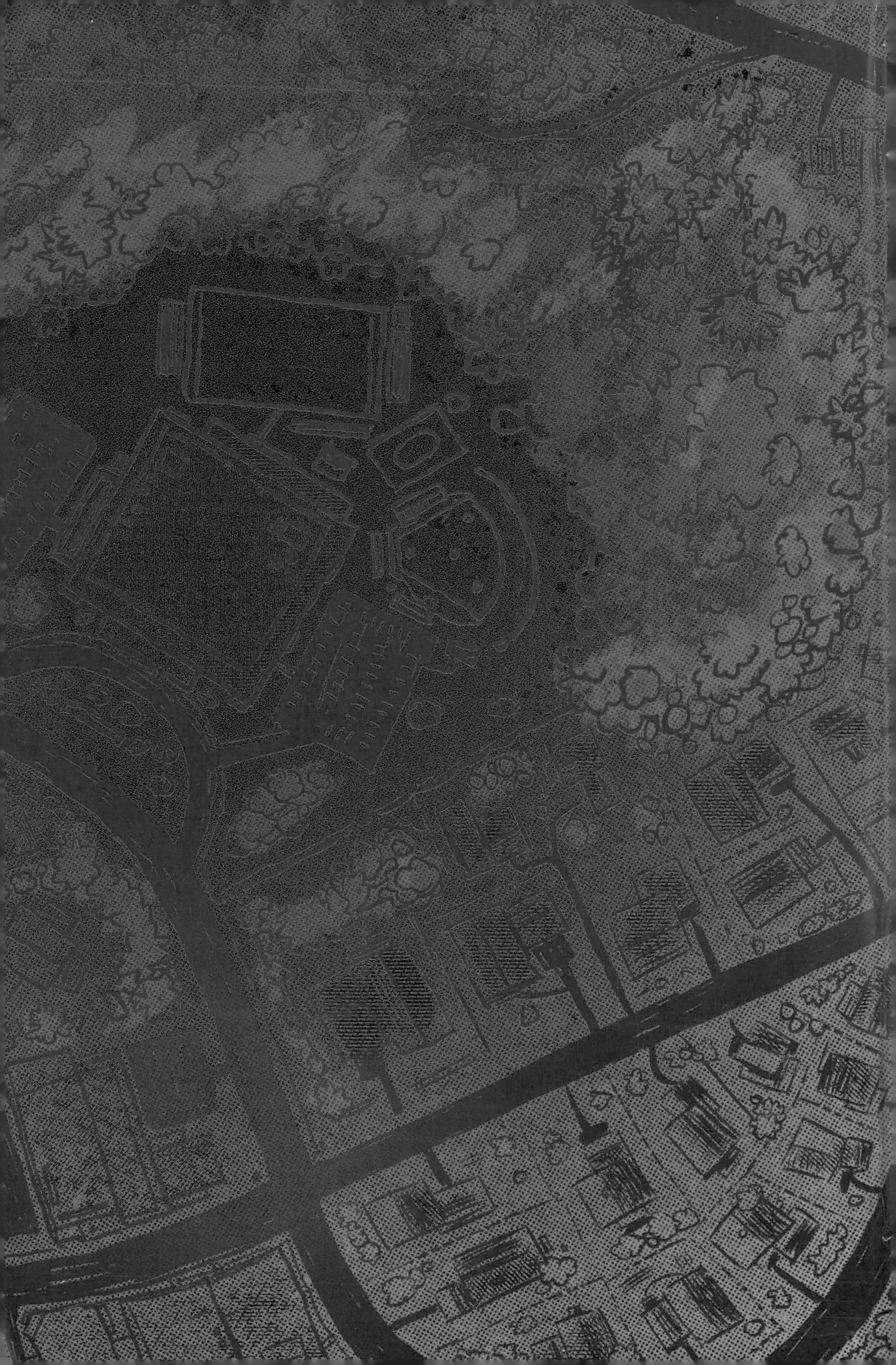

Last Exit to FERAL

LITTLE TOWN. UNDERGROUND.

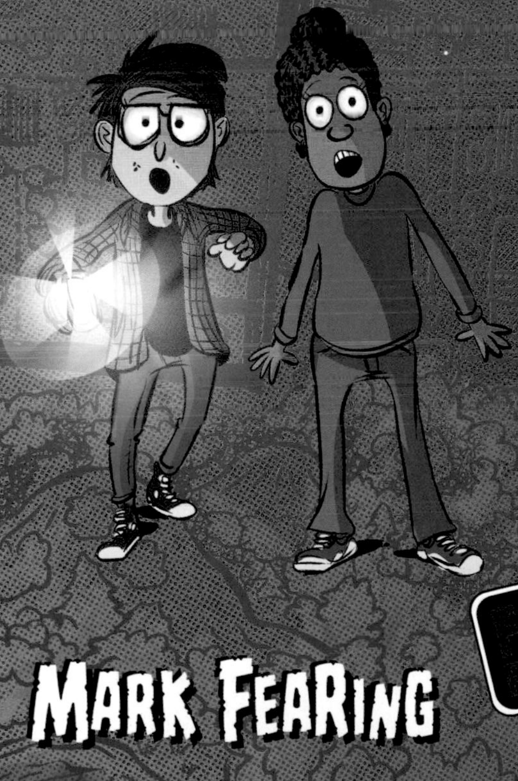

[redacted]

MARK FEARING

HOLIDAY HOUSE NEW YORK

For Jodie, Vickie, Scott, Jerry, and Dolores. And everyone else who lives in Feral.

HOLIDAY HOUSE is registered in the U.S. Patent and Trademark Office.

Printed and bound in May 2023 at C&C Offset, Shenzhen, China.

The artwork was created with pencil and finished with digital ink and paint.

www.holidayhouse.com

First Edition

10 9 8 7 6 5 4 3 2 1

Library of Congress Cataloging-in-Publication Data is available.

ISBN: 978-0-8234-4866-1 (hardcover)

ISBN: 978-0-8234-5601-7 (paperback)

CONTENTS

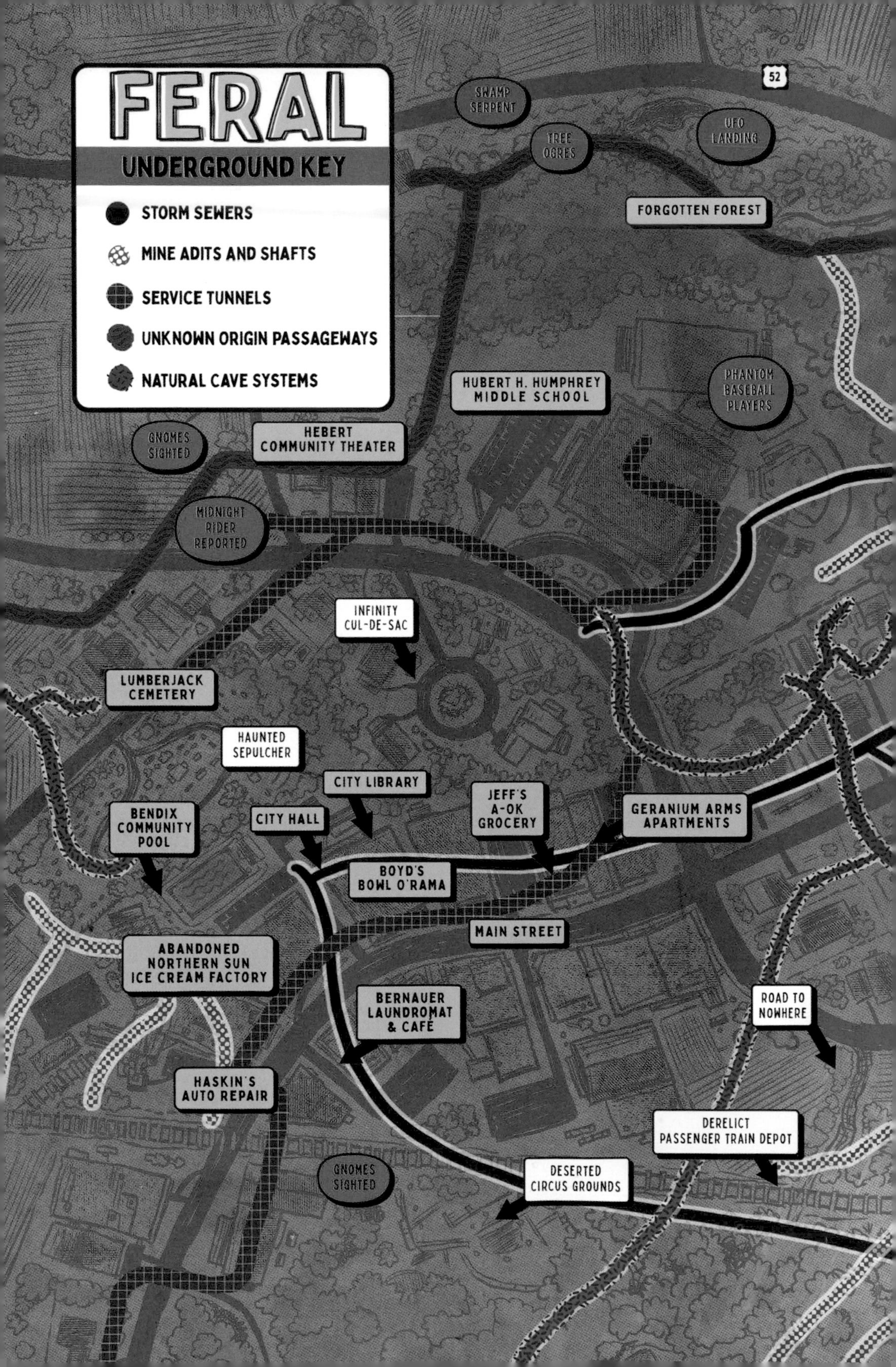
FERAL
UNDERGROUND KEY
STORM SEWERS
MINE ADITS AND SHAFTS
SERVICE TUNNELS
UNKNOWN ORIGIN PASSAGEWAYS
NATURAL CAVE SYSTEMS
52
SWAMP SERPENT
TREE OGRES
UFO LANDING
FORGOTTEN FOREST
HUBERT H. HUMPHREY MIDDLE SCHOOL
PHANTOM BASEBALL PLAYERS
GNOMES SIGHTED
HEBERT COMMUNITY THEATER
MIDNIGHT RIDER REPORTED
INFINITY CUL-DE-SAC
LUMBERJACK CEMETERY
HAUNTED SEPULCHER
CITY LIBRARY
JEFF'S A-OK GROCERY
GERANIUM ARMS APARTMENTS
BENDIX COMMUNITY POOL
CITY HALL
BOYD'S BOWL O'RAMA
MAIN STREET
ABANDONED NORTHERN SUN ICE CREAM FACTORY
BERNAUER LAUNDROMAT & CAFÉ
ROAD TO NOWHERE
HASKIN'S AUTO REPAIR
DERELICT PASSENGER TRAIN DEPOT
GNOMES SIGHTED
DESERTED CIRCUS GROUNDS

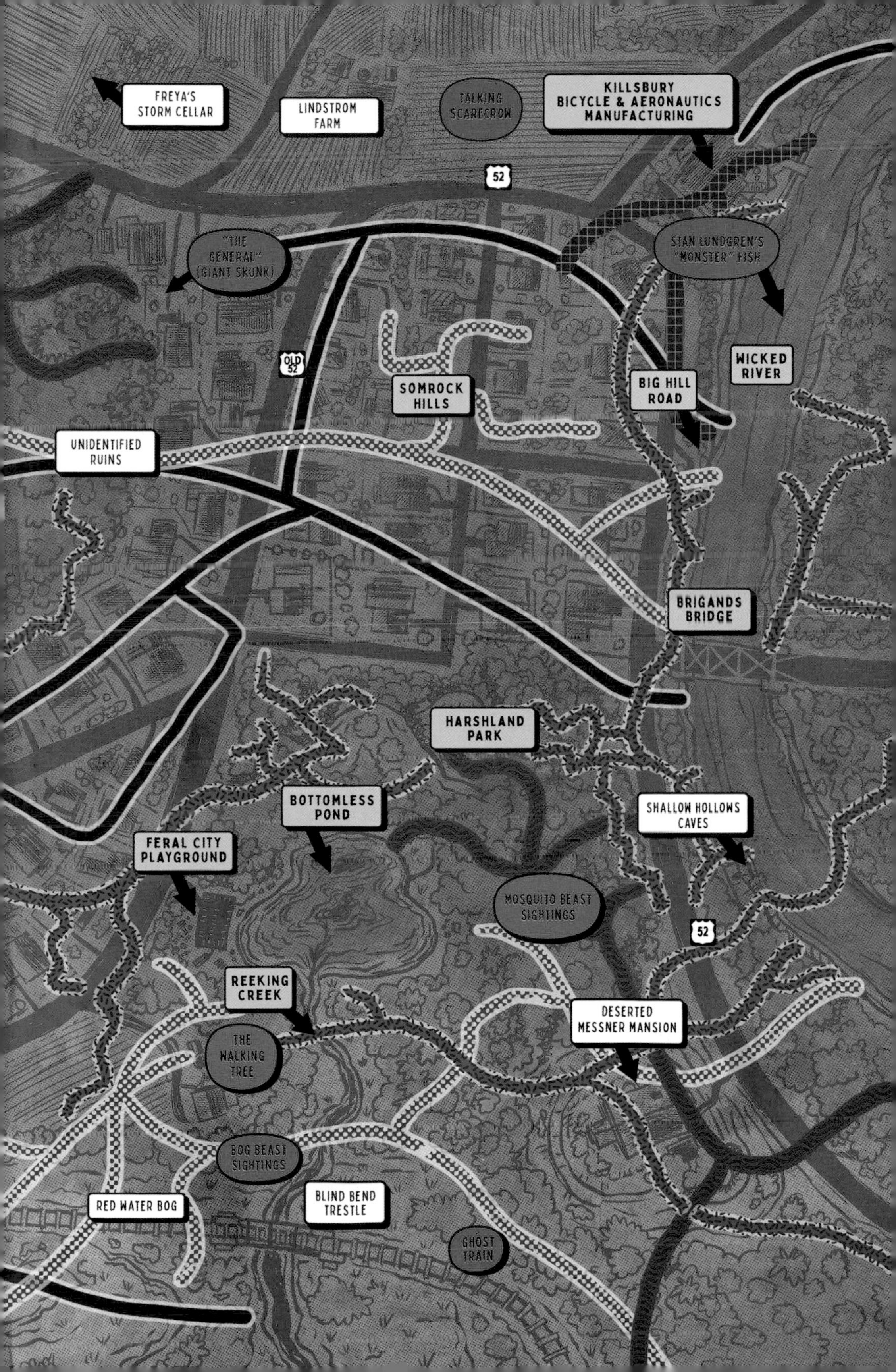
FREYA'S STORM CELLAR
LINDSTROM FARM
TALKING SCARECROW
KILLSBURY BICYCLE & AERONAUTICS MANUFACTURING
52
"THE GENERAL" (GIANT SKUNK)
STAN LUNDGREN'S "MONSTER" FISH
OLD 52
SOMROCK HILLS
BIG HILL ROAD
WICKED RIVER
UNIDENTIFIED RUINS
BRIGANDS BRIDGE
HARSHLAND PARK
BOTTOMLESS POND
SHALLOW HOLLOWS CAVES
FERAL CITY PLAYGROUND
MOSQUITO BEAST SIGHTINGS
52
REEKING CREEK
DESERTED MESSNER MANSION
THE WALKING TREE
BOG BEAST SIGHTINGS
RED WATER BOG
BLIND BEND TRESTLE
GHOST TRAIN

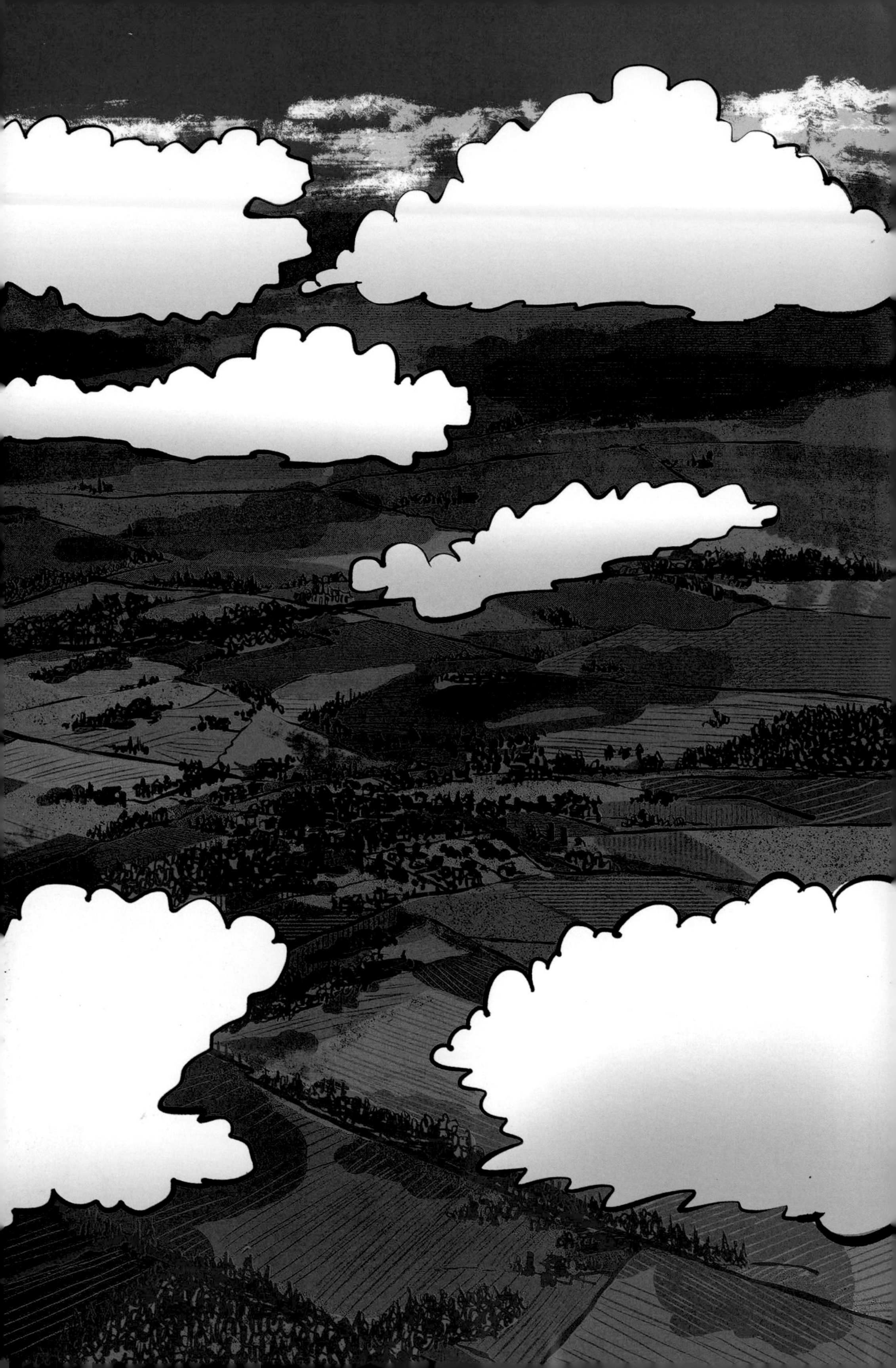

PROLOGUE

Lillian Veronica Bushkin (age 8)
& Ichabod Messner (age 10)

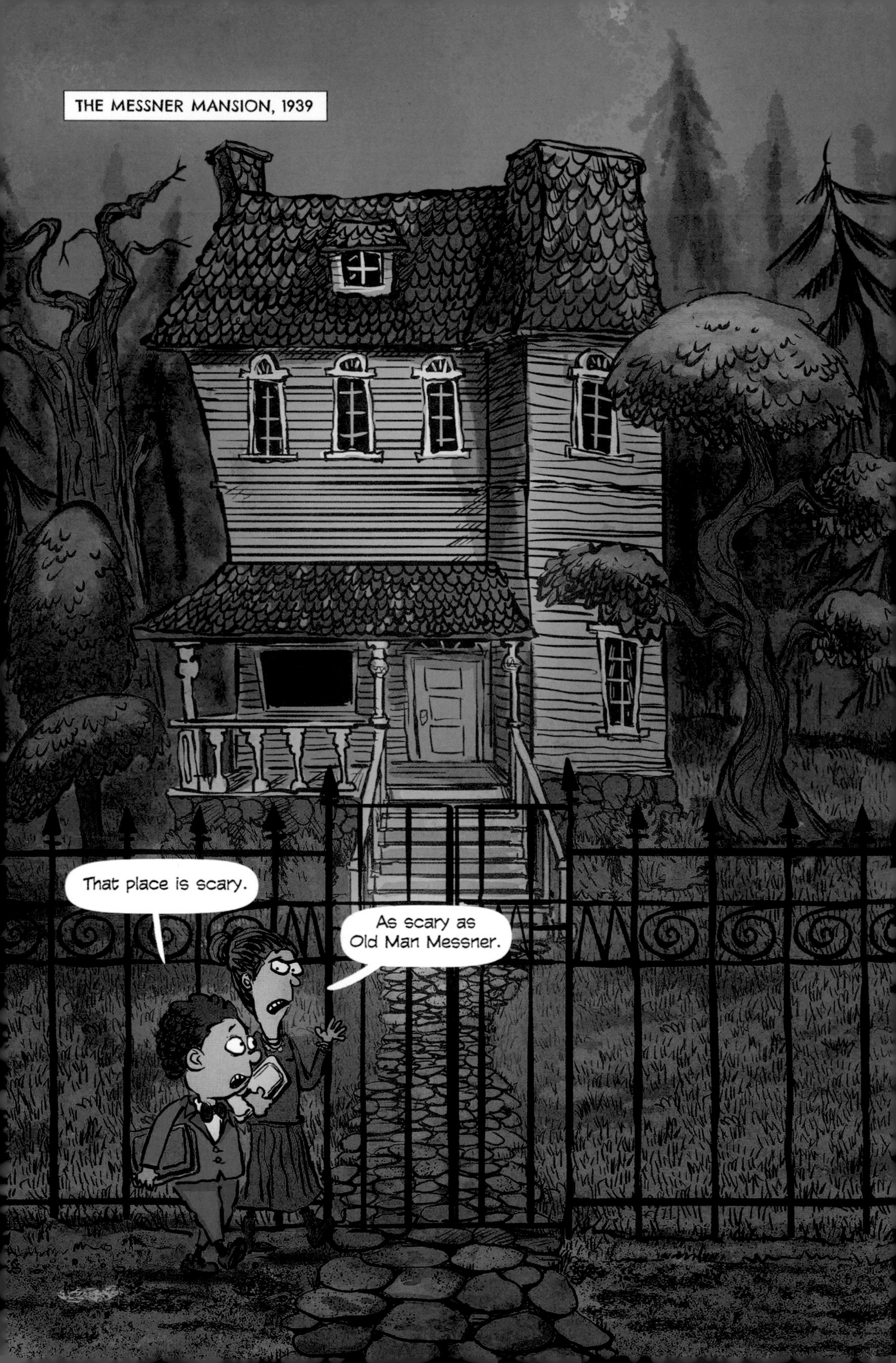
THE MESSNER MANSION, 1939
That place is scary.
As scary as Old Man Messner.

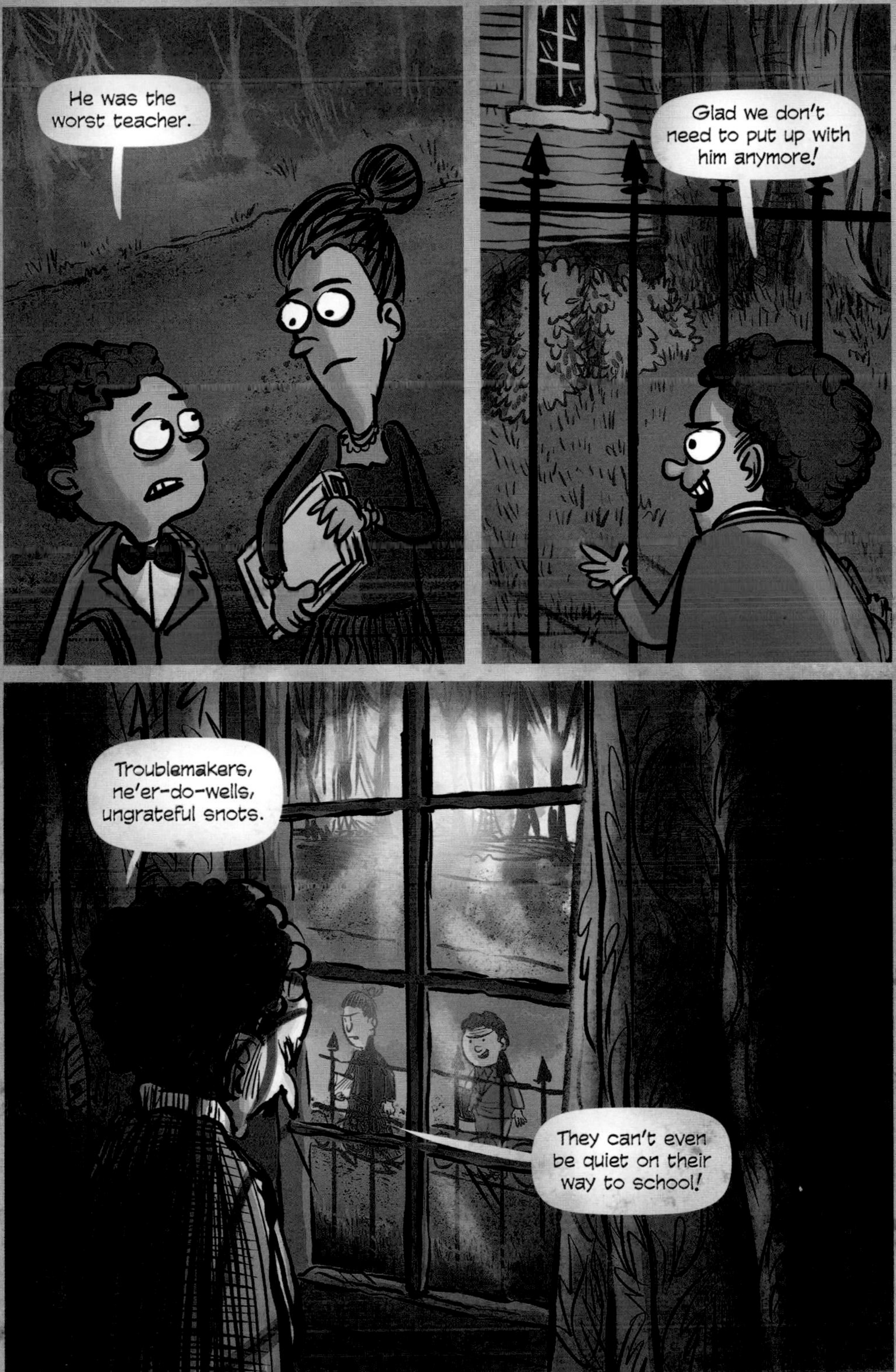
He was the worst teacher.
Glad we don't need to put up with him anymore!
Troublemakers, ne'er-do-wells, ungrateful snots.
They can't even be quiet on their way to school!

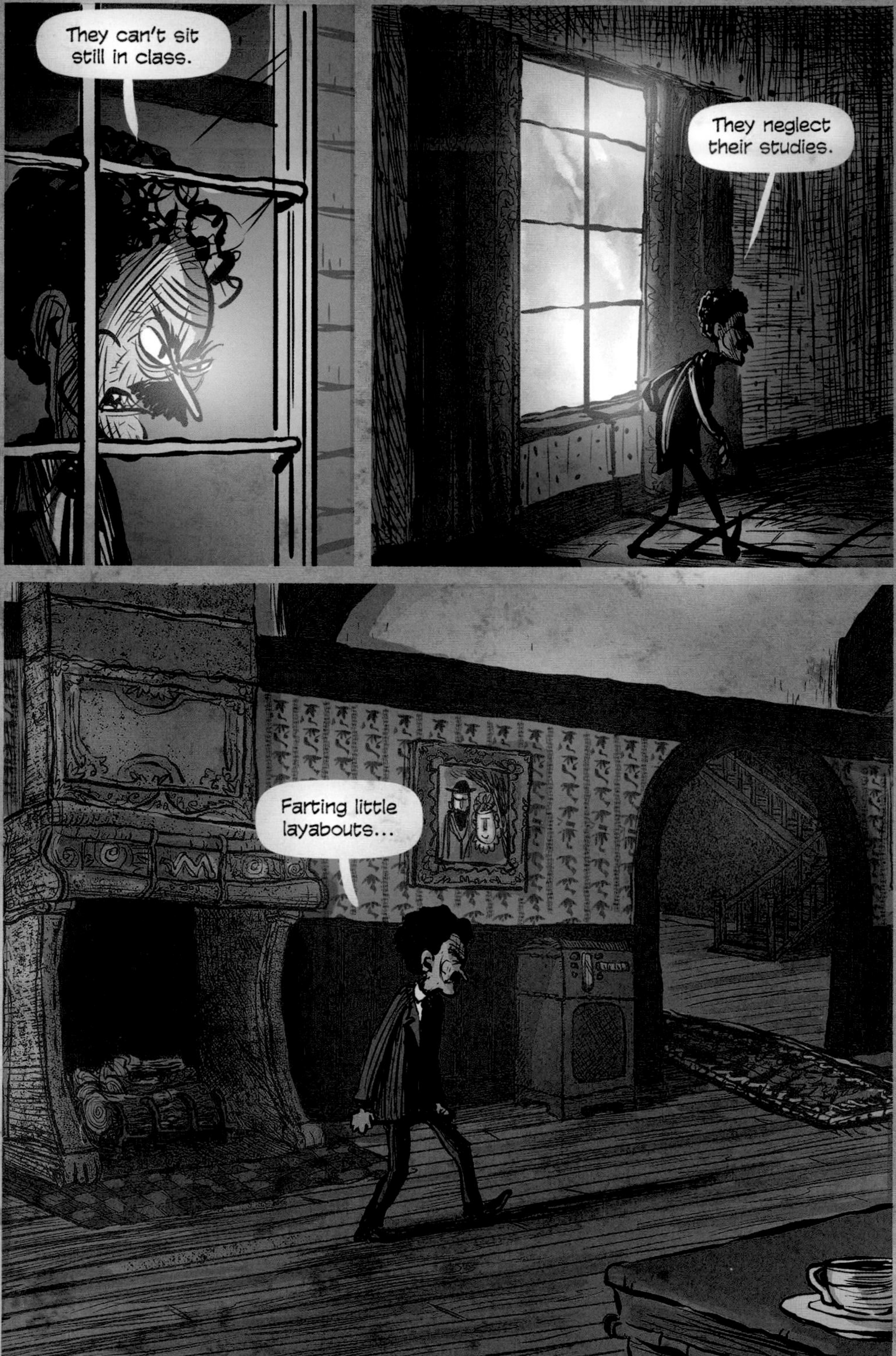
They can't sit still in class.
They neglect their studies.
Farting little layabouts...

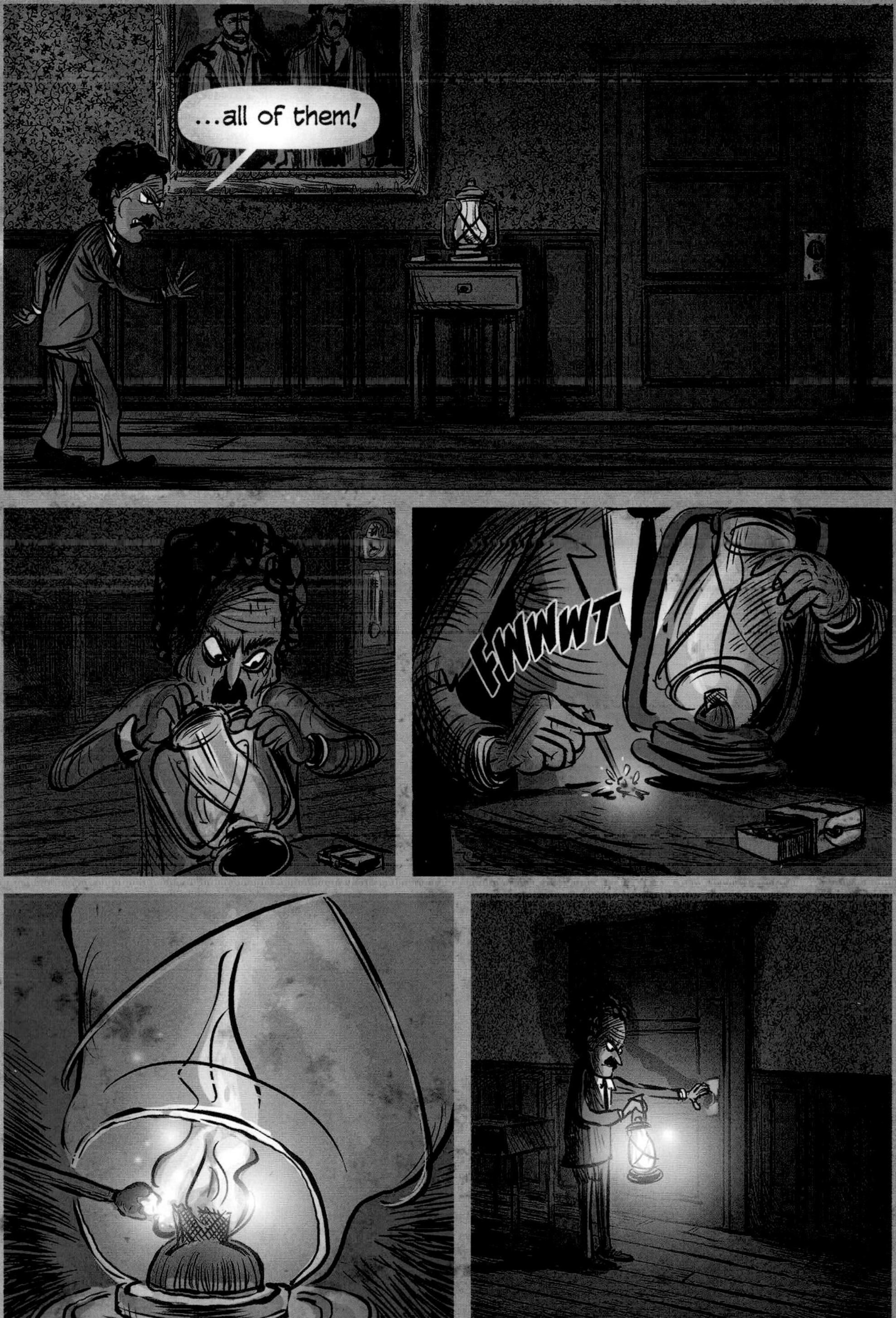
...all of them!
FWWWT

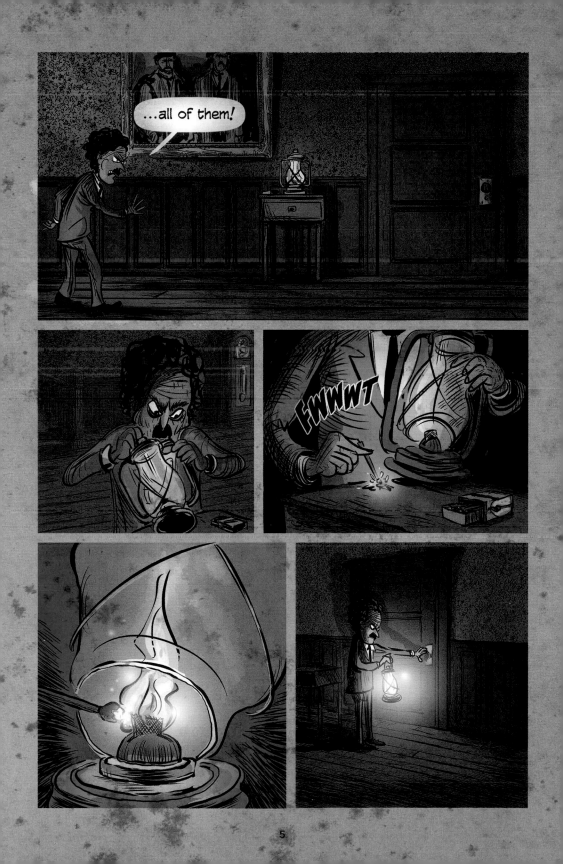

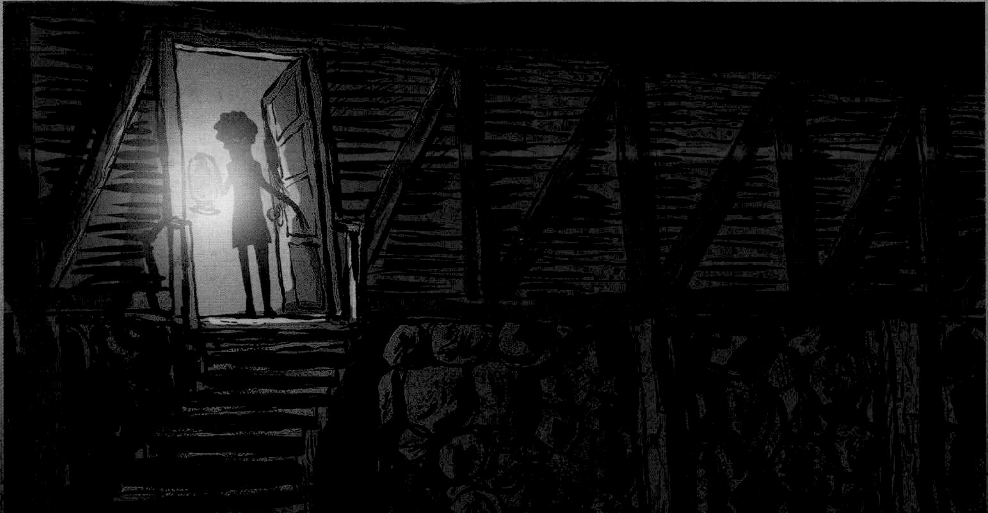

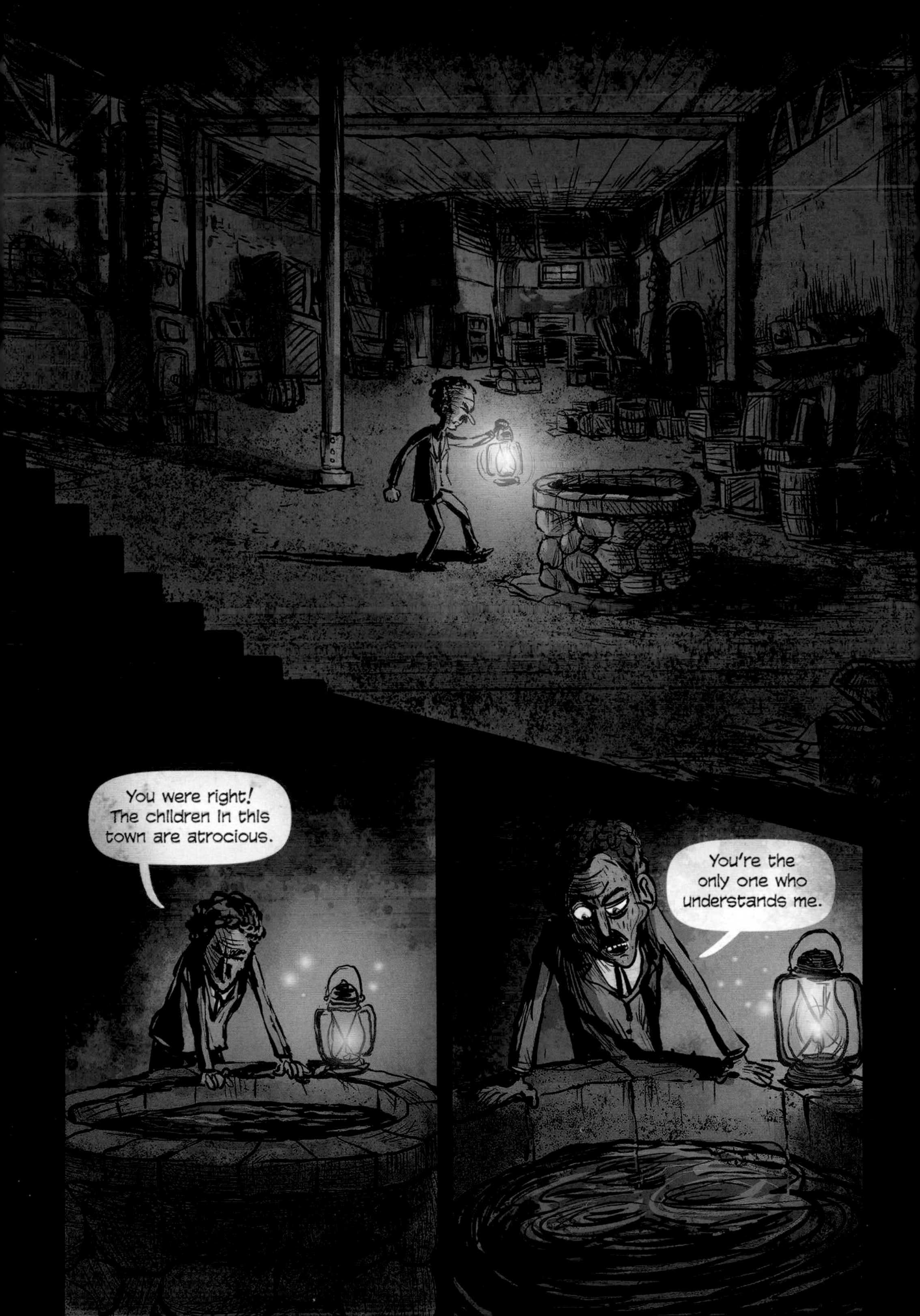
You were right! The children in this town are atrocious.
You're the only one who understands me.

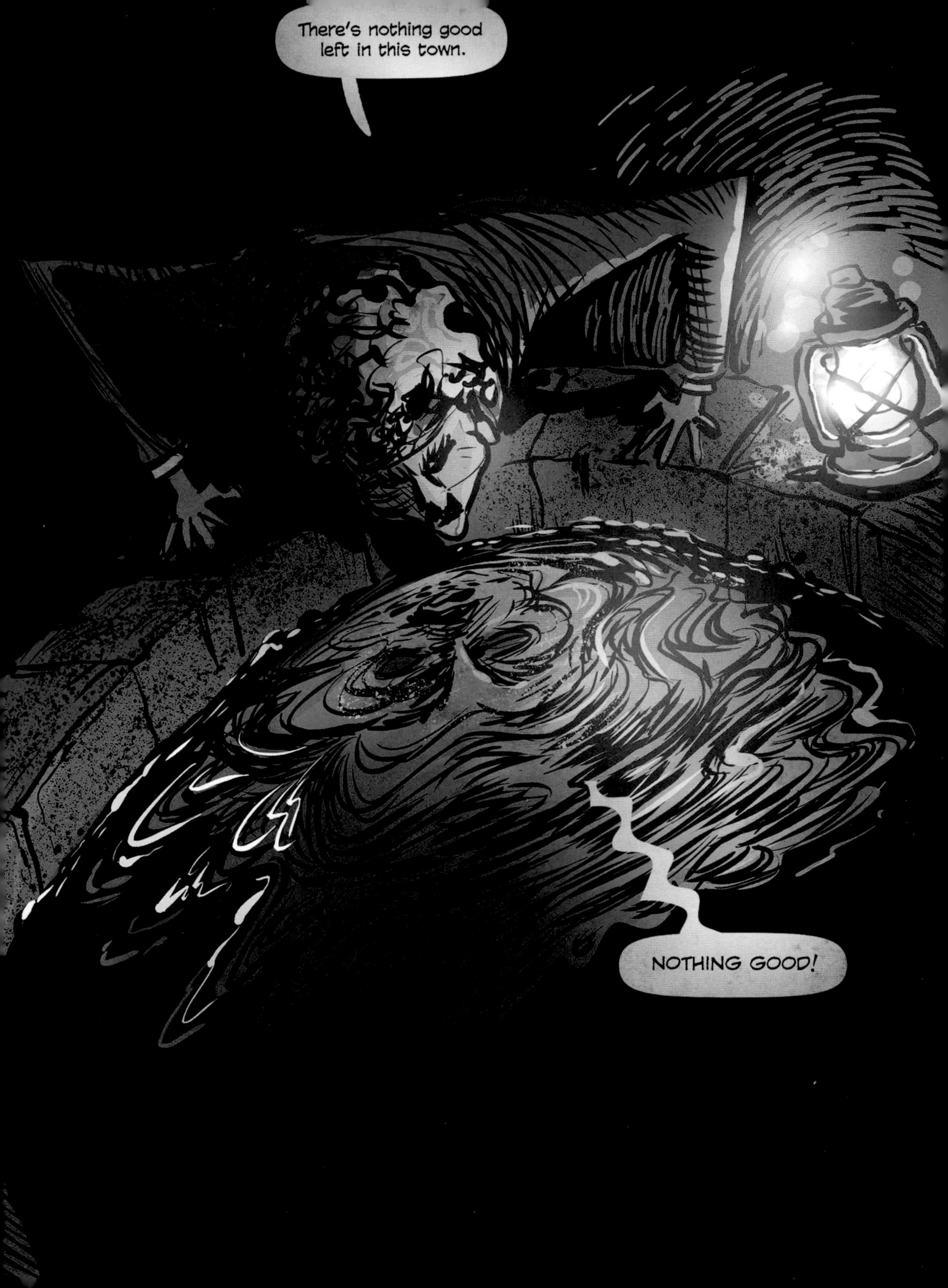
There's nothing good left in this town.
NOTHING GOOD!

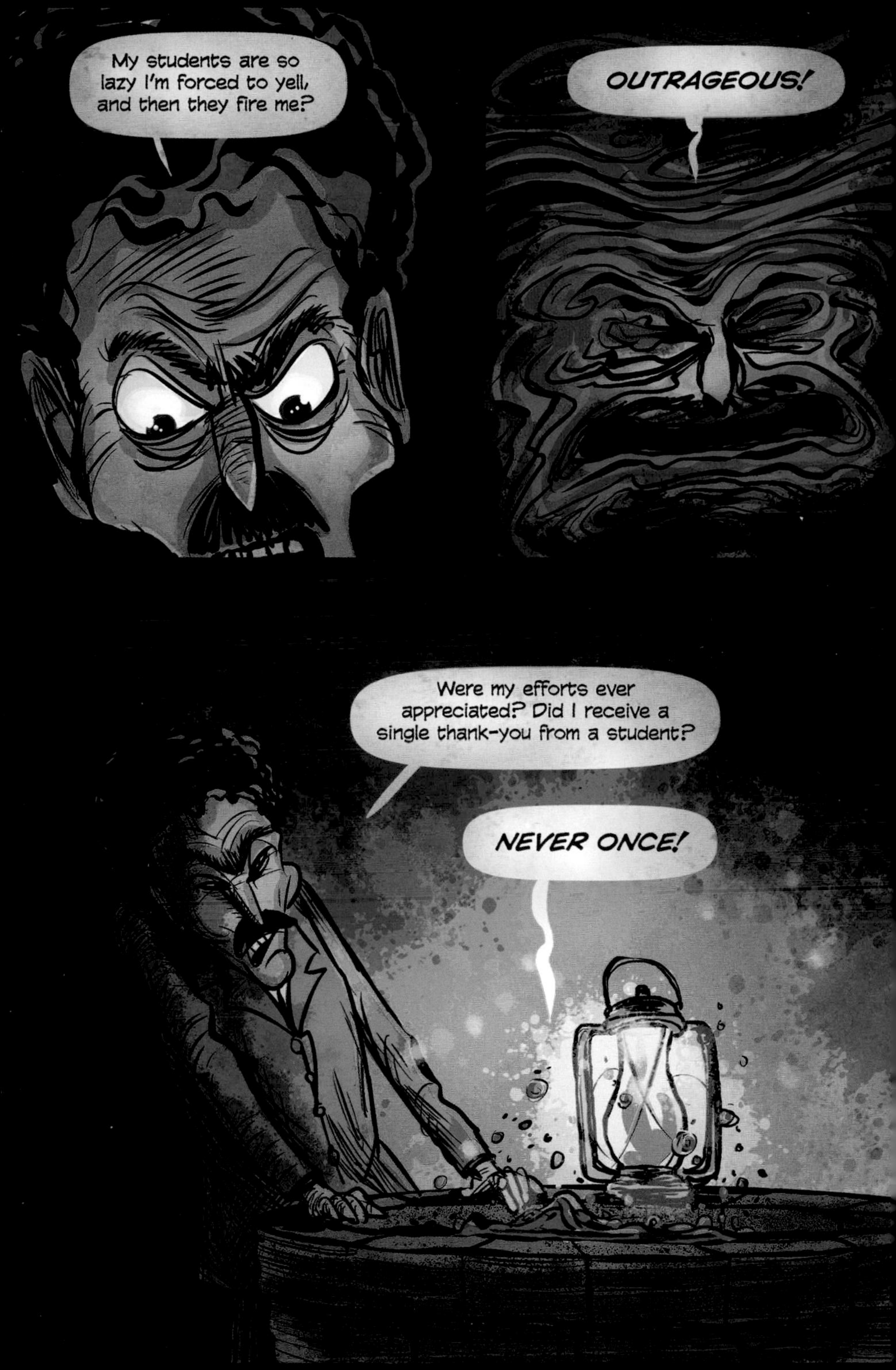
My students are so lazy I'm forced to yell, and then they fire me?
OUTRAGEOUS!
Were my efforts ever appreciated? Did I receive a single thank-you from a student?
NEVER ONCE!

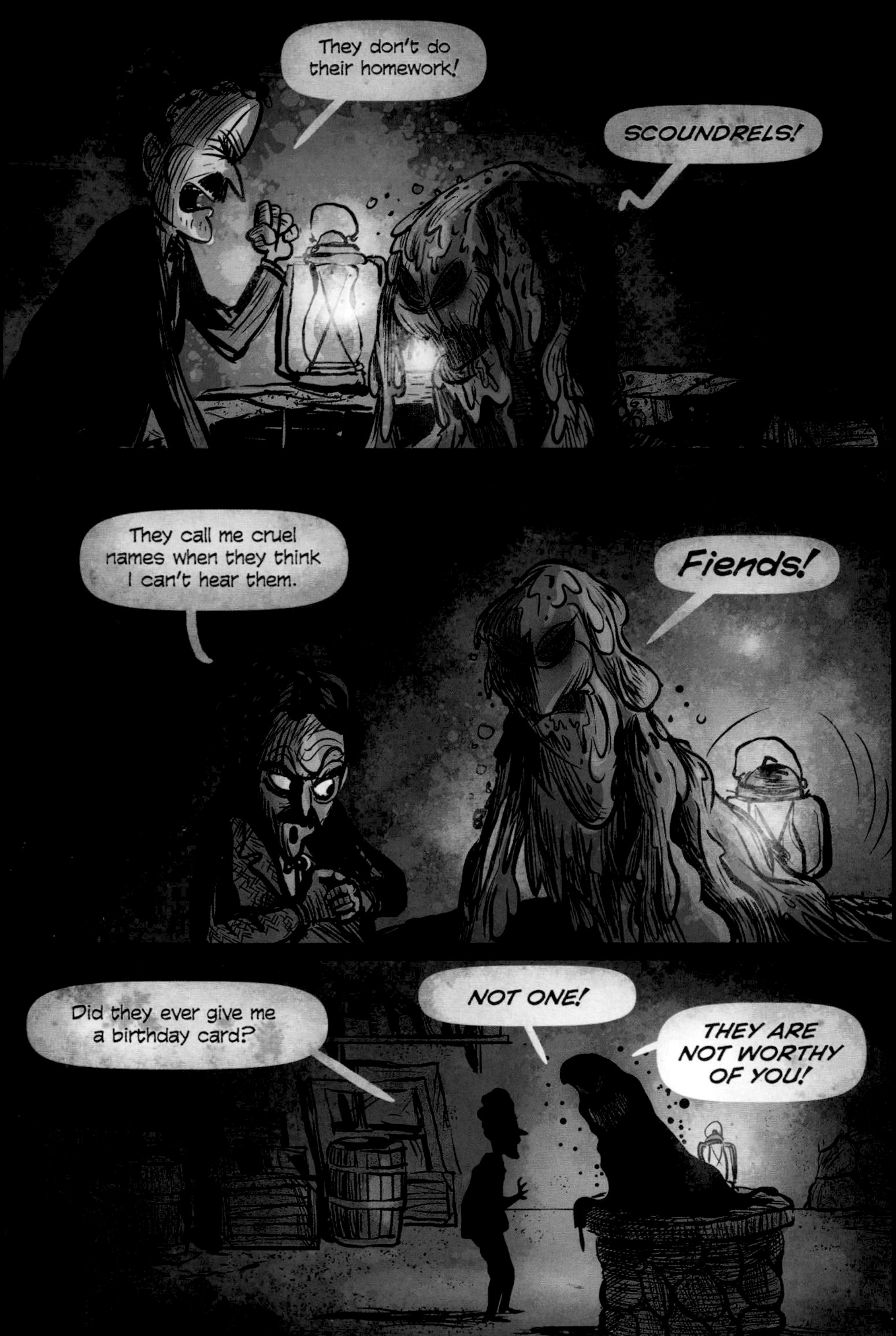
They don't do their homework!
SCOUNDRELS!
They call me cruel names when they think I can't hear them.
Fiends!
Did they ever give me a birthday card?
NOT ONE!
THEY ARE NOT WORTHY OF YOU!

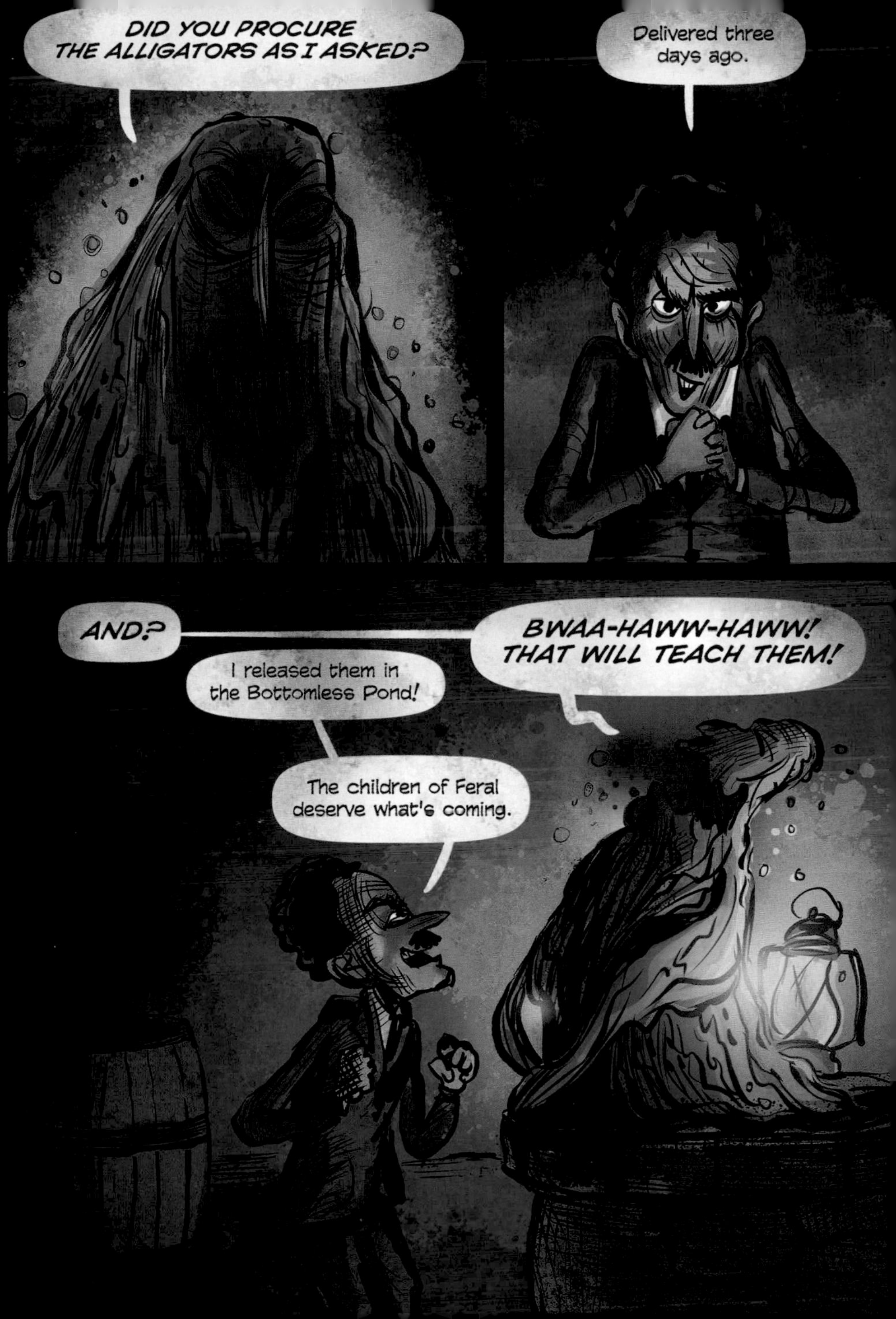
DID YOU PROCURE THE ALLIGATORS AS I ASKED?
Delivered three days ago.
AND?
I released them in the Bottomless Pond!
The children of Feral deserve what's coming.
BWAA-HAWW-HAWW! THAT WILL TEACH THEM!

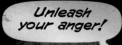

Unleash your anger!

I hereby curse this town. Anything that goes bump in the night will be welcome here!

I swear with all my anger, all my hate, I will have my revenge and one day...

...I *will* bring this town down!

BLARBBB

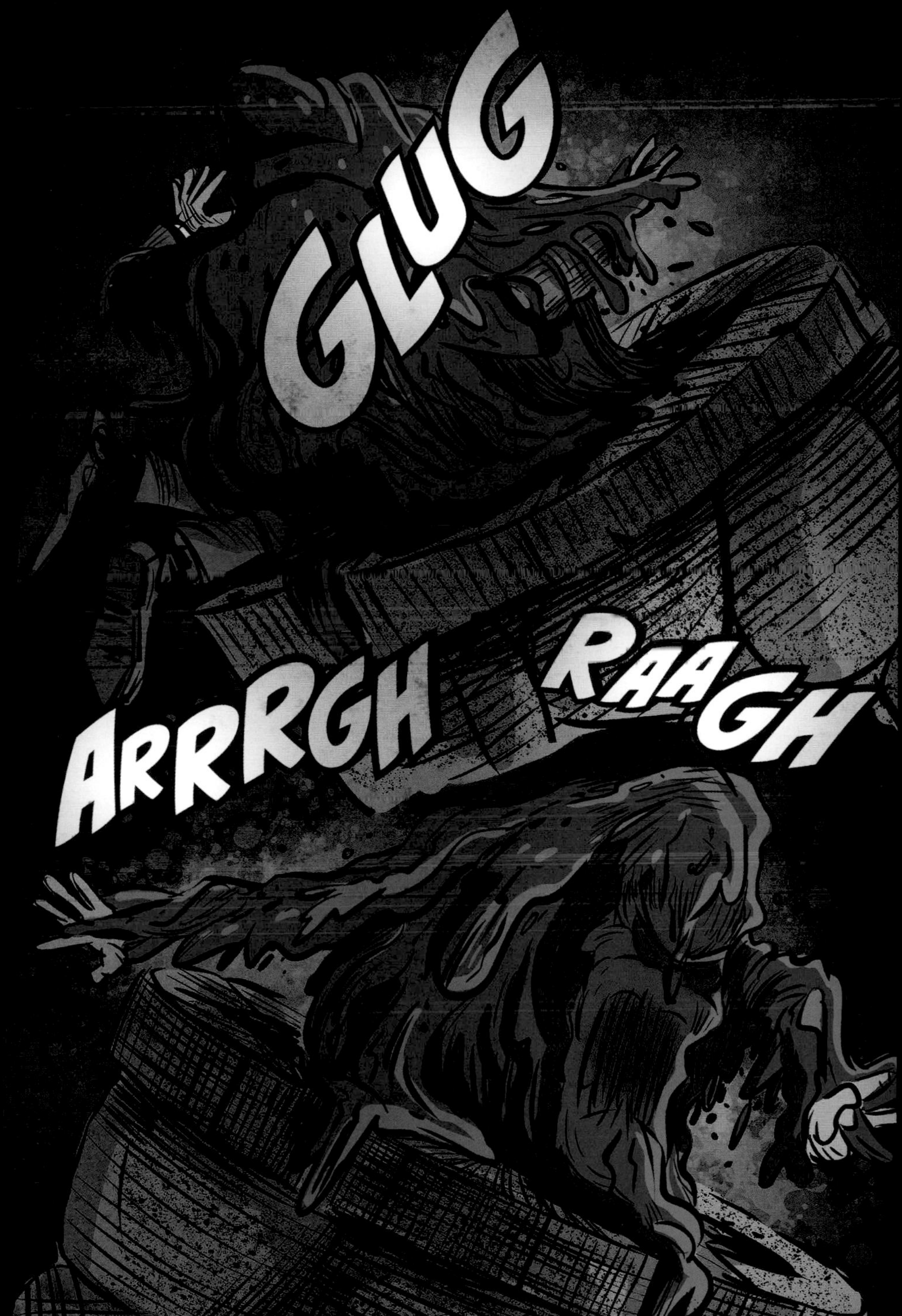
GLUG
ARRRGH
RAAGH

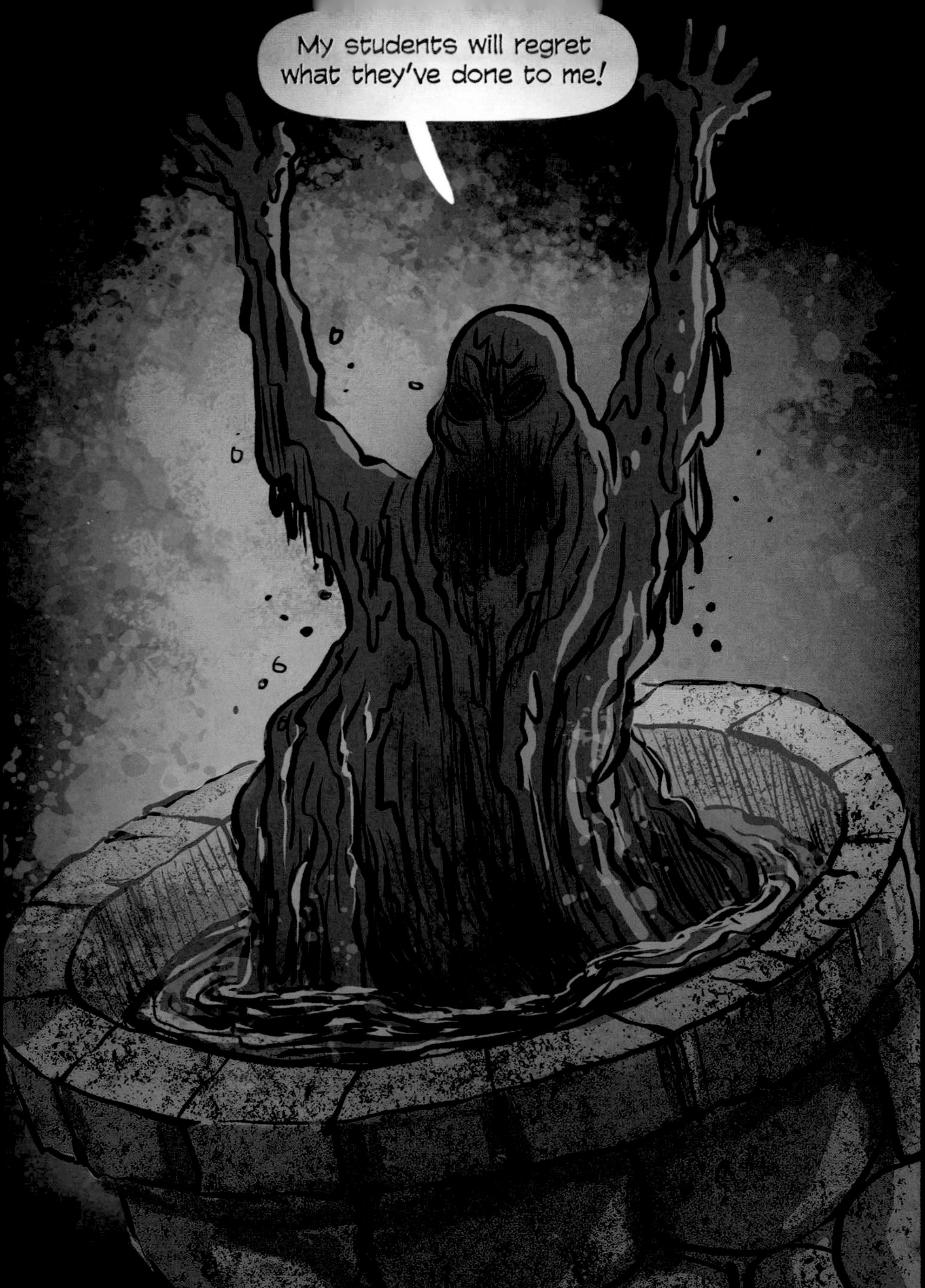
My students will regret what they've done to me!

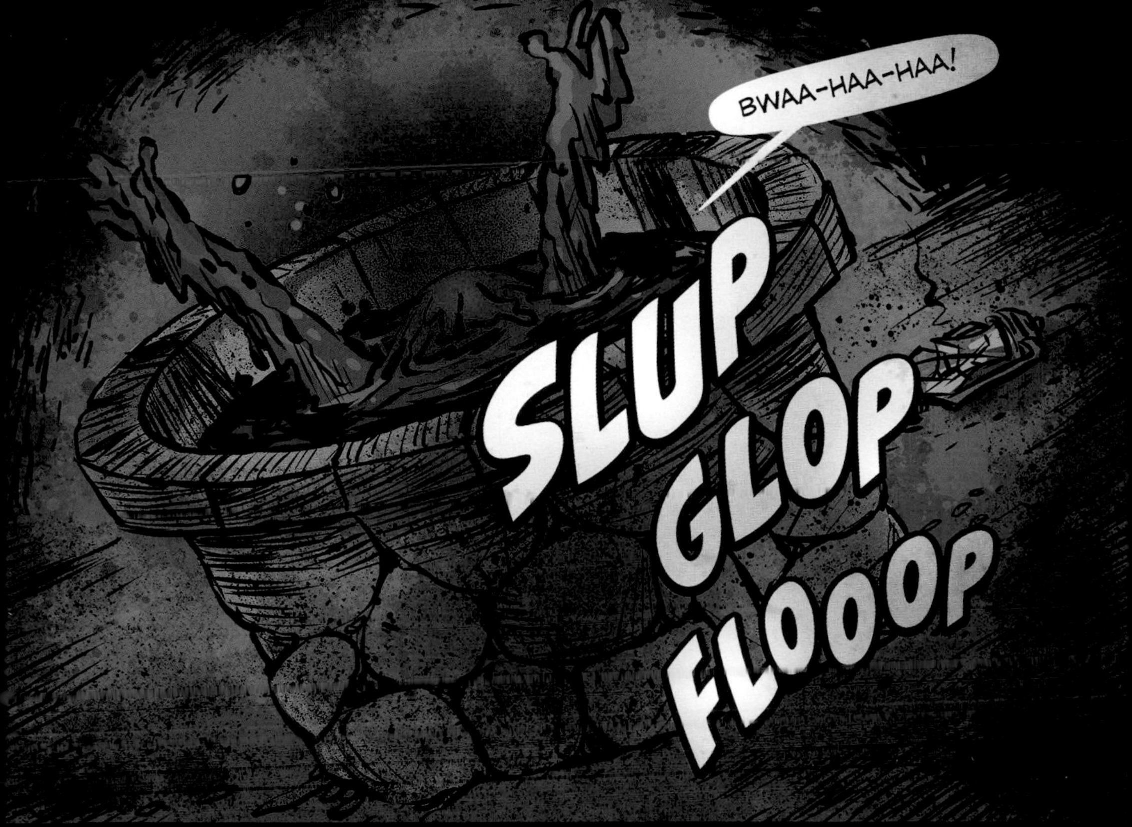
BWAA-HAA-HAA!
SLUP
GLOP
FLOOOP
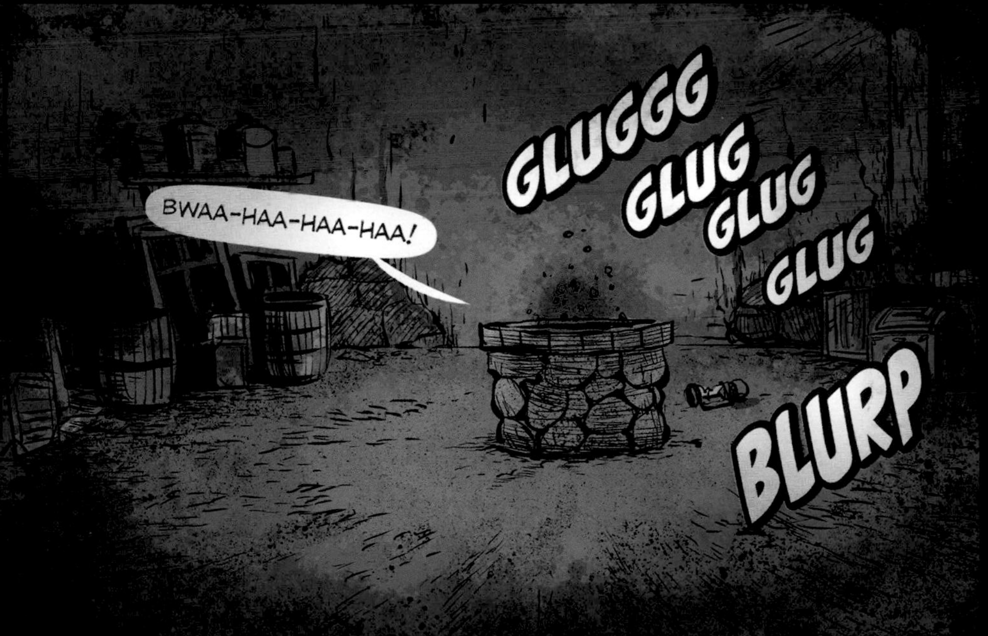
BWAA-HAA-HAA-HAA!
GLUGGG
GLUG
GLUG
GLUG
BLURP

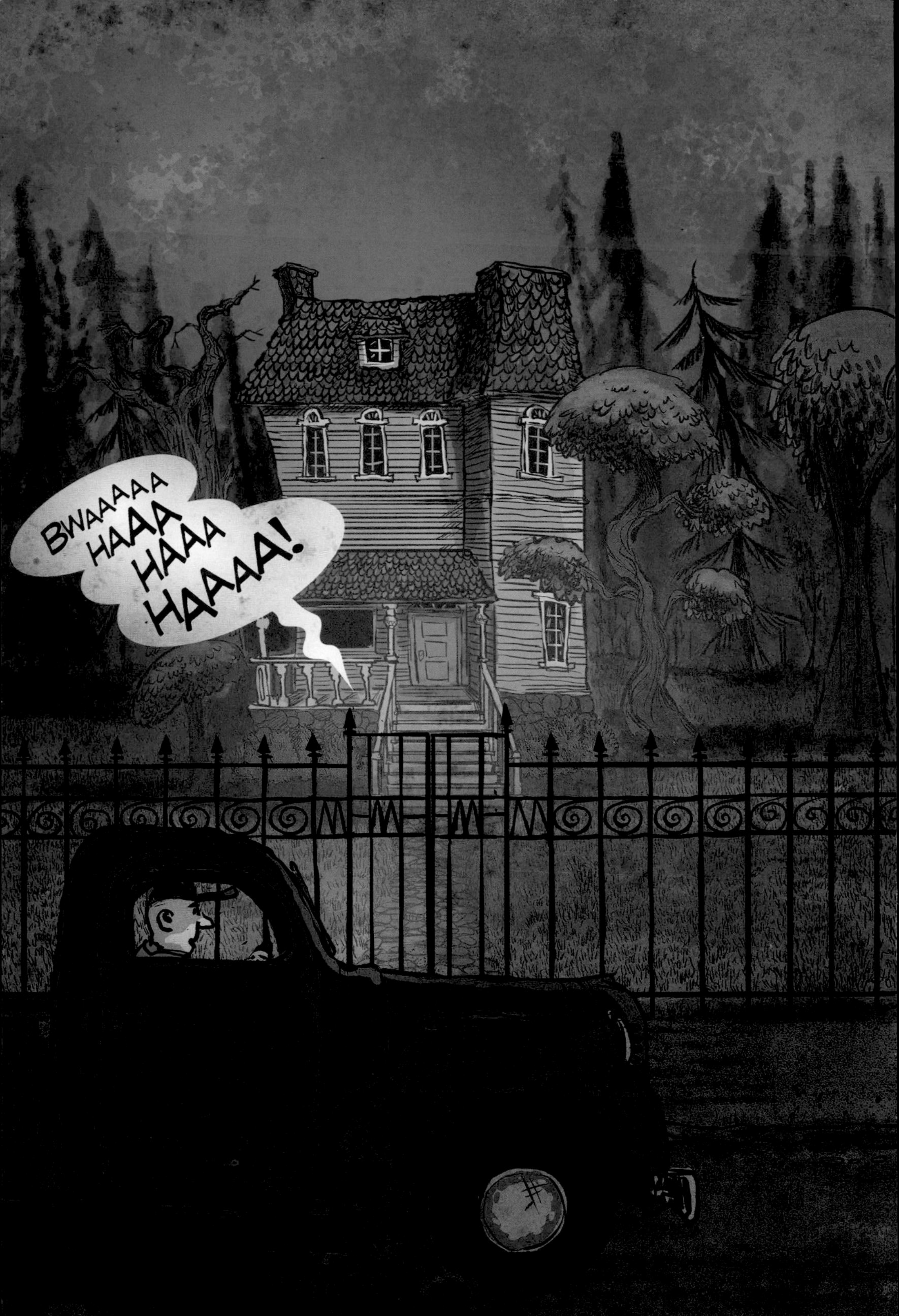
BWAAAAA HAAA HAAA HAAAA!

CHAPTER 1

VISIT FERAL
THE CAMPING CAPITAL!

Can
Har

Doe—
Hasn't stopped raining
in 4 days. Strange
noises at night. Look
forward to getting home
soon—
        Jerry

Dolores Kulhavek
2800 Ammate Av.
Sandia NM 47105

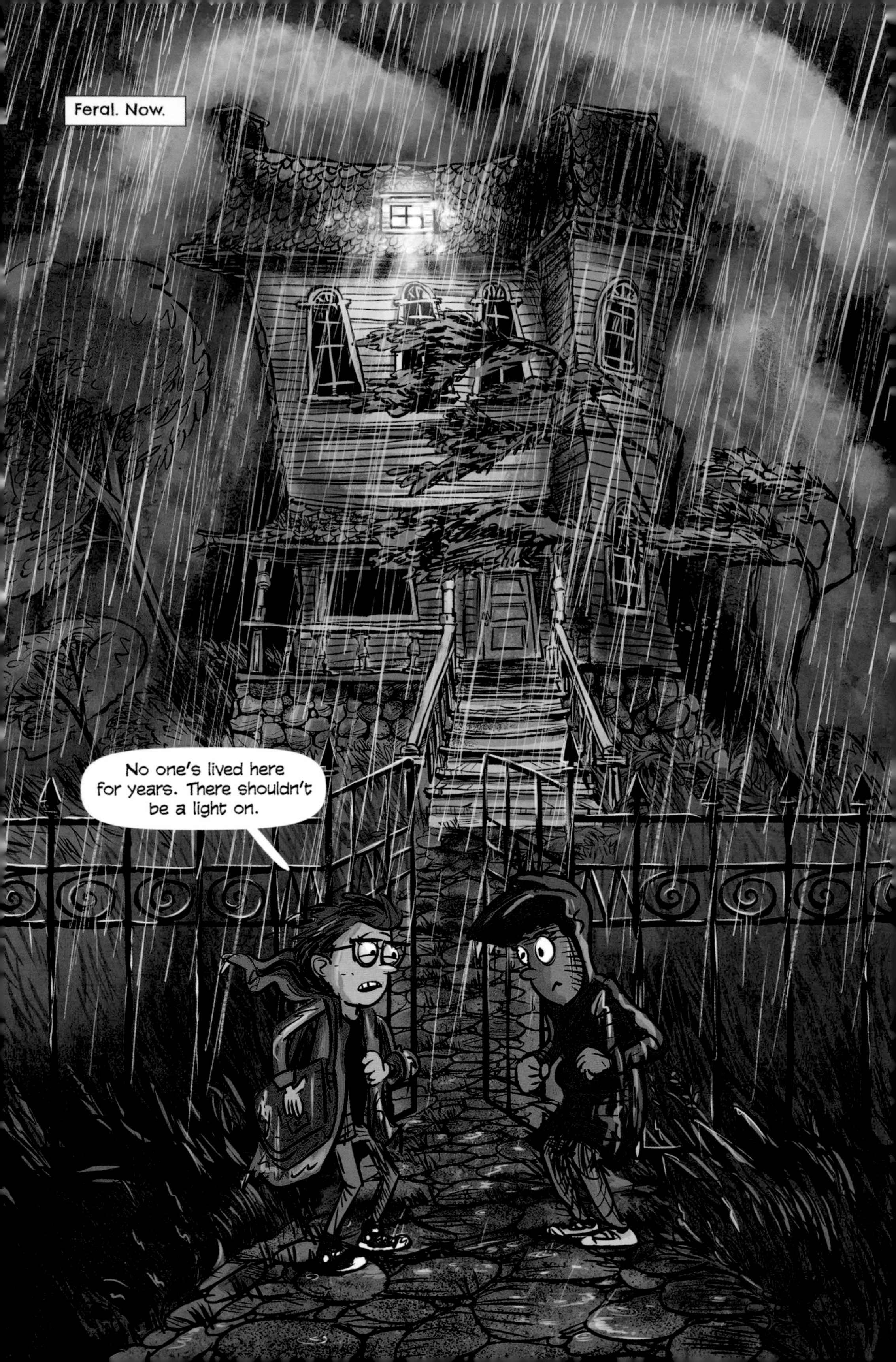
Feral. Now.
No one's lived here for years. There shouldn't be a light on.

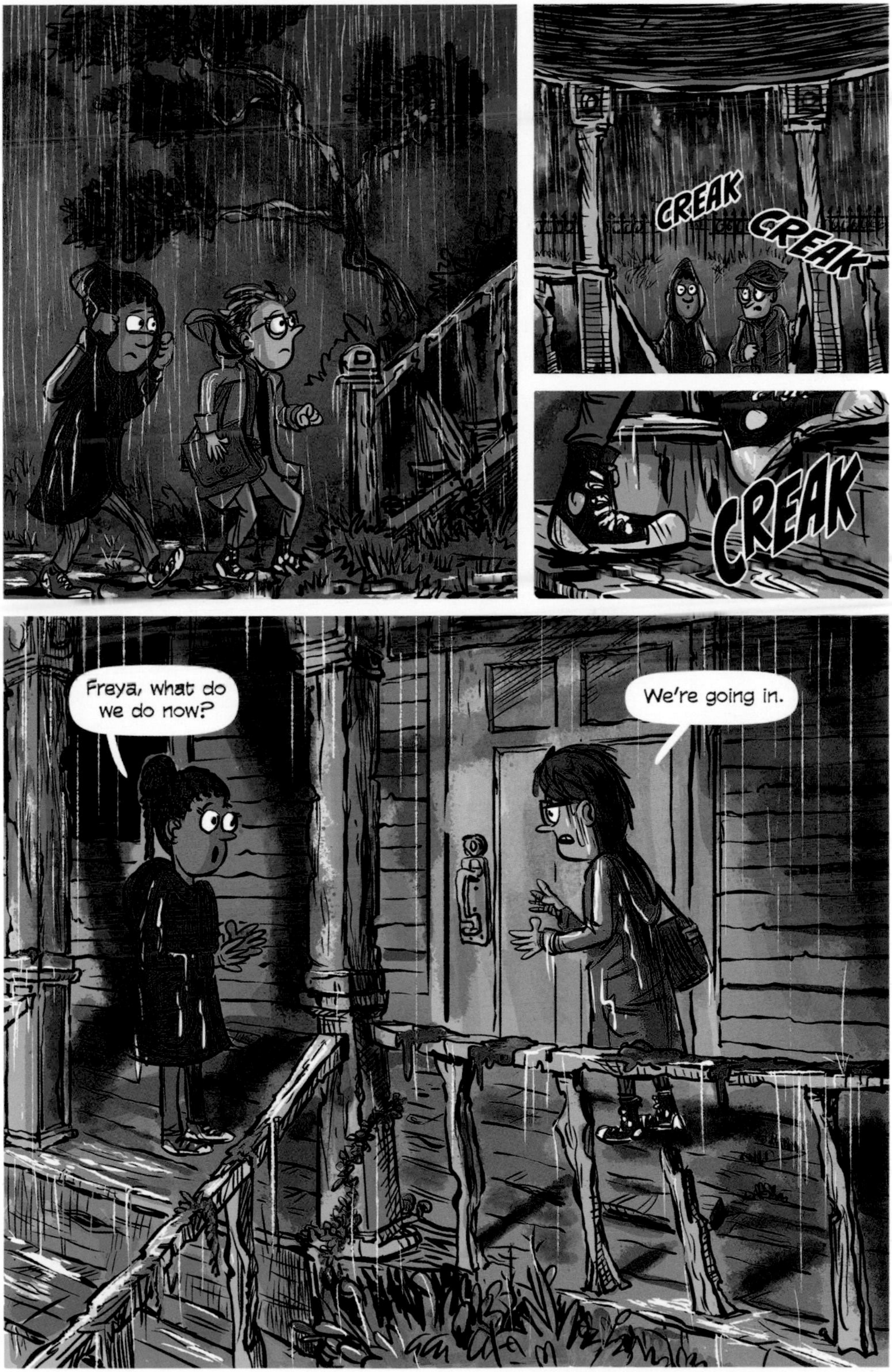
CREAK
CREAK
CREAK
Freya, what do we do now?
We're going in.

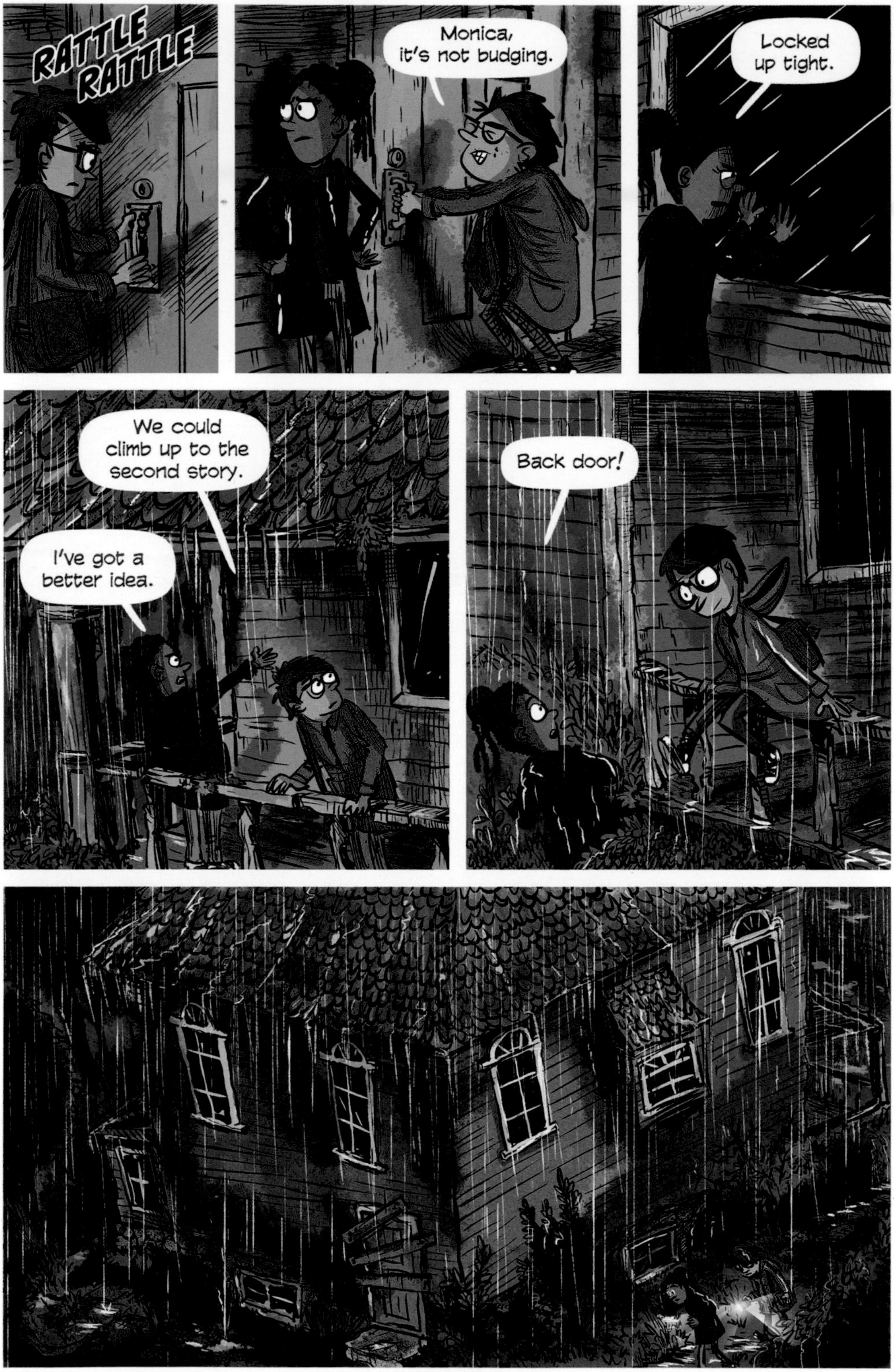
RATTLE RATTLE
Monica, it's not budging.
Locked up tight.
We could climb up to the second story.
I've got a better idea.
Back door!

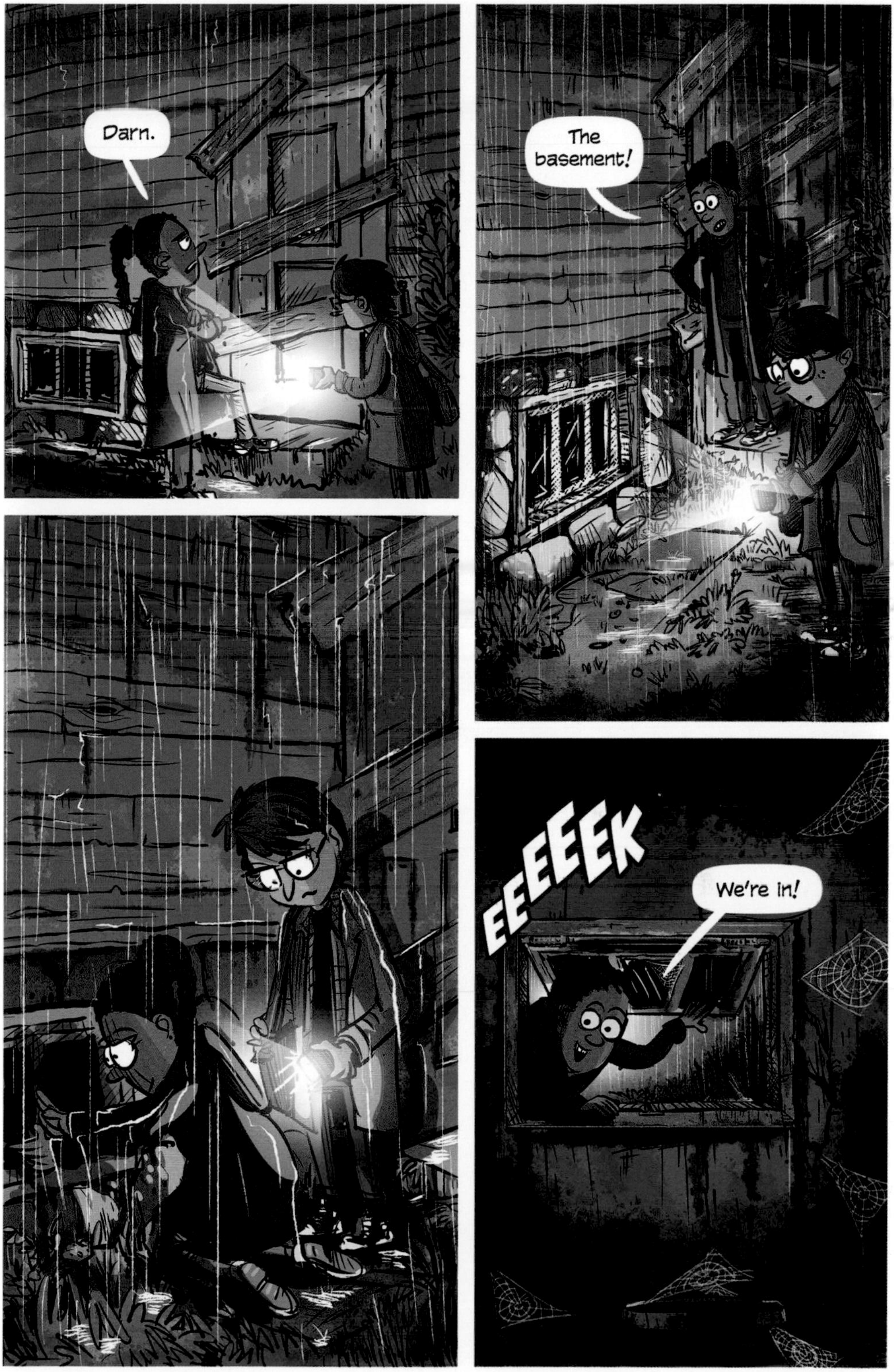
Darn.
The basement!
EEEEEK
We're in!

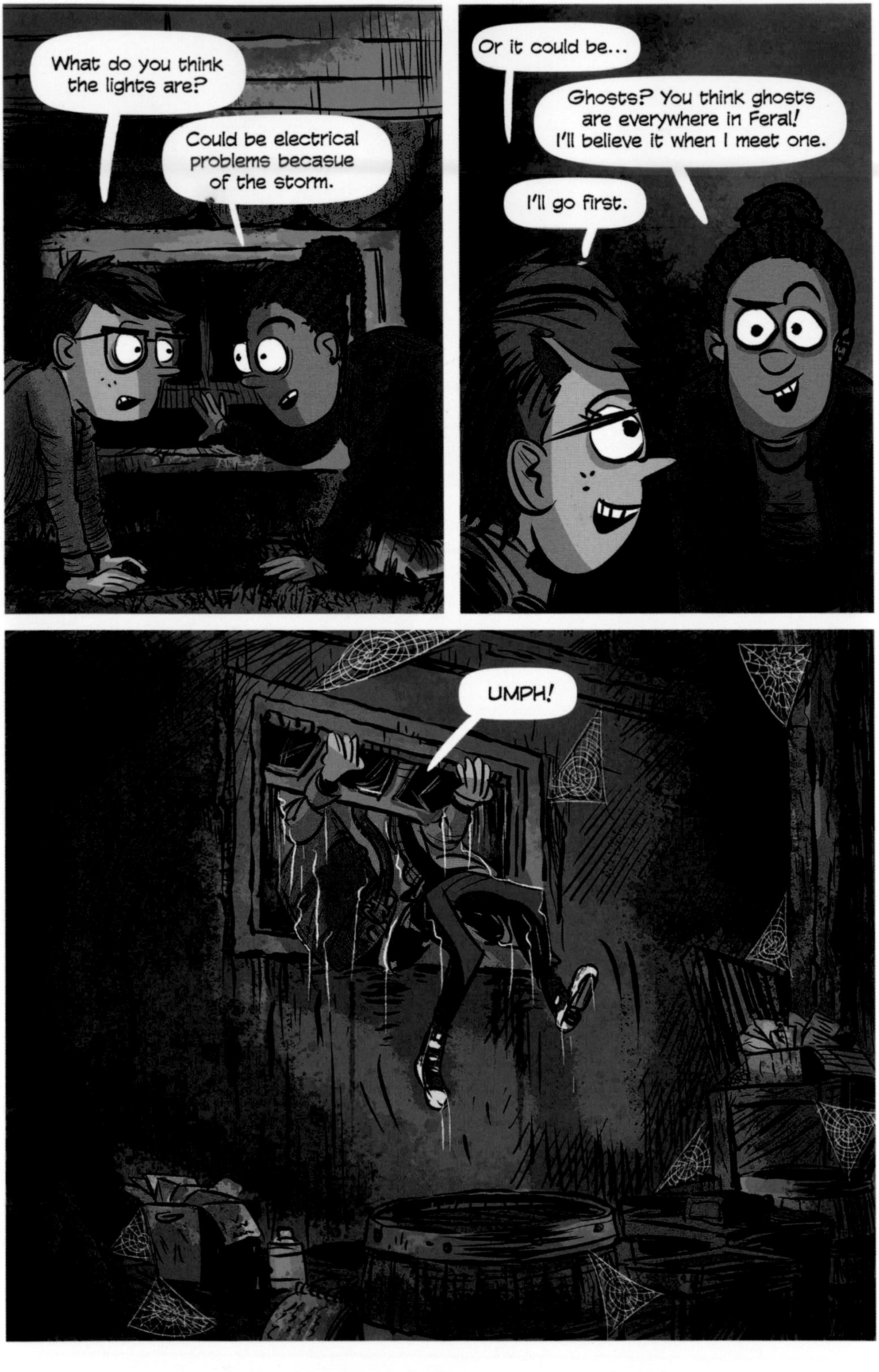
What do you think the lights are?
Could be electrical problems becasue of the storm.
Or it could be...
Ghosts? You think ghosts are everywhere in Feral! I'll believe it when I meet one.
I'll go first.
UMPH!

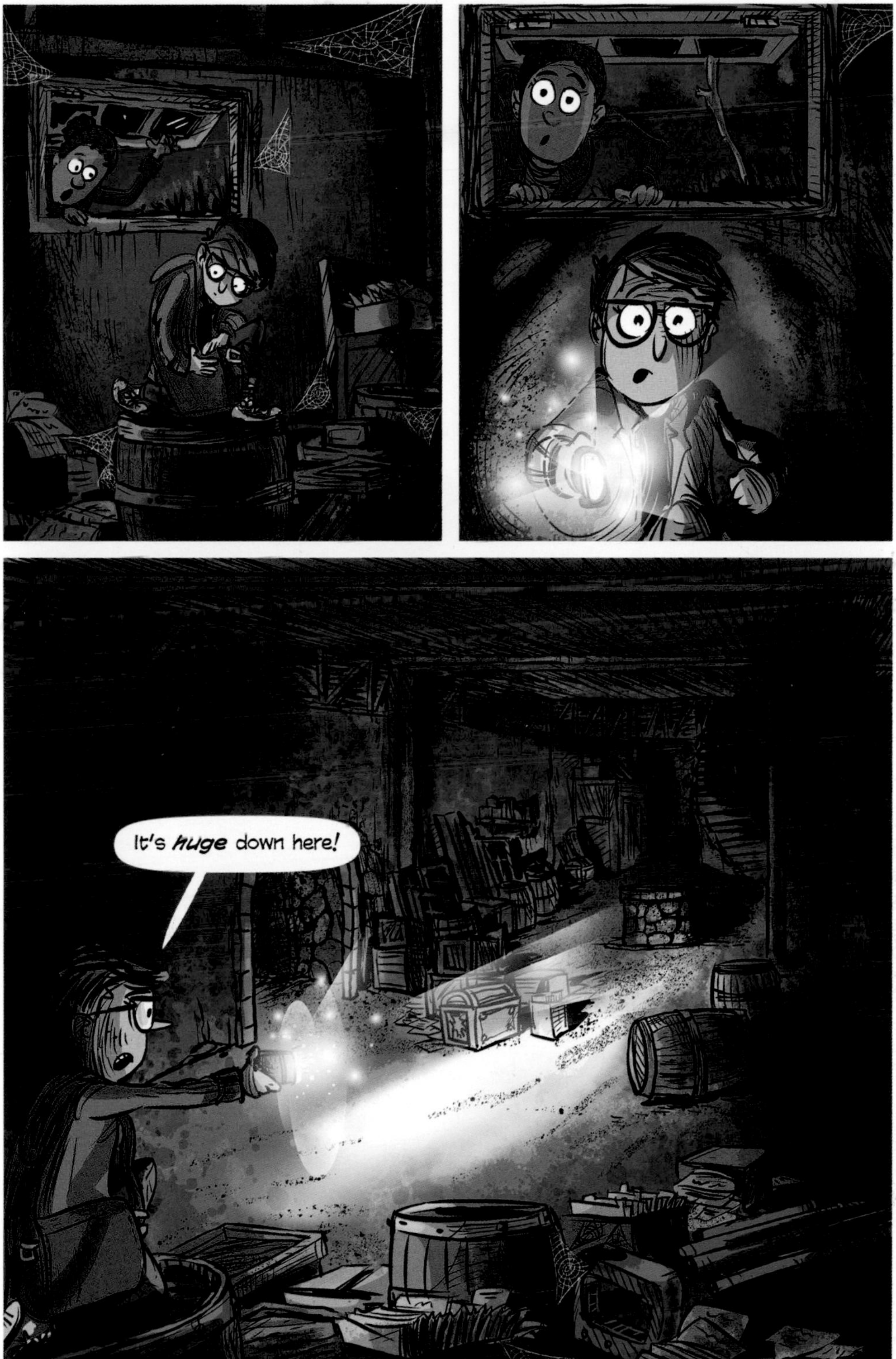
It's *huge* down here!

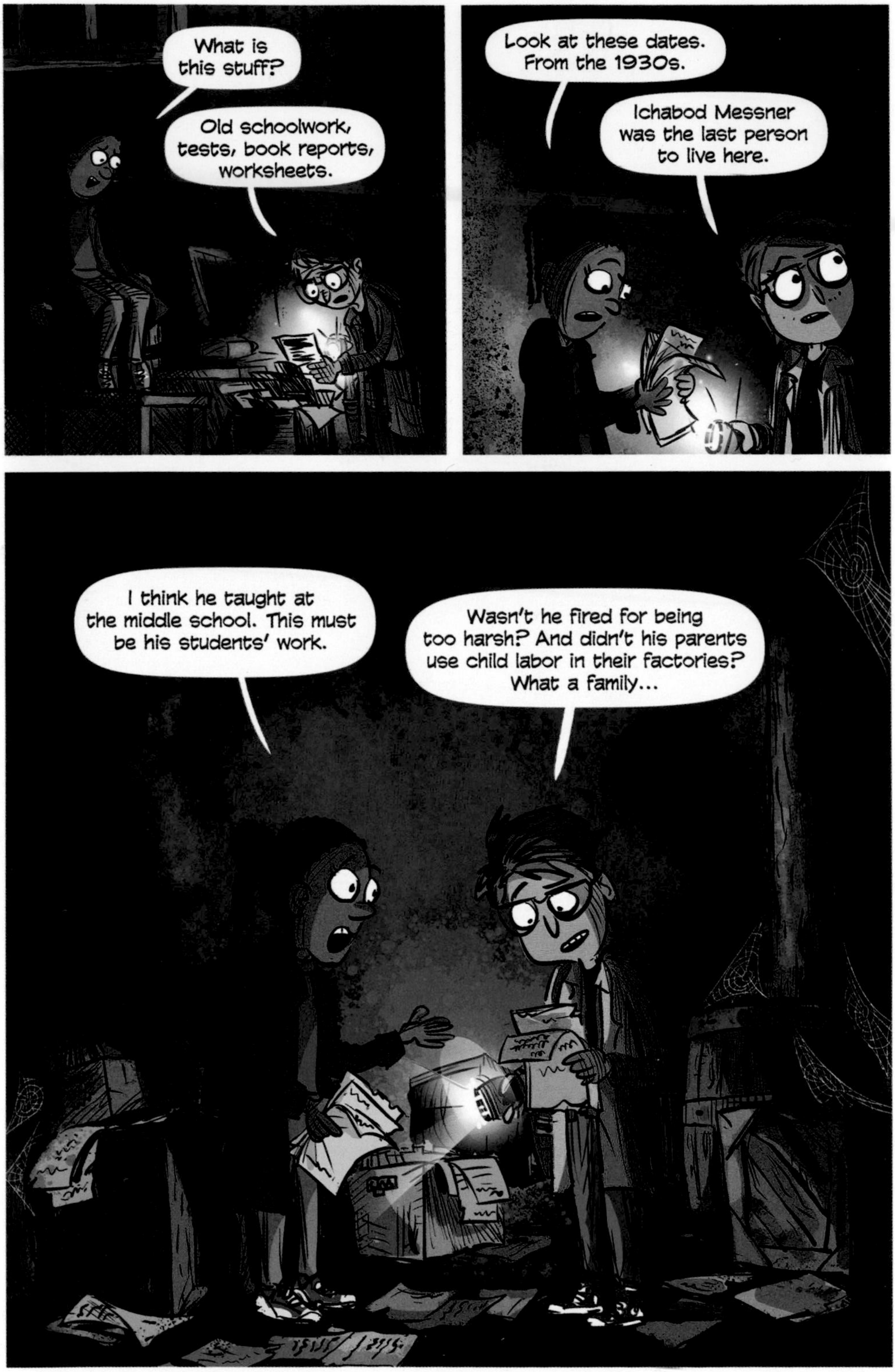
What is this stuff?
Old schoolwork, tests, book reports, worksheets.
Look at these dates. From the 1930s.
Ichabod Messner was the last person to live here.
I think he taught at the middle school. This must be his students' work.
Wasn't he fired for being too harsh? And didn't his parents use child labor in their factories? What a family...

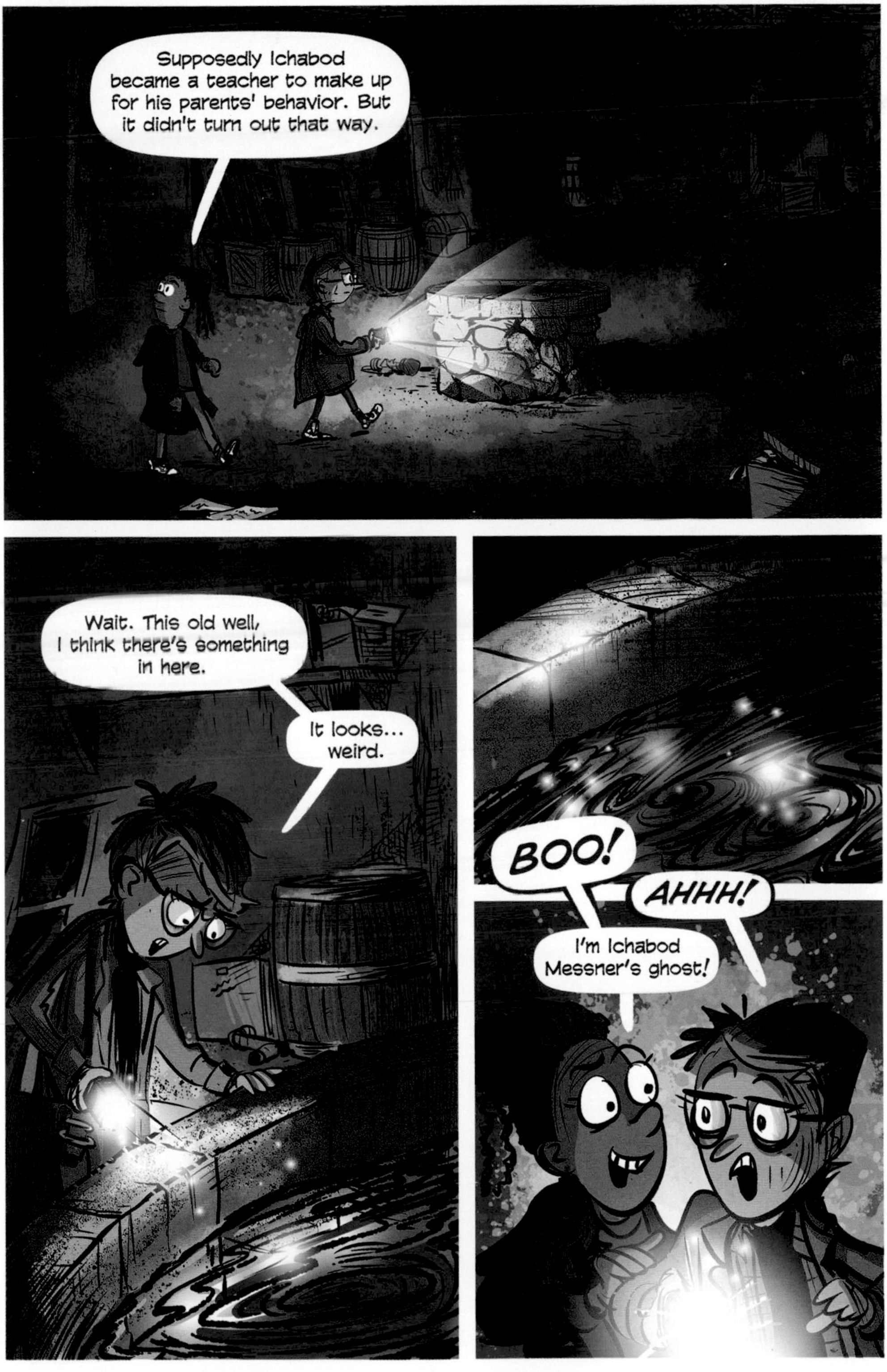
Supposedly Ichabod became a teacher to make up for his parents' behavior. But it didn't turn out that way.
Wait. This old well, I think there's something in here.
It looks... weird.
BOO!
AHHH!
I'm Ichabod Messner's ghost!

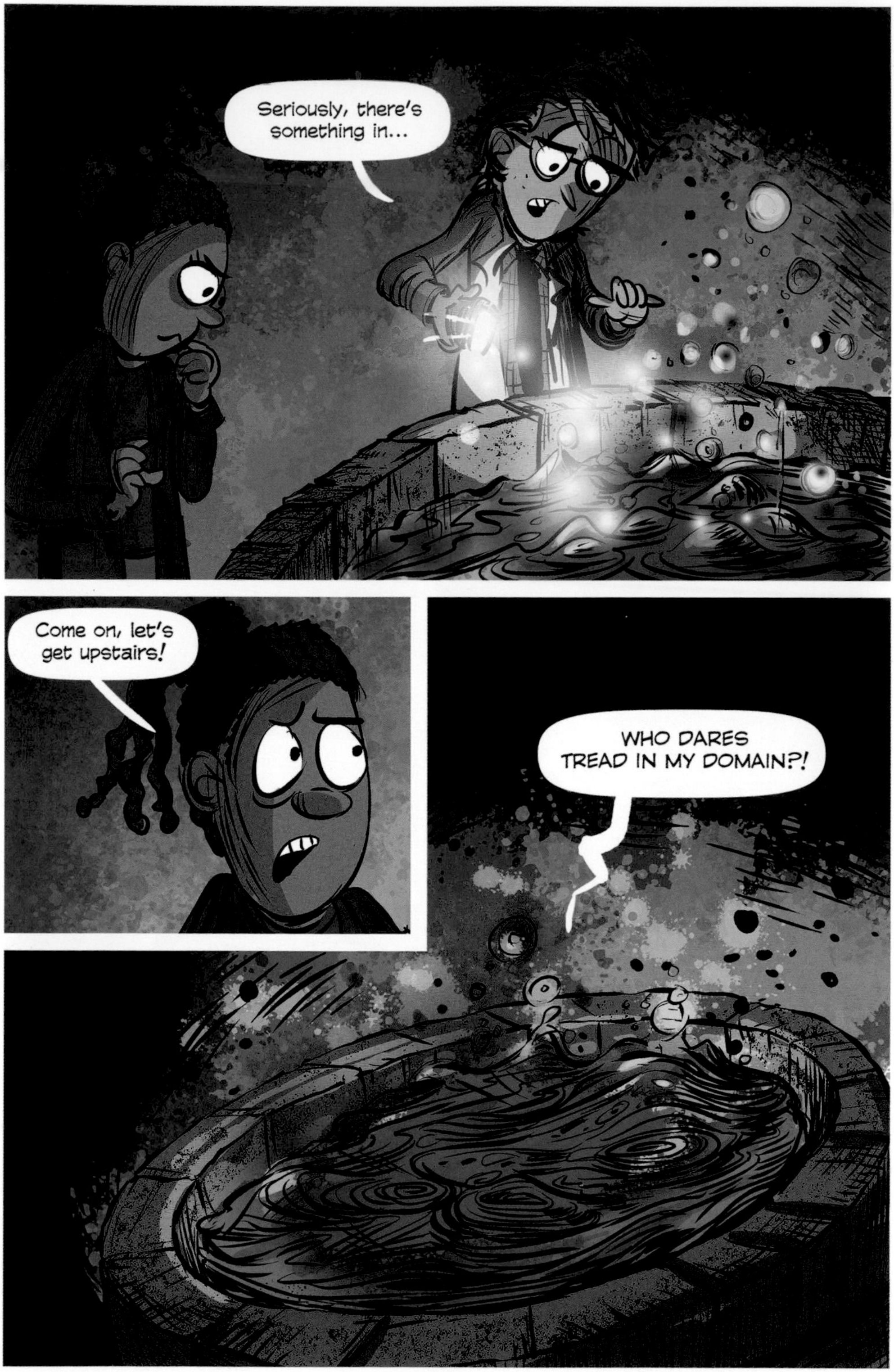
Seriously, there's something in...
Come on, let's get upstairs!
WHO DARES TREAD IN MY DOMAIN?!

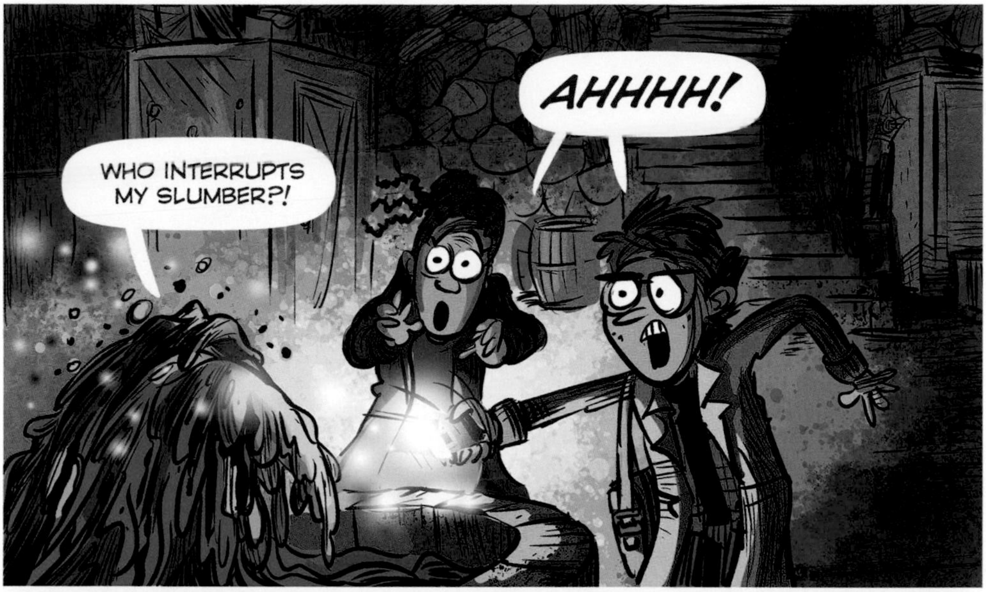
WHO INTERRUPTS MY SLUMBER?!
AHHHH!

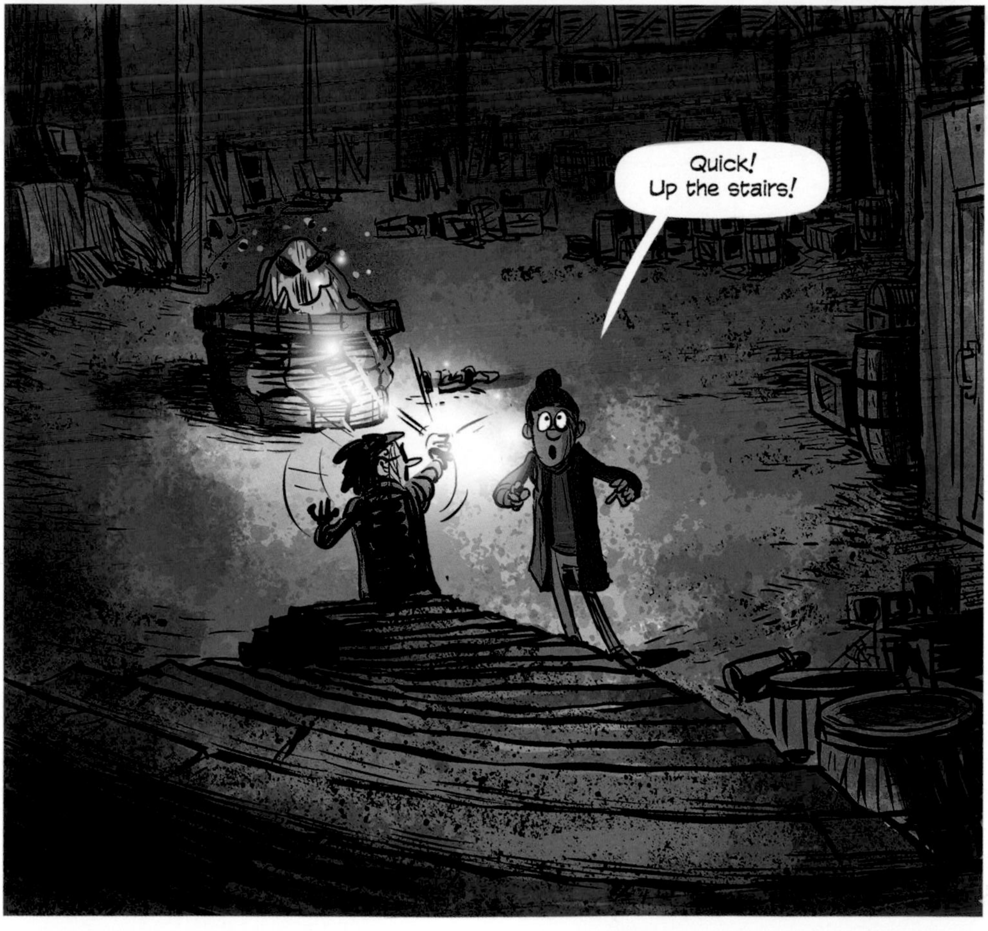
Quick! Up the stairs!

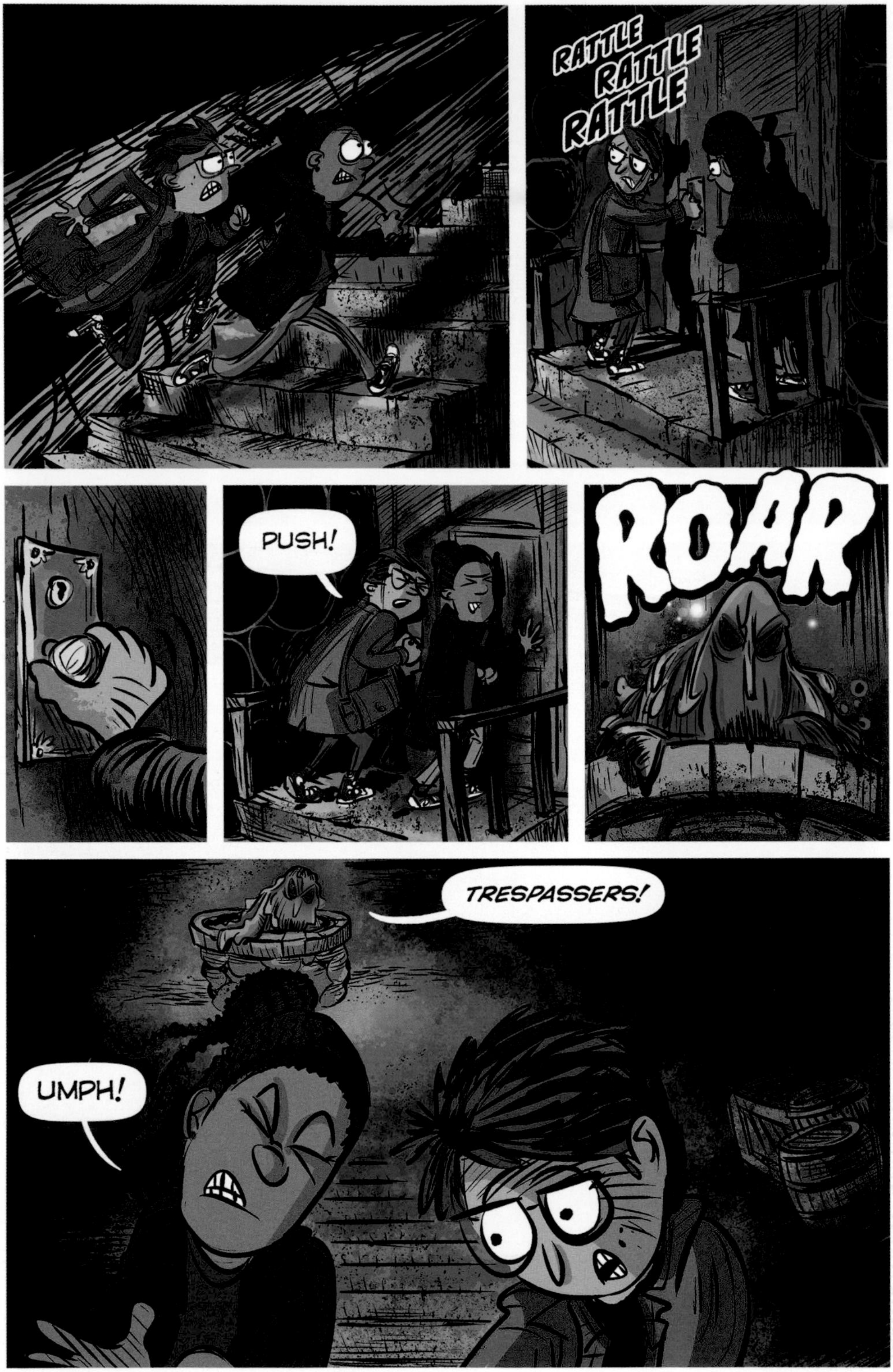
RATTLE
RATTLE
RATTLE
PUSH!
ROAR
TRESPASSERS!
UMPH!

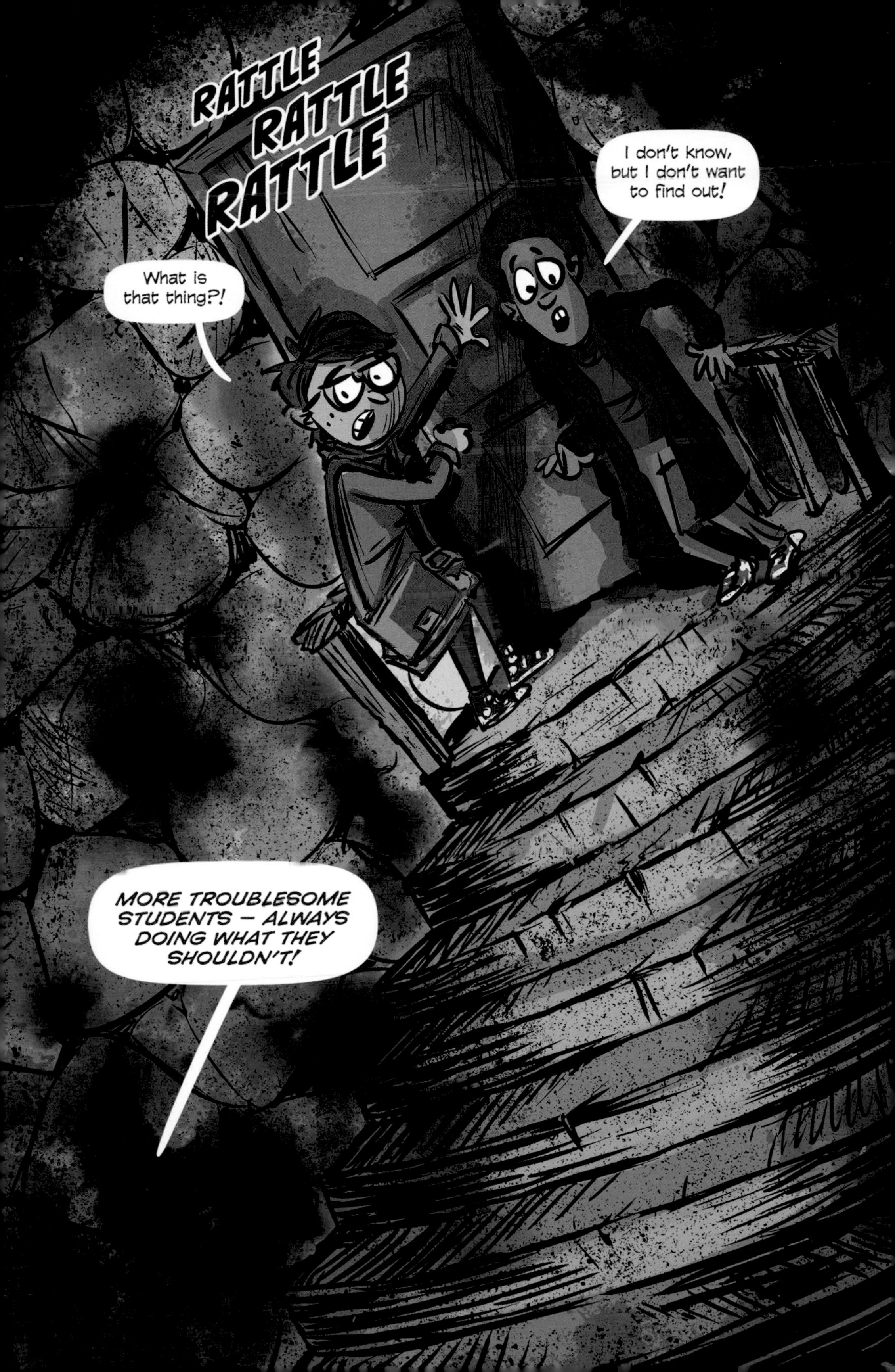
RATTLE RATTLE RATTLE
What is that thing?!
I don't know, but I don't want to find out!
MORE TROUBLESOME STUDENTS — ALWAYS DOING WHAT THEY SHOULDN'T!

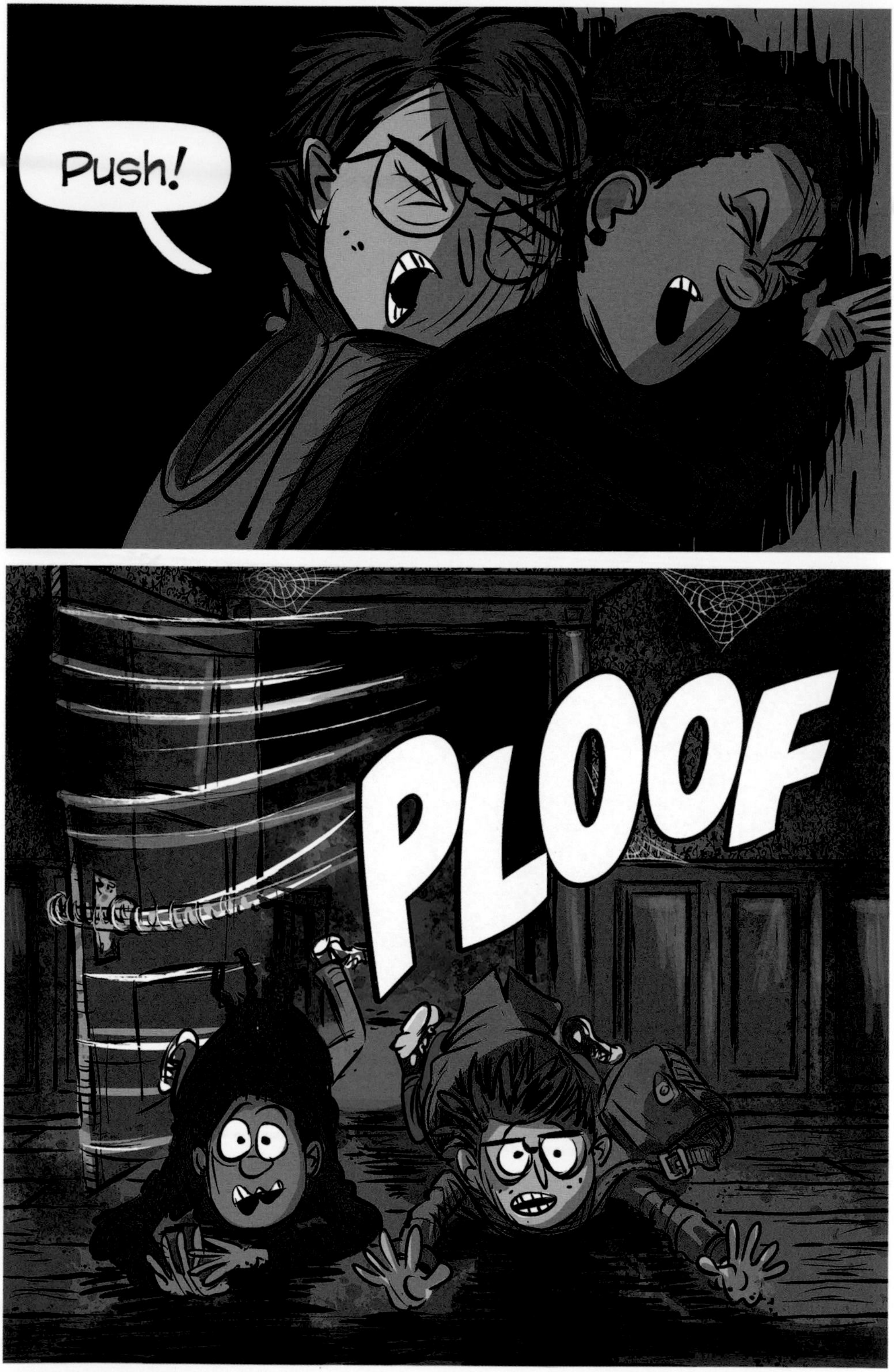
Push!
PLOOF

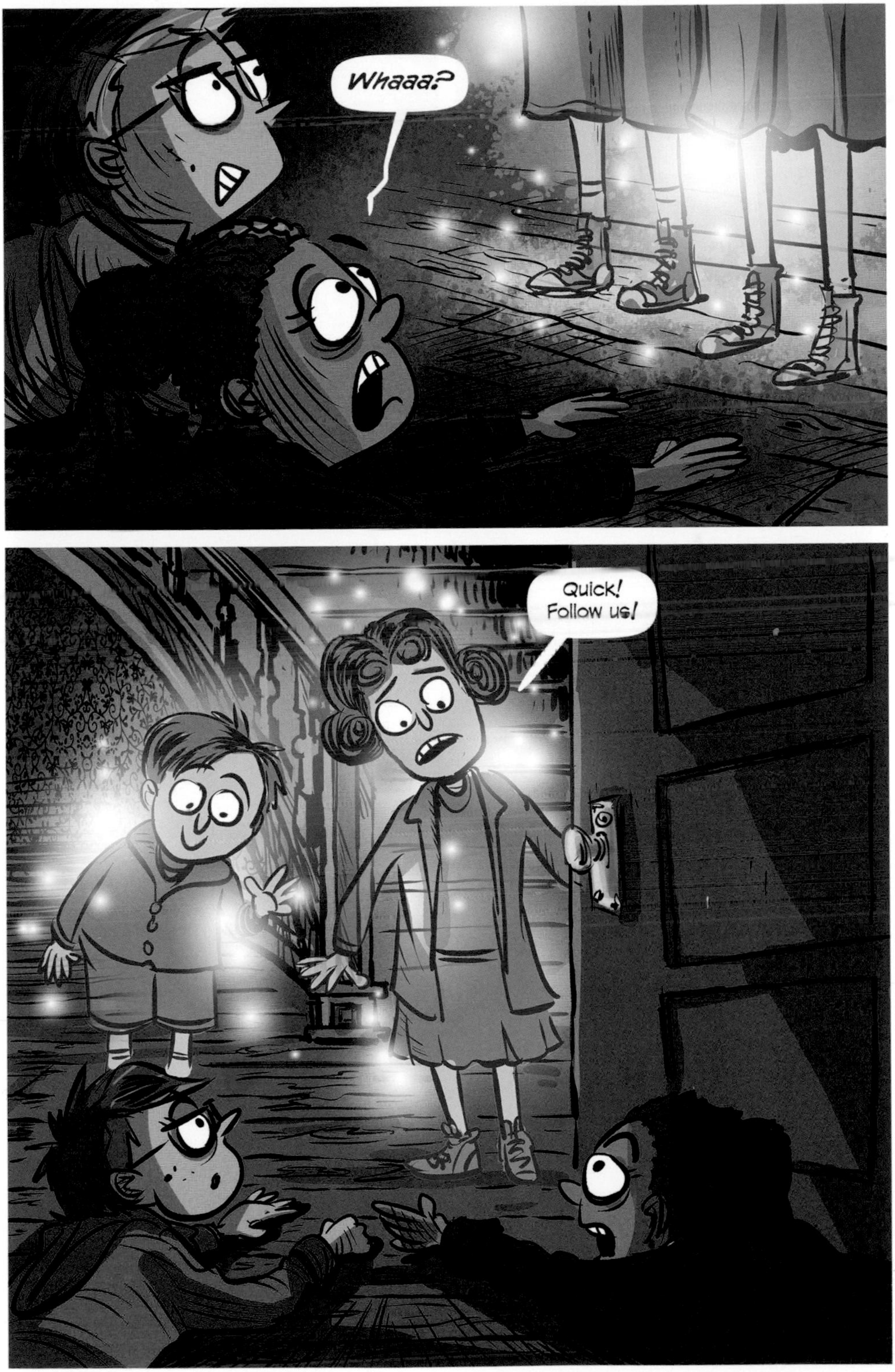
Whaaa?
Quick! Follow us!

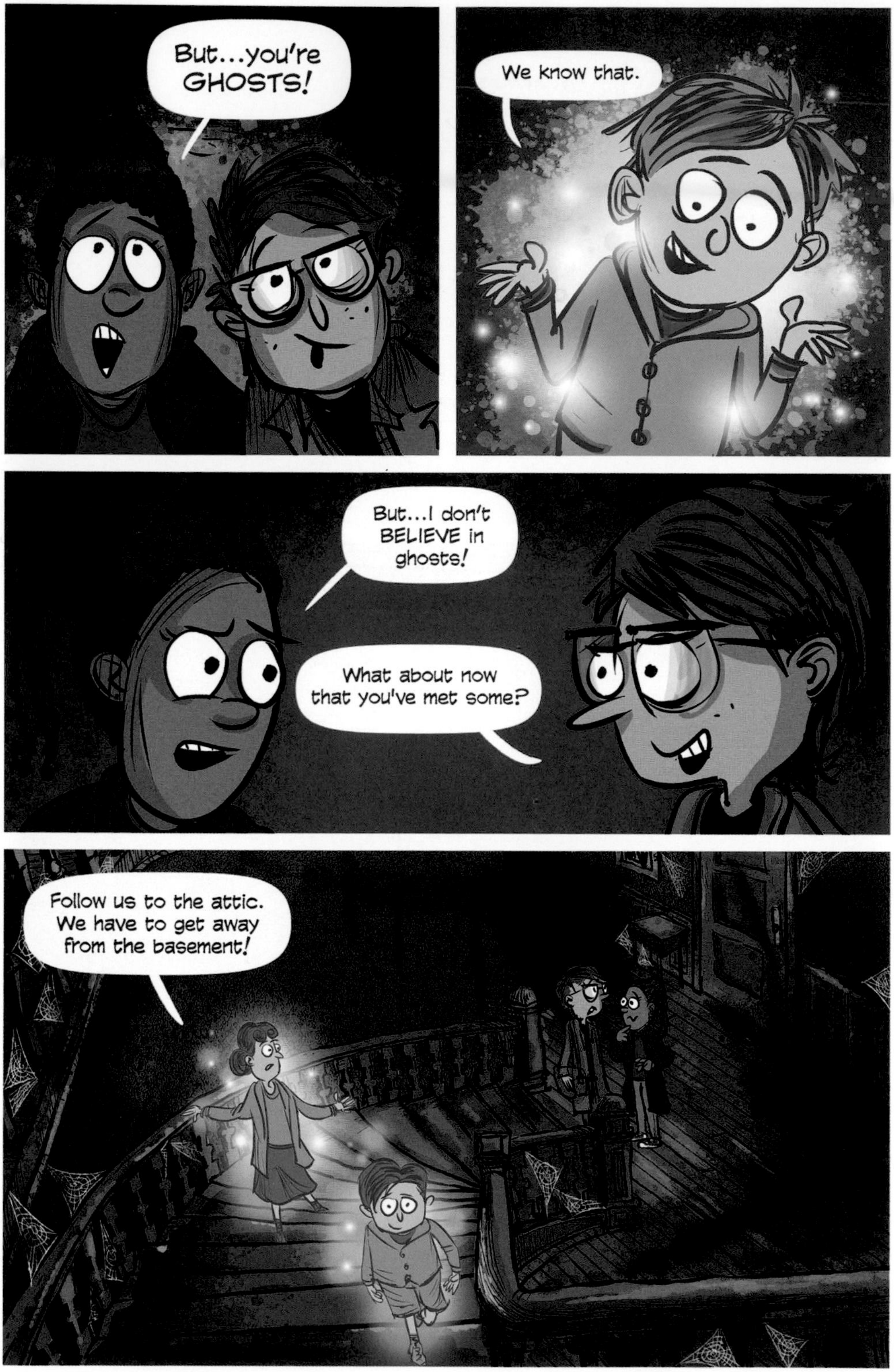
But...you're GHOSTS!
We know that.
But...I don't BELIEVE in ghosts!
What about now that you've met some?
Follow us to the attic. We have to get away from the basement!

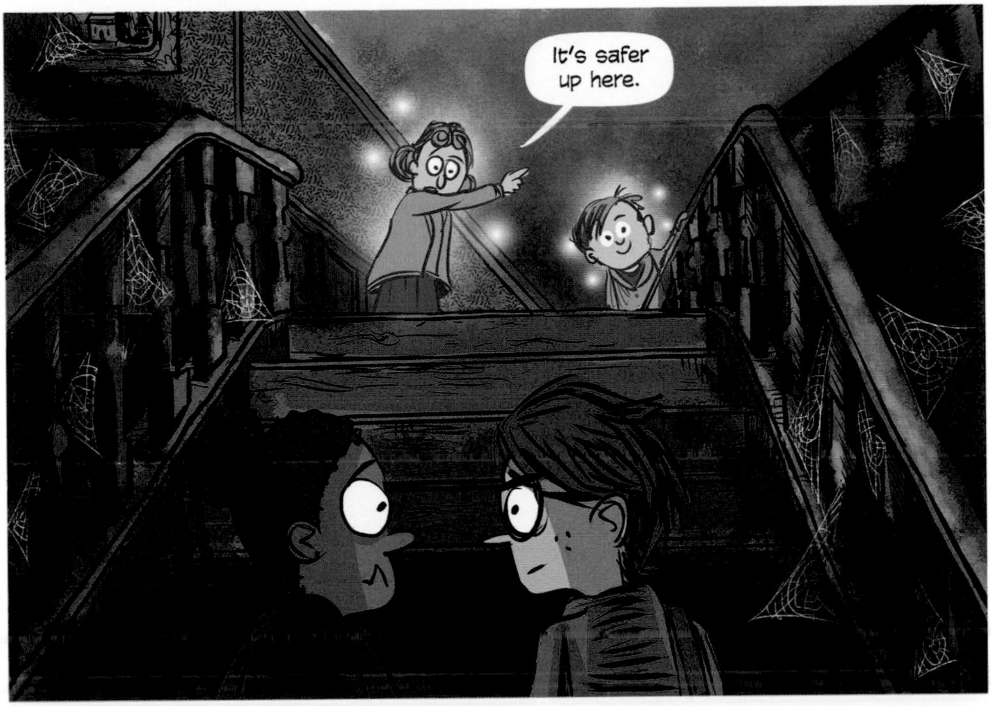
It's safer up here.

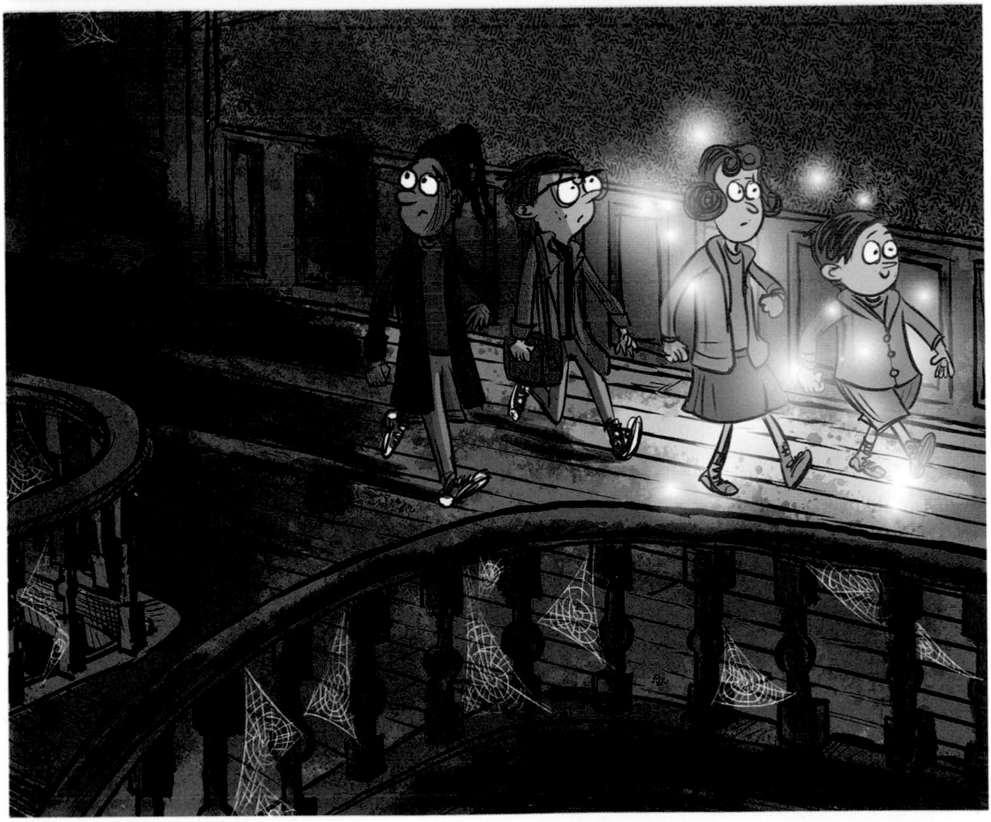

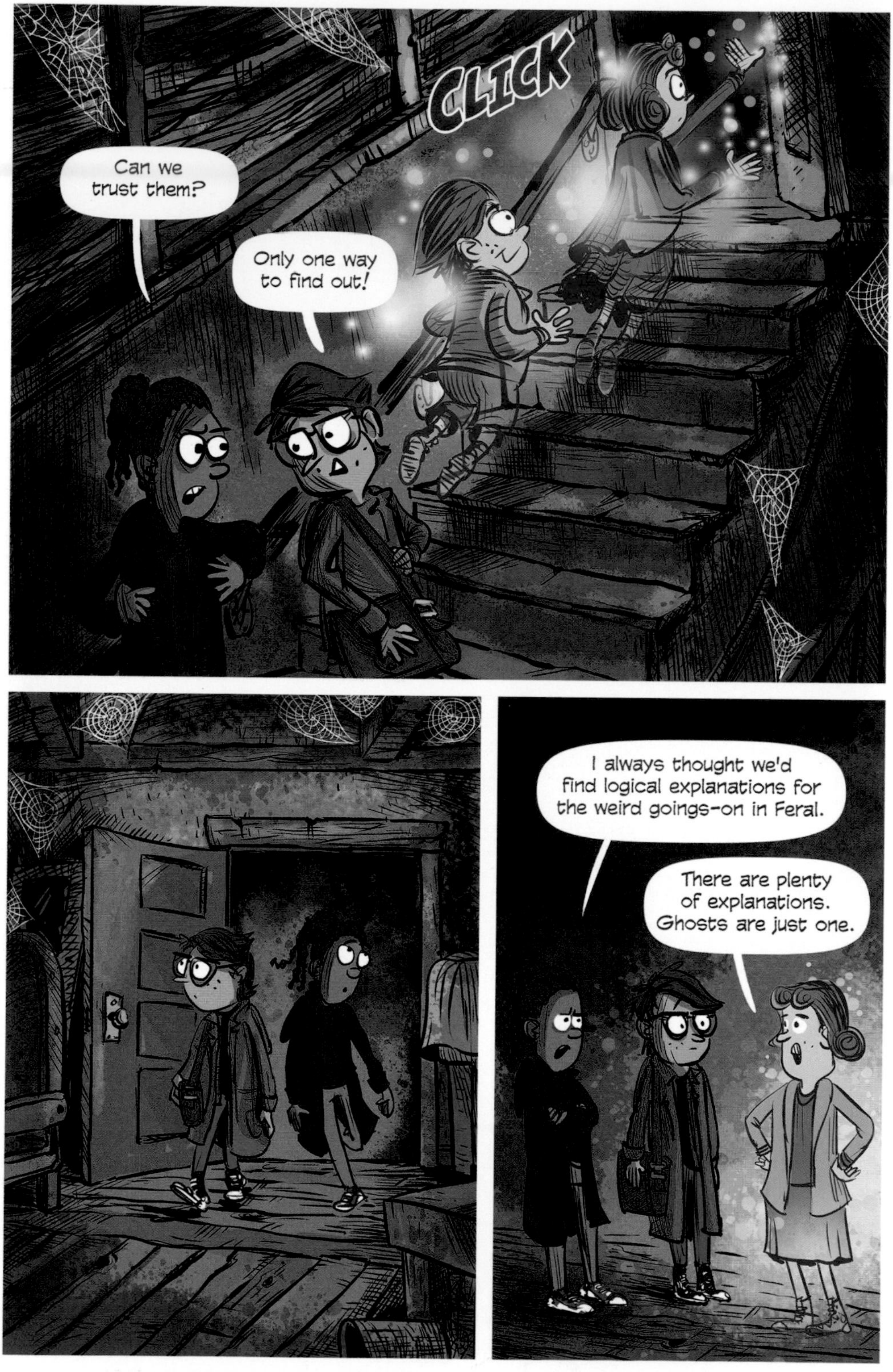
CLICK
Can we trust them?
Only one way to find out!
I always thought we'd find logical explanations for the weird goings-on in Feral.
There are plenty of explanations. Ghosts are just one.

CHAPTER 2

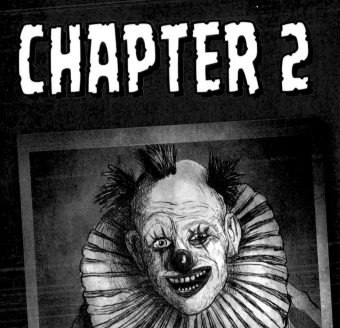

Blinky the clown —
Feral circus

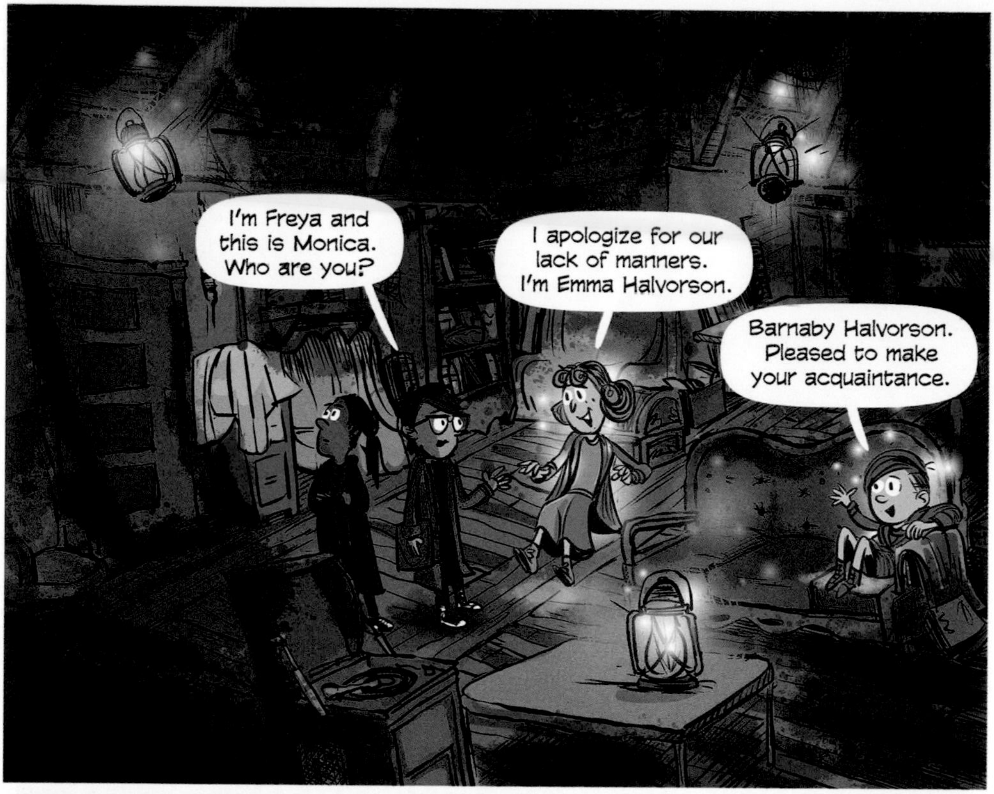
I'm Freya and this is Monica. Who are you?
I apologize for our lack of manners. I'm Emma Halvorson.
Barnaby Halvorson. Pleased to make your acquaintance.

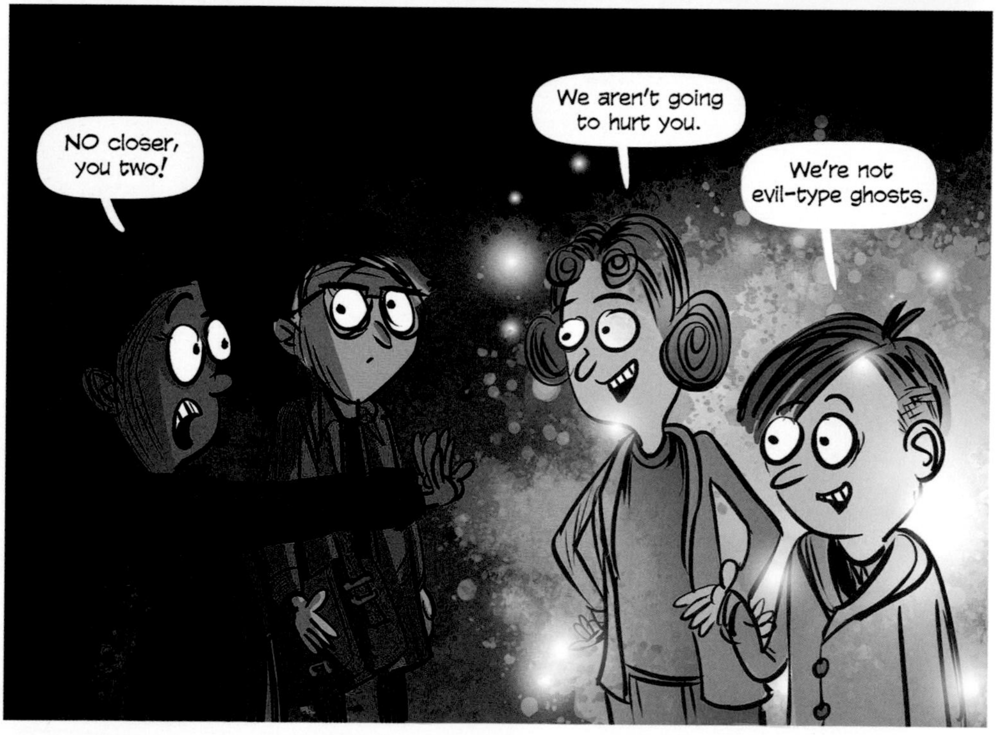
NO closer, you two!
We aren't going to hurt you.
We're not evil-type ghosts.

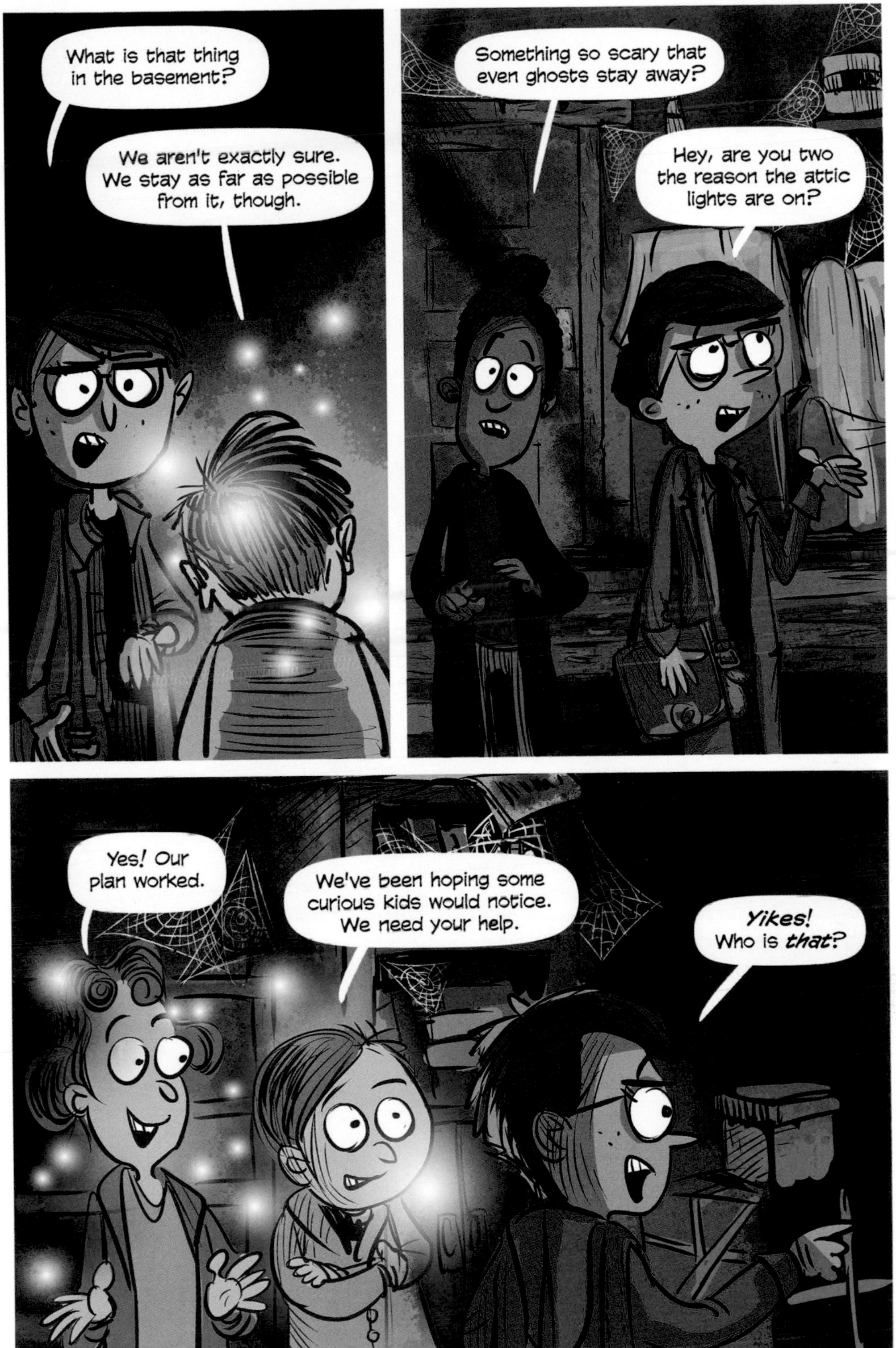
What is that thing in the basement?
We aren't exactly sure. We stay as far as possible from it, though.
Something so scary that even ghosts stay away?
Hey, are you two the reason the attic lights are on?
Yes! Our plan worked.
We've been hoping some curious kids would notice. We need your help.
Yikes! Who is ***that***?

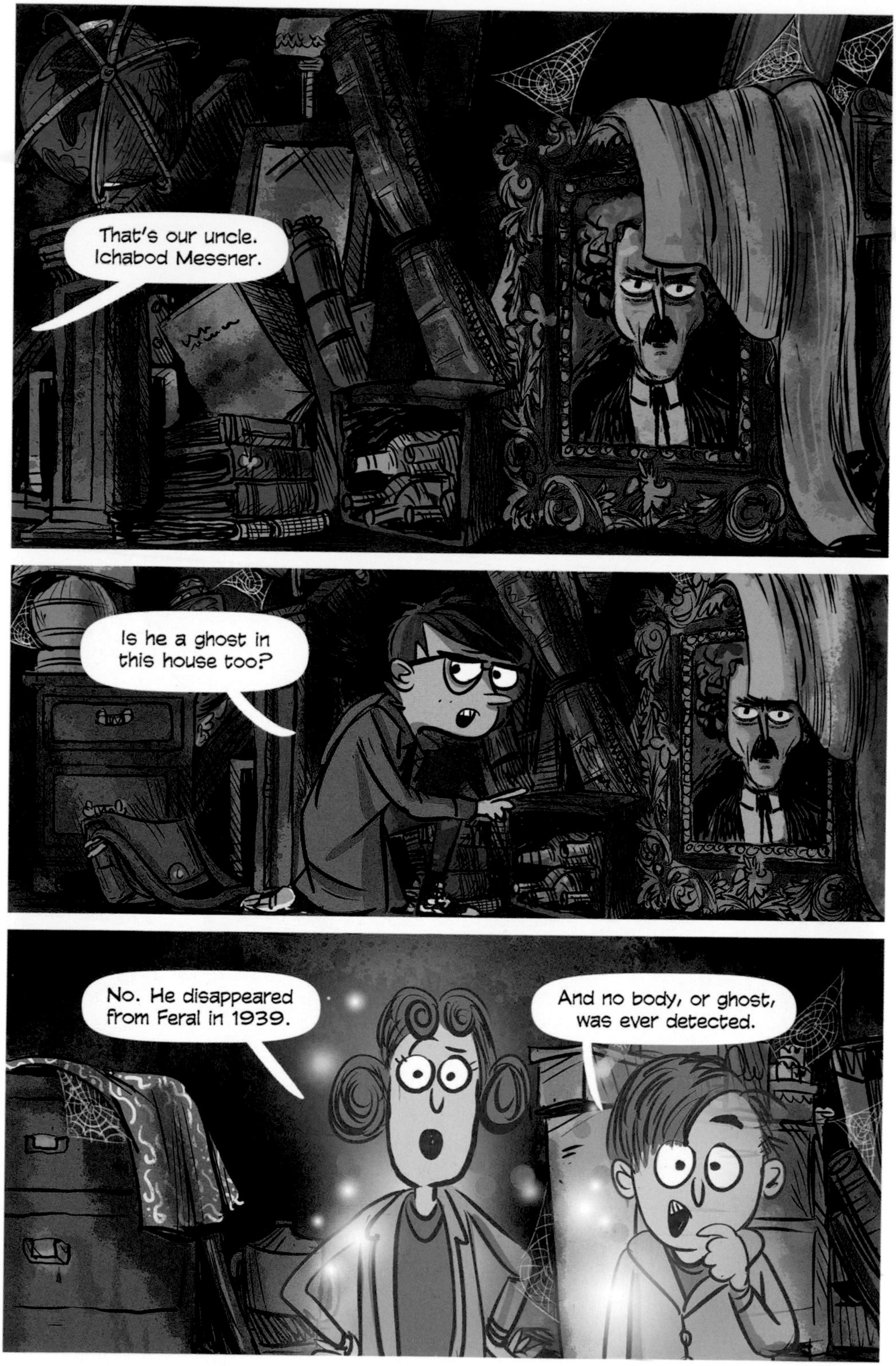
That's our uncle. Ichabod Messner.
Is he a ghost in this house too?
No. He disappeared from Feral in 1939.
And no body, or ghost, was ever detected.

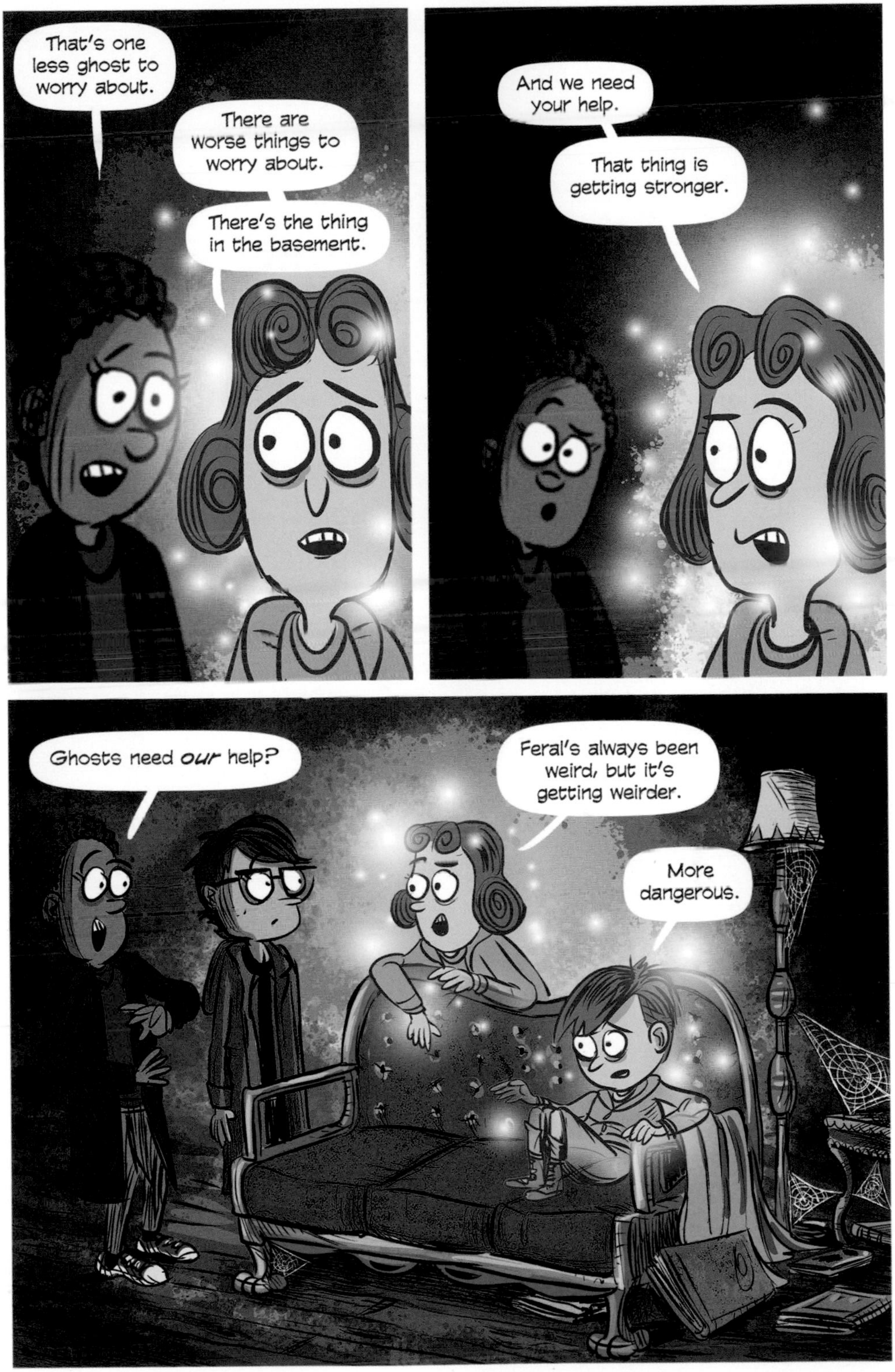
That's one less ghost to worry about.
There are worse things to worry about.
There's the thing in the basement.
And we need your help.
That thing is getting stronger.
Ghosts need *our* help?
Feral's always been weird, but it's getting weirder.
More dangerous.

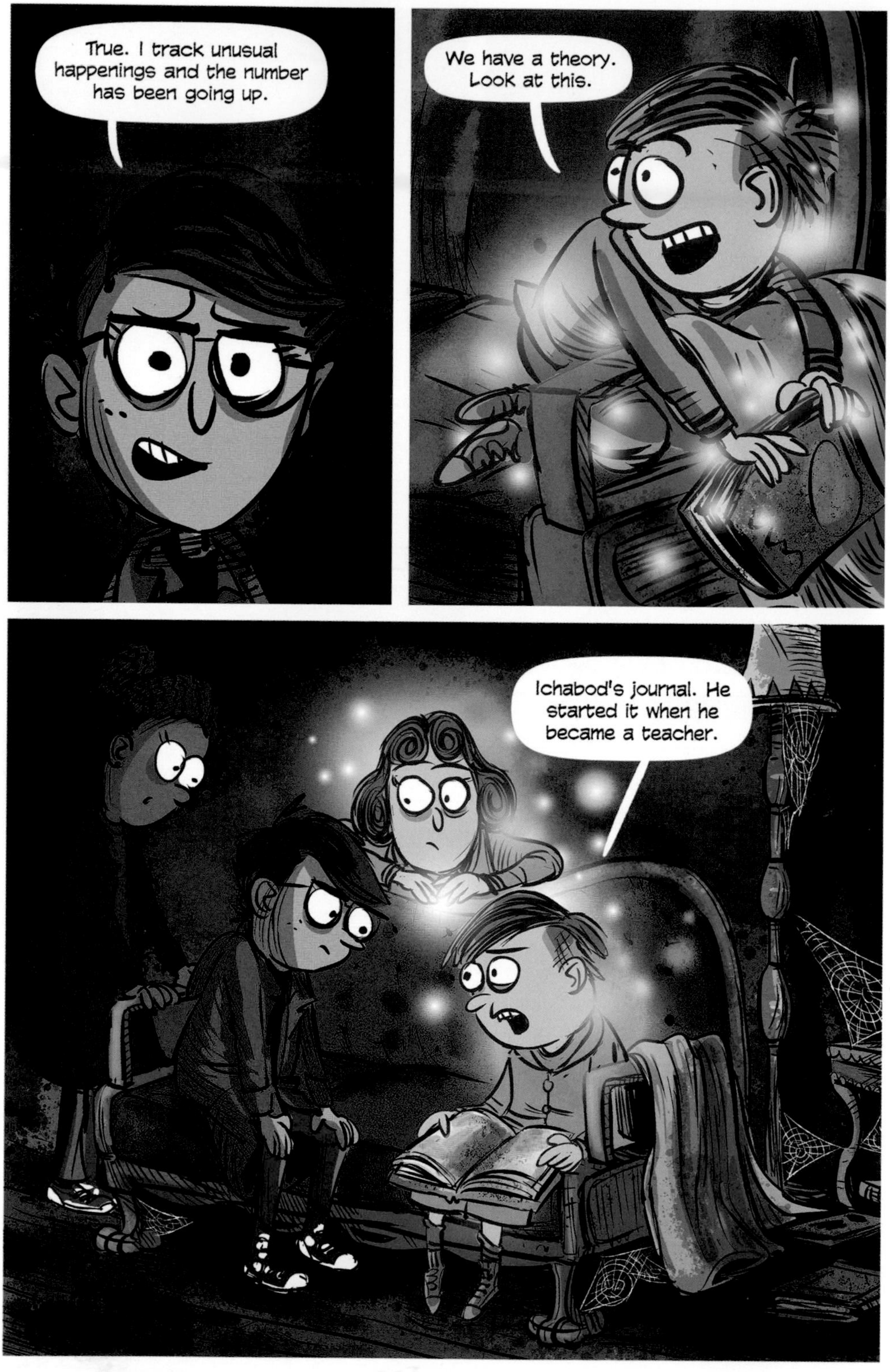
True. I track unusual happenings and the number has been going up.
We have a theory. Look at this.
Ichabod's journal. He started it when he became a teacher.

September 7, 1920.
It was my first day of teaching and it all went aces! I love my students! I know I can make a difference with these great kids.
He loved it at first. He really cared about the children of Feral.
But as the years went by, things got... weird.
April 4, 1927.
I believe my students are playing tricks on me. The town shuns me because of my family and offers no kindness. I'm seeing Feral in a whole new way. Unnamed things lurk in the dark. And I like those things.

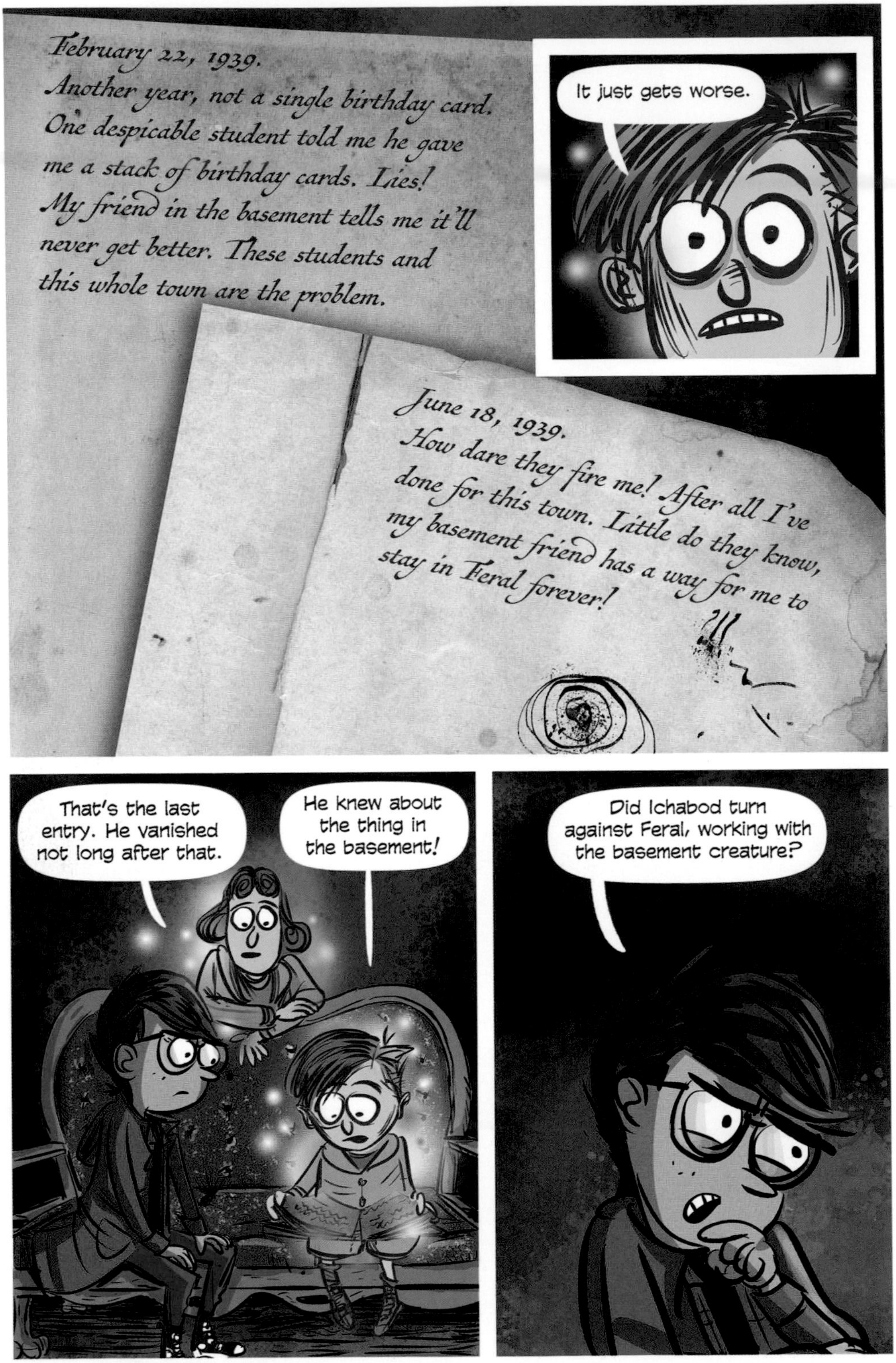
February 22, 1939.
Another year, not a single birthday card. One despicable student told me he gave me a stack of birthday cards. Lies! My friend in the basement tells me it'll never get better. These students and this whole town are the problem.
It just gets worse.
June 18, 1939.
How dare they fire me! After all I've done for this town. Little do they know, my basement friend has a way for me to stay in Feral forever!
That's the last entry. He vanished not long after that.
He knew about the thing in the basement!
Did Ichabod turn against Feral, working with the basement creature?

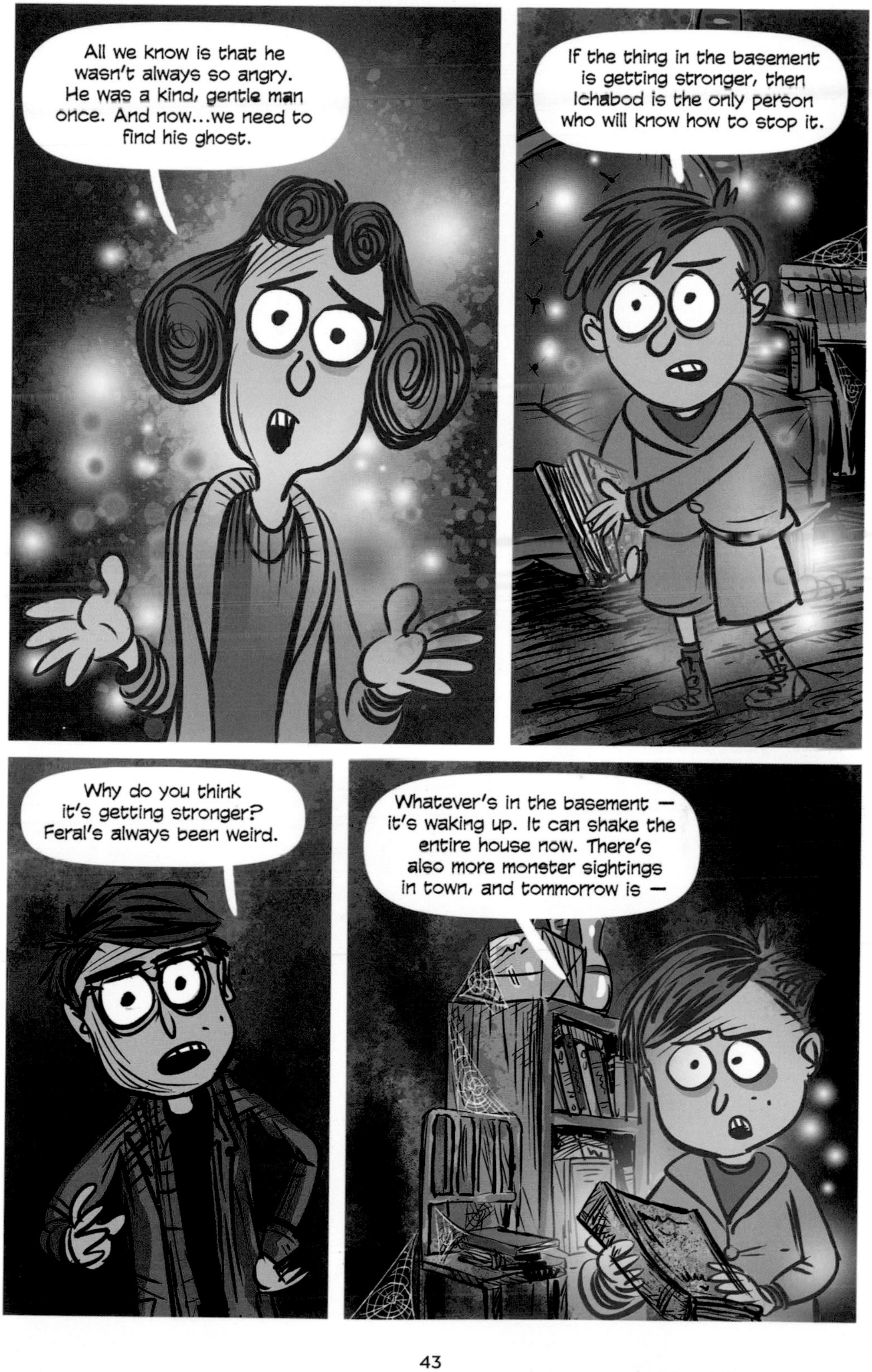
All we know is that he wasn't always so angry. He was a kind, gentle man once. And now...we need to find his ghost.
If the thing in the basement is getting stronger, then Ichabod is the only person who will know how to stop it.
Why do you think it's getting stronger? Feral's always been weird.
Whatever's in the basement — it's waking up. It can shake the entire house now. There's also more monster sightings in town, and tommorrow is —

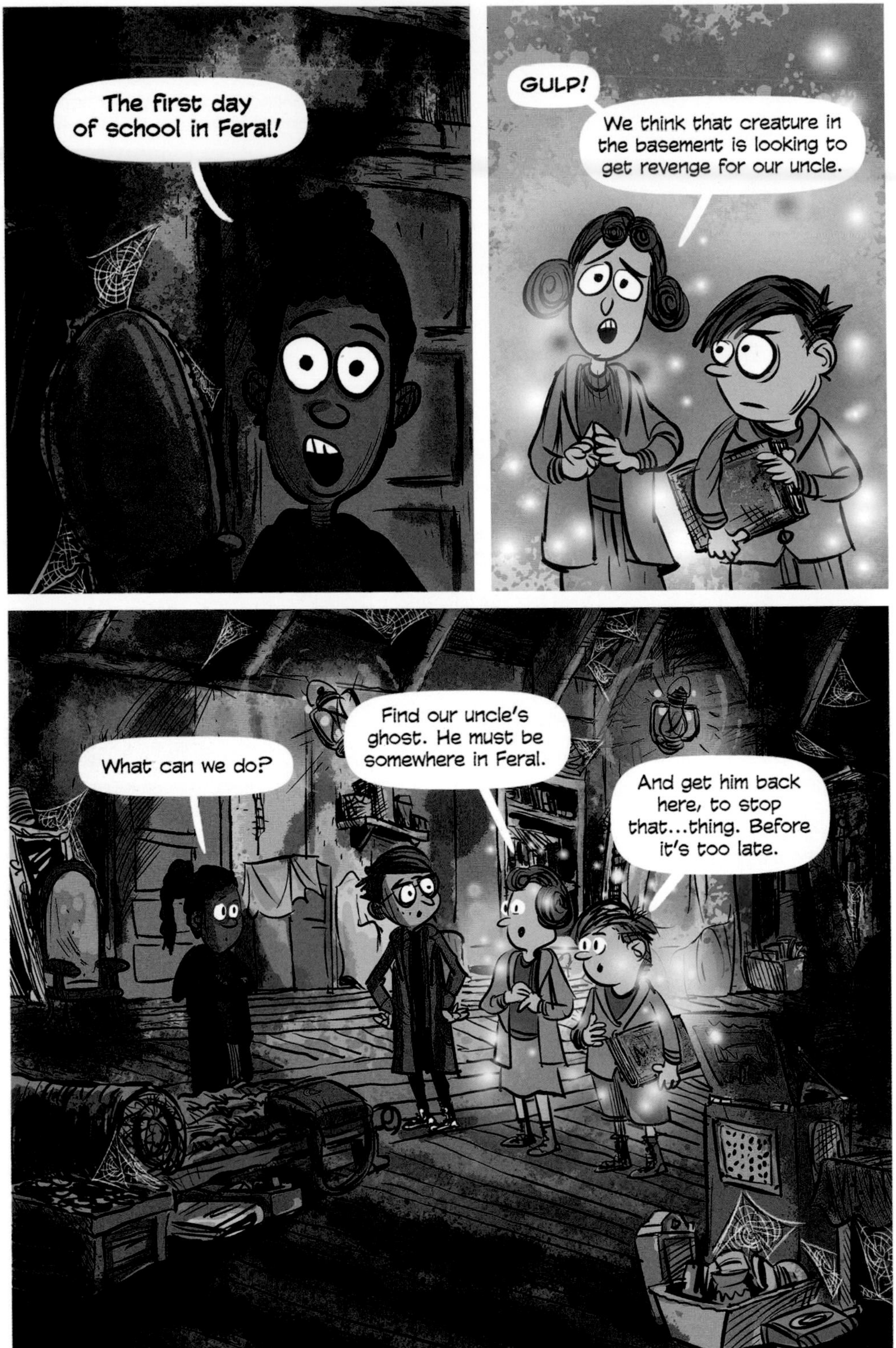
The first day of school in Feral!
GULP!
We think that creature in the basement is looking to get revenge for our uncle.
What can we do?
Find our uncle's ghost. He must be somewhere in Feral.
And get him back here, to stop that...thing. Before it's too late.

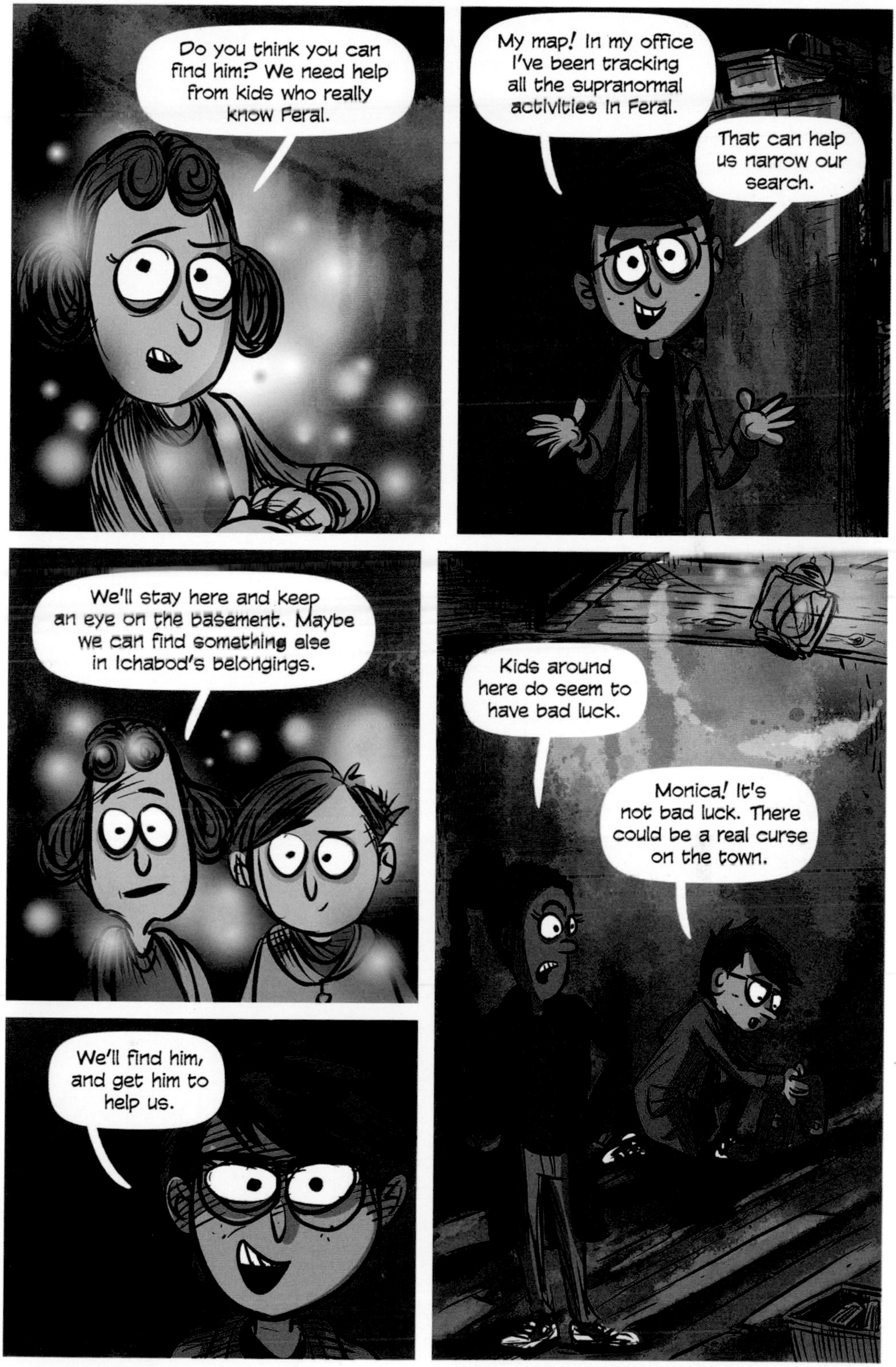
Do you think you can find him? We need help from kids who really know Feral.
My map! In my office I've been tracking all the supranormal activities in Feral.
That can help us narrow our search.
We'll stay here and keep an eye on the basement. Maybe we can find something else in Ichabod's belongings.
We'll find him, and get him to help us.
Kids around here do seem to have bad luck.
Monica! It's not bad luck. There could be a real curse on the town.

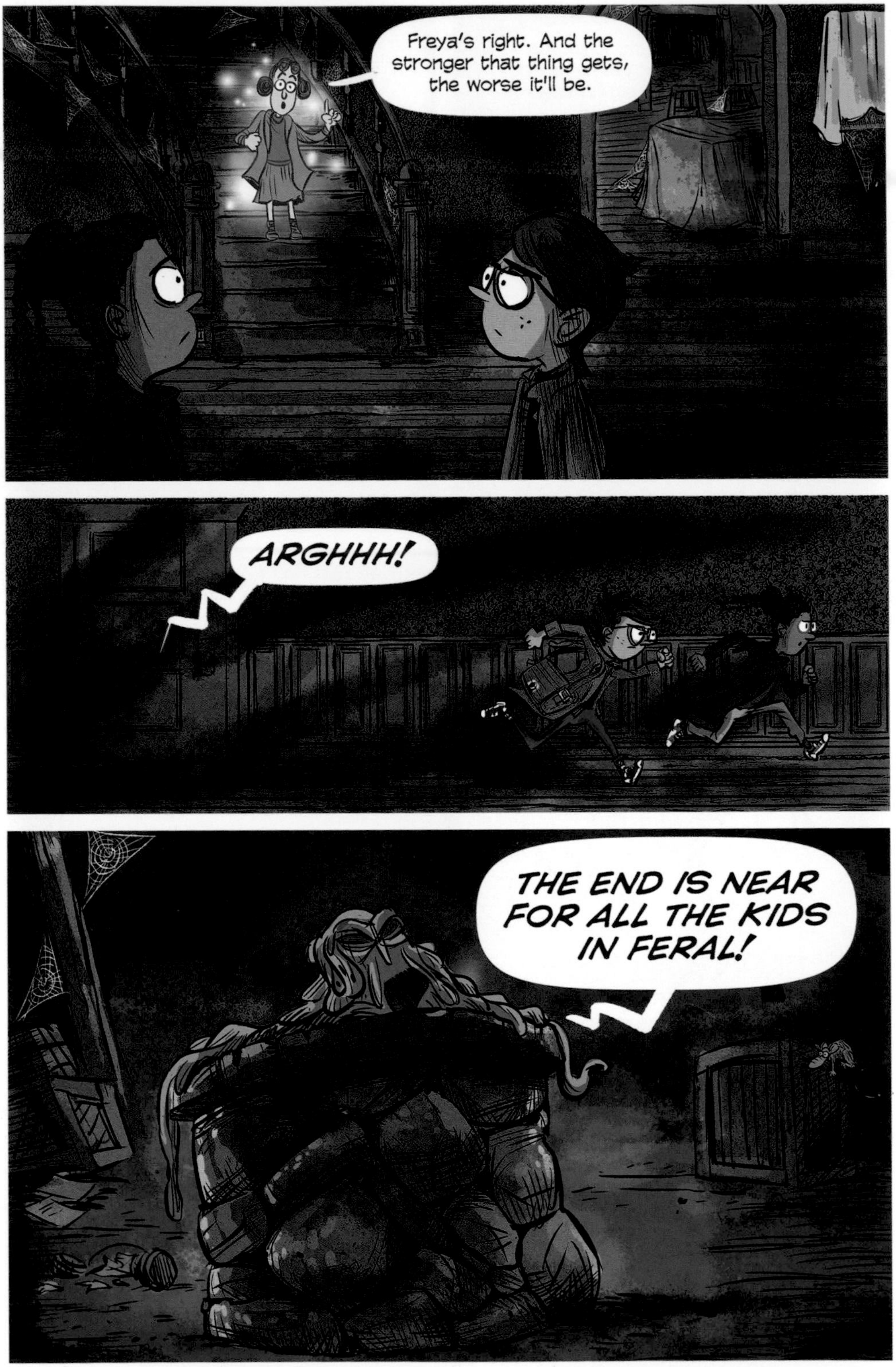
Freya's right. And the stronger that thing gets, the worse it'll be.
ARGHHH!
THE END IS NEAR FOR ALL THE KIDS IN FERAL!

CHAPTER 3

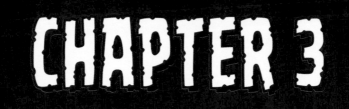

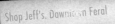

JEFF'S A-OK GROCERY
JEFF'S A-OK GROCERY
Shop Jeff's. Downtown Feral
Stopped in this town.
Something weird about it.
Need to look into it.
Jodella Fearingski
Kita Street
Winslow AZ
86047

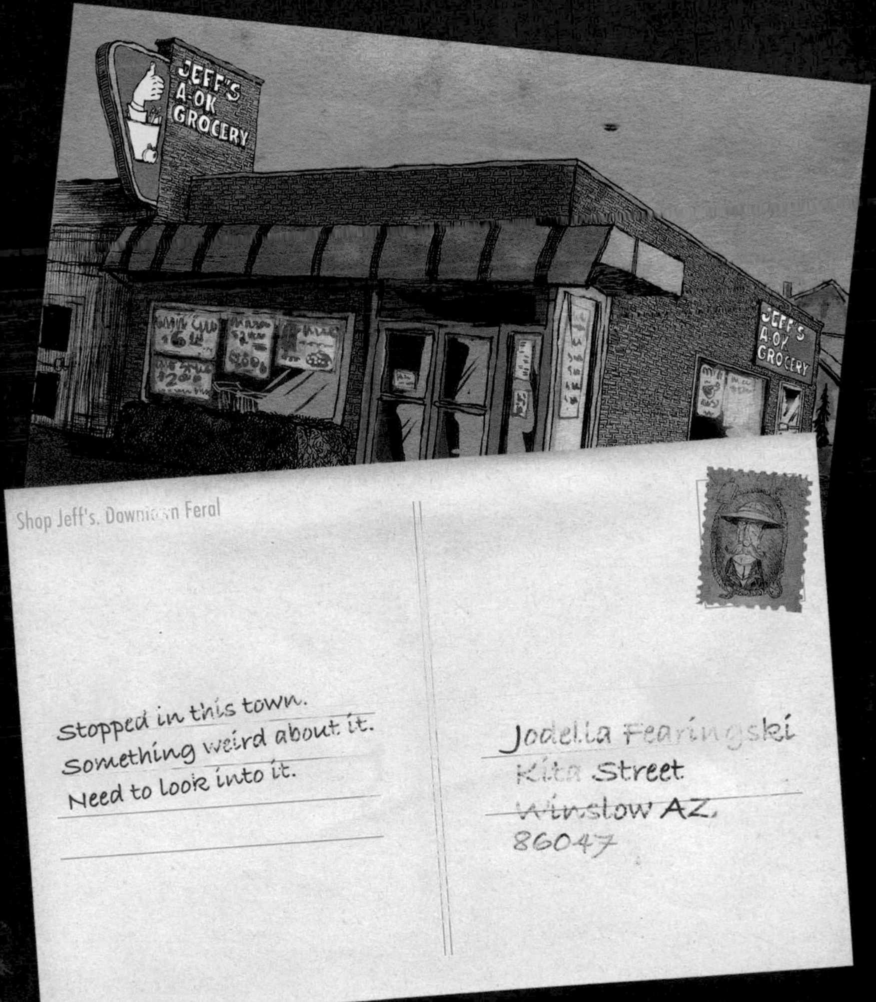

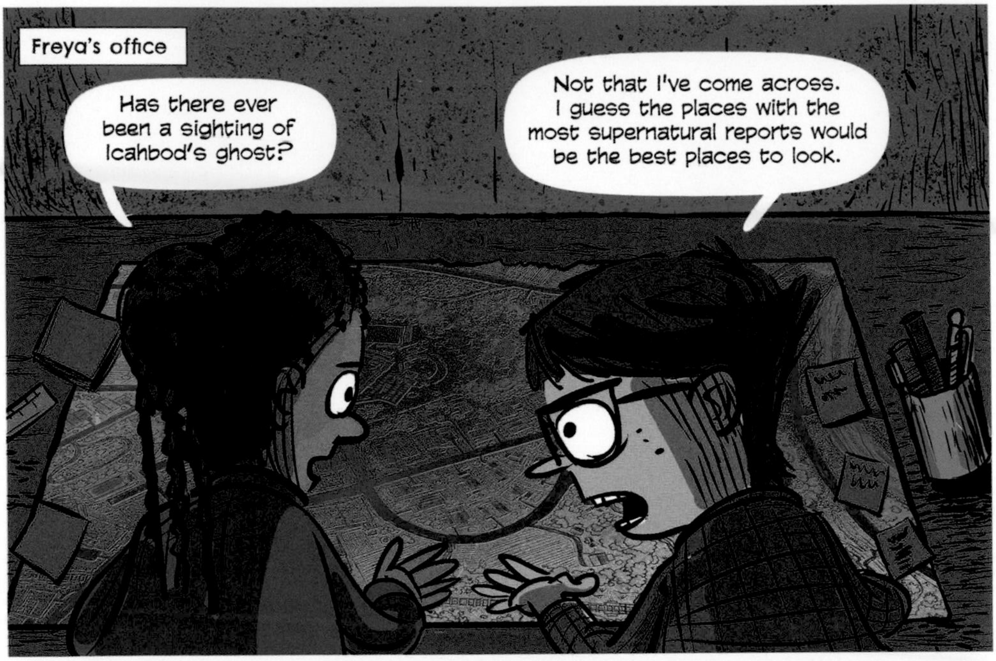
Freya's office
Has there ever been a sighting of Icahbod's ghost?
Not that I've come across. I guess the places with the most supernatural reports would be the best places to look.

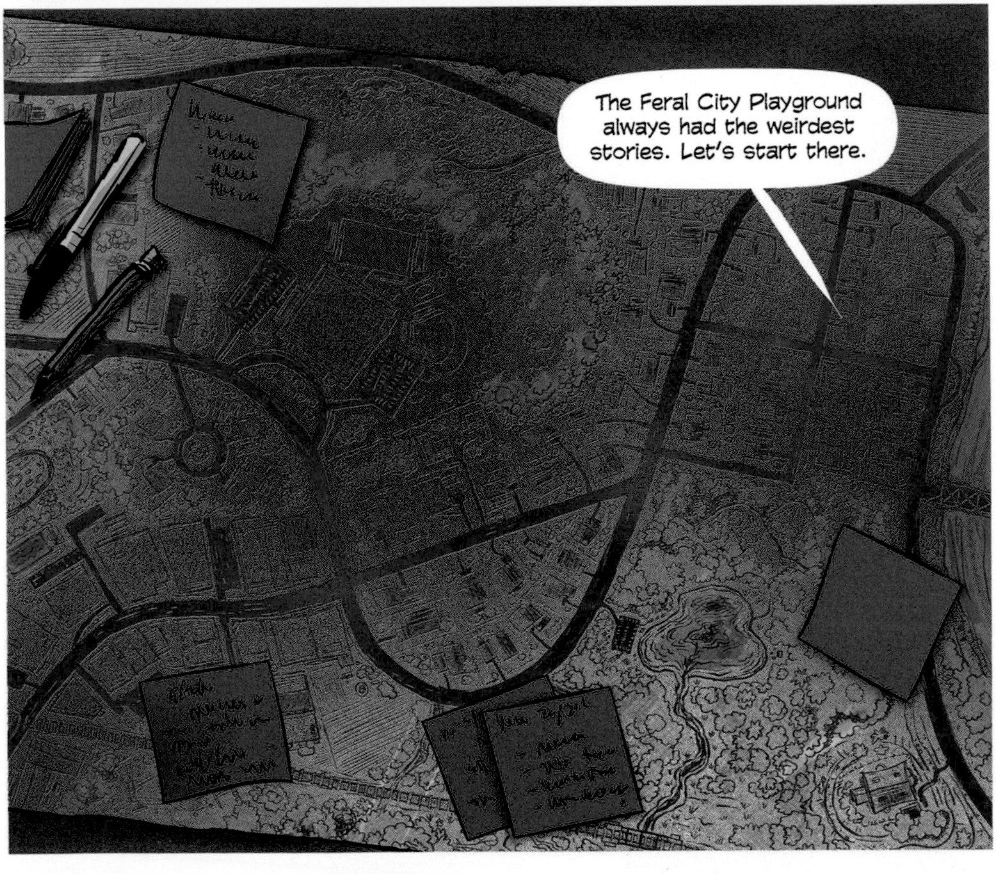
The Feral City Playground always had the weirdest stories. Let's start there.

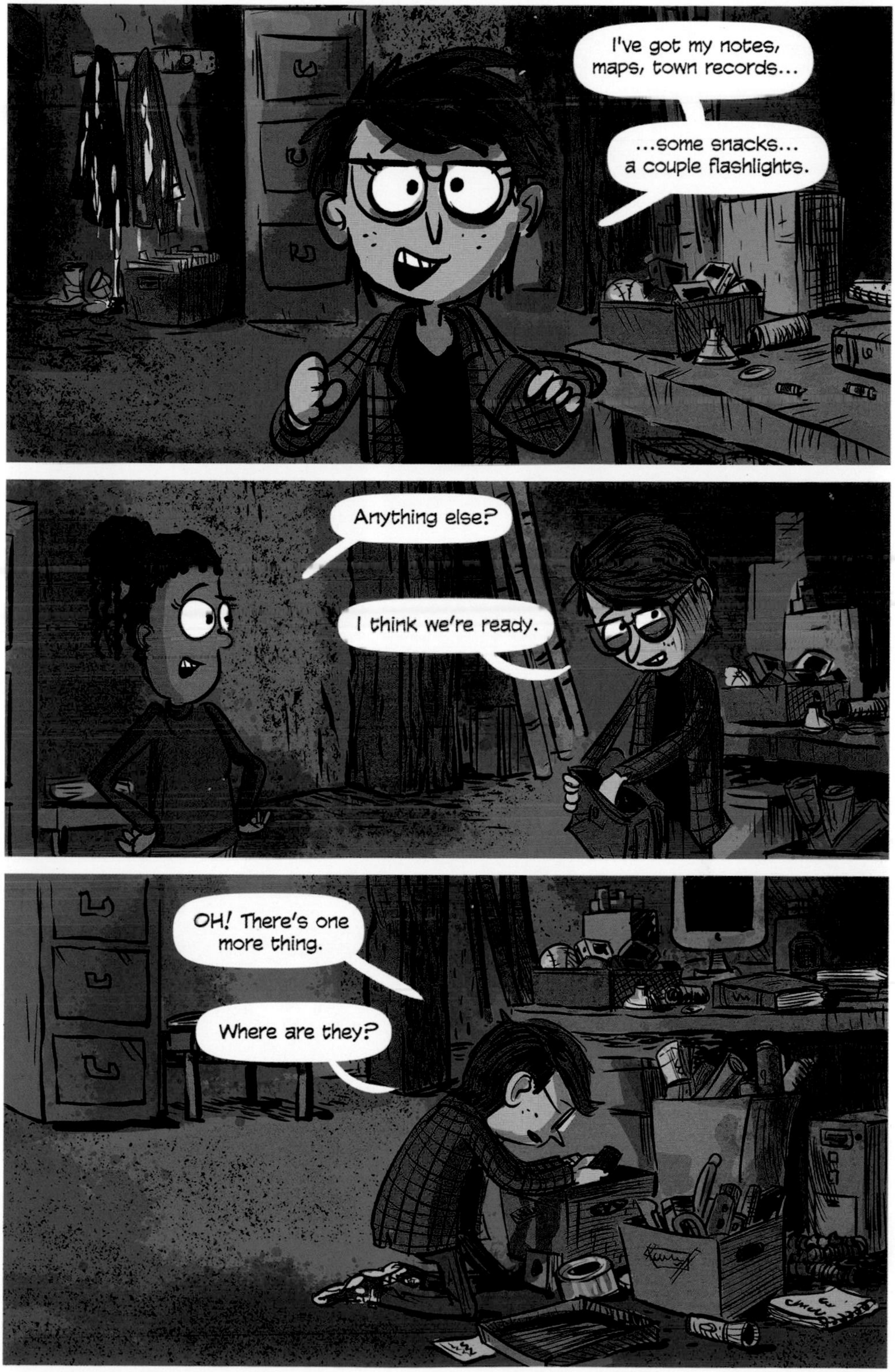
I've got my notes, maps, town records...
...some snacks... a couple flashlights.
Anything else?
I think we're ready.
OH! There's one more thing.
Where are they?

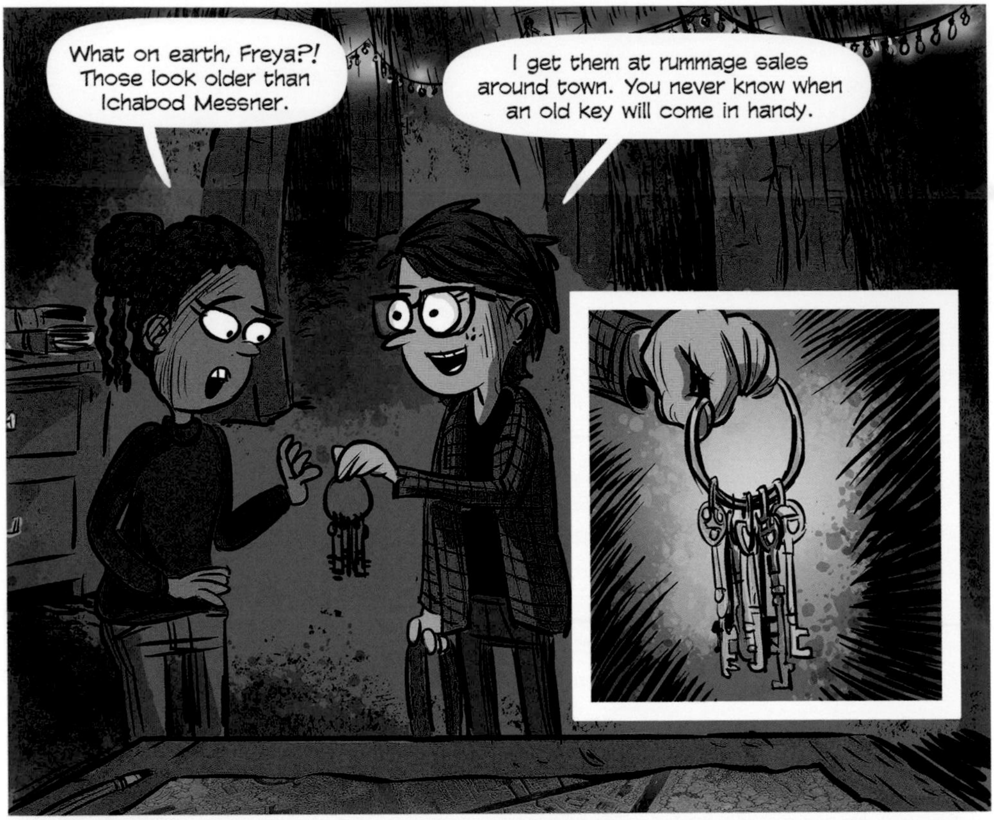
What on earth, Freya?! Those look older than Ichabod Messner.
I get them at rummage sales around town. You never know when an old key will come in handy.

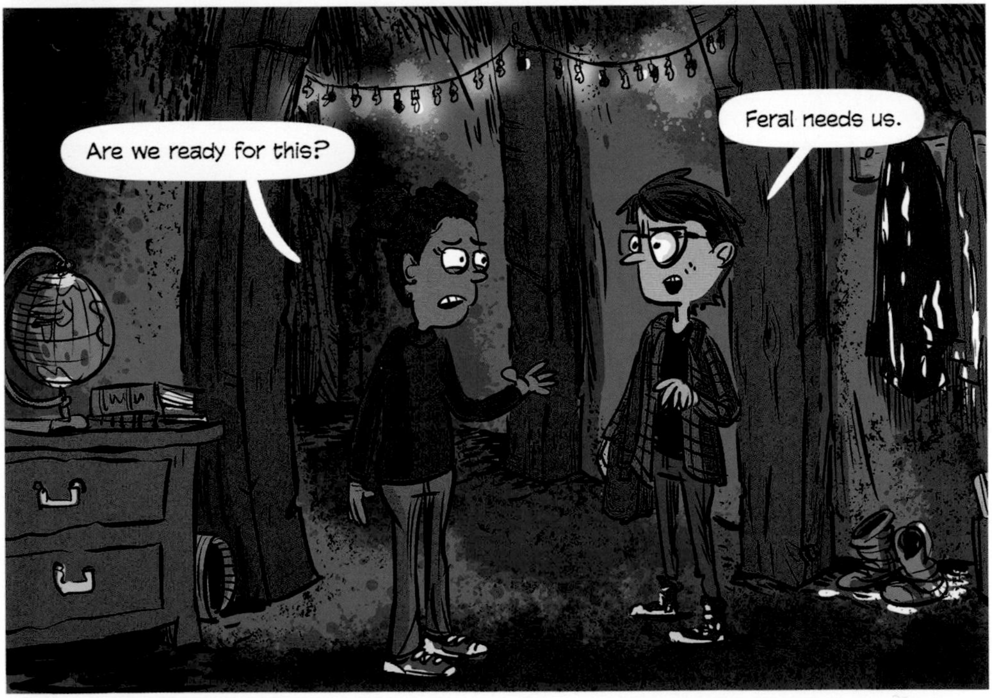
Are we ready for this?
Feral needs us.

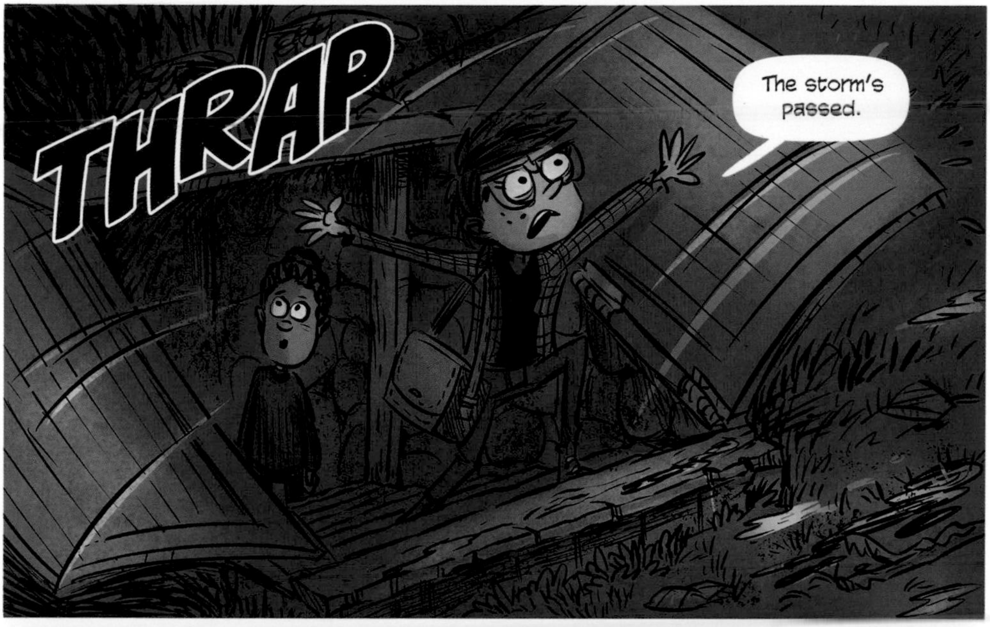
THRAP
The storm's passed.

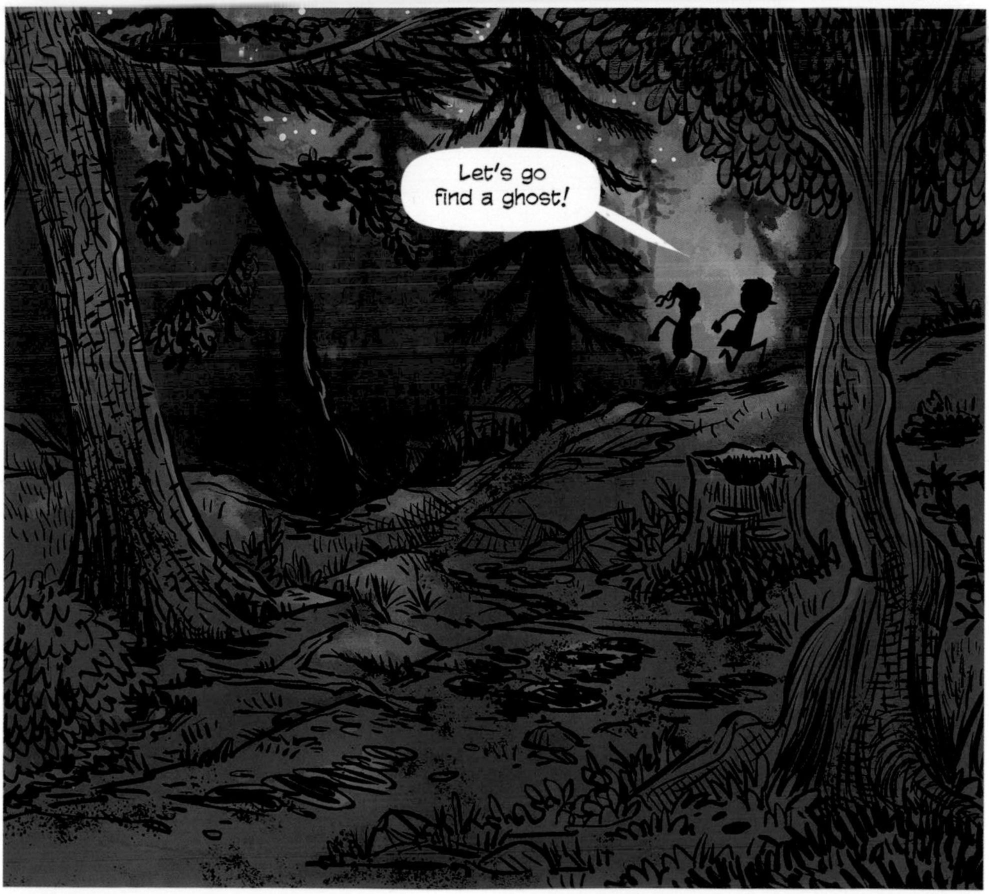
Let's go find a ghost!

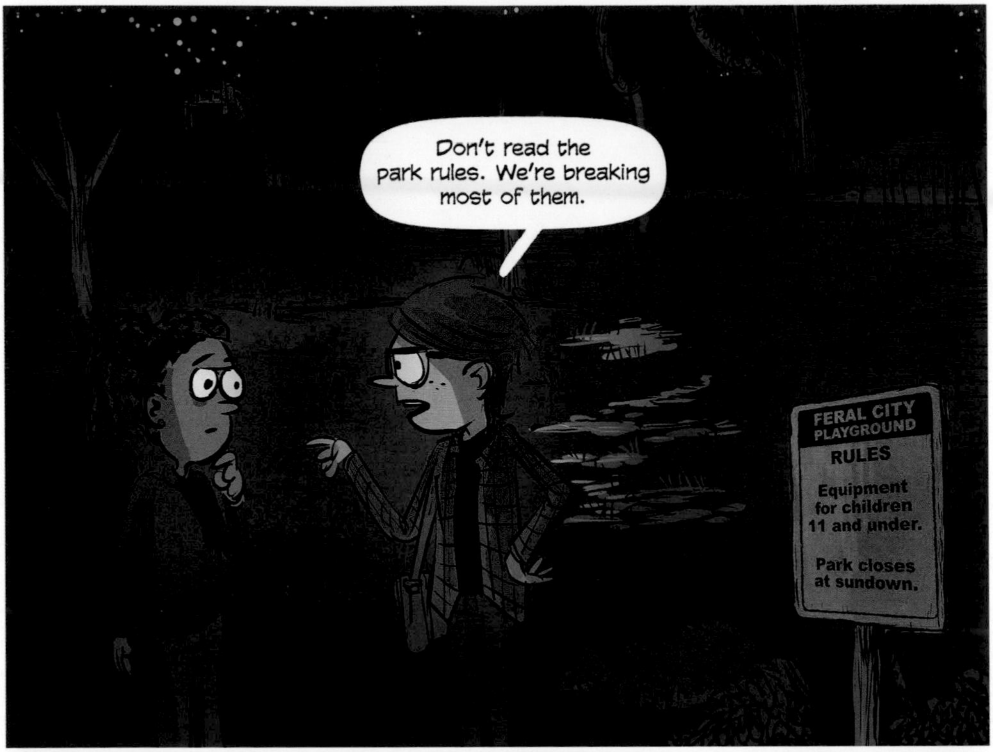
Don't read the park rules. We're breaking most of them.
FERAL CITY PLAYGROUND
RULES
Equipment for children 11 and under.
Park closes at sundown.

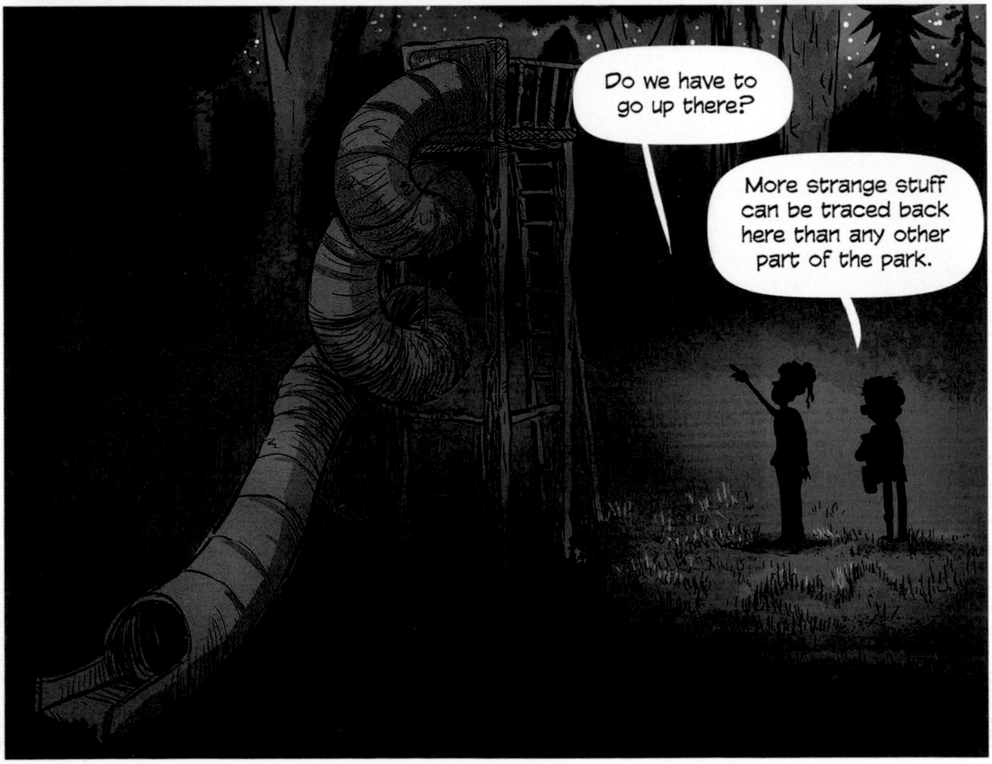
Do we have to go up there?
More strange stuff can be traced back here than any other part of the park.

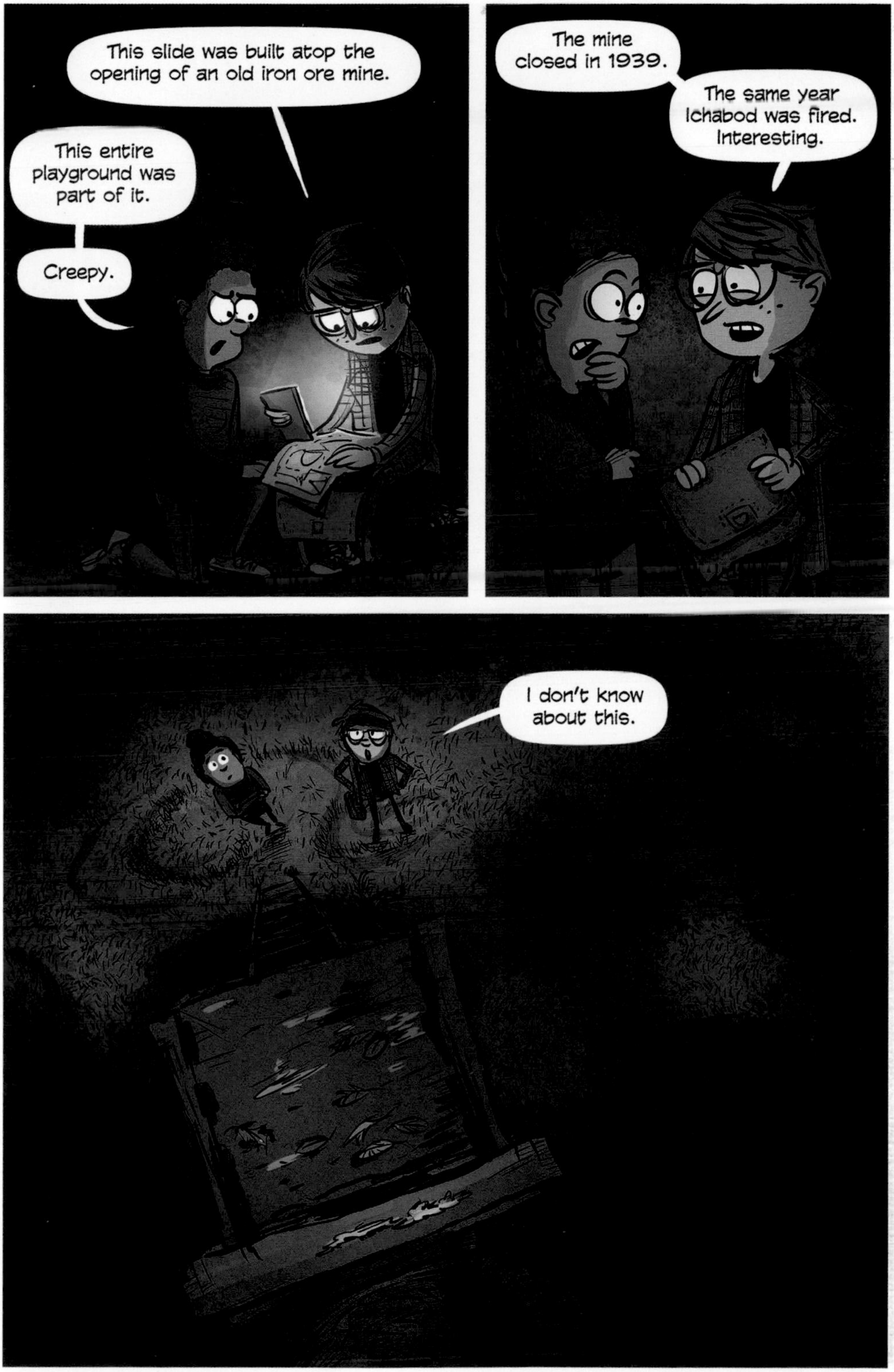
This slide was built atop the opening of an old iron ore mine.
This entire playground was part of it.
Creepy.
The mine closed in 1939.
The same year Ichabod was fired. Interesting.
I don't know about this.

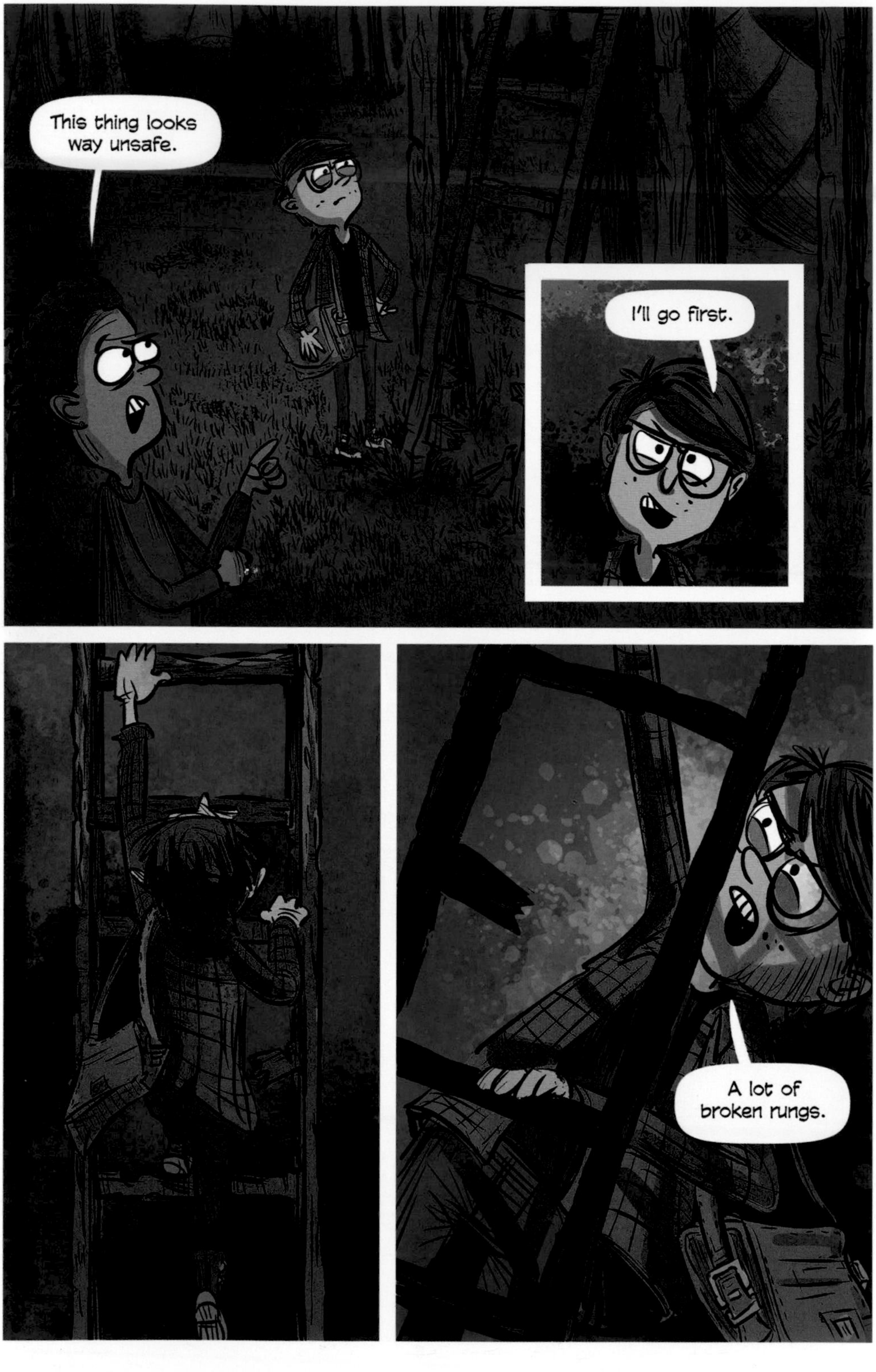
This thing looks way unsafe.
I'll go first.
A lot of broken rungs.

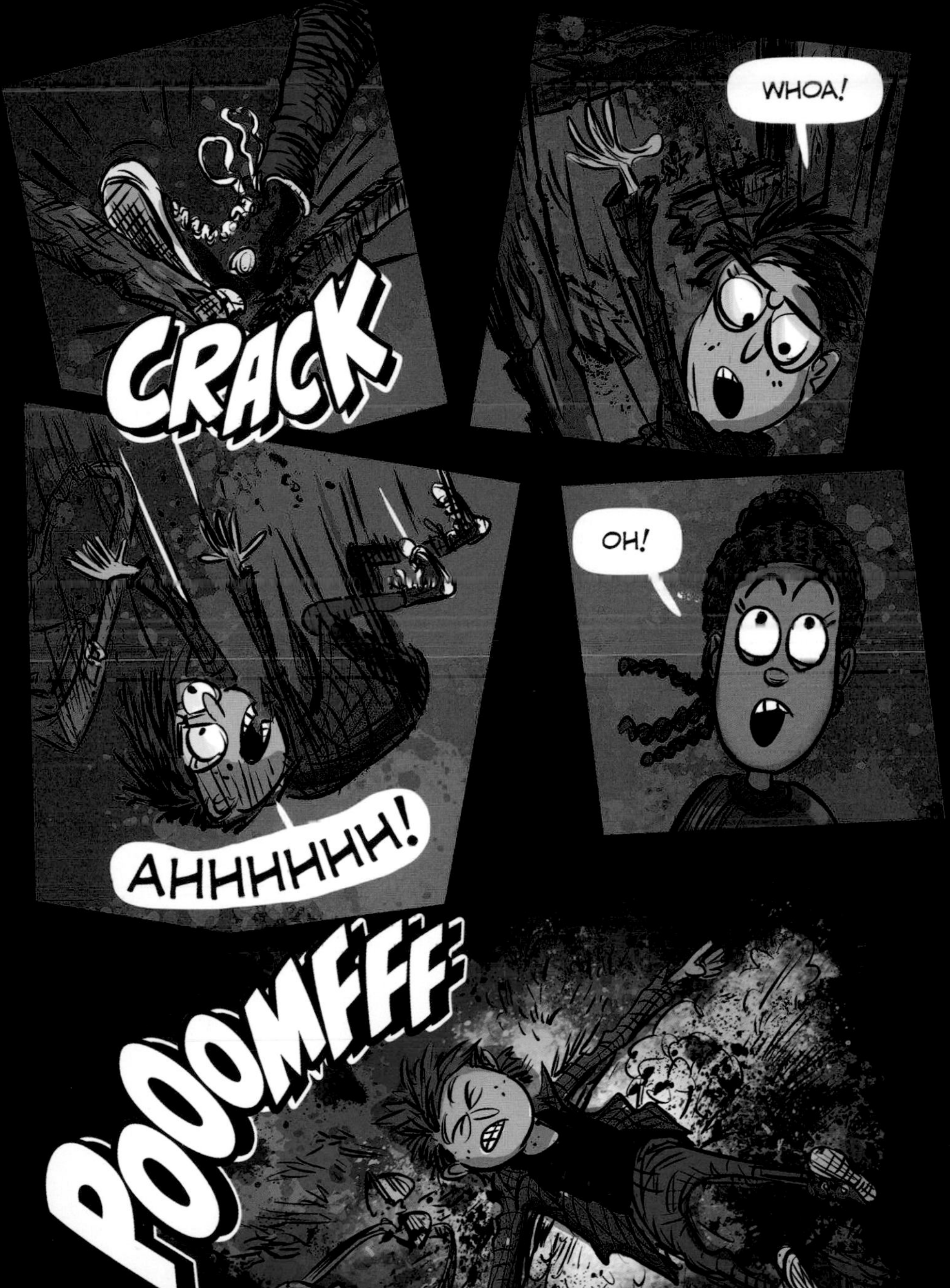
CRACK
WHOA!
AHHHHHH!
OH!
POOOMFFF

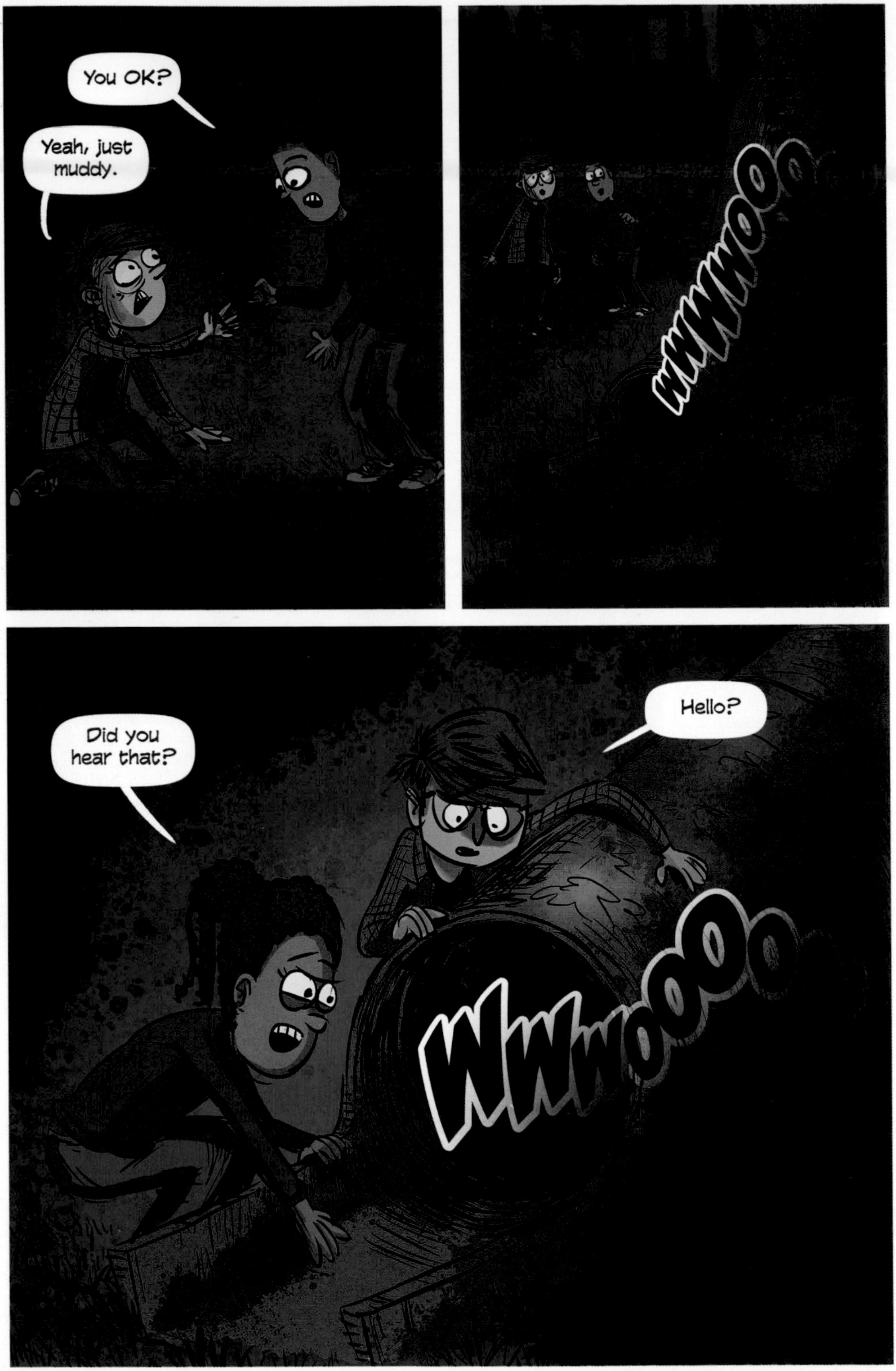
You OK?
Yeah, just muddy.
WWWWOOOO
Did you hear that?
Hello?
WWWOOOOO

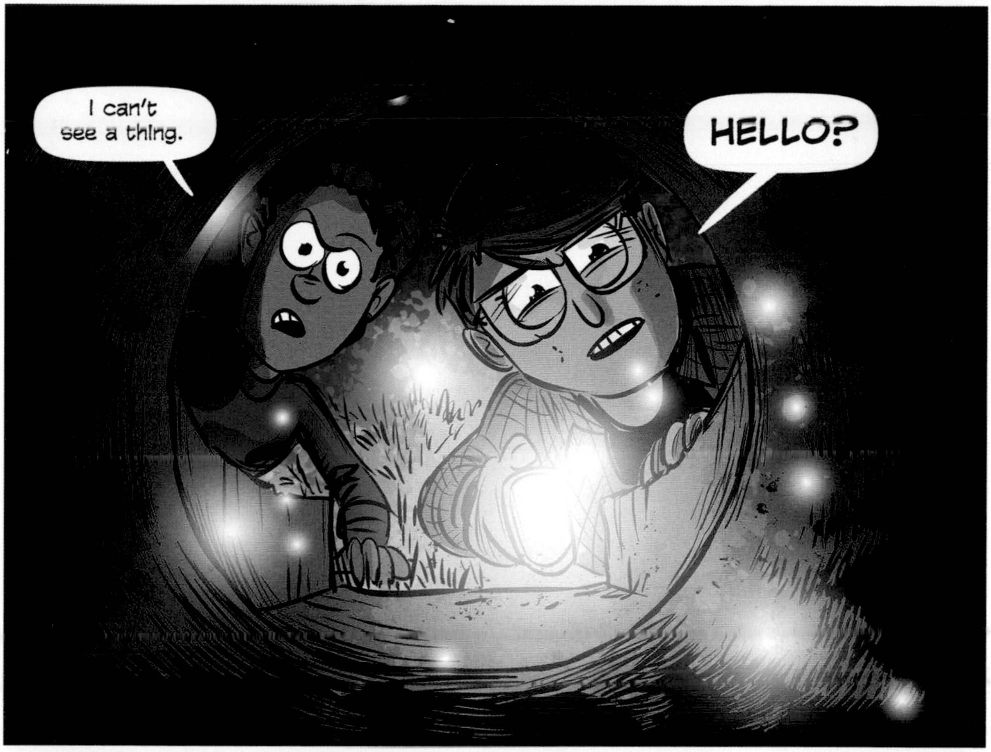
I can't see a thing.
HELLO?

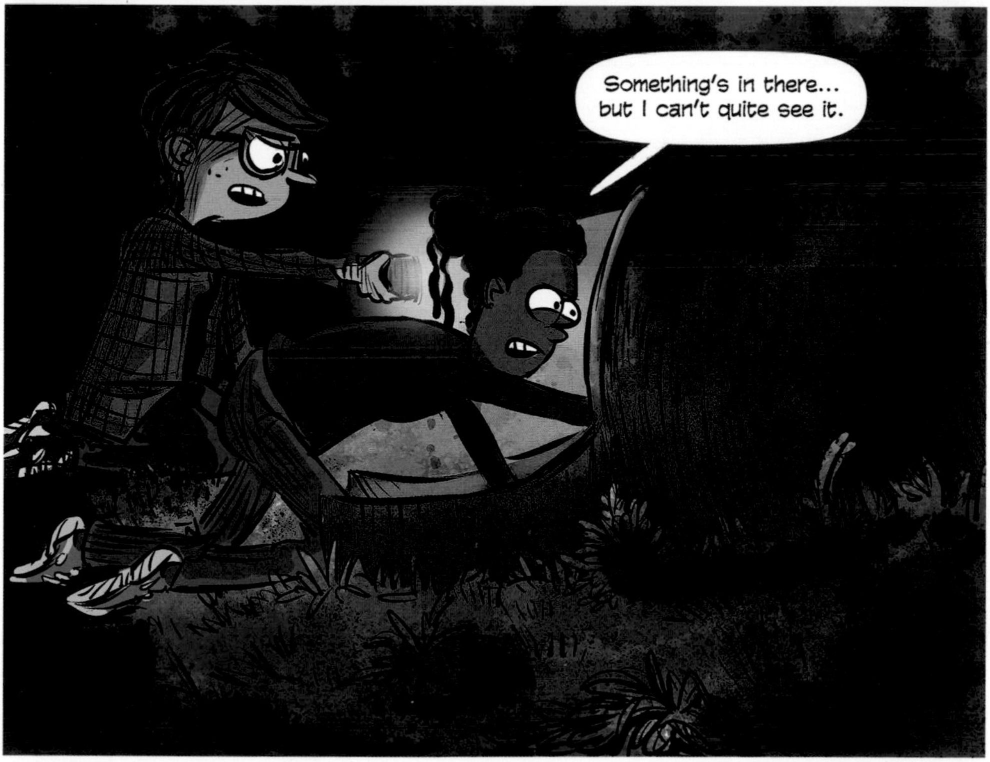
Something's in there... but I can't quite see it.

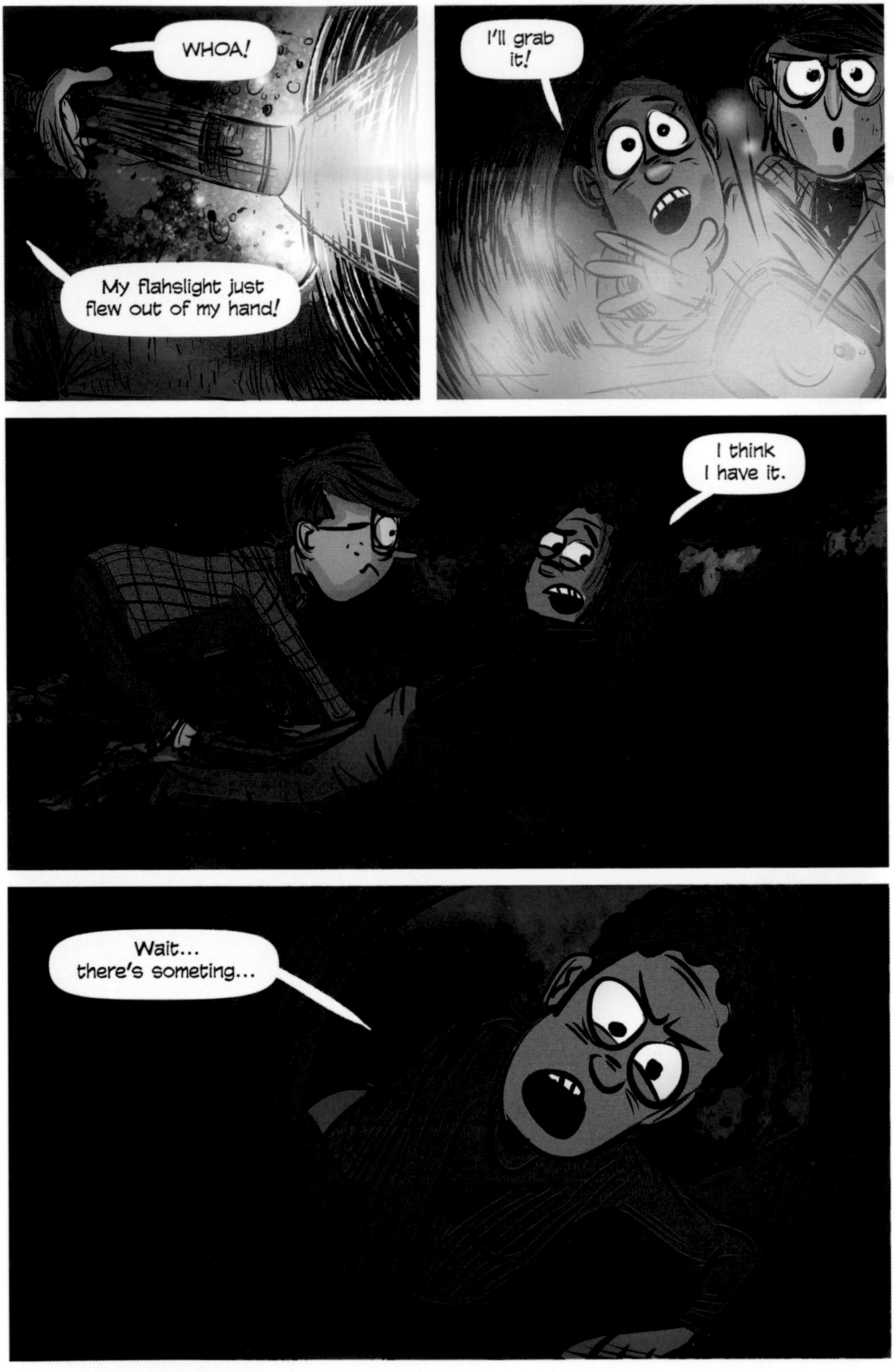
WHOA!
My flahslight just flew out of my hand!
I'll grab it!
I think I have it.
Wait... there's someting...

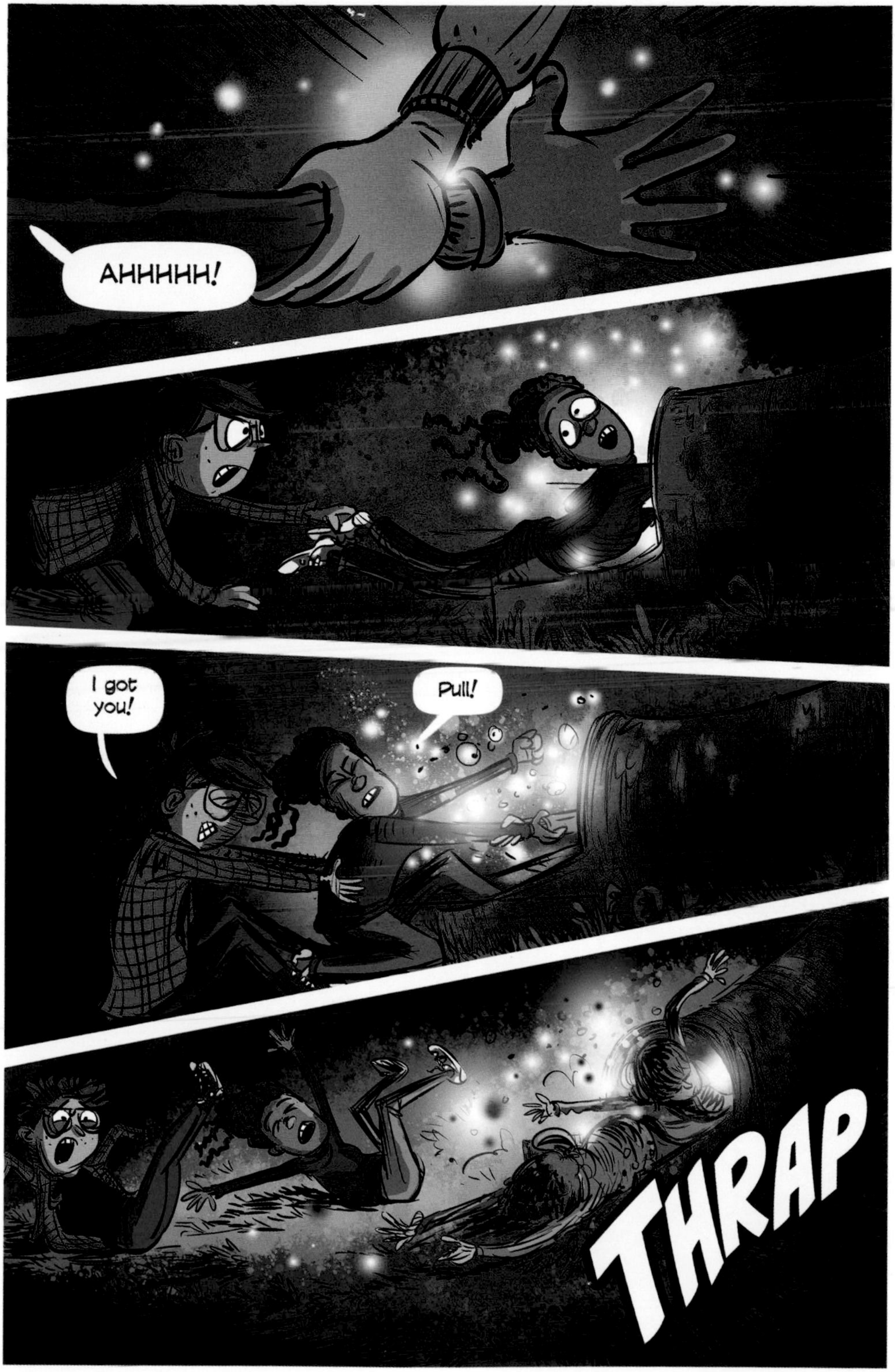
AHHHHH!
I got you!
Pull!
THRAP

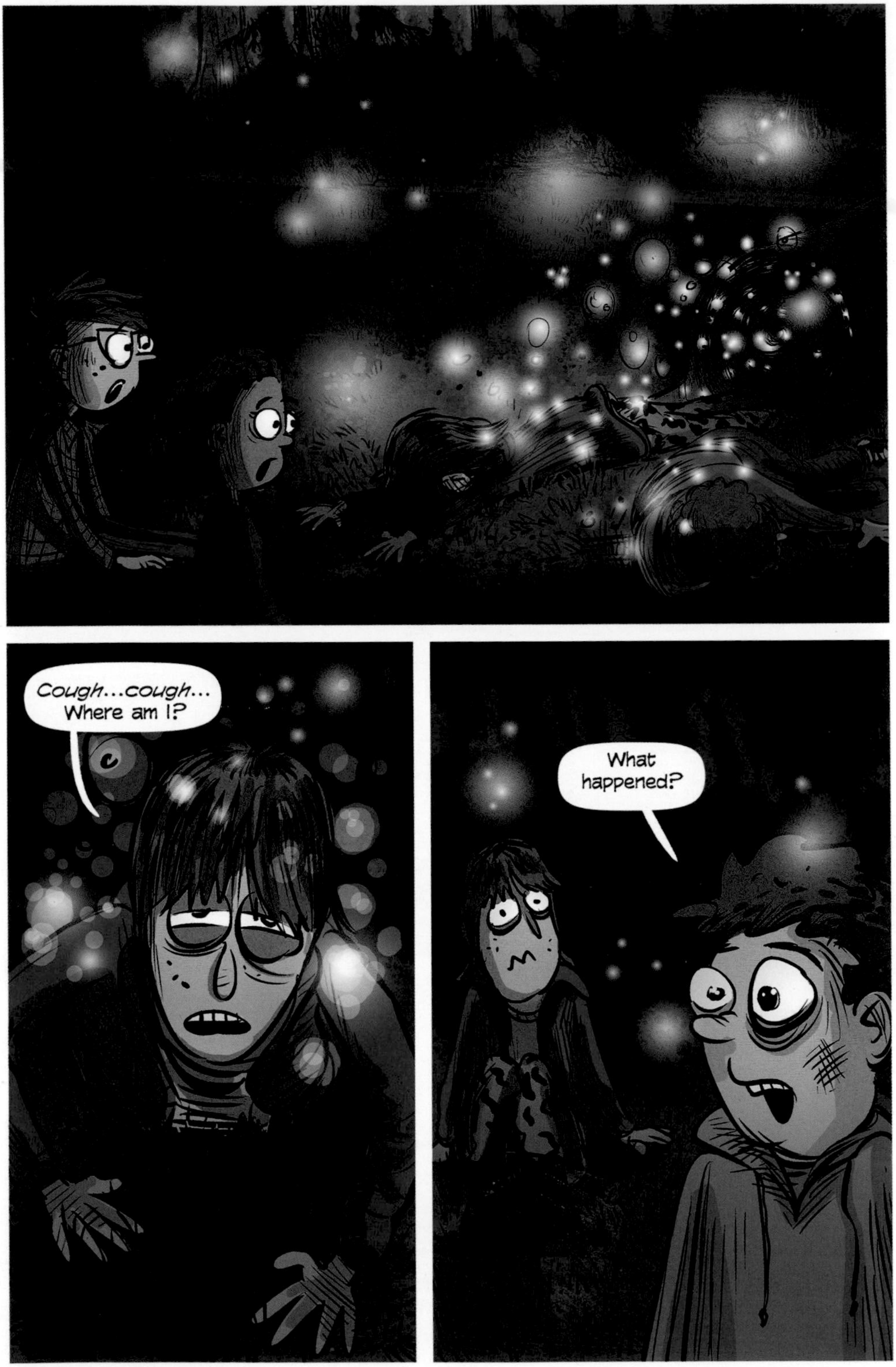
Cough...*cough*... Where am I?
What happened?

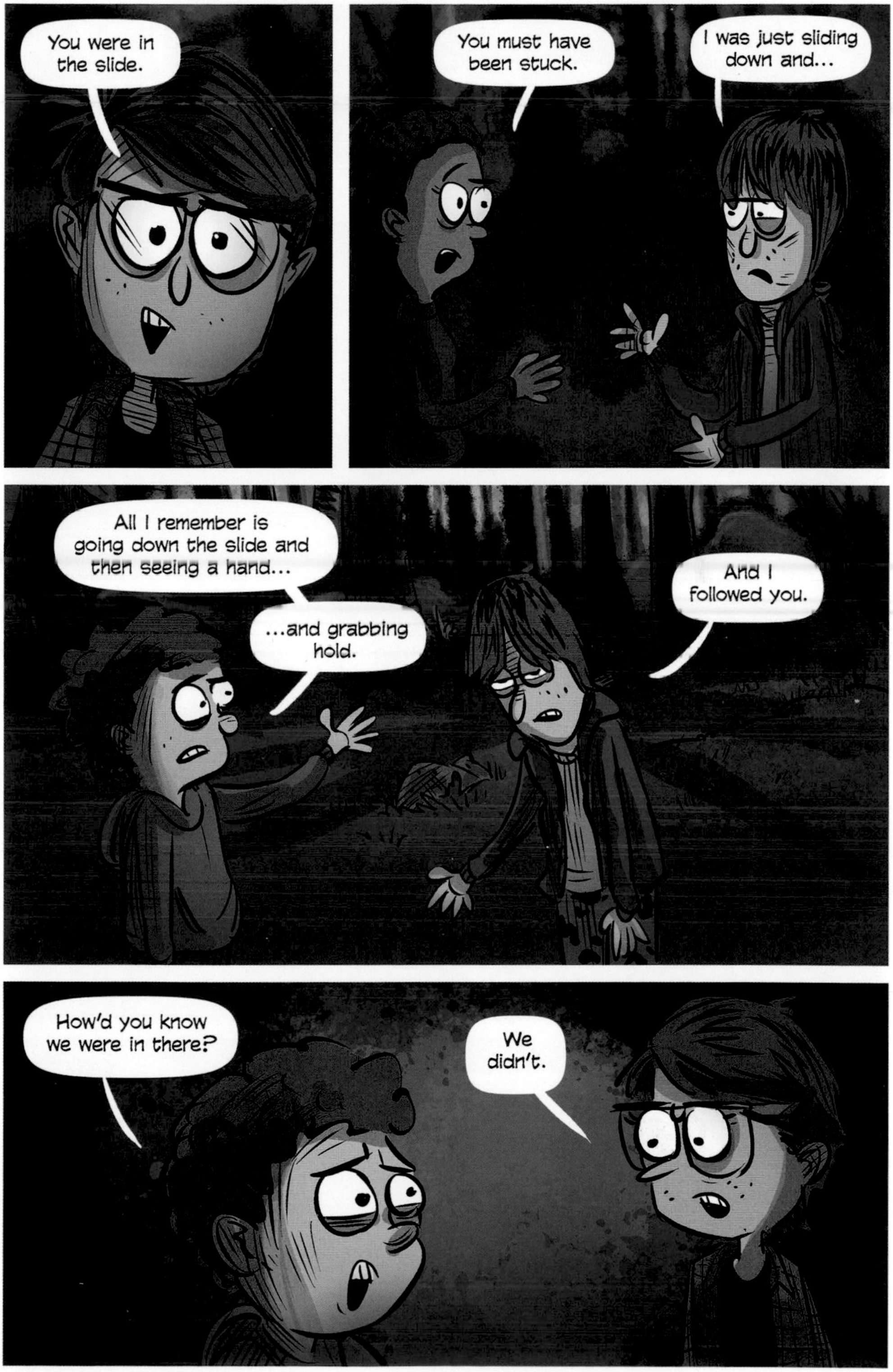
You were in the slide.
You must have been stuck.
I was just sliding down and...
All I remember is going down the slide and then seeing a hand...
...and grabbing hold.
And I followed you.
How'd you know we were in there?
We didn't.

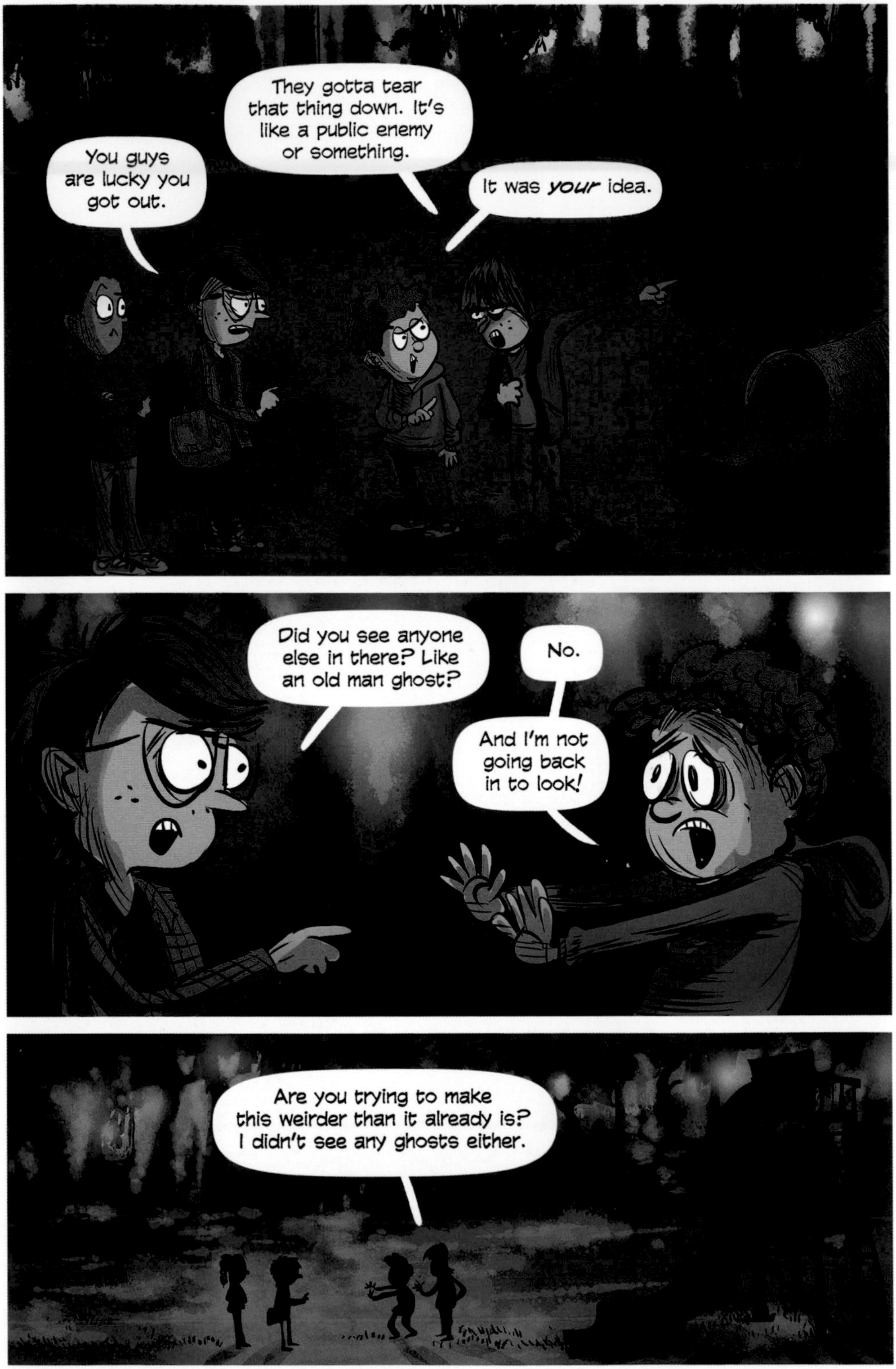
You guys are lucky you got out.
They gotta tear that thing down. It's like a public enemy or something.
It was *your* idea.
Did you see anyone else in there? Like an old man ghost?
No.
And I'm not going back in to look!
Are you trying to make this weirder than it already is? I didn't see any ghosts either.

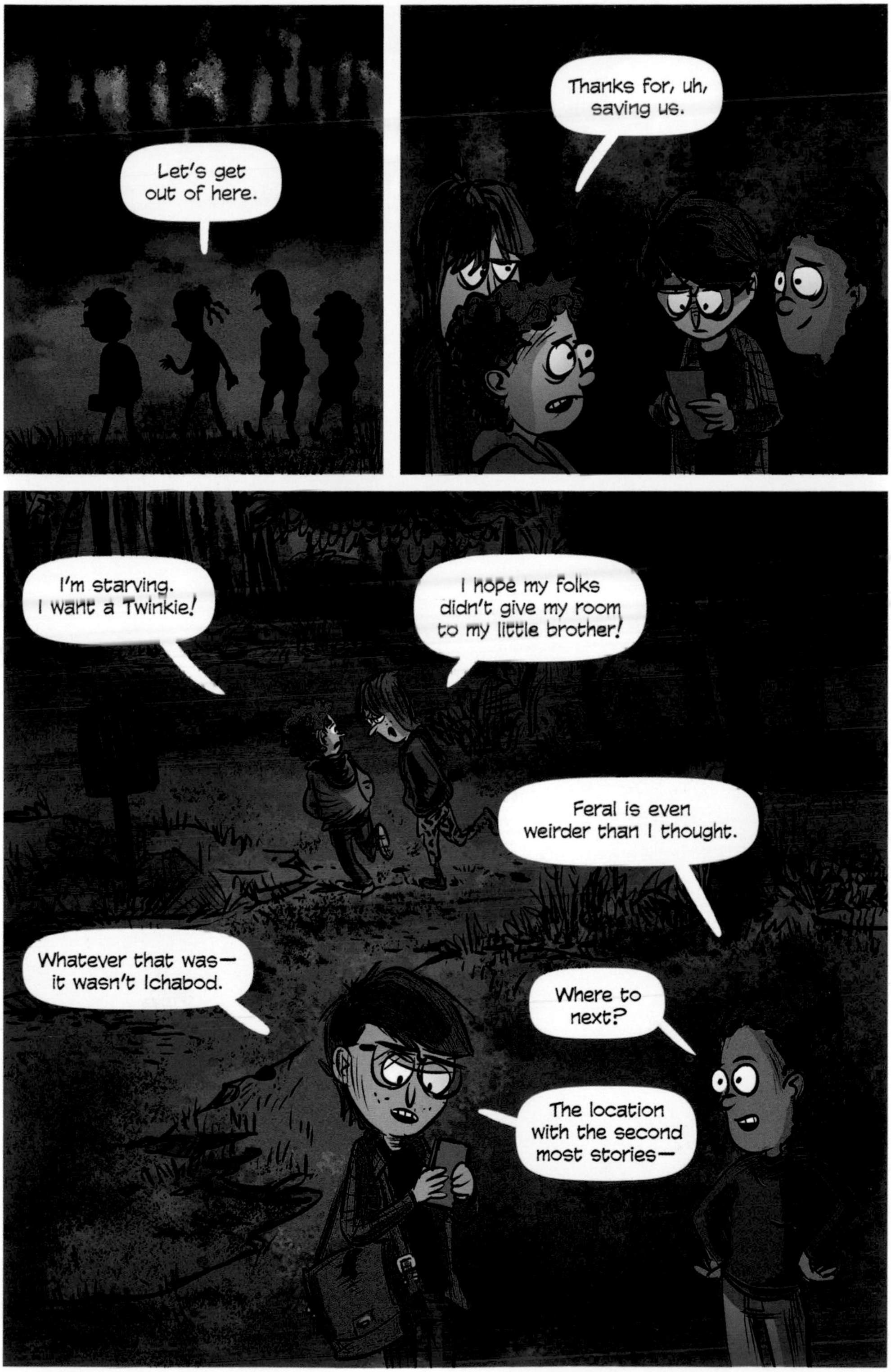
Let's get out of here.
Thanks for, uh, saving us.
I'm starving. I want a Twinkie!
I hope my folks didn't give my room to my little brother!
Feral is even weirder than I thought.
Whatever that was— it wasn't Ichabod.
Where to next?
The location with the second most stories—

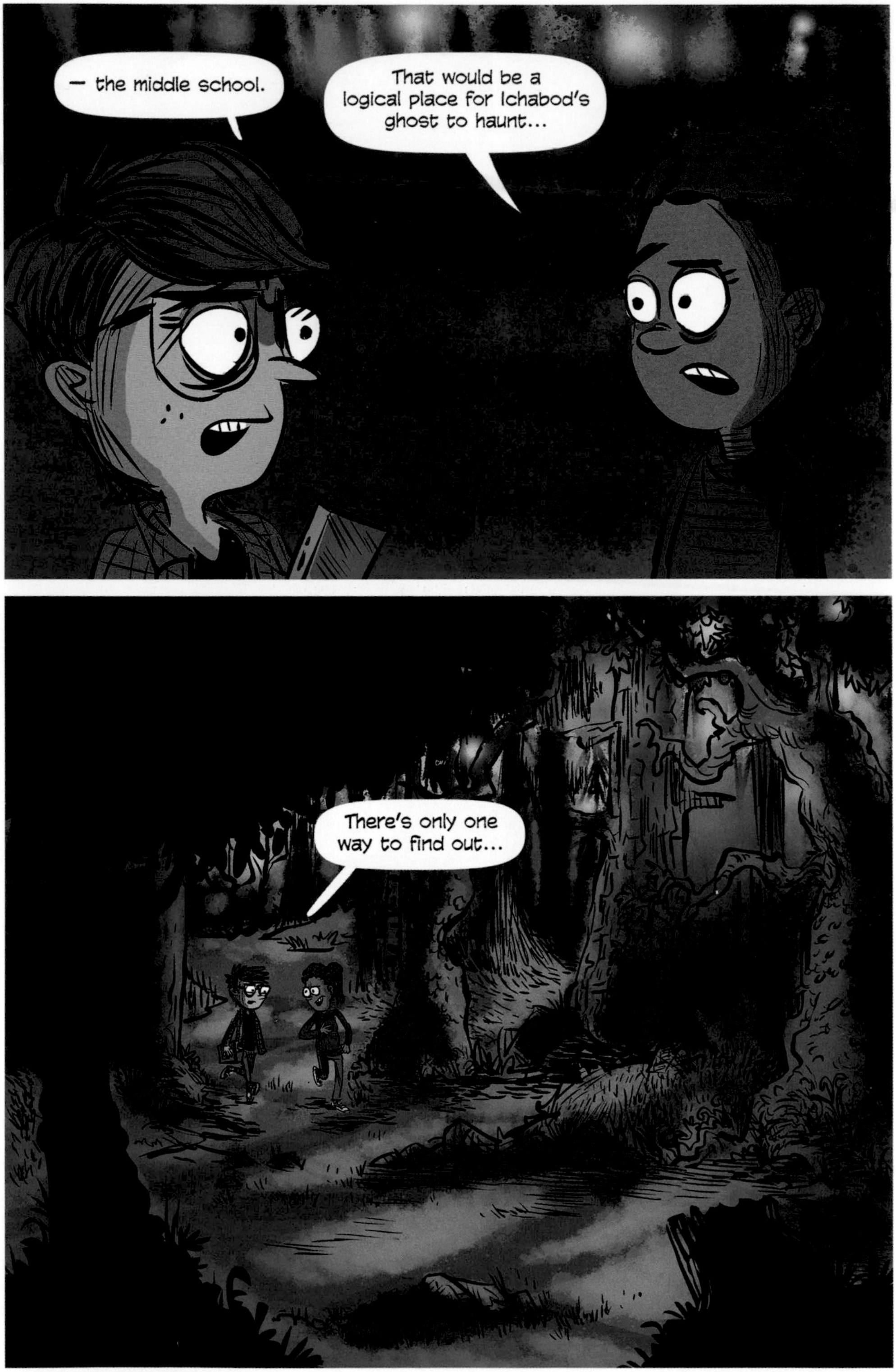
— the middle school.
That would be a logical place for Ichabod's ghost to haunt...
There's only one way to find out...

CHAPTER 4

County Road 52 Rest Area
In Beautiful Feral

I don't know why they make
a postcard of a rest stop, but
that's not the only odd thing
about this town.
Be home soonish—
Scott

The Gordon Family
3688 Almond Tree Lane
13455

12¢

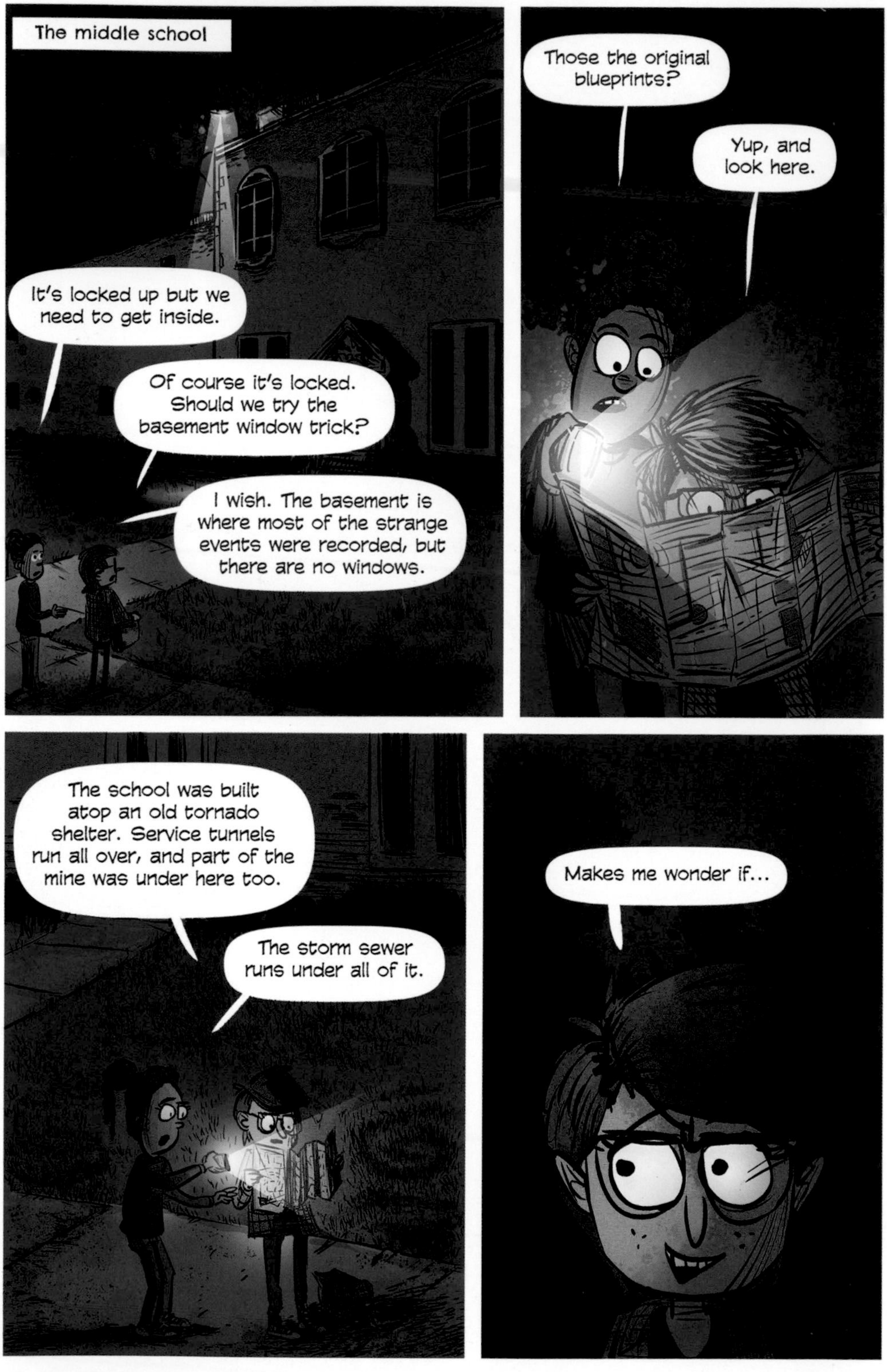
The middle school
It's locked up but we need to get inside.
Of course it's locked. Should we try the basement window trick?
I wish. The basement is where most of the strange events were recorded, but there are no windows.
Those the original blueprints?
Yup, and look here.
The school was built atop an old tornado shelter. Service tunnels run all over, and part of the mine was under here too.
The storm sewer runs under all of it.
Makes me wonder if...

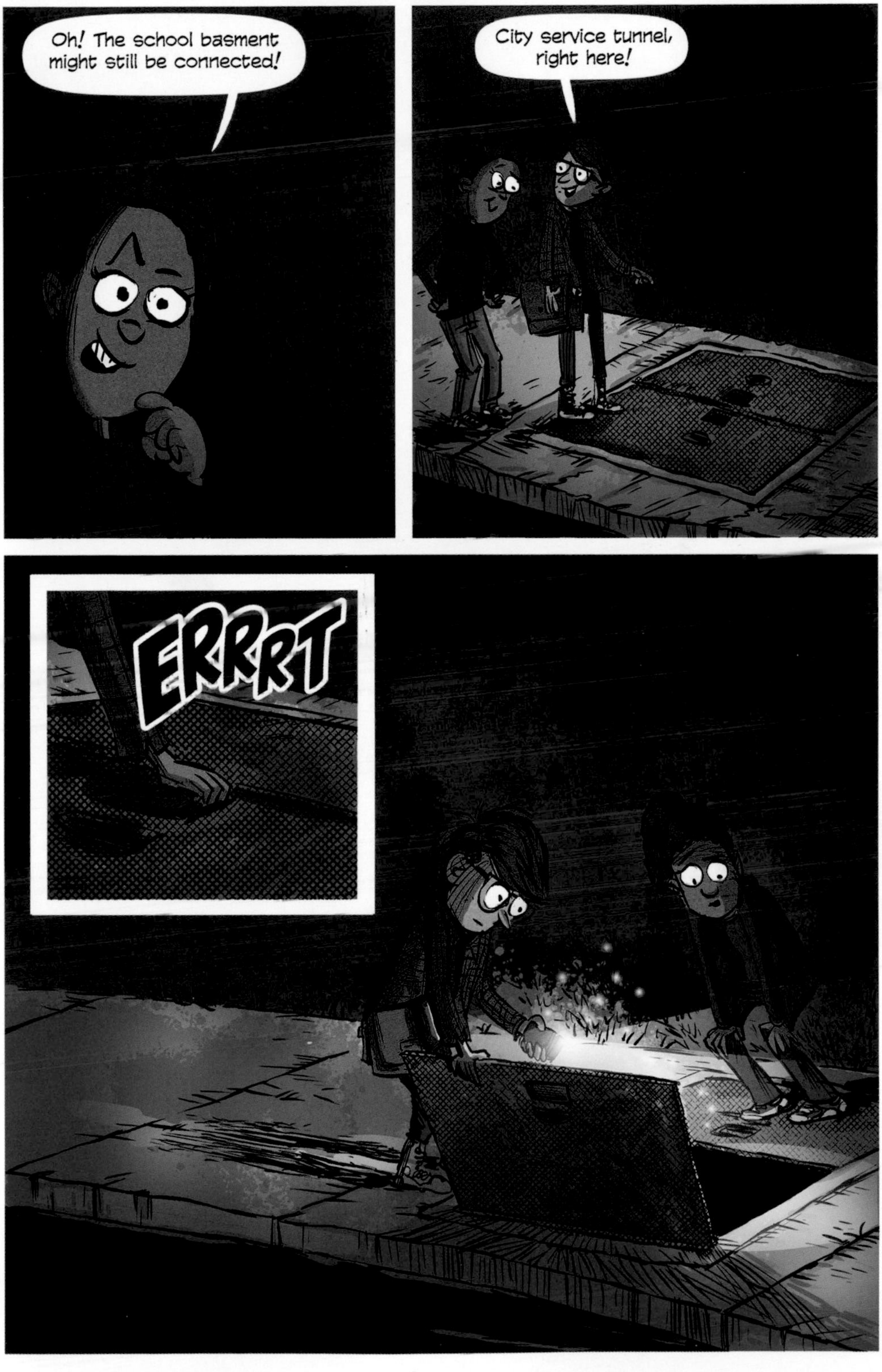
Oh! The school basment might still be connected!
City service tunnel, right here!
ERRRT

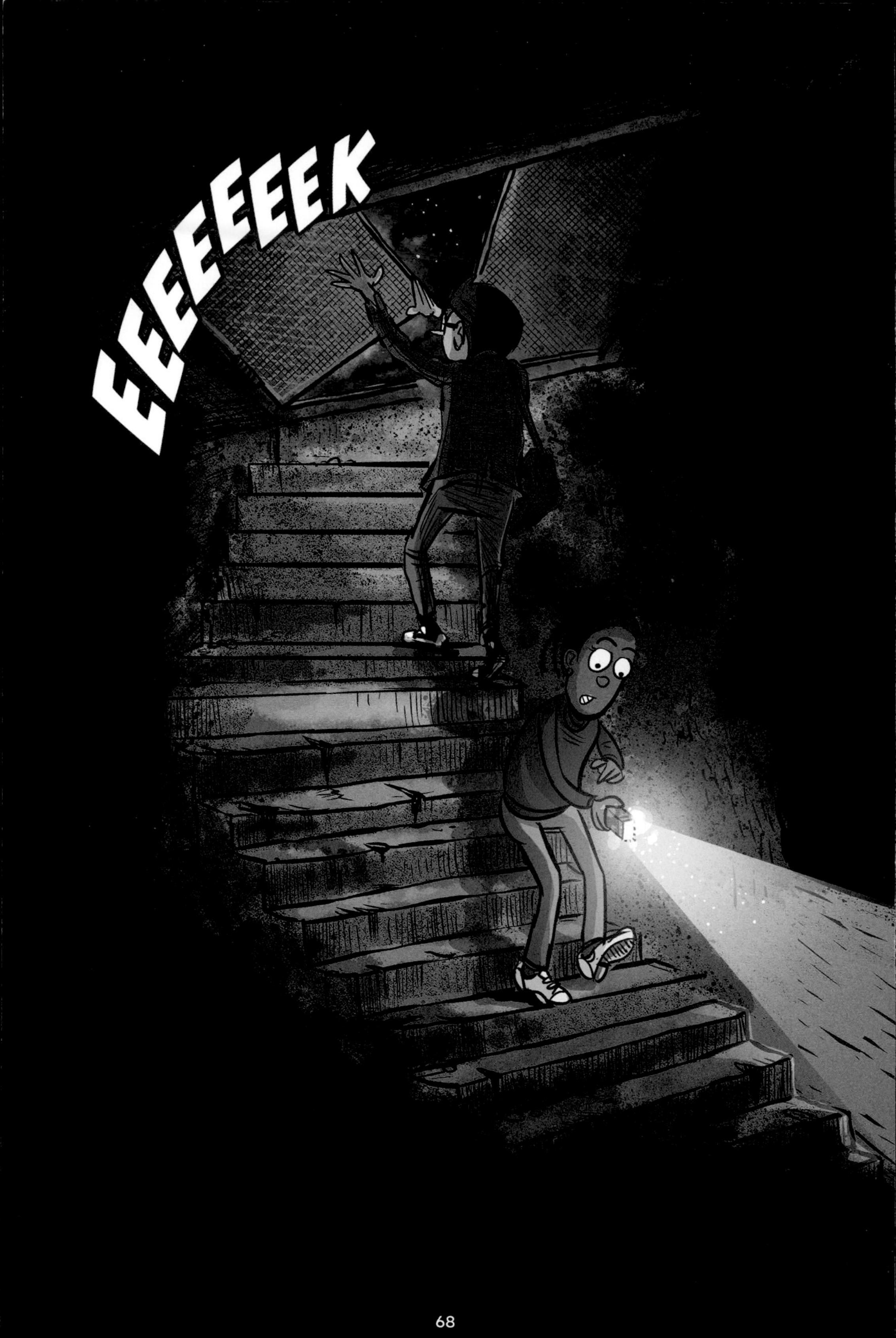
EEEEEEEK

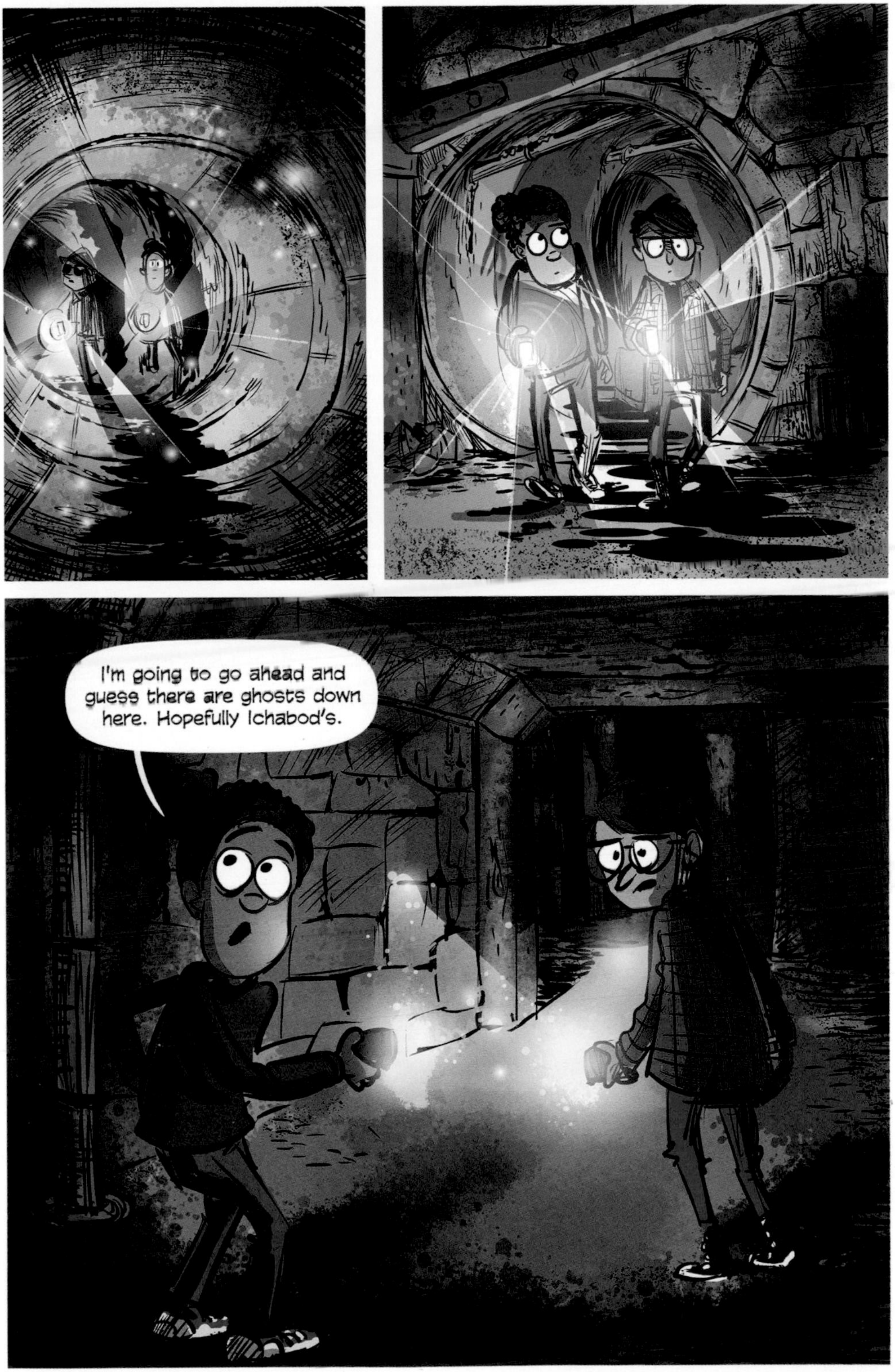
I'm going to go ahead and guess there are ghosts down here. Hopefully Ichabod's.

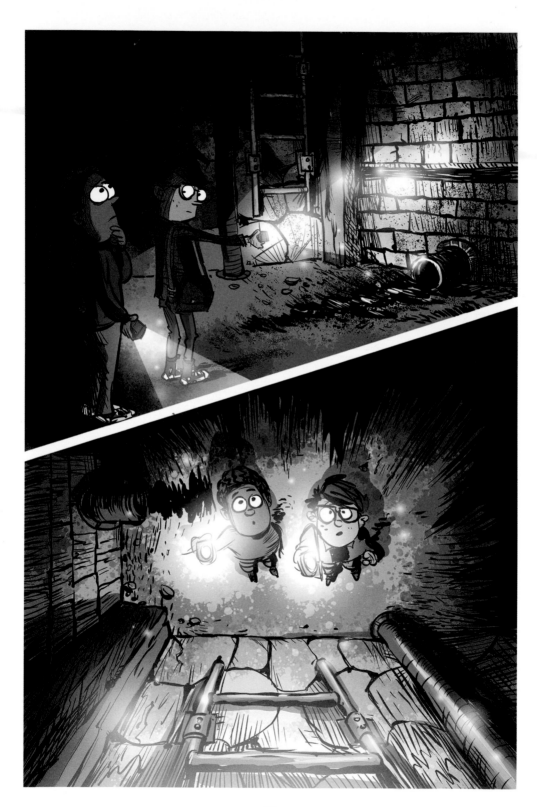

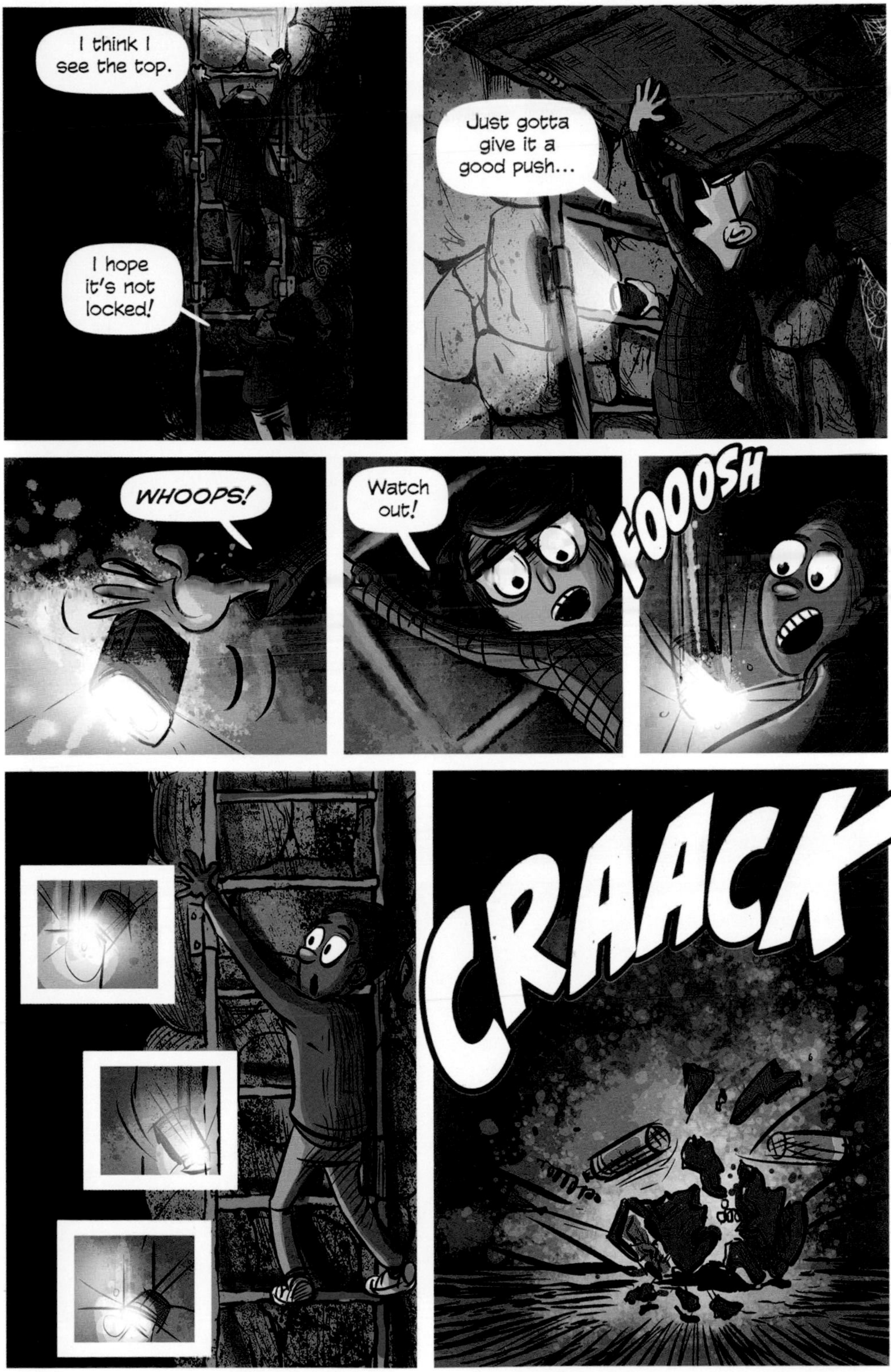
I think I see the top.
I hope it's not locked!
Just gotta give it a good push...
WHOOPS!
Watch out!
FOOOSH
CRAACK

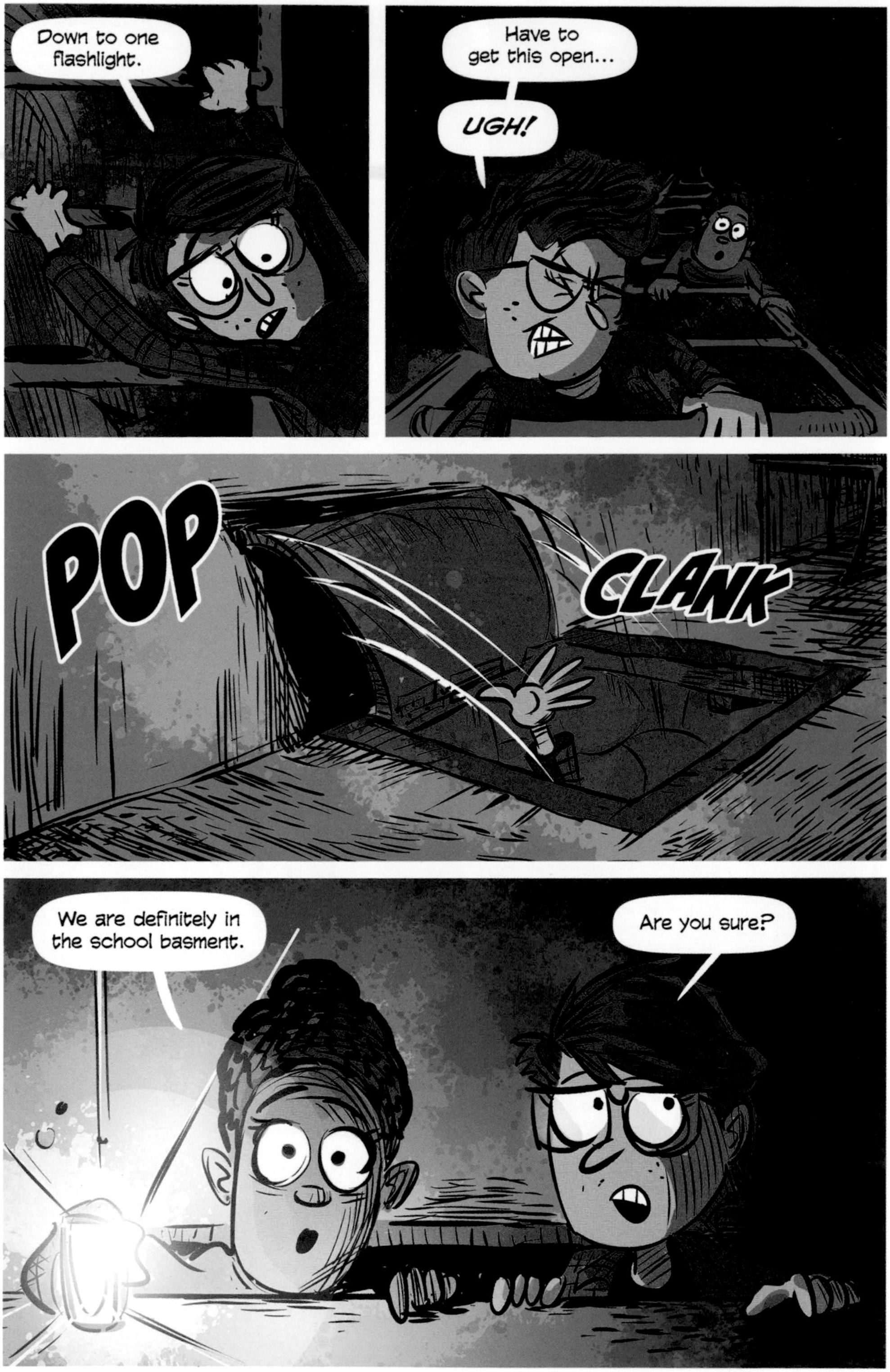
Down to one flashlight.
Have to get this open...
UGH!
POP
CLANK
We are definitely in the school basment.
Are you sure?

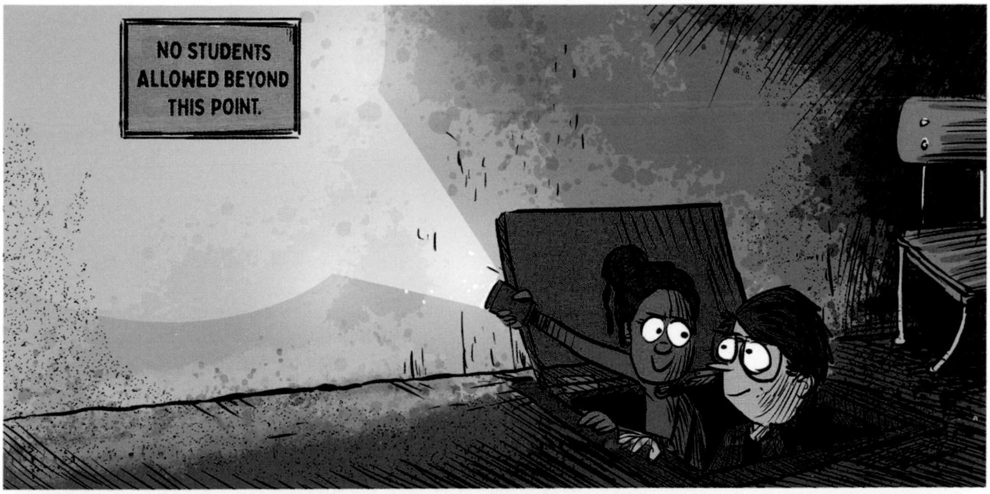
NO STUDENTS
ALLOWED BEYOND
THIS POINT.

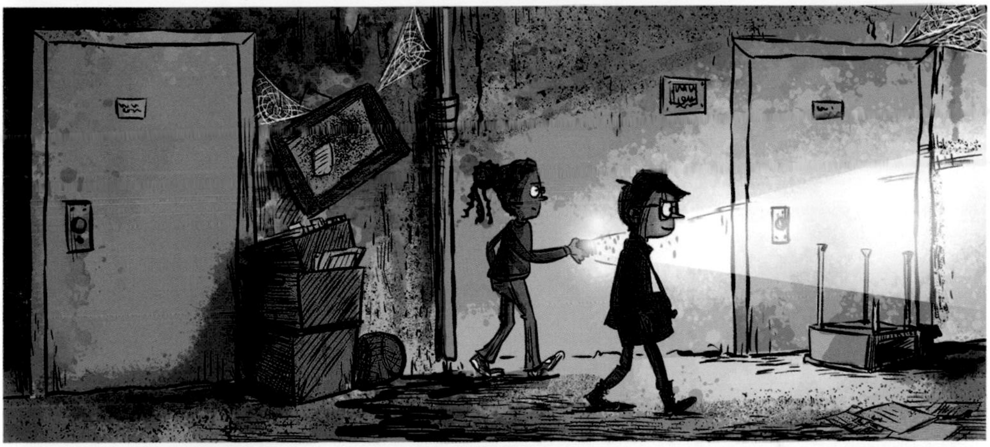

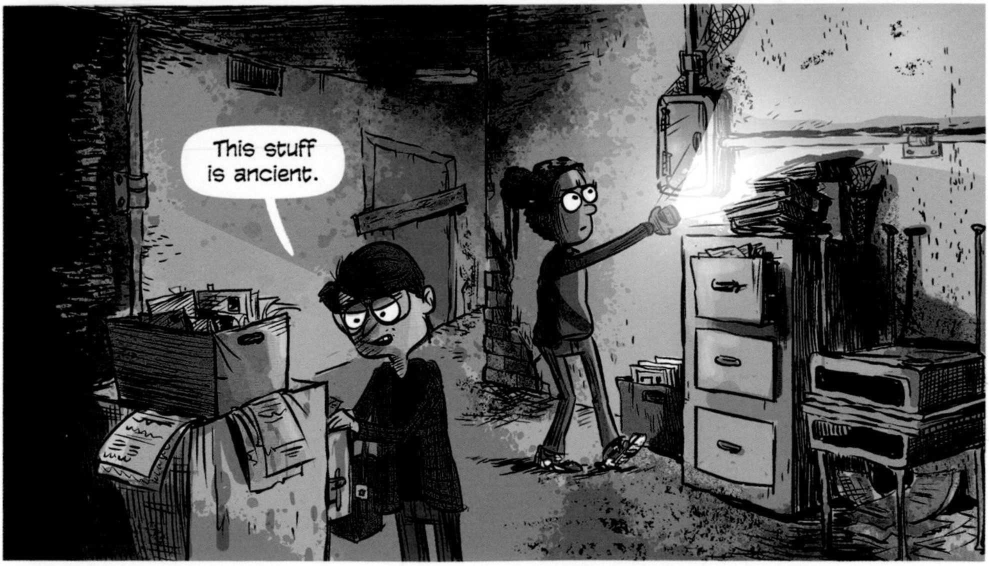
This stuff is ancient.

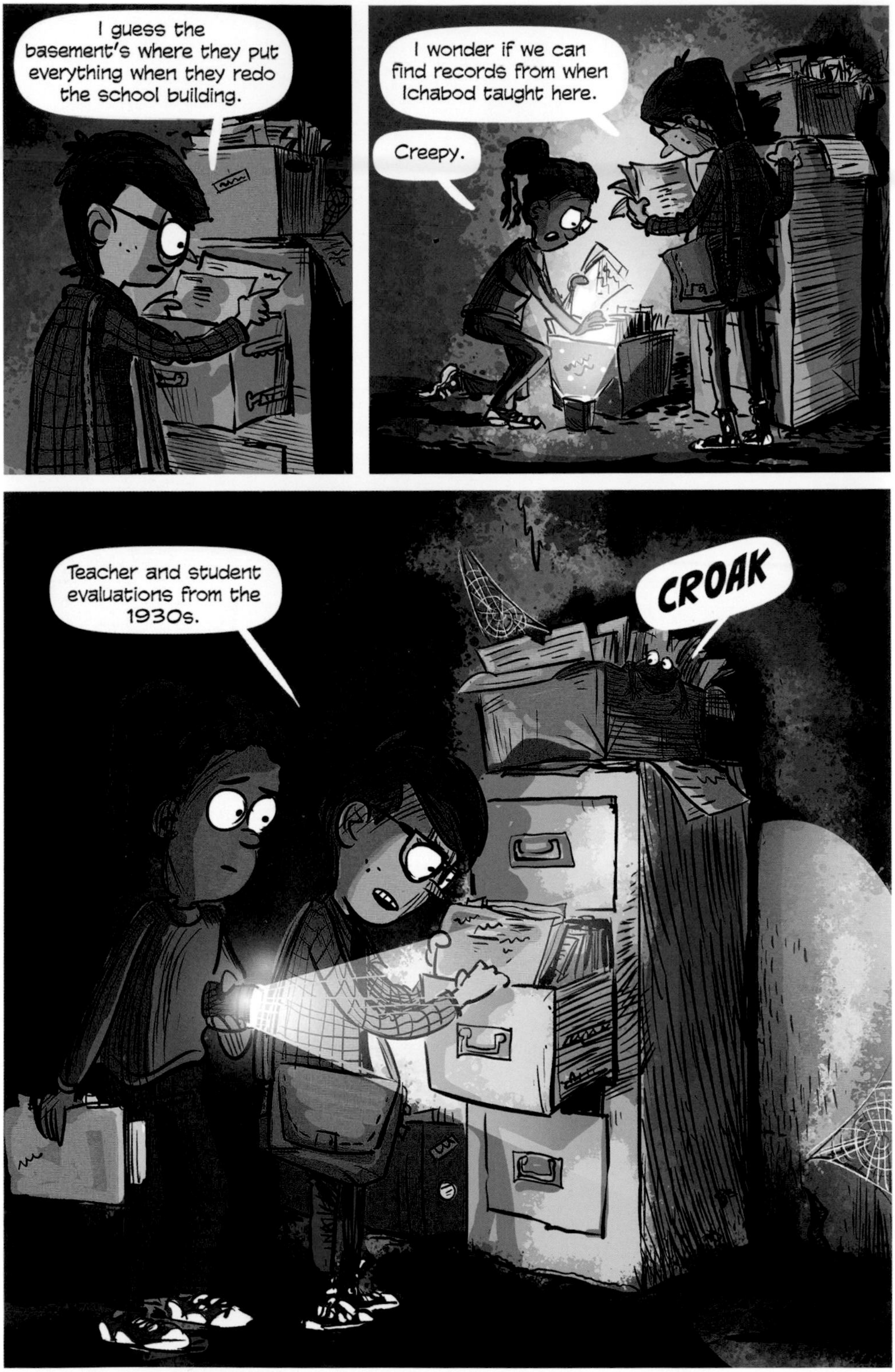
I guess the basement's where they put everything when they redo the school building.
I wonder if we can find records from when Ichabod taught here.
Creepy.
Teacher and student evaluations from the 1930s.
CROAK

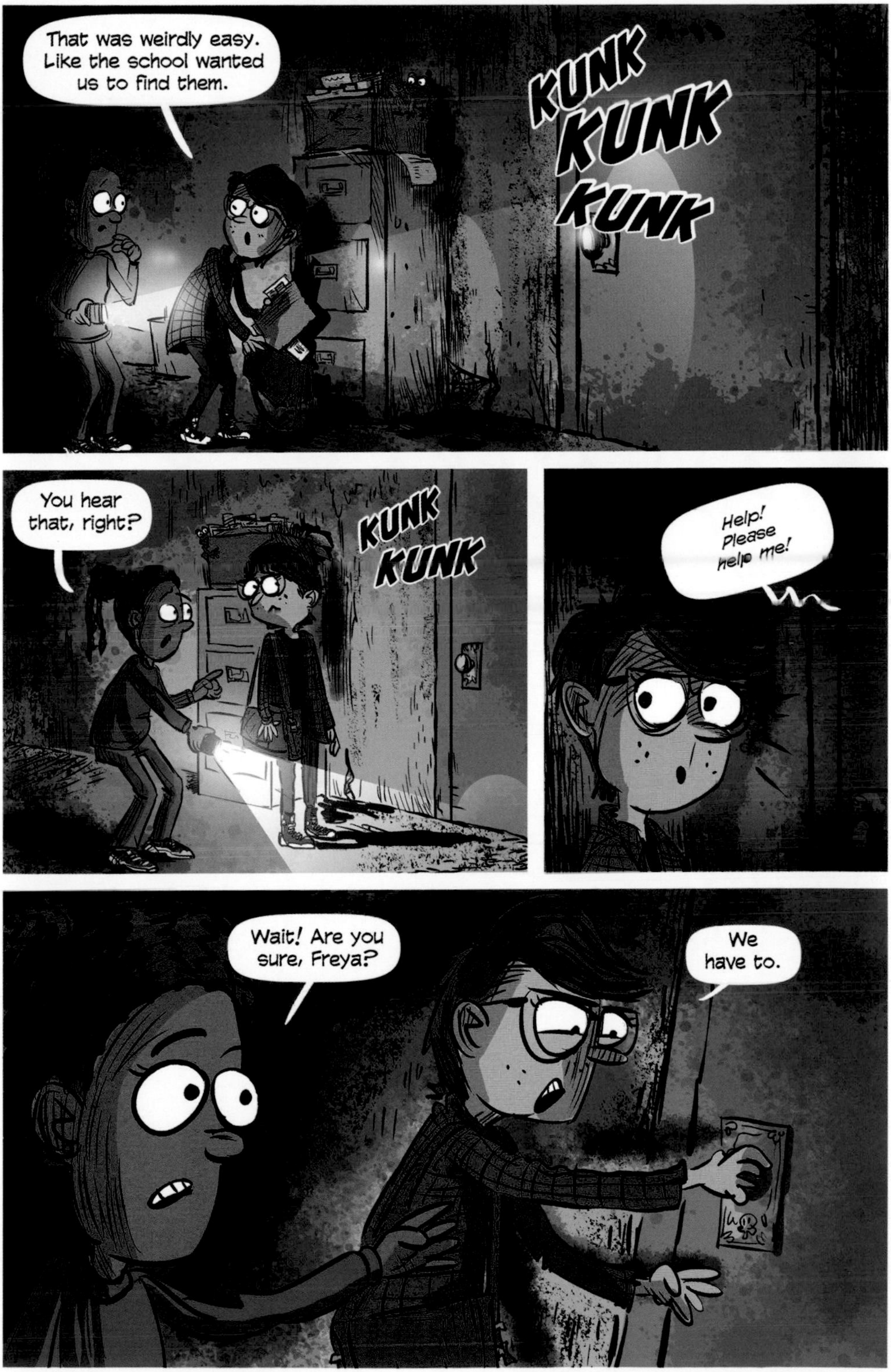
That was weirdly easy. Like the school wanted us to find them.
KUNK KUNK KUNK
You hear that, right?
KUNK KUNK
Help! Please help me!
Wait! Are you sure, Freya?
We have to.

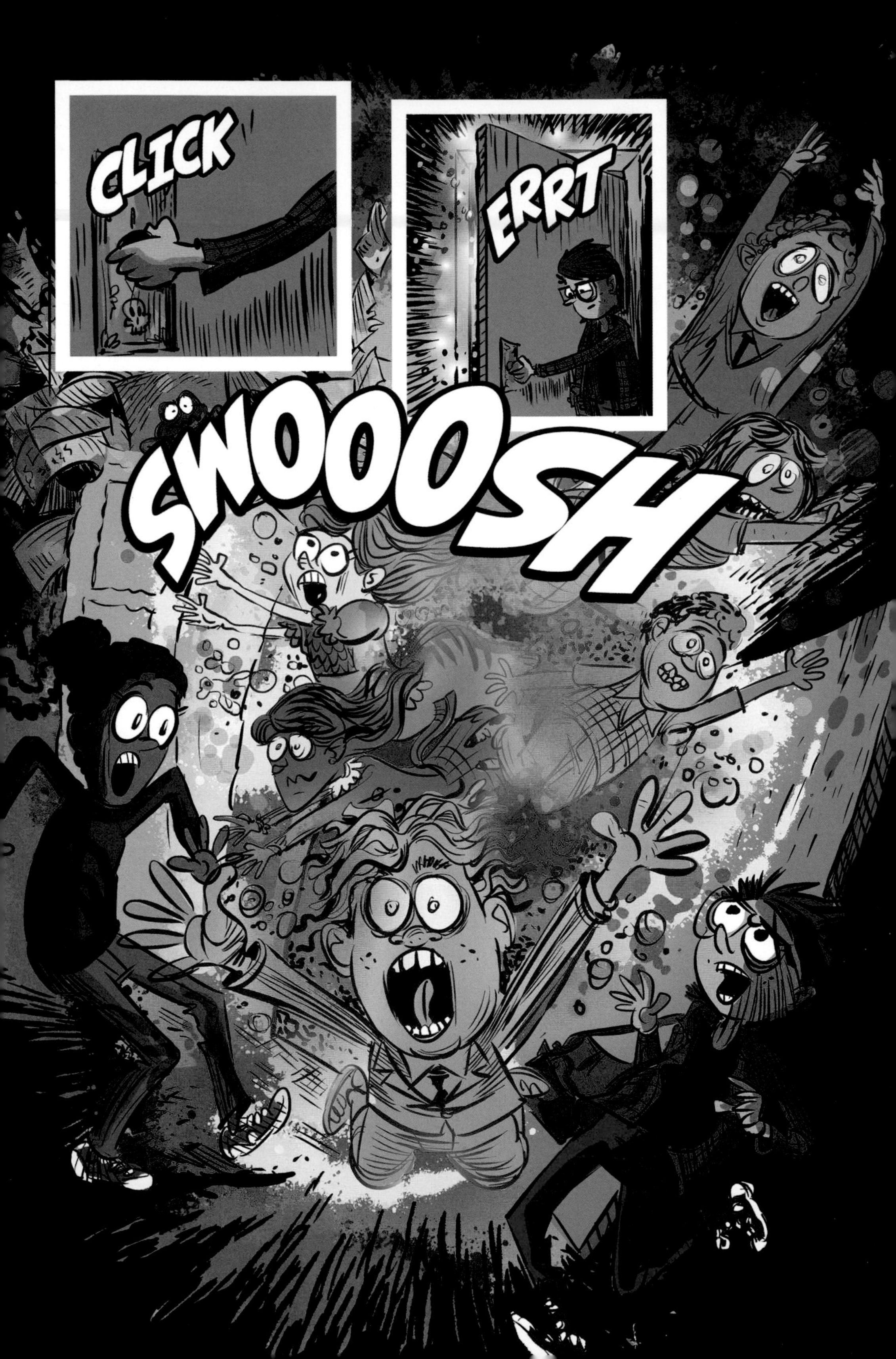
CLICK
ERRT
SWOOOSH

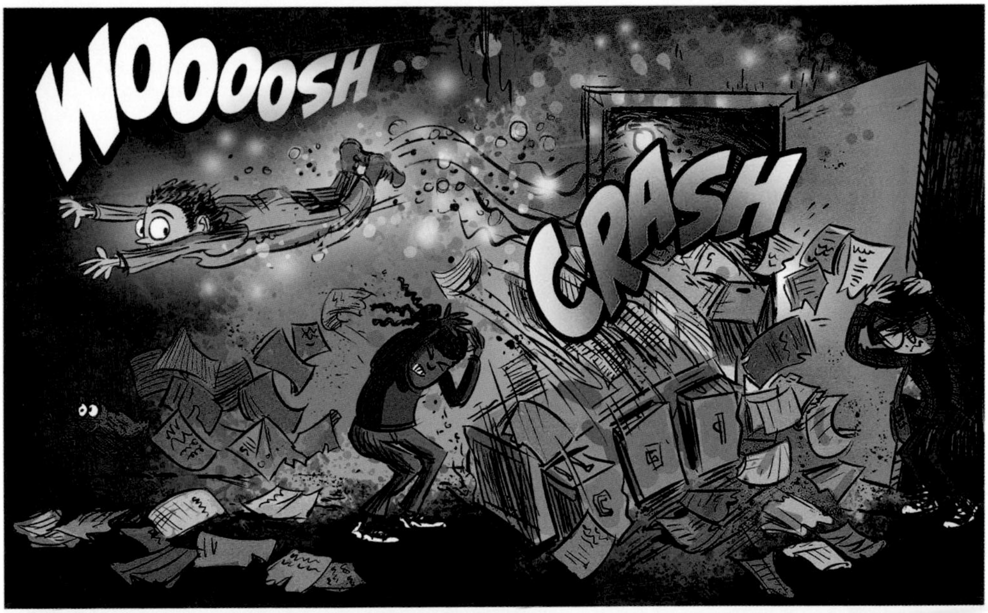
WOOOOSH
CRASH

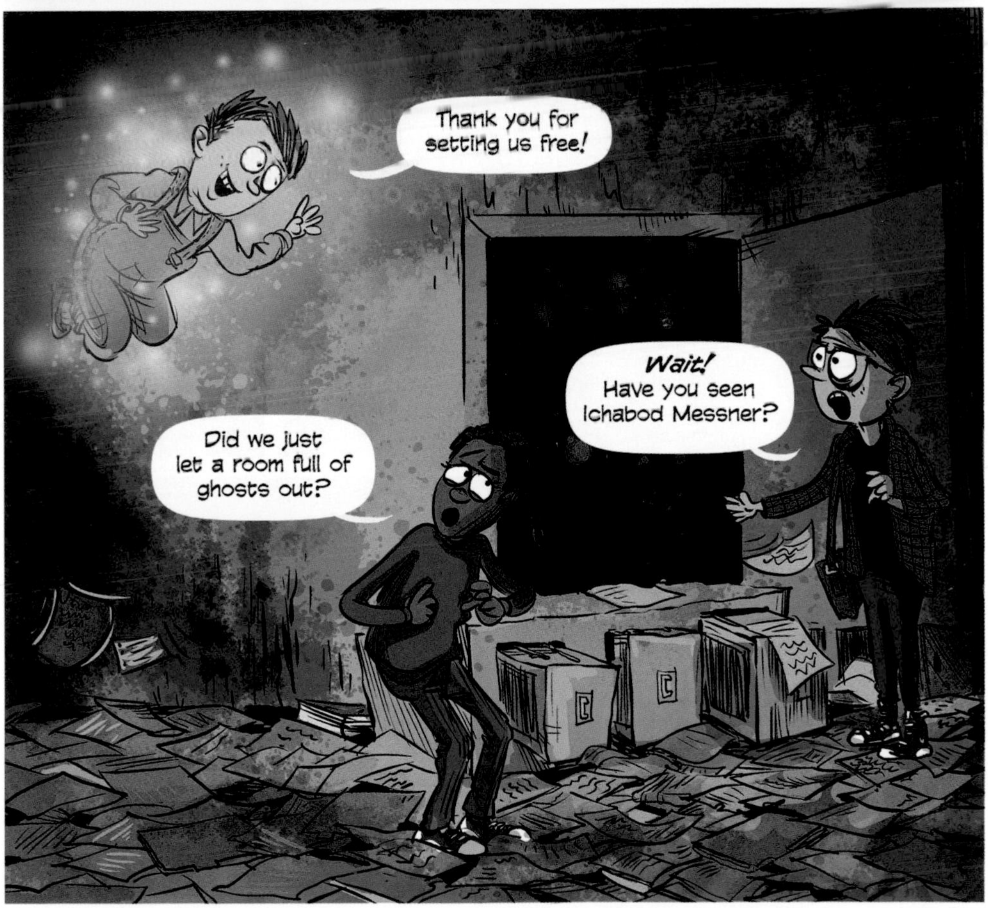
Thank you for setting us free!
Did we just let a room full of ghosts out?
Wait! Have you seen Ichabod Messner?

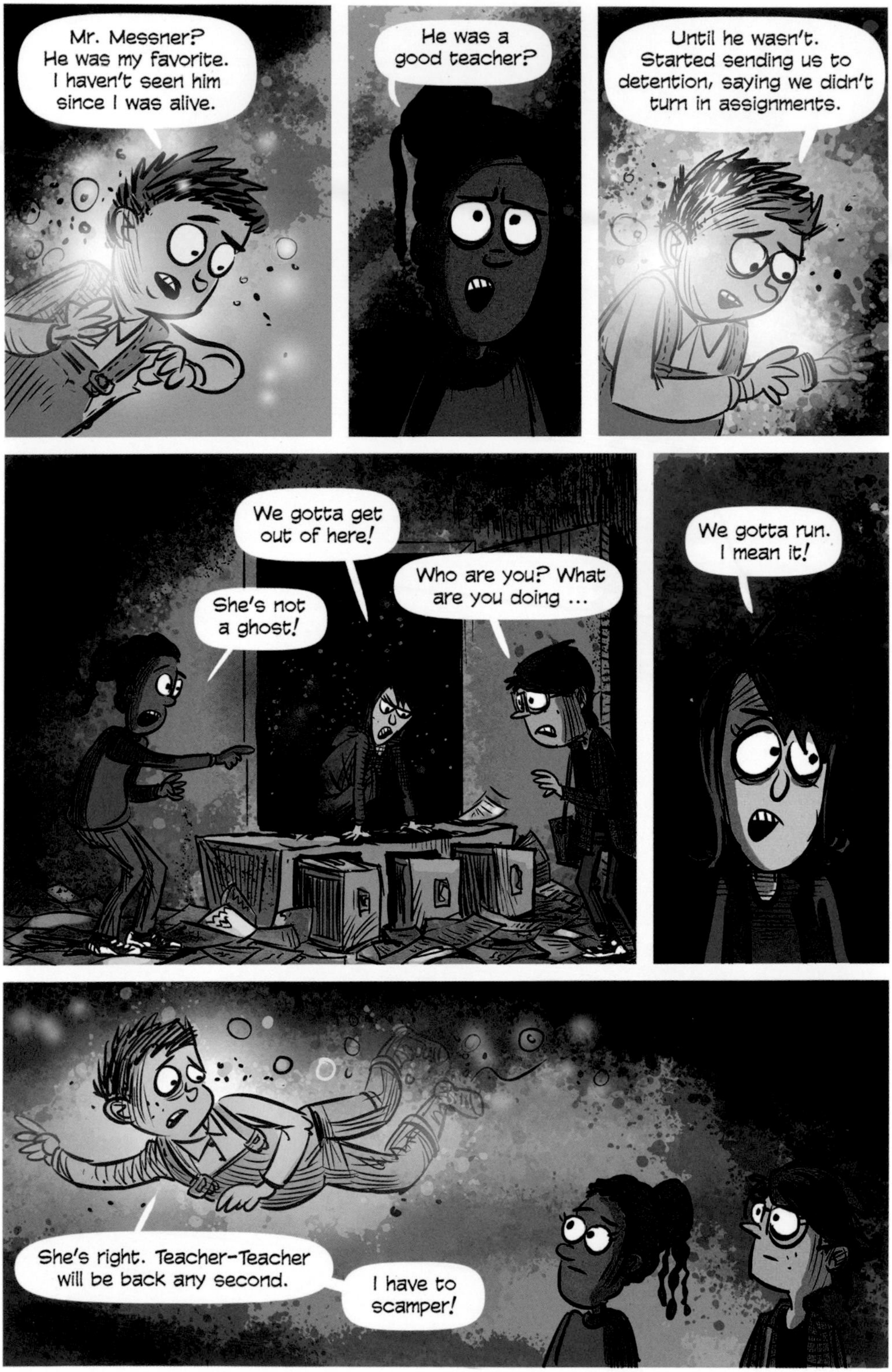
Mr. Messner? He was my favorite. I haven't seen him since I was alive.
He was a good teacher?
Until he wasn't. Started sending us to detention, saying we didn't turn in assignments.
We gotta get out of here!
She's not a ghost!
Who are you? What are you doing ...
We gotta run. I mean it!
She's right. Teacher-Teacher will be back any second.
I have to scamper!

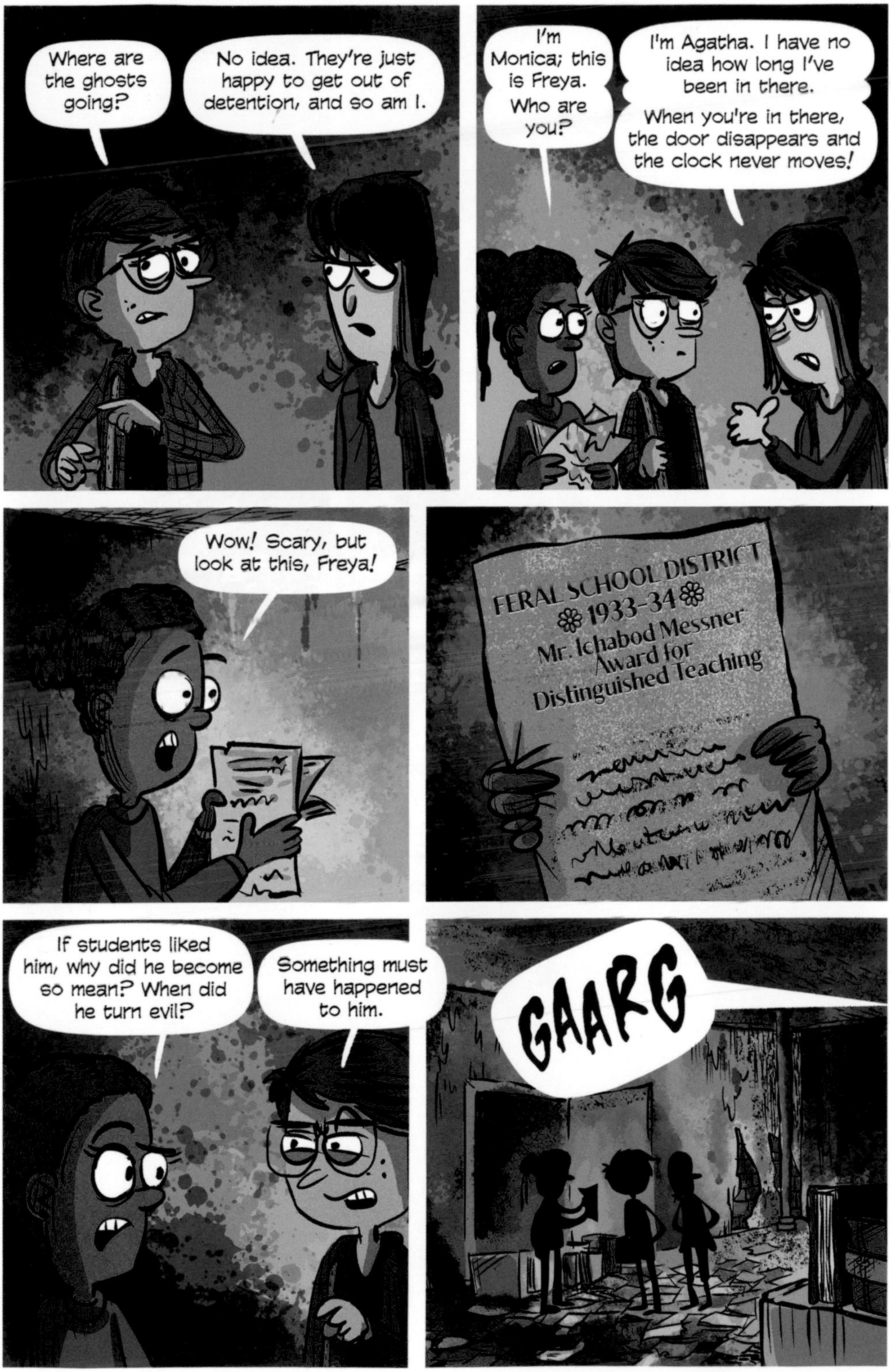
Where are the ghosts going?
No idea. They're just happy to get out of detention, and so am I.
I'm Monica; this is Freya. Who are you?
I'm Agatha. I have no idea how long I've been in there.
When you're in there, the door disappears and the clock never moves!
Wow! Scary, but look at this, Freya!
FERAL SCHOOL DISTRICT
1933-34
Mr. Ichabod Messner
Award for
Distinguished Teaching
If students liked him, why did he become so mean? When did he turn evil?
Something must have happened to him.
GAARG

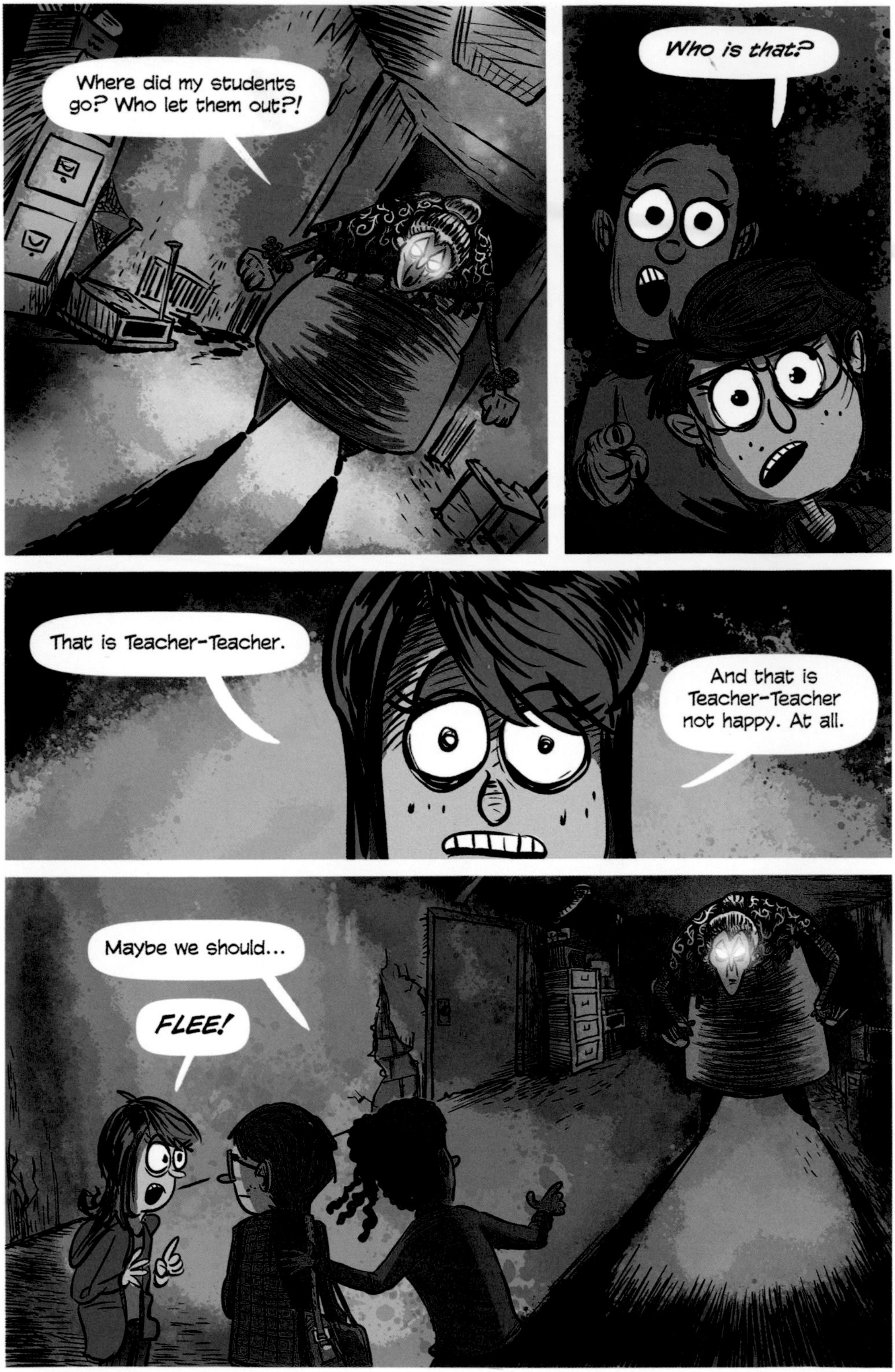
Where did my students go? Who let them out?!
Who is that?
That is Teacher-Teacher.
And that is Teacher-Teacher not happy. At all.
Maybe we should...
FLEE!

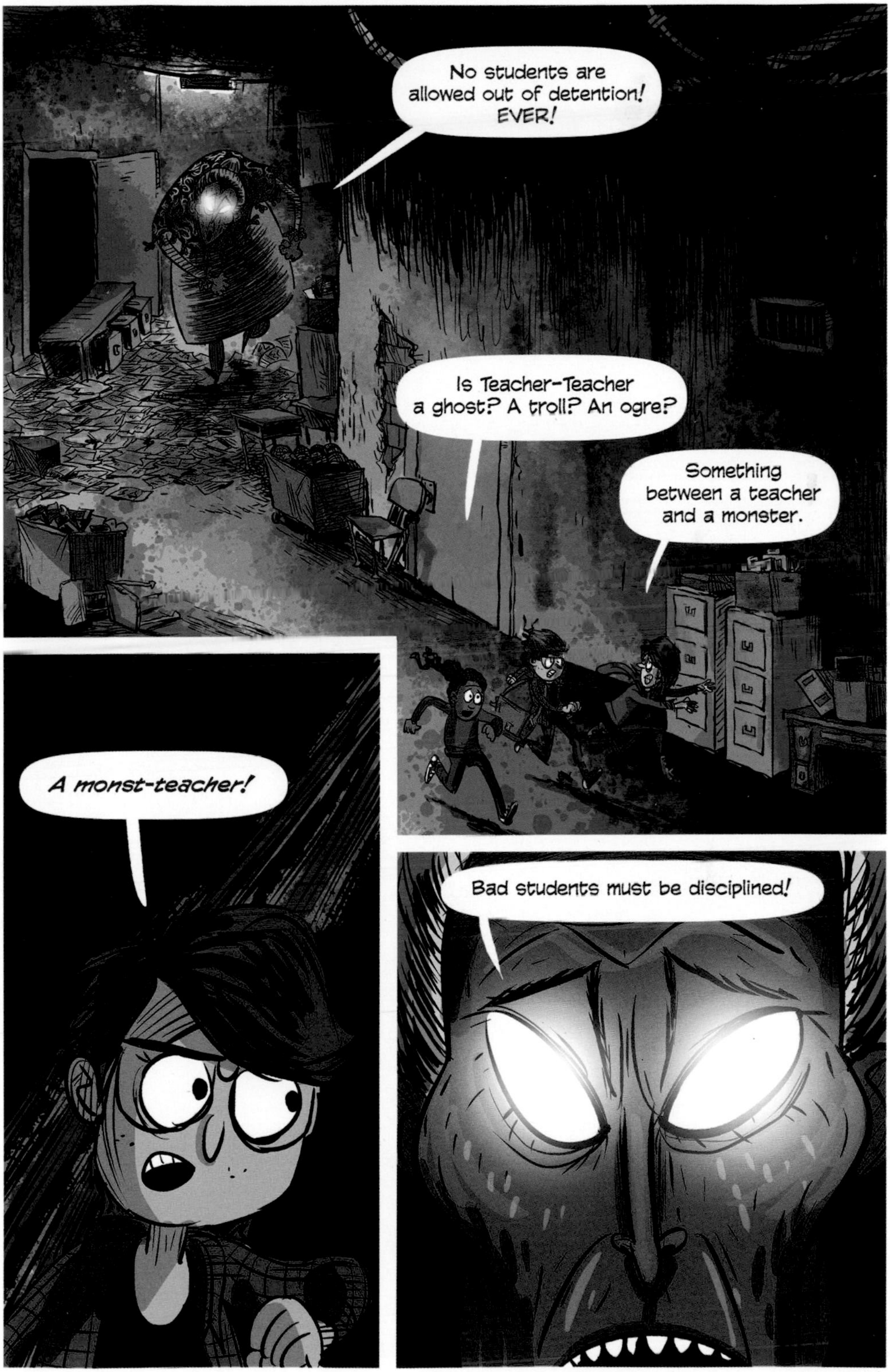
No students are allowed out of detention! EVER!
Is Teacher-Teacher a ghost? A troll? An ogre?
Something between a teacher and a monster.
A monst-teacher!
Bad students must be disciplined!

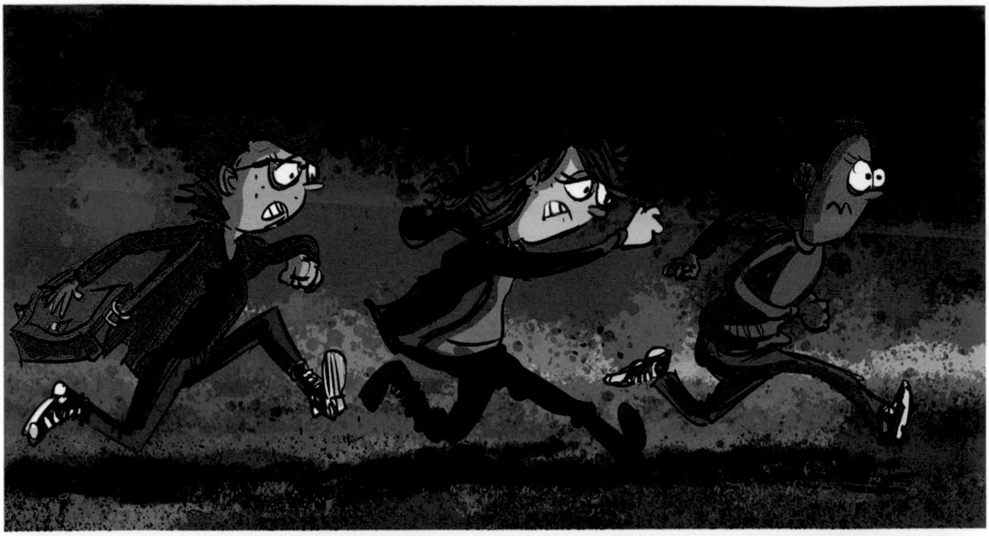

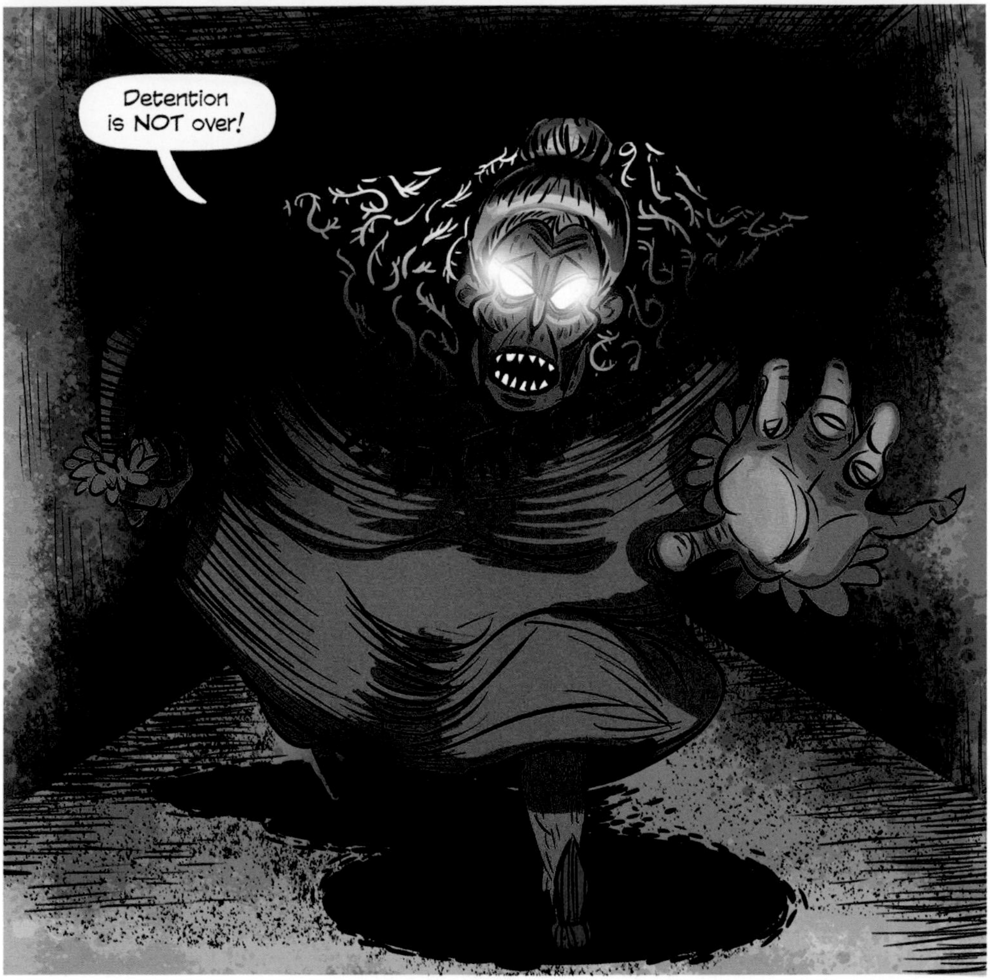
Detention is NOT over!

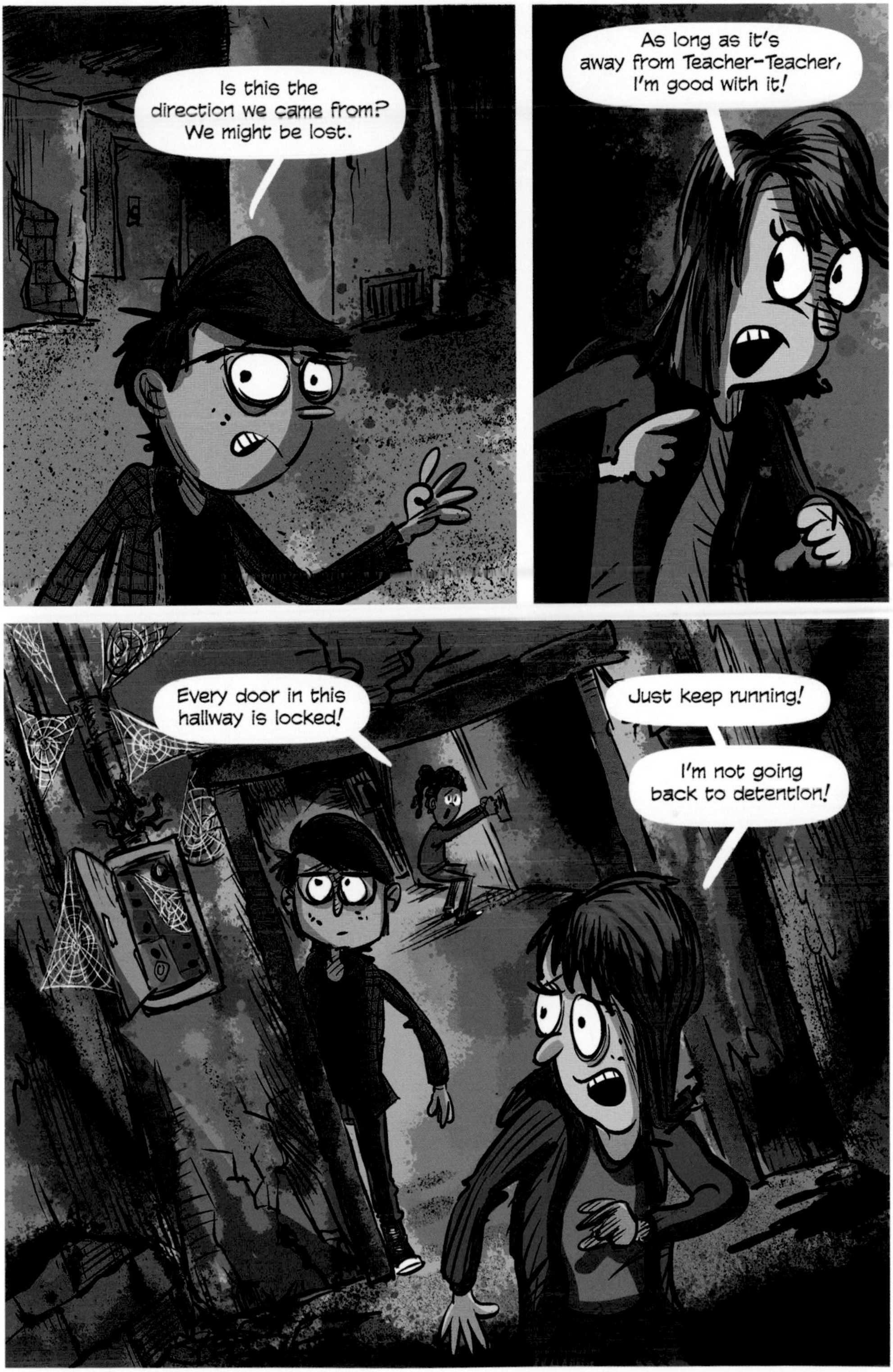
Is this the direction we came from? We might be lost.
As long as it's away from Teacher-Teacher, I'm good with it!
Every door in this hallway is locked!
Just keep running!
I'm not going back to detention!

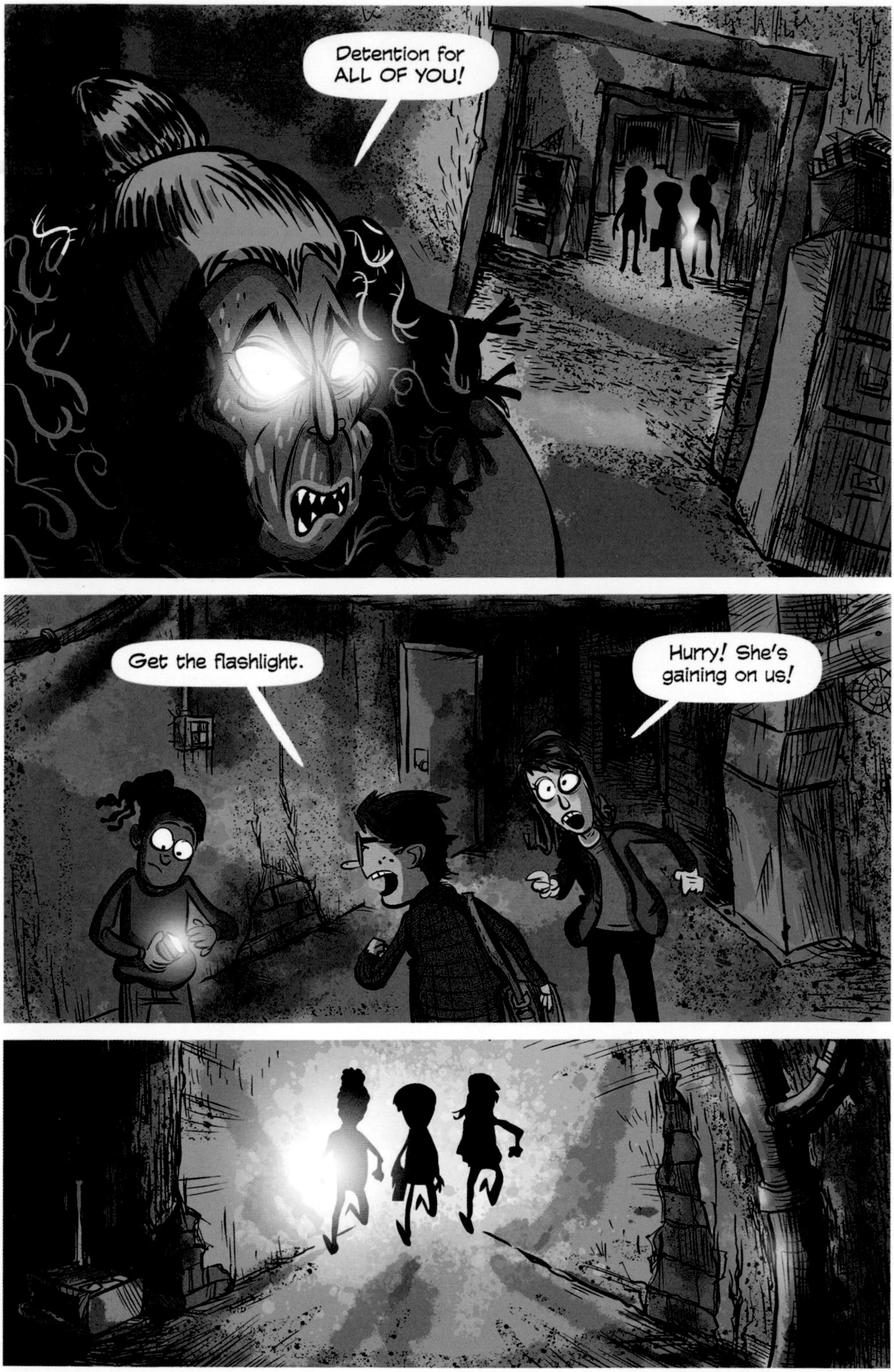
Detention for ALL OF YOU!
Get the flashlight.
Hurry! She's gaining on us!

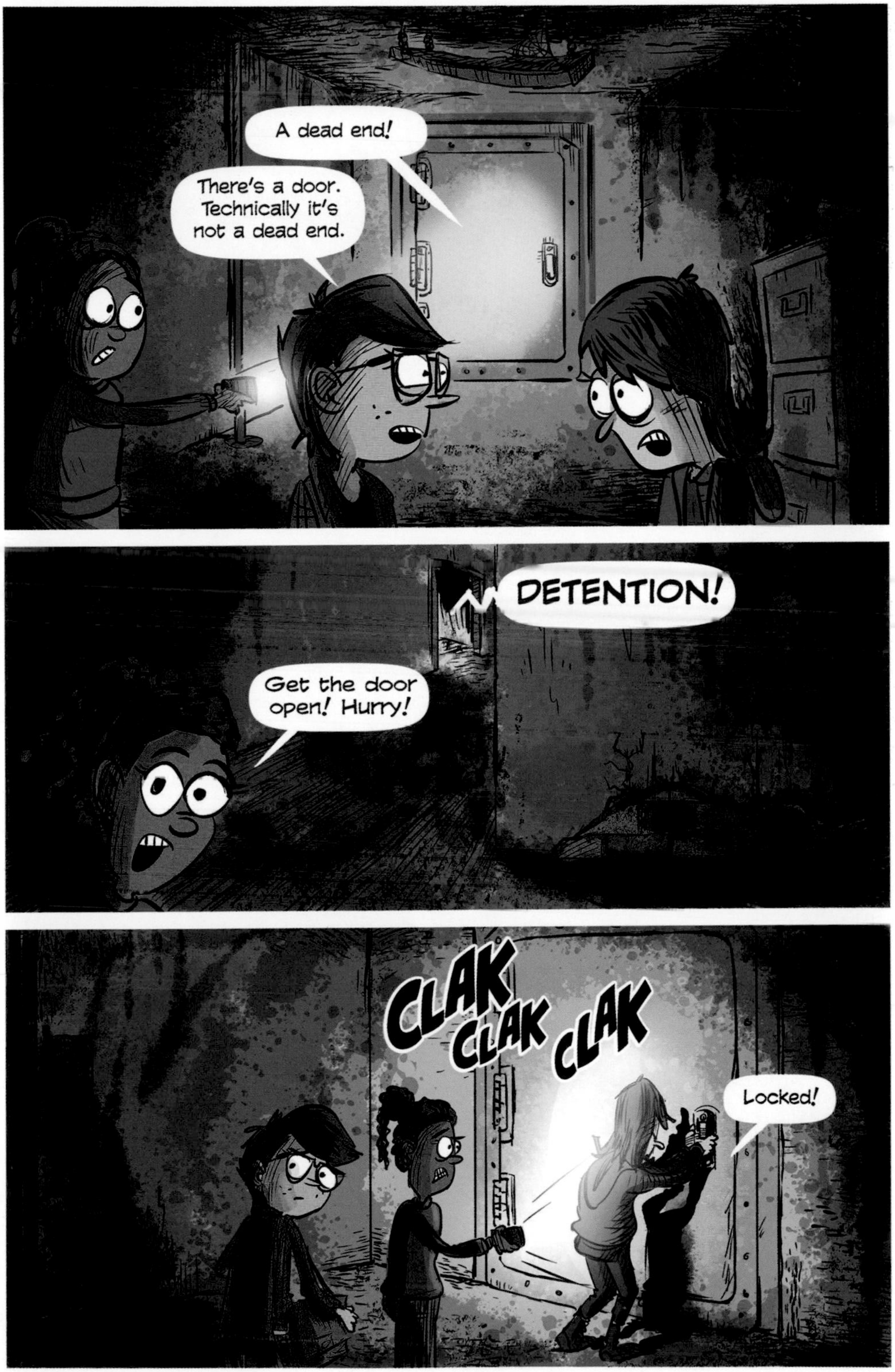
A dead end!
There's a door. Technically it's not a dead end.
DETENTION!
Get the door open! Hurry!
CLAK CLAK CLAK
Locked!

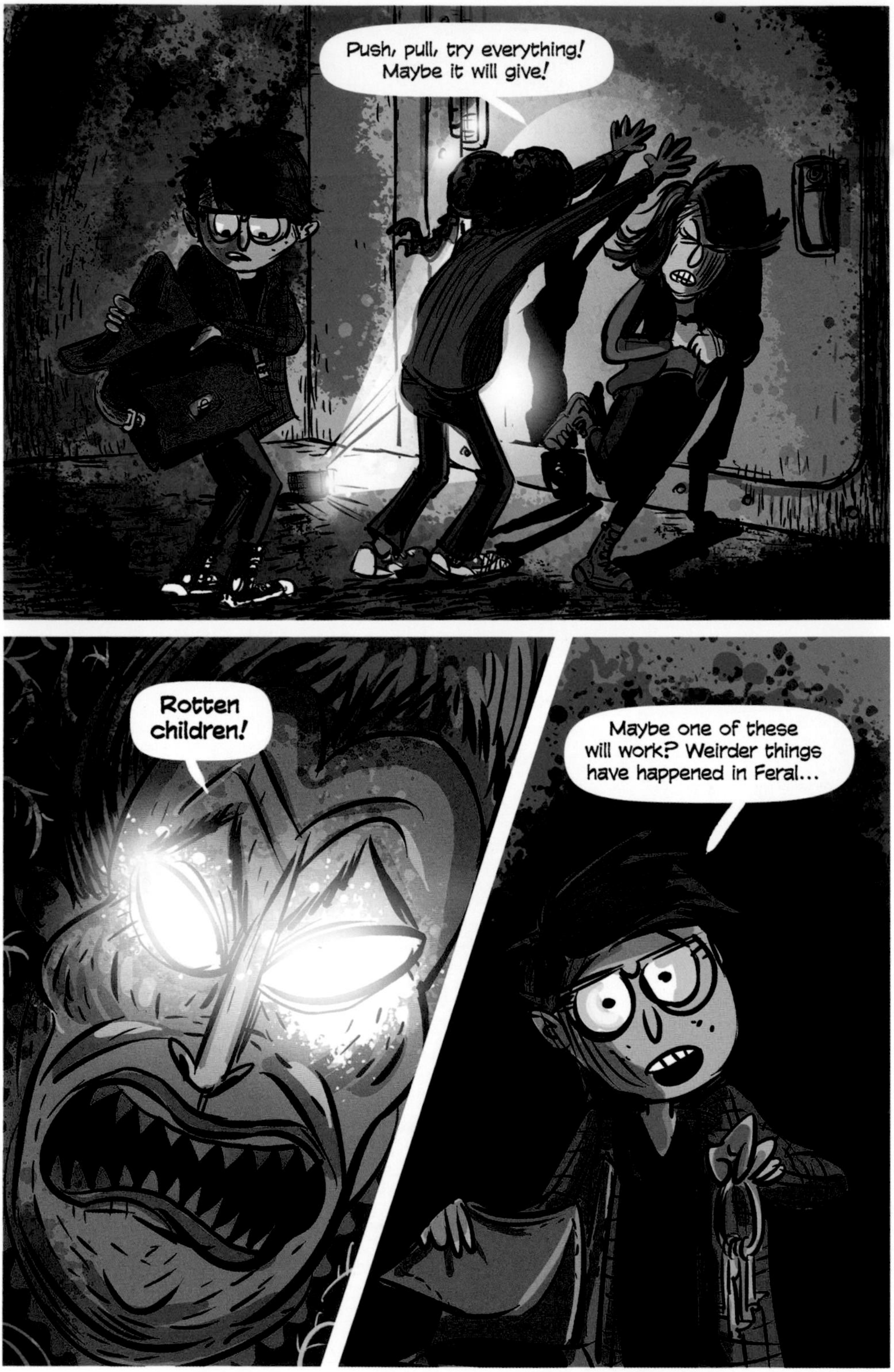
Push, pull, try everything! Maybe it will give!
Rotten children!
Maybe one of these will work? Weirder things have happened in Feral...

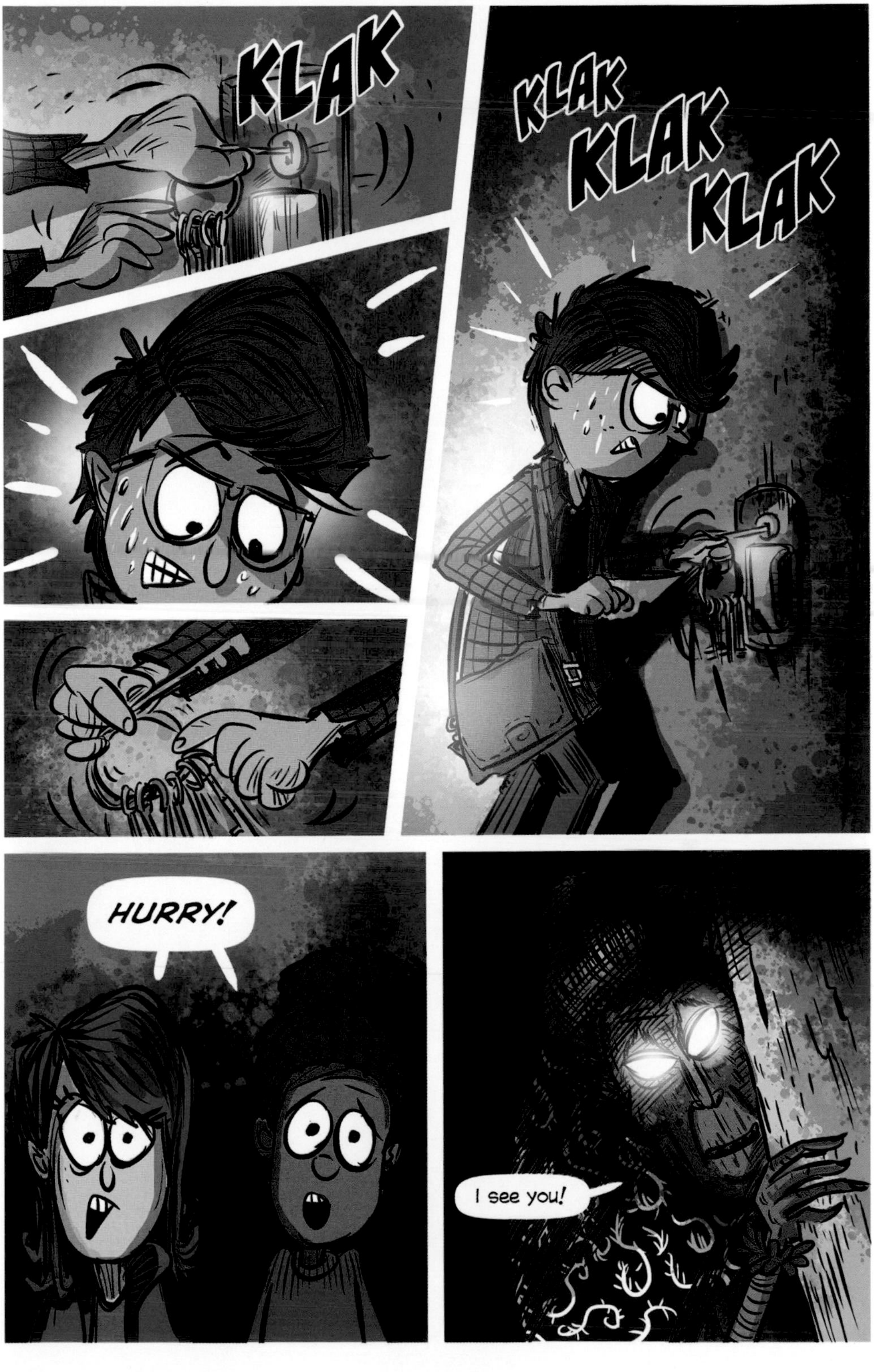
KLAK
KLAK
KLAK
KLAK
HURRY!
I see you!

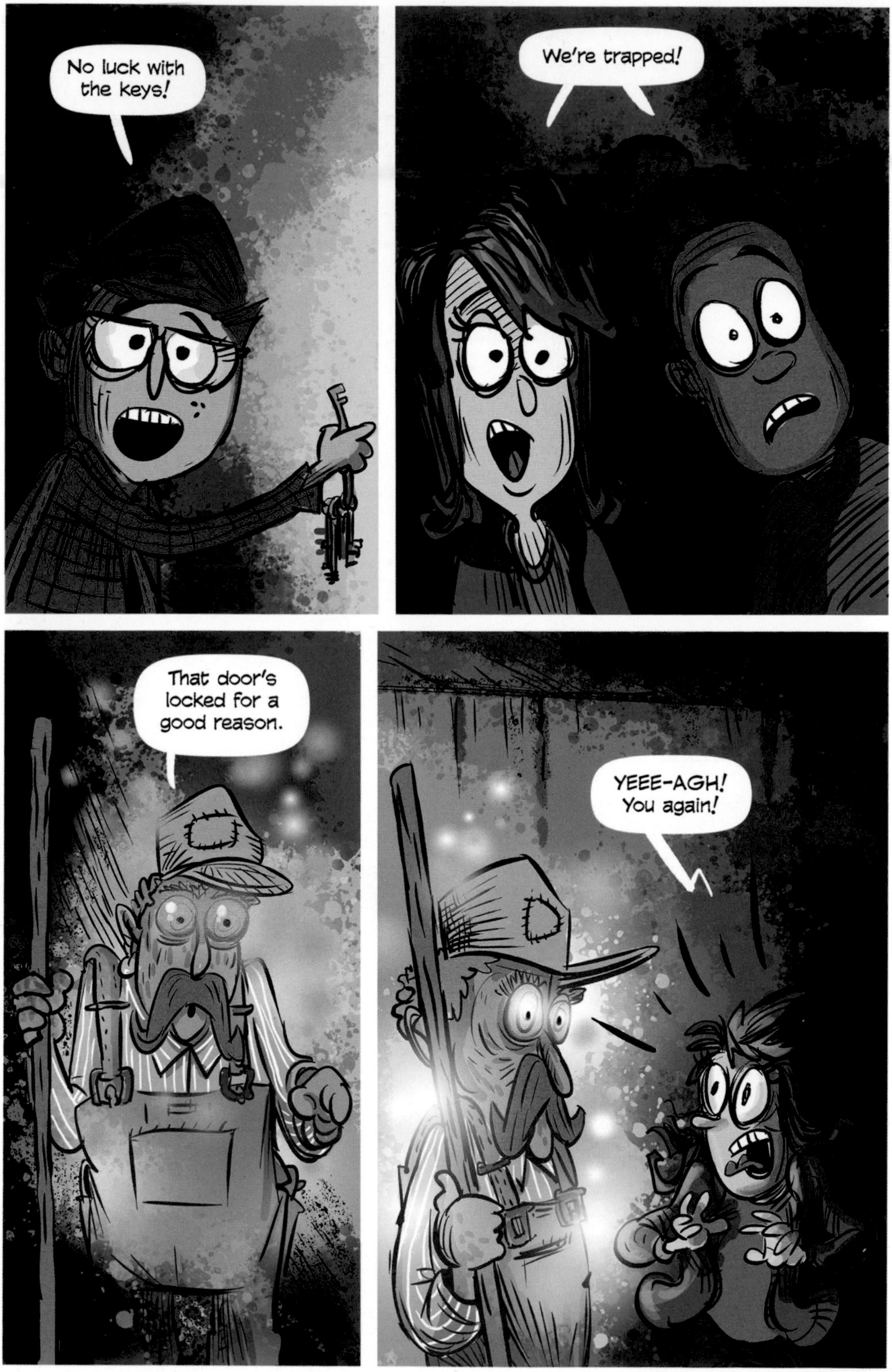
No luck with the keys!
We're trapped!
That door's locked for a good reason.
YEEE-AGH! You again!

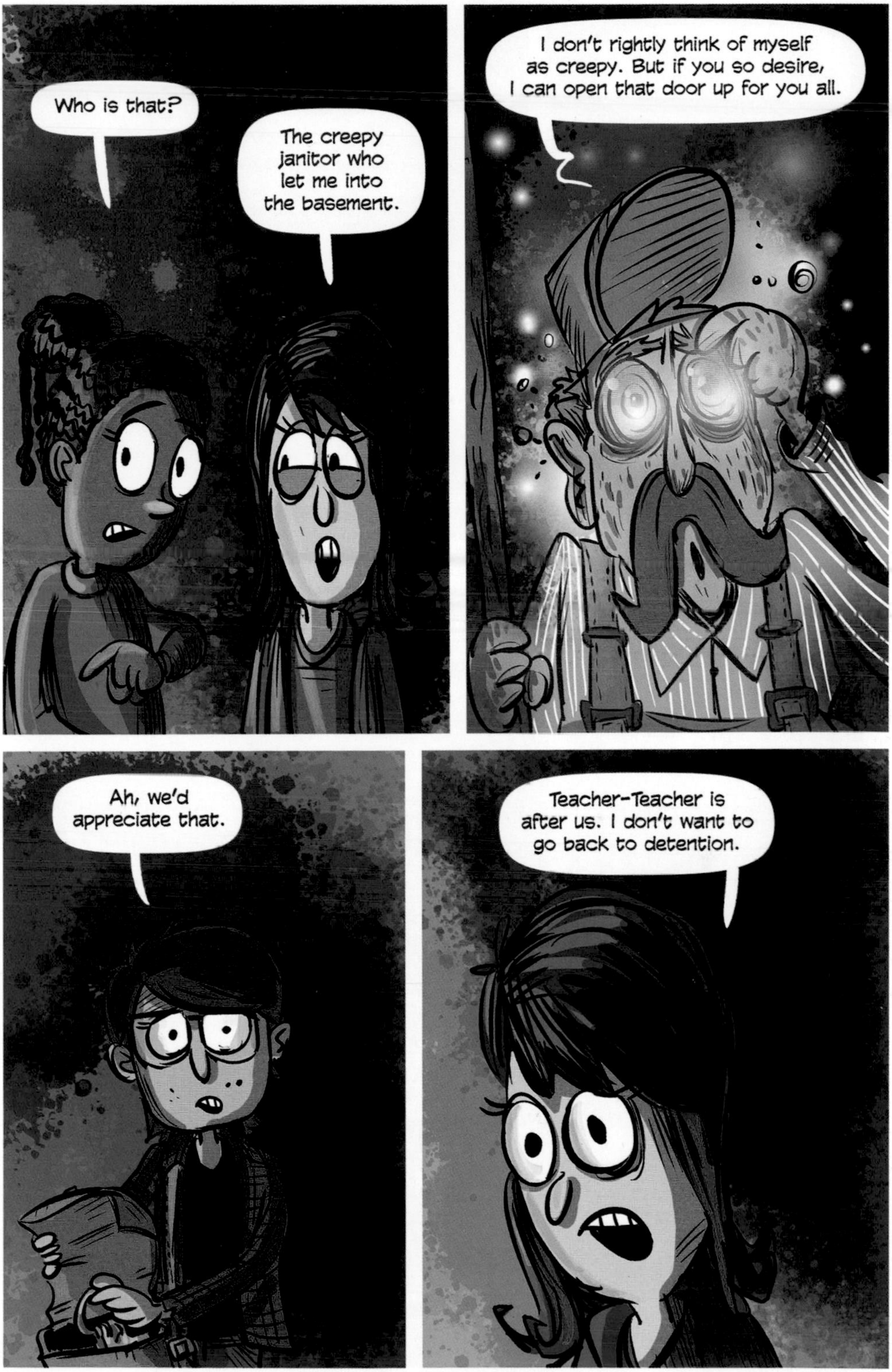
Who is that?
The creepy janitor who let me into the basement.
I don't rightly think of myself as creepy. But if you so desire, I can open that door up for you all.
Ah, we'd appreciate that.
Teacher-Teacher is after us. I don't want to go back to detention.

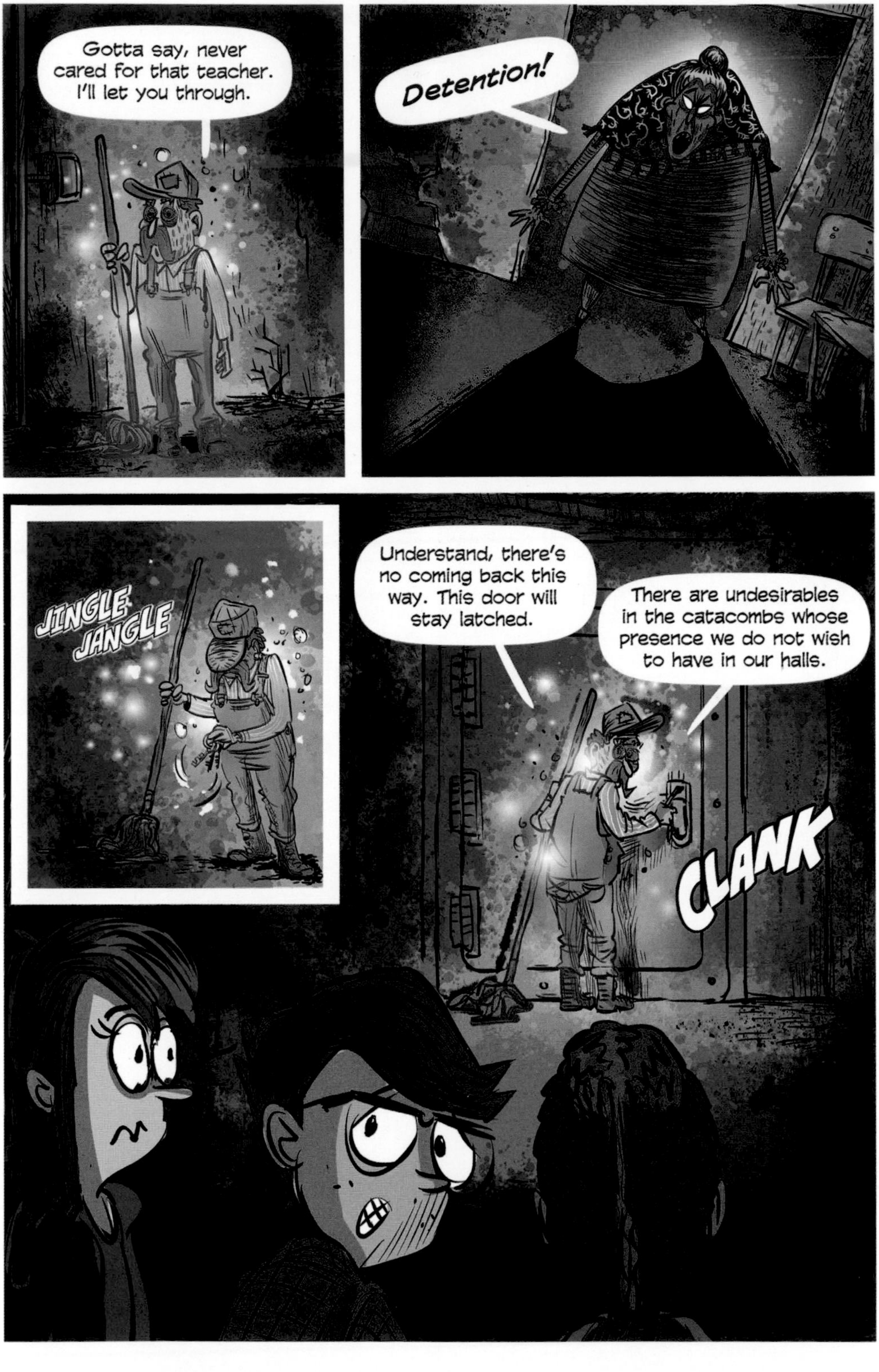
Gotta say, never cared for that teacher. I'll let you through.
Detention!
JINGLE JANGLE
Understand, there's no coming back this way. This door will stay latched.
There are undesirables in the catacombs whose presence we do not wish to have in our halls.
CLANK

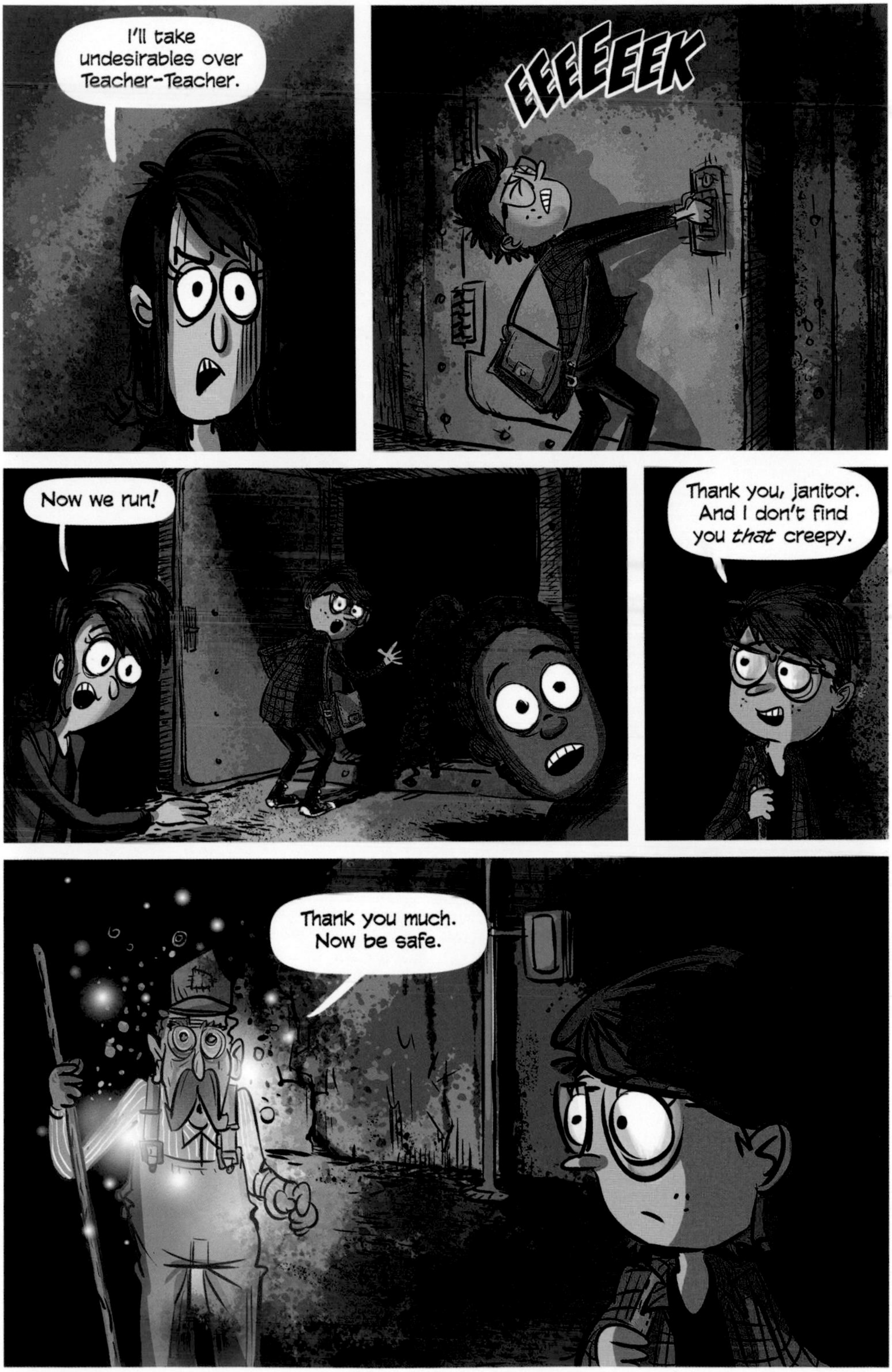
I'll take undesirables over Teacher-Teacher.
EEEEEEK
Now we run!
Thank you, janitor. And I don't find you *that* creepy.
Thank you much. Now be safe.

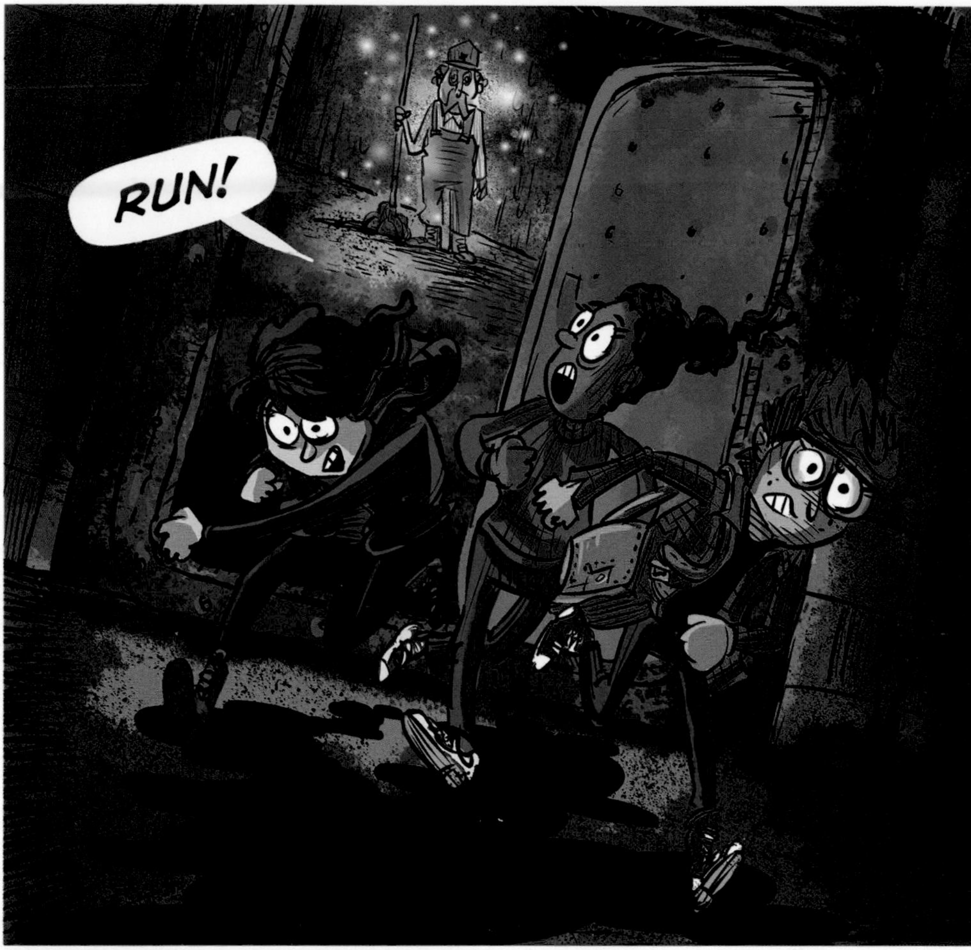
RUN!

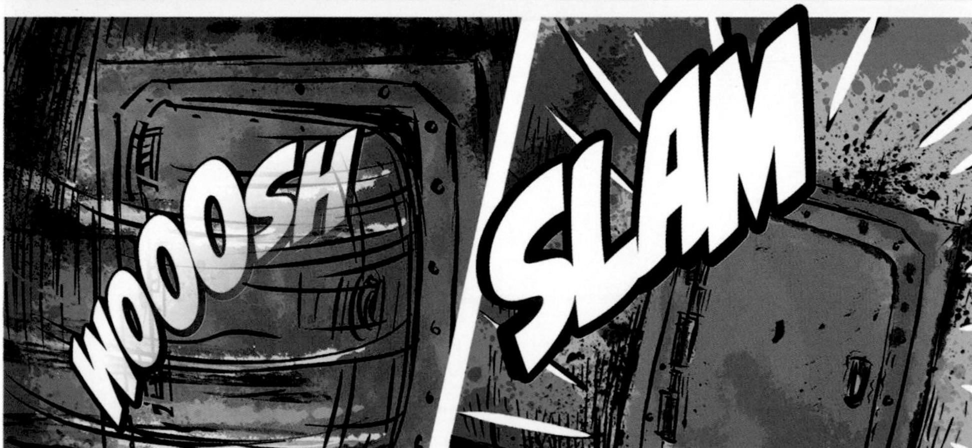
WOOOSH
SLAM

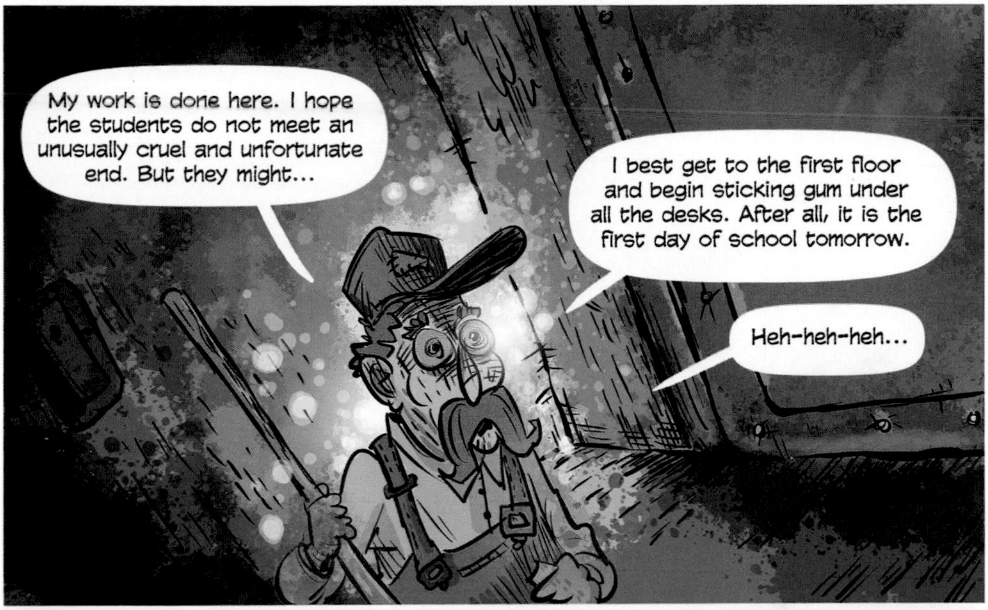
My work is done here. I hope the students do not meet an unusually cruel and unfortunate end. But they might...
I best get to the first floor and begin sticking gum under all the desks. After all, it is the first day of school tomorrow.
Heh-heh-heh...

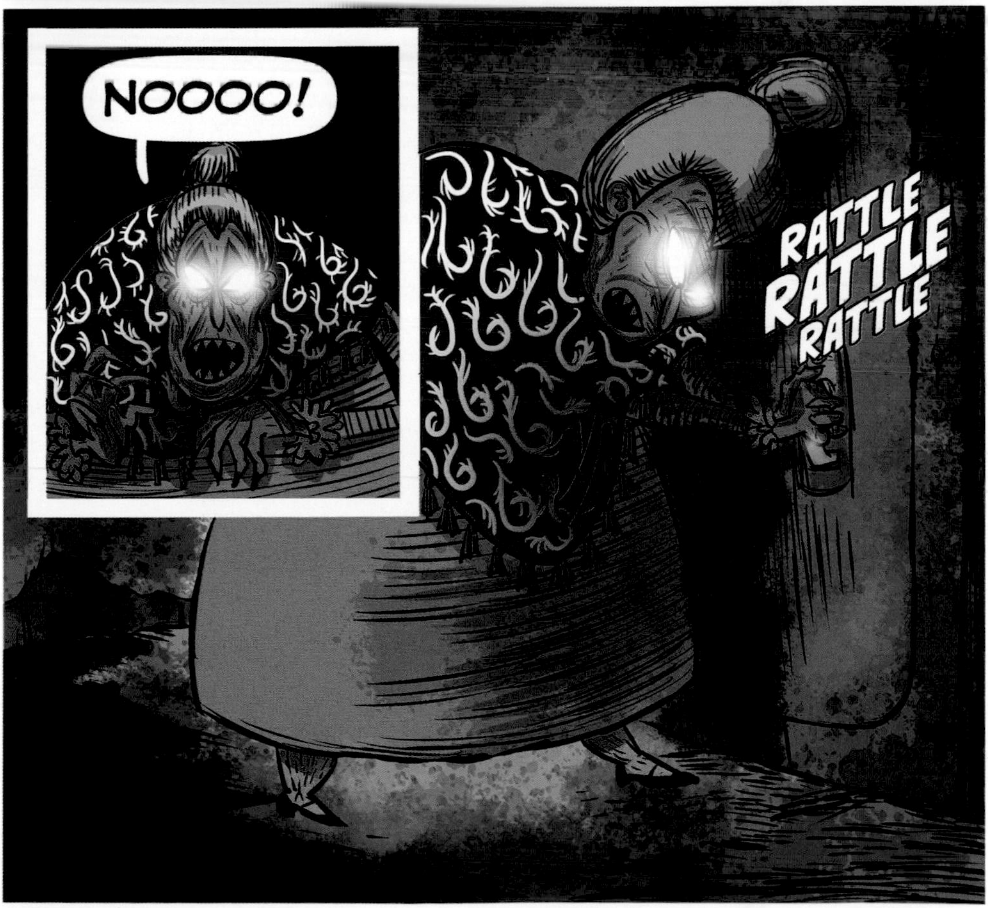
NOOOO!
RATTLE
RATTLE
RATTLE

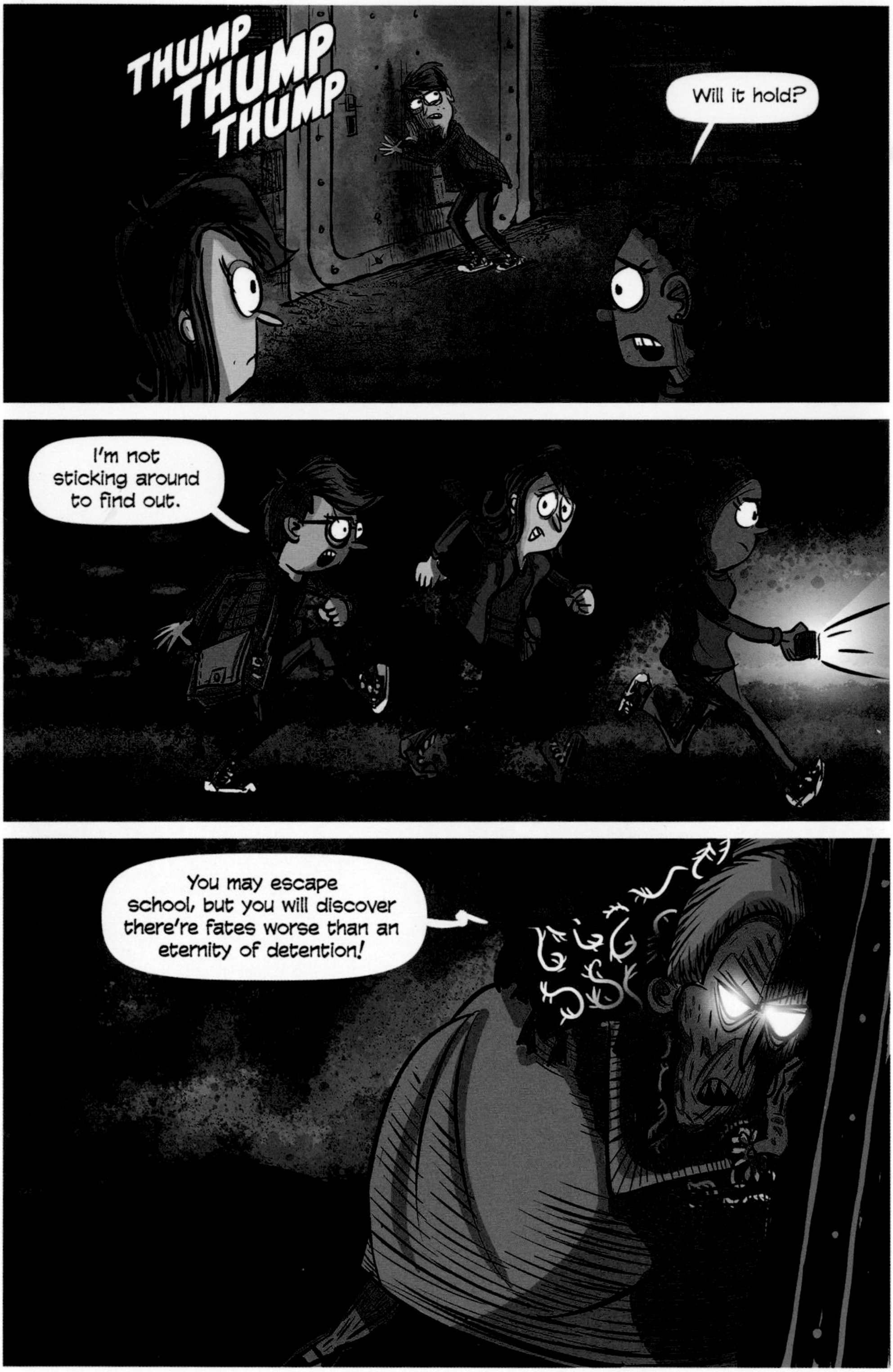
THUMP
THUMP
THUMP
Will it hold?
I'm not sticking around to find out.
You may escape school, but you will discover there're fates worse than an eternity of detention!

CHAPTER 5

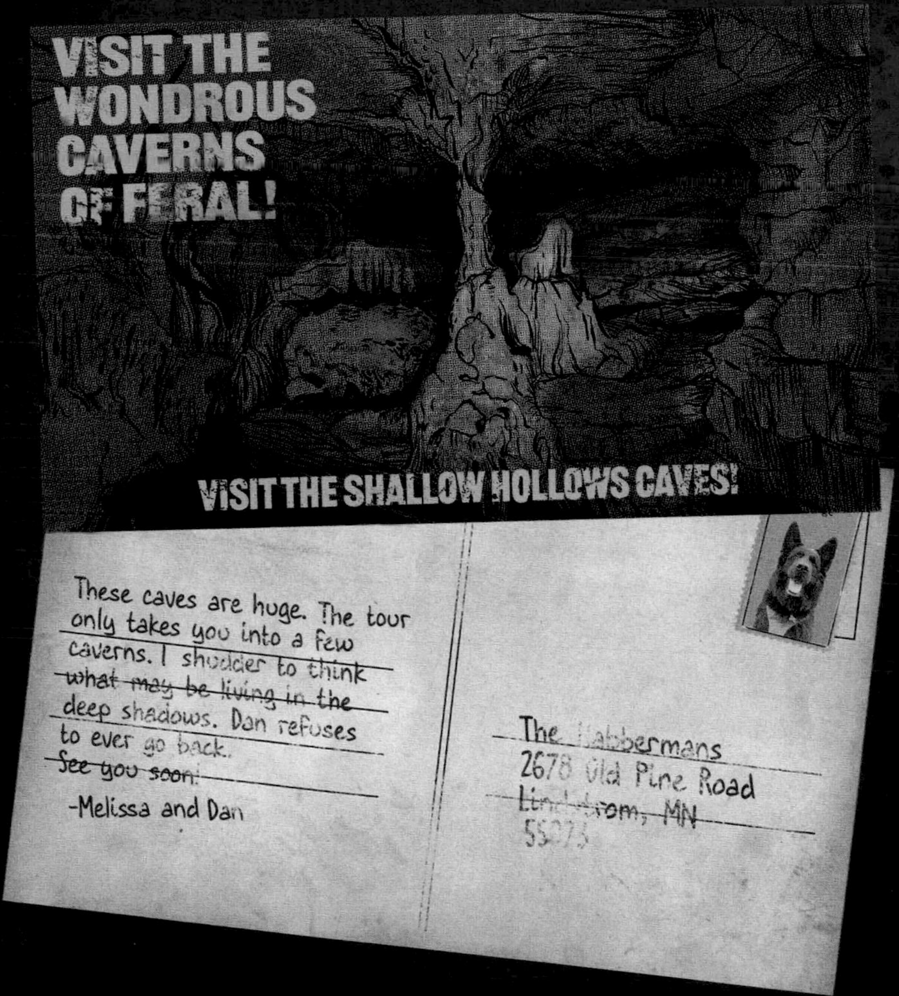
VISIT THE WONDROUS CAVERNS OF FERAL!
VISIT THE SHALLOW HOLLOWS CAVES!
These caves are huge. The tour only takes you into a few caverns. I shudder to think what may be living in the deep shadows. Dan refuses to ever go back.
See you soon!
-Melissa and Dan
The Habbermans
2678 Old Pine Road
Lindstrom, MN

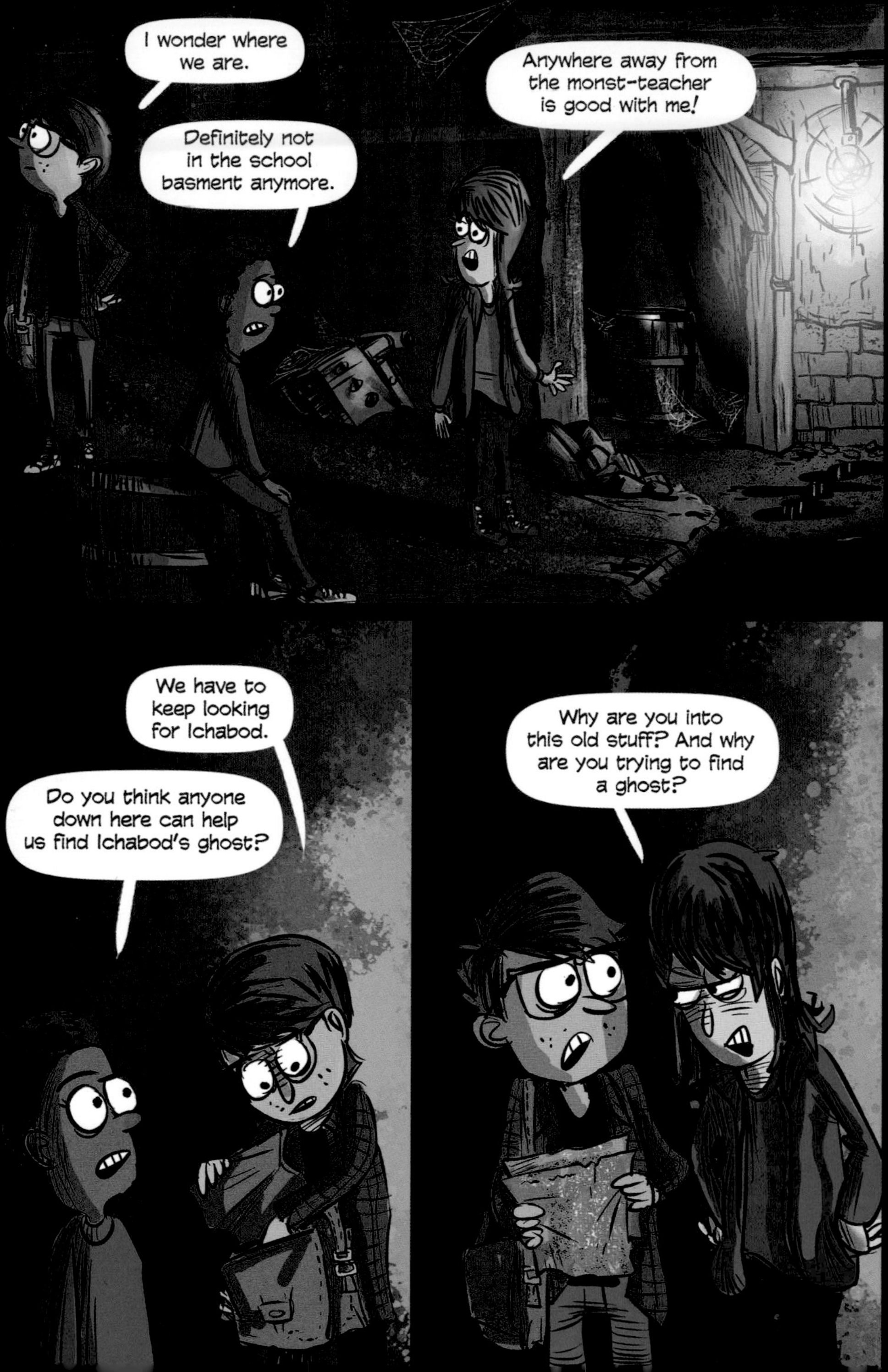
I wonder where we are.
Definitely not in the school basment anymore.
Anywhere away from the monst-teacher is good with me!
We have to keep looking for Ichabod.
Do you think anyone down here can help us find Ichabod's ghost?
Why are you into this old stuff? And why are you trying to find a ghost?

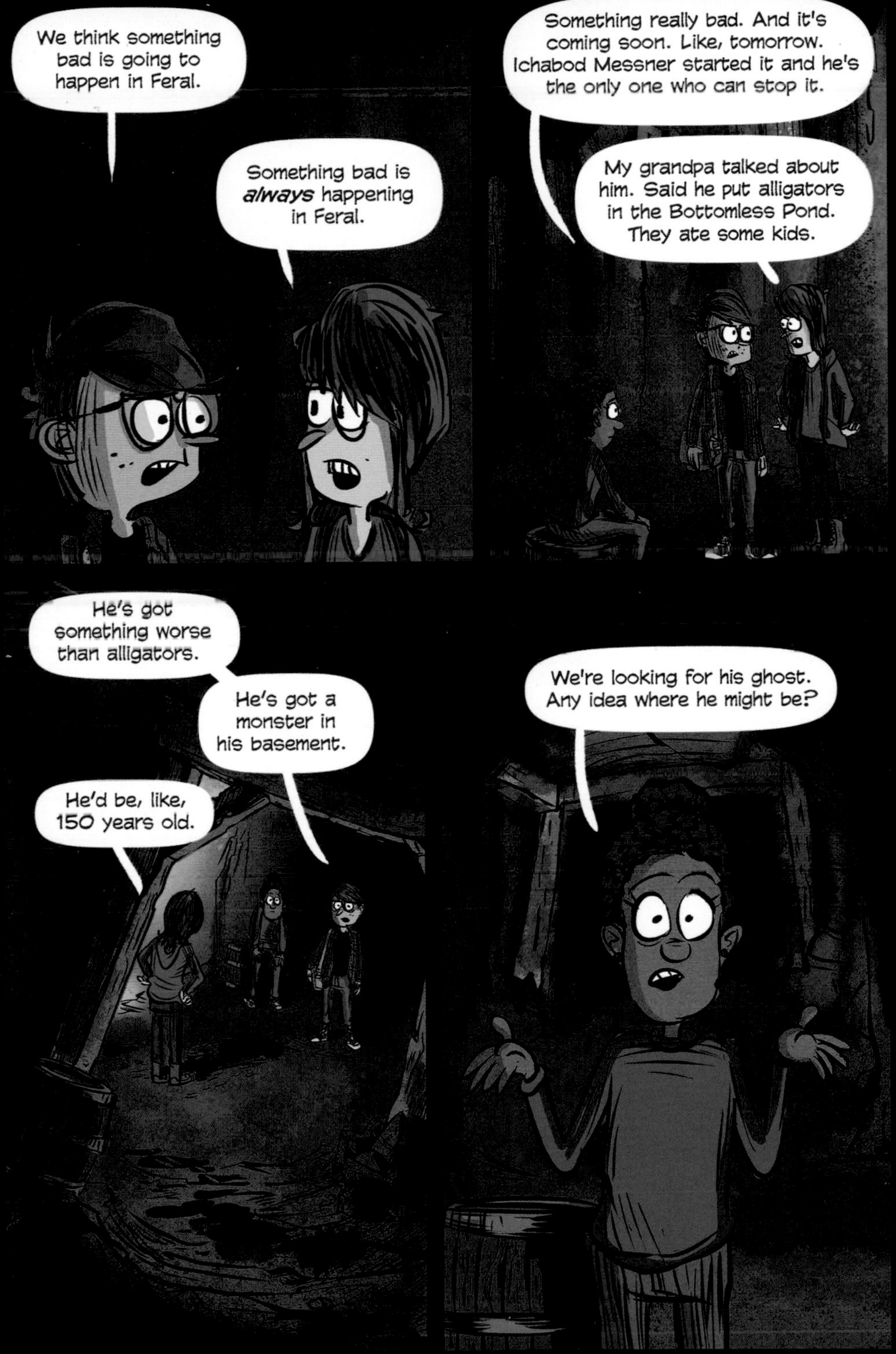
We think something bad is going to happen in Feral.
Something bad is *always* happening in Feral.
Something really bad. And it's coming soon. Like, tomorrow. Ichabod Messner started it and he's the only one who can stop it.
My grandpa talked about him. Said he put alligators in the Bottomless Pond. They ate some kids.
He's got something worse than alligators.
He's got a monster in his basement.
He'd be, like, 150 years old.
We're looking for his ghost. Any idea where he might be?

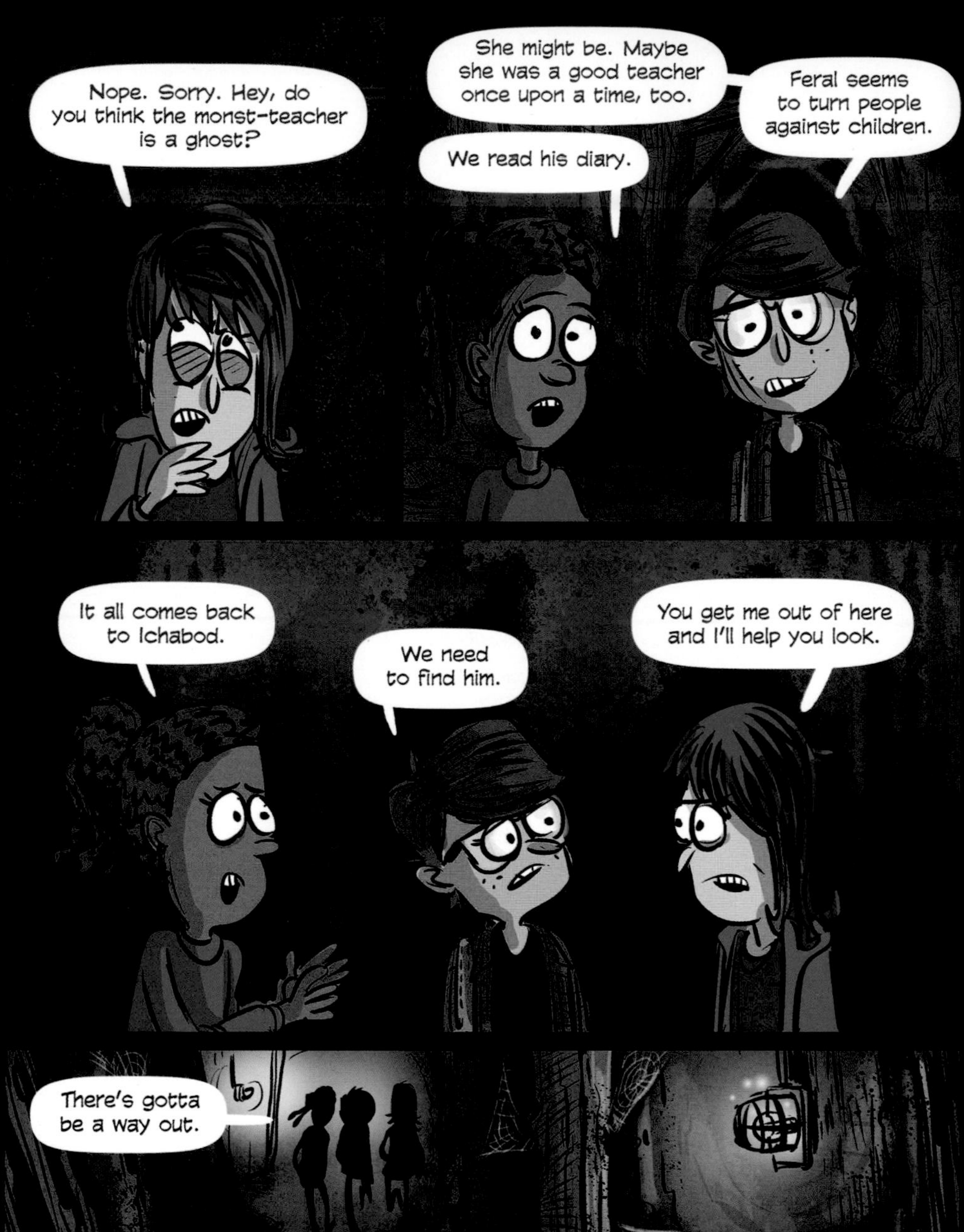
Nope. Sorry. Hey, do you think the monst-teacher is a ghost?
She might be. Maybe she was a good teacher once upon a time, too.
We read his diary.
Feral seems to turn people against children.
It all comes back to Ichabod.
We need to find him.
You get me out of here and I'll help you look.
There's gotta be a way out.

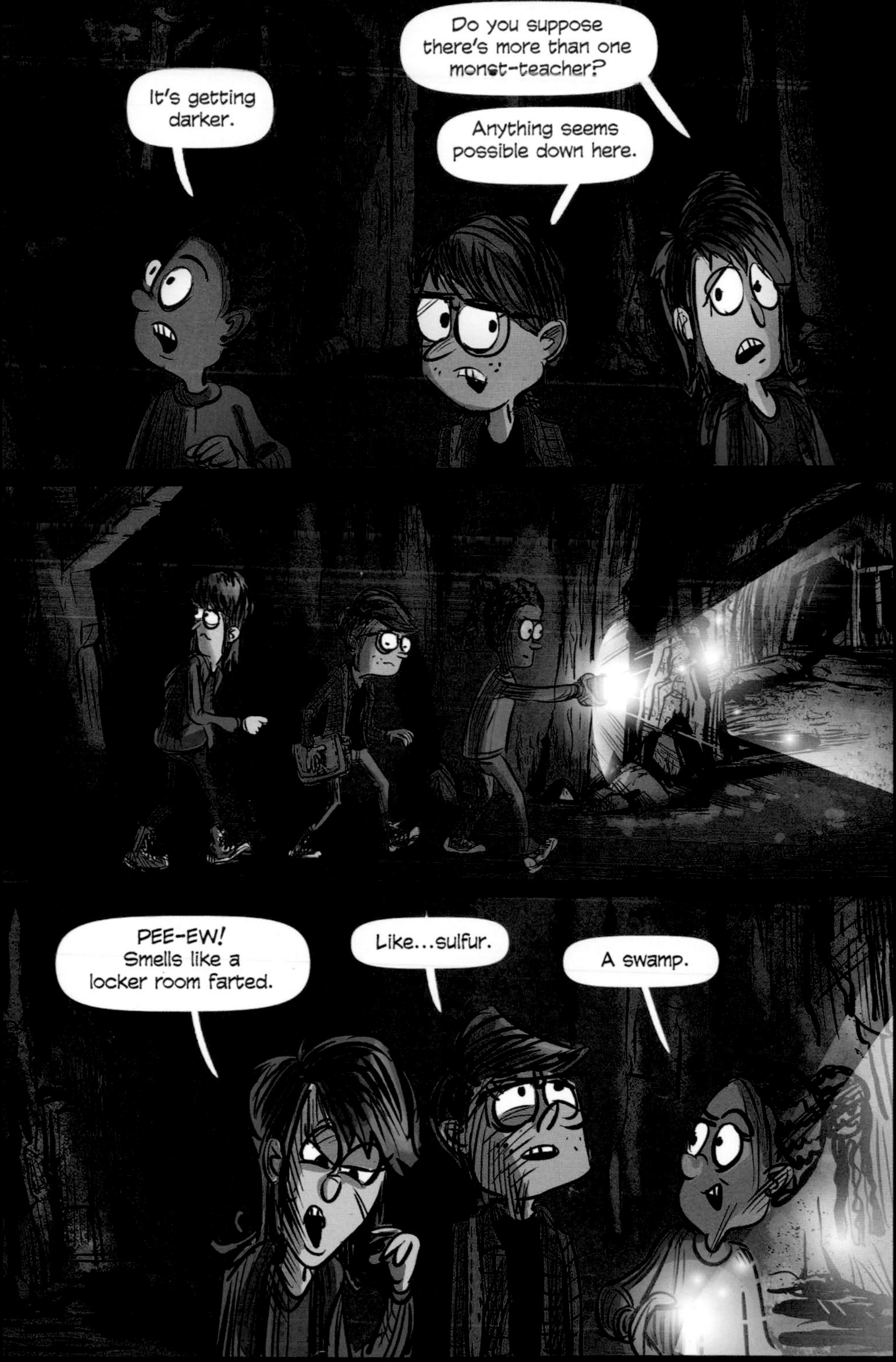
It's getting darker.
Do you suppose there's more than one monst-teacher?
Anything seems possible down here.
PEE-EW! Smells like a locker room farted.
Like...sulfur.
A swamp.

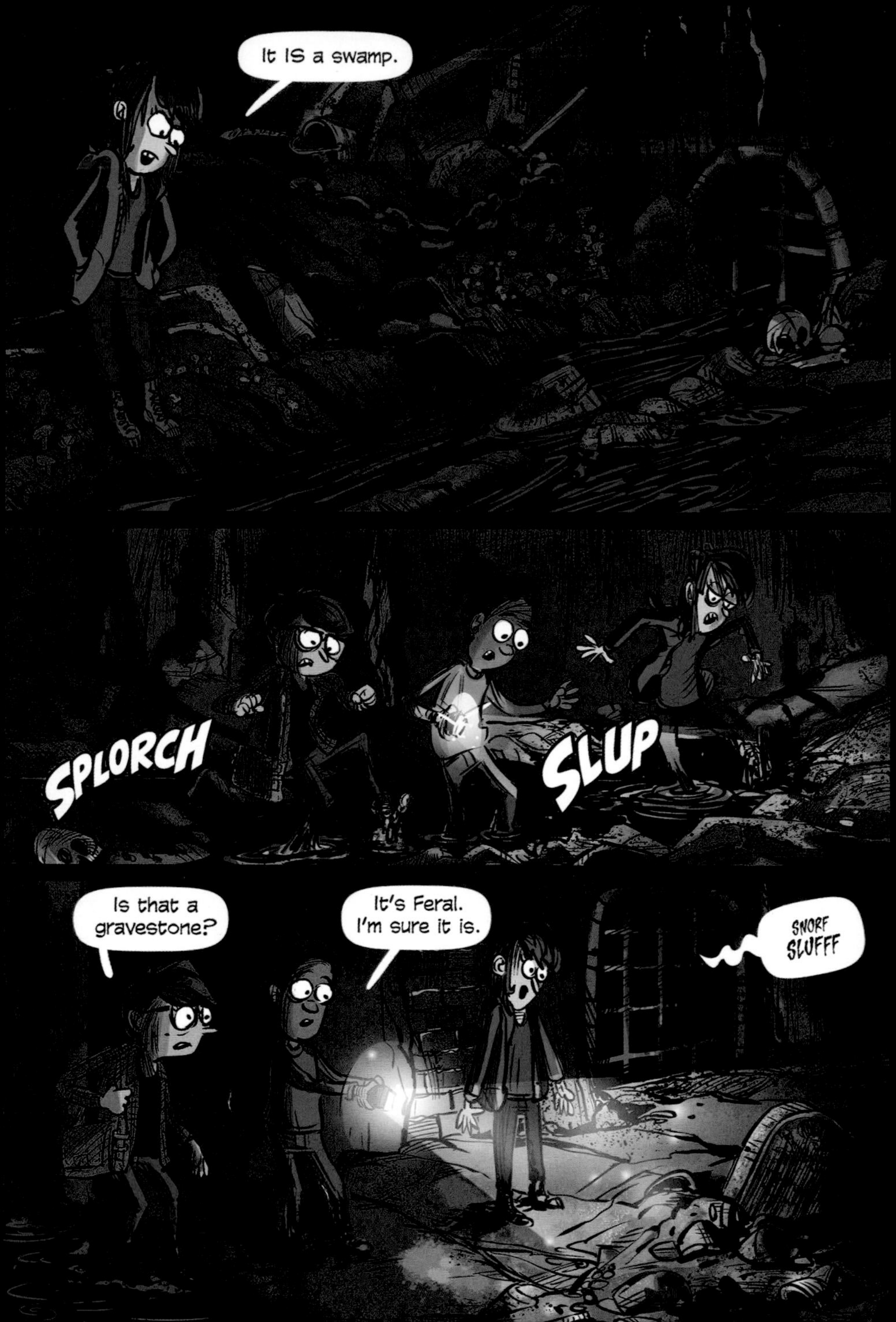
It IS a swamp.
SPLORCH
SLUP
Is that a gravestone?
It's Feral. I'm sure it is.
SNORF SLUFFF

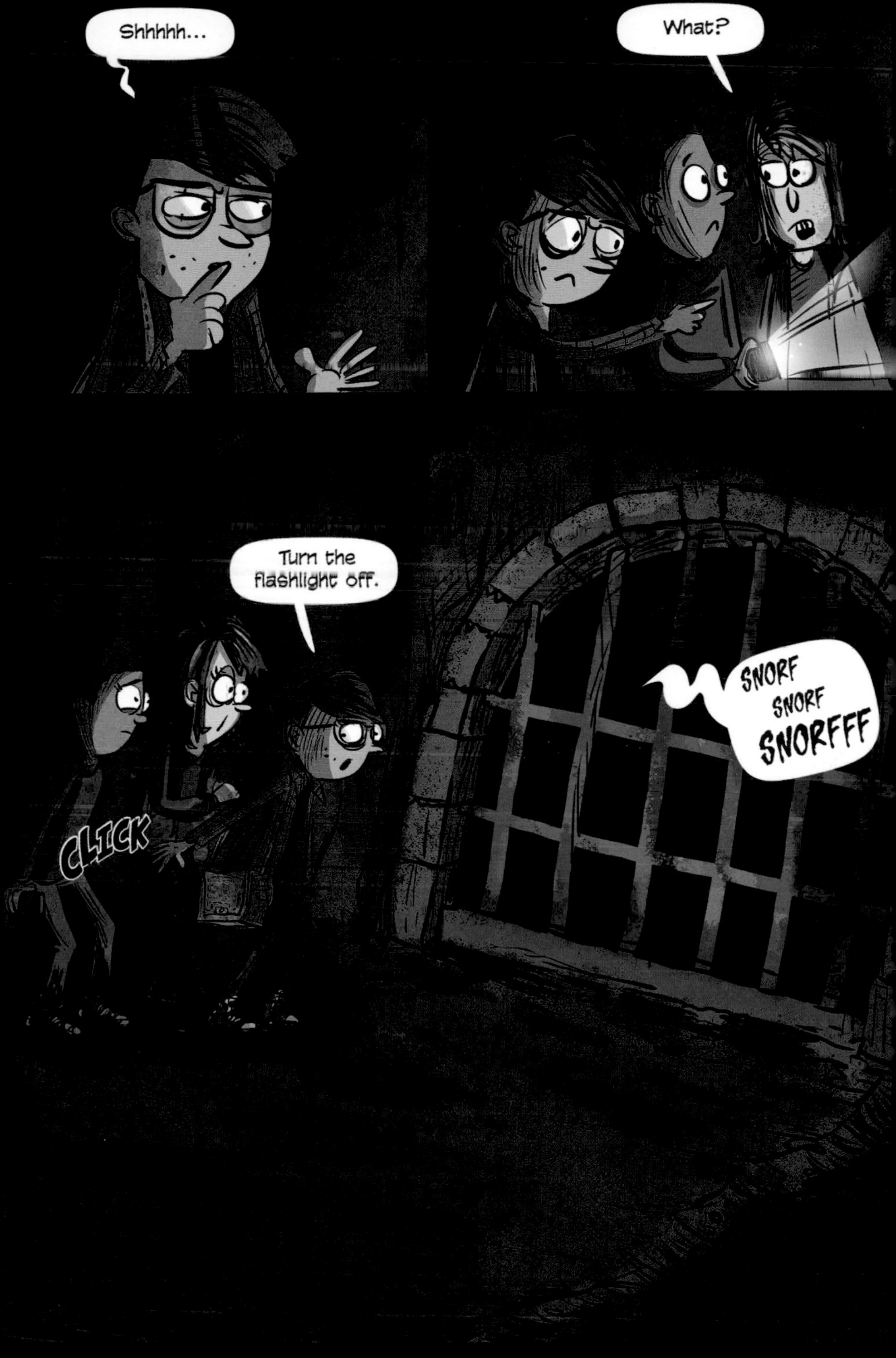
Shhhhh...
What?
Turn the flashlight off.
CLICK
SNORF SNORF SNORFFF

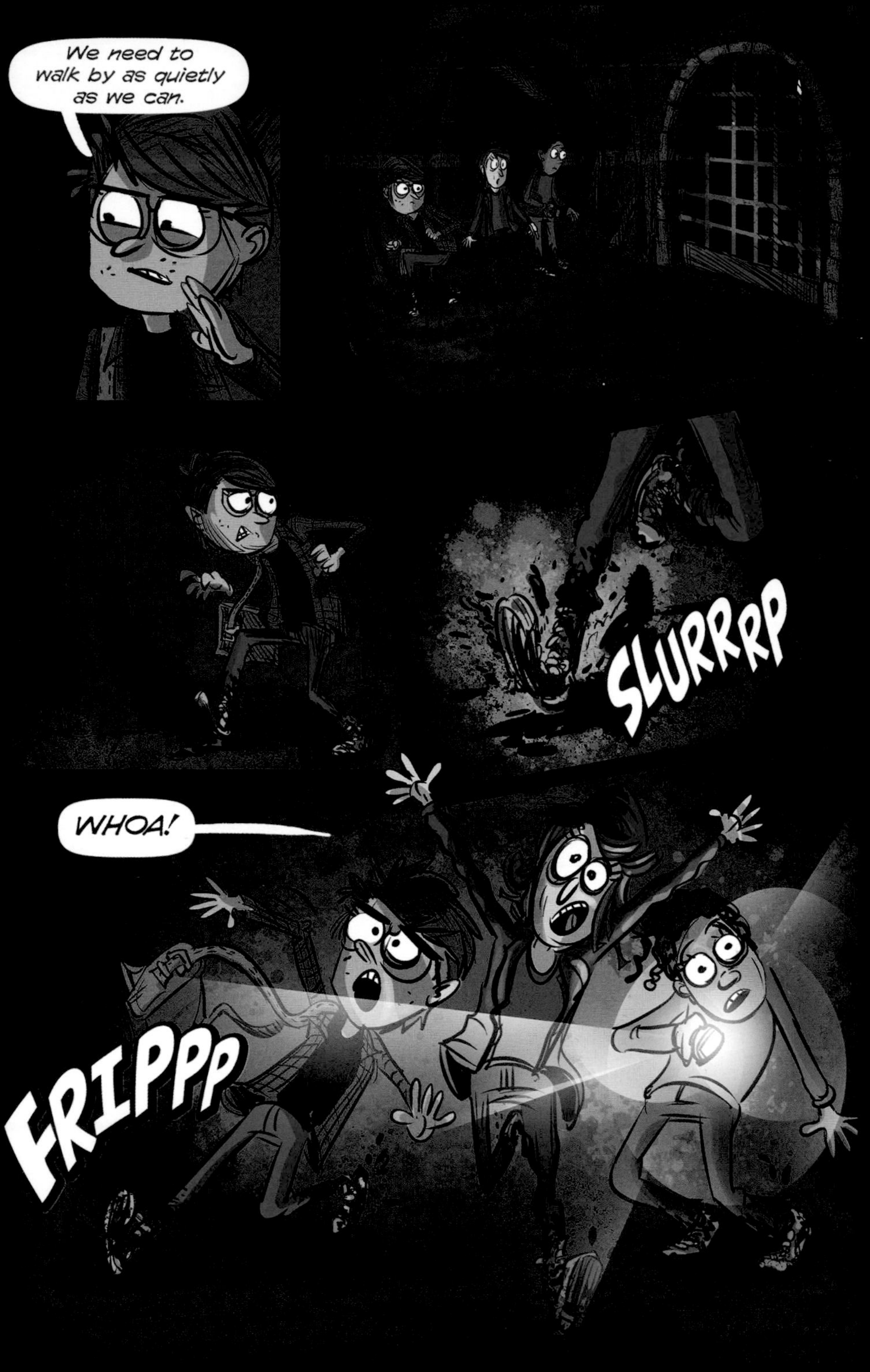
We need to walk by as quietly as we can.
SLURRRP
WHOA!
FRIPPP

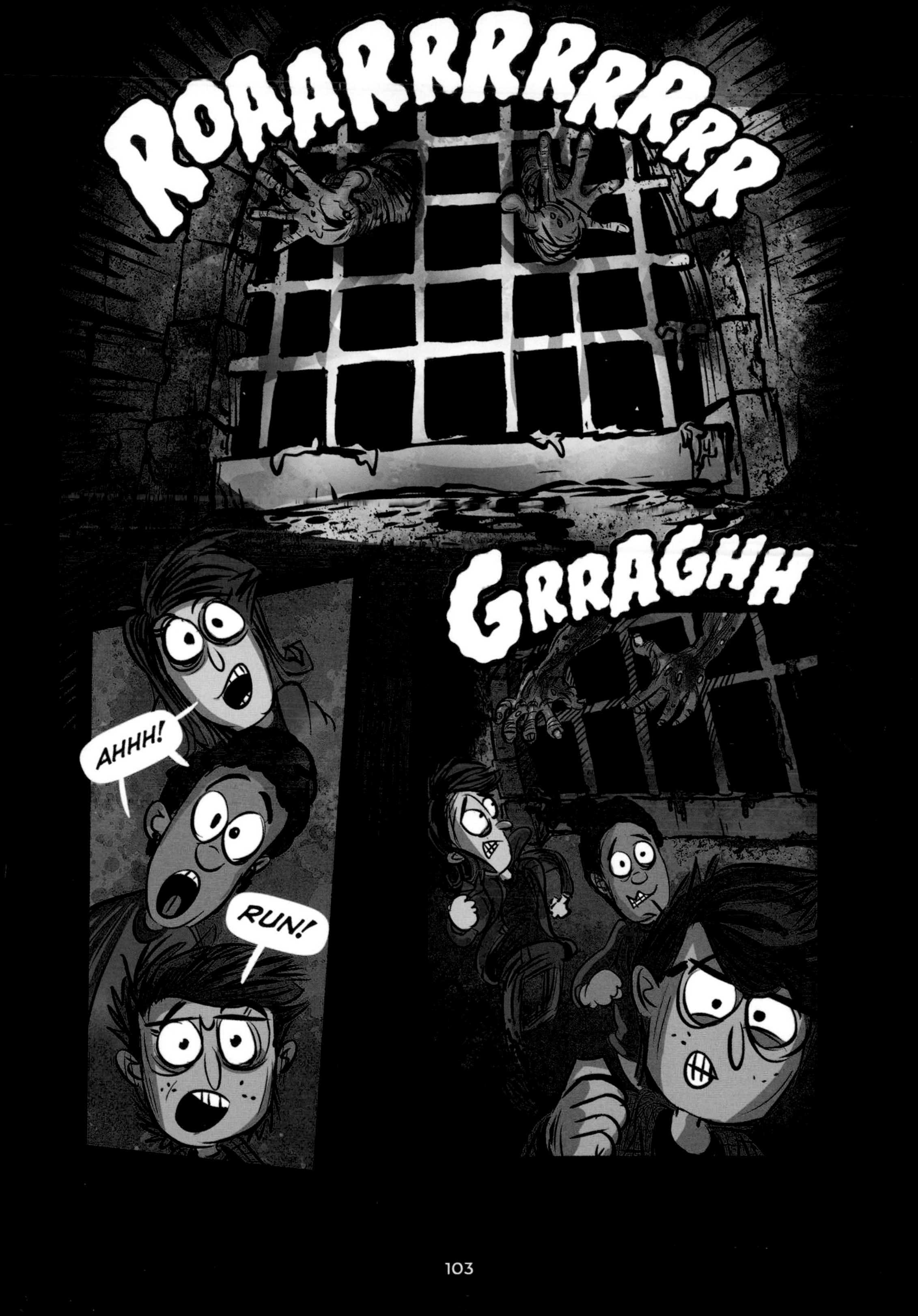
ROAARRRRRRRRR
AHHH!
RUN!
GRRAGHH

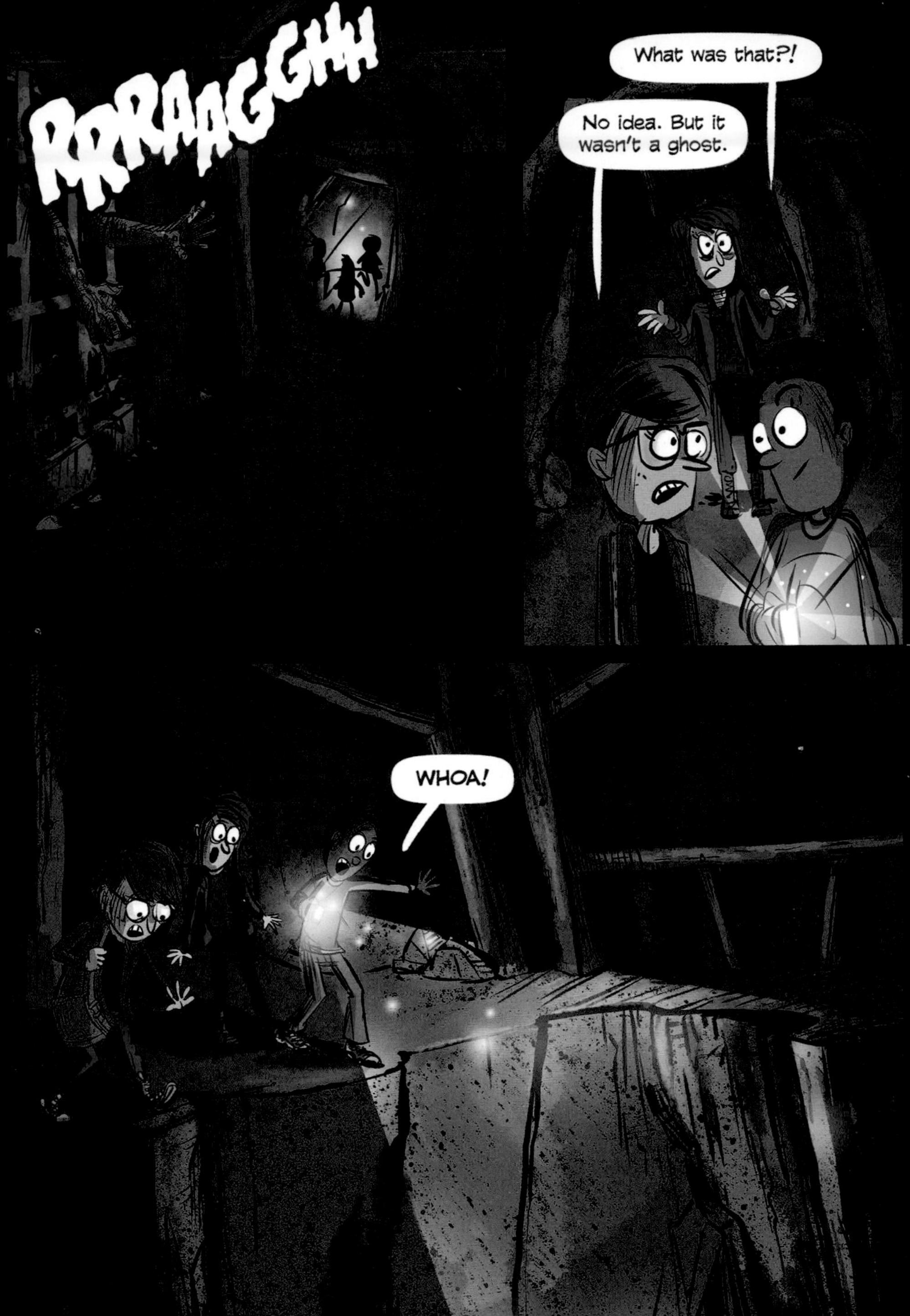
RRRAAGGHH
What was that?!
No idea. But it wasn't a ghost.
WHOA!

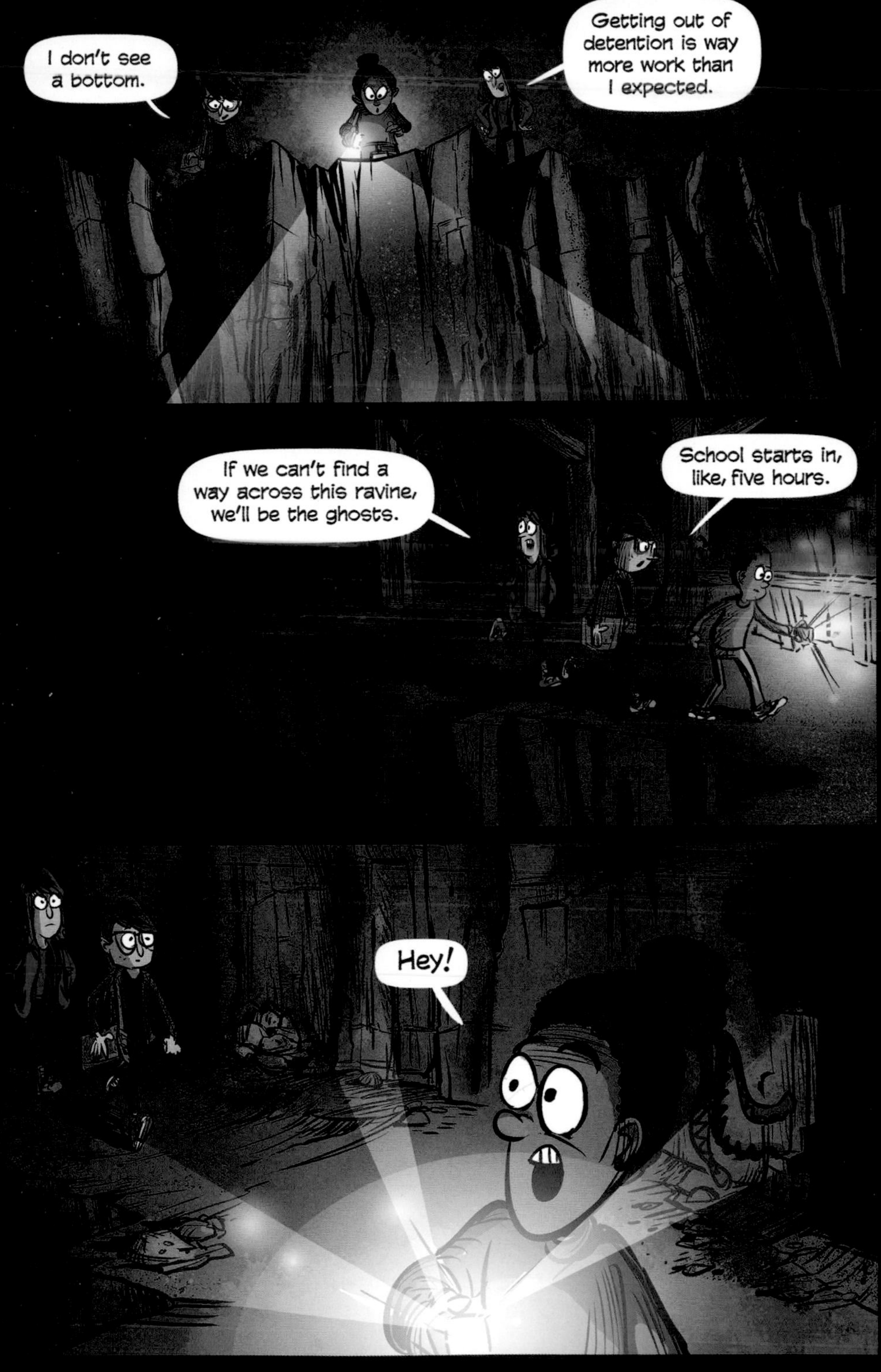
I don't see a bottom.
Getting out of detention is way more work than I expected.
If we can't find a way across this ravine, we'll be the ghosts.
School starts in, like, five hours.
Hey!

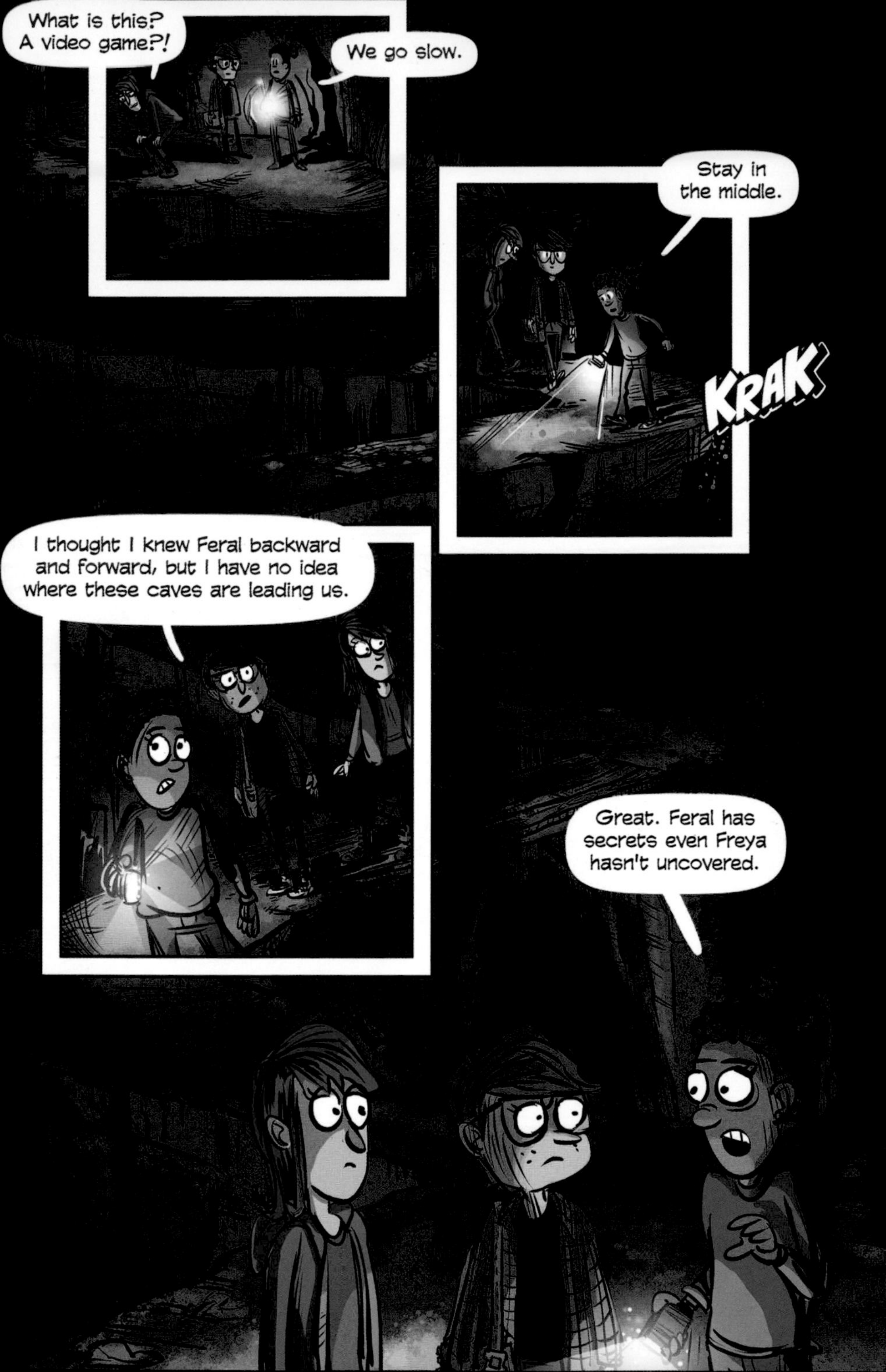
What is this? A video game?!
We go slow.
Stay in the middle.
KRAK
I thought I knew Feral backward and forward, but I have no idea where these caves are leading us.
Great. Feral has secrets even Freya hasn't uncovered.

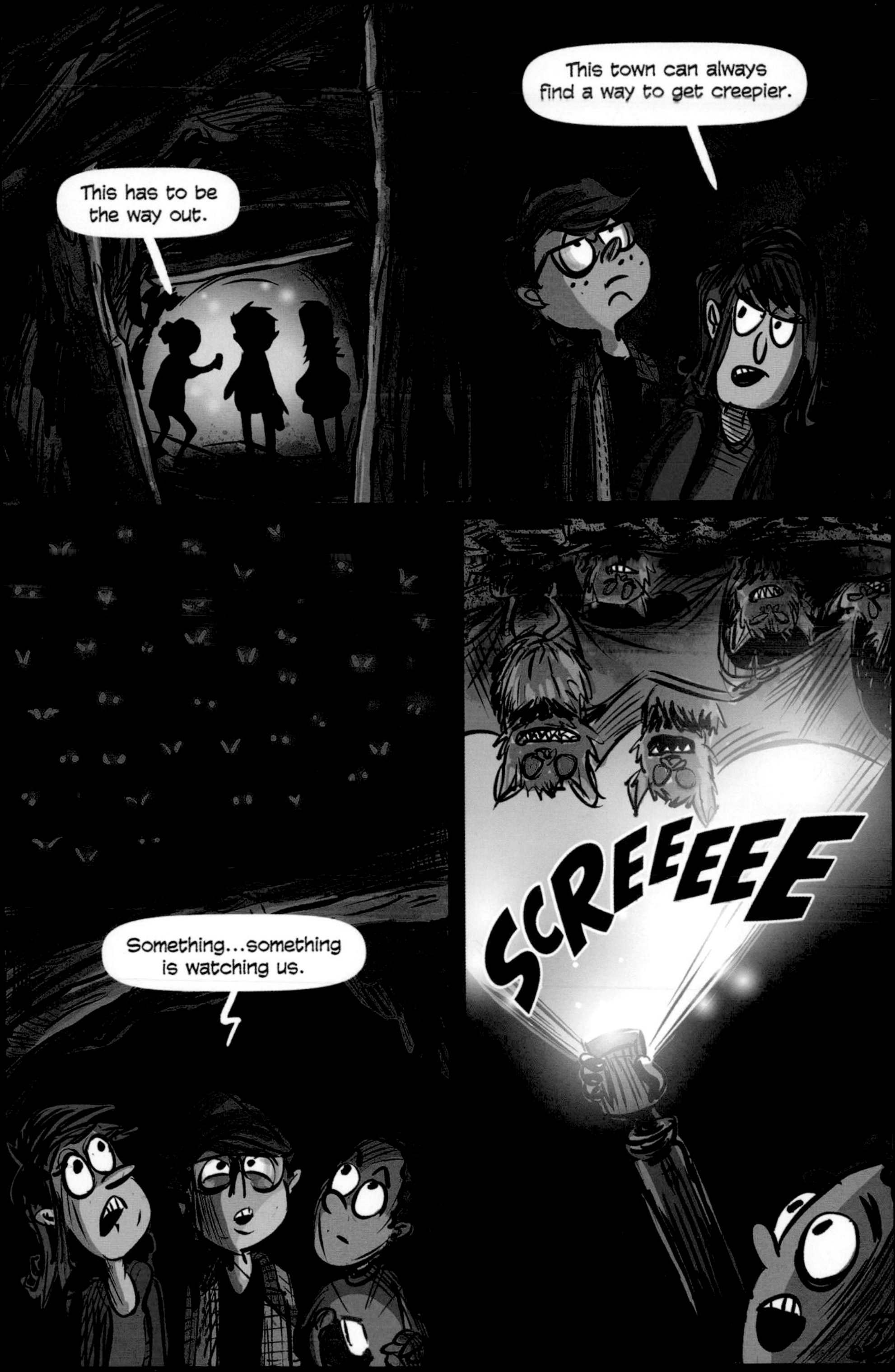
This has to be the way out.
This town can always find a way to get creepier.
Something...something is watching us.
SCREEEEE

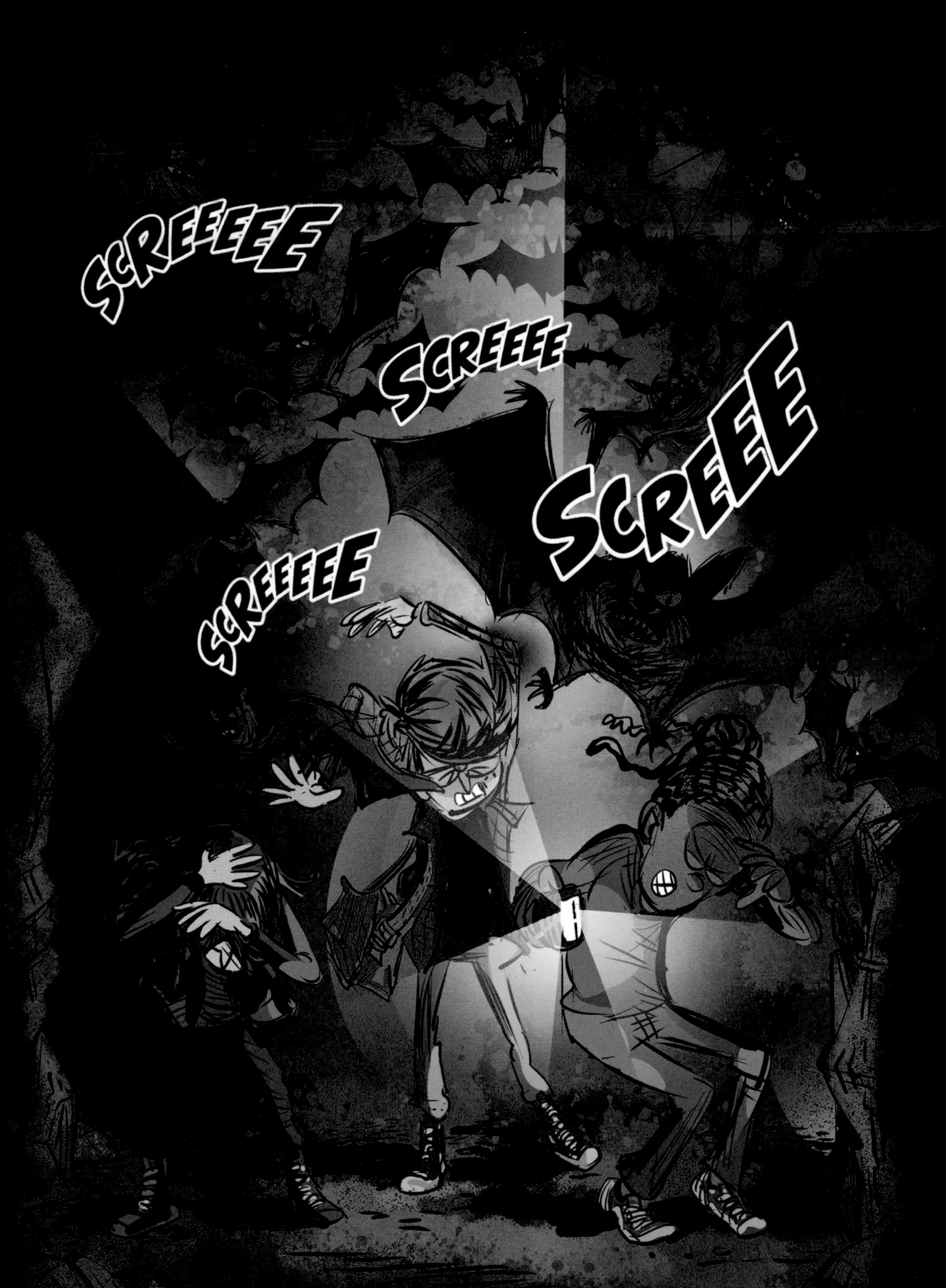
SCREEEEE
SCREEEE
SCREEE
SCREEEEE

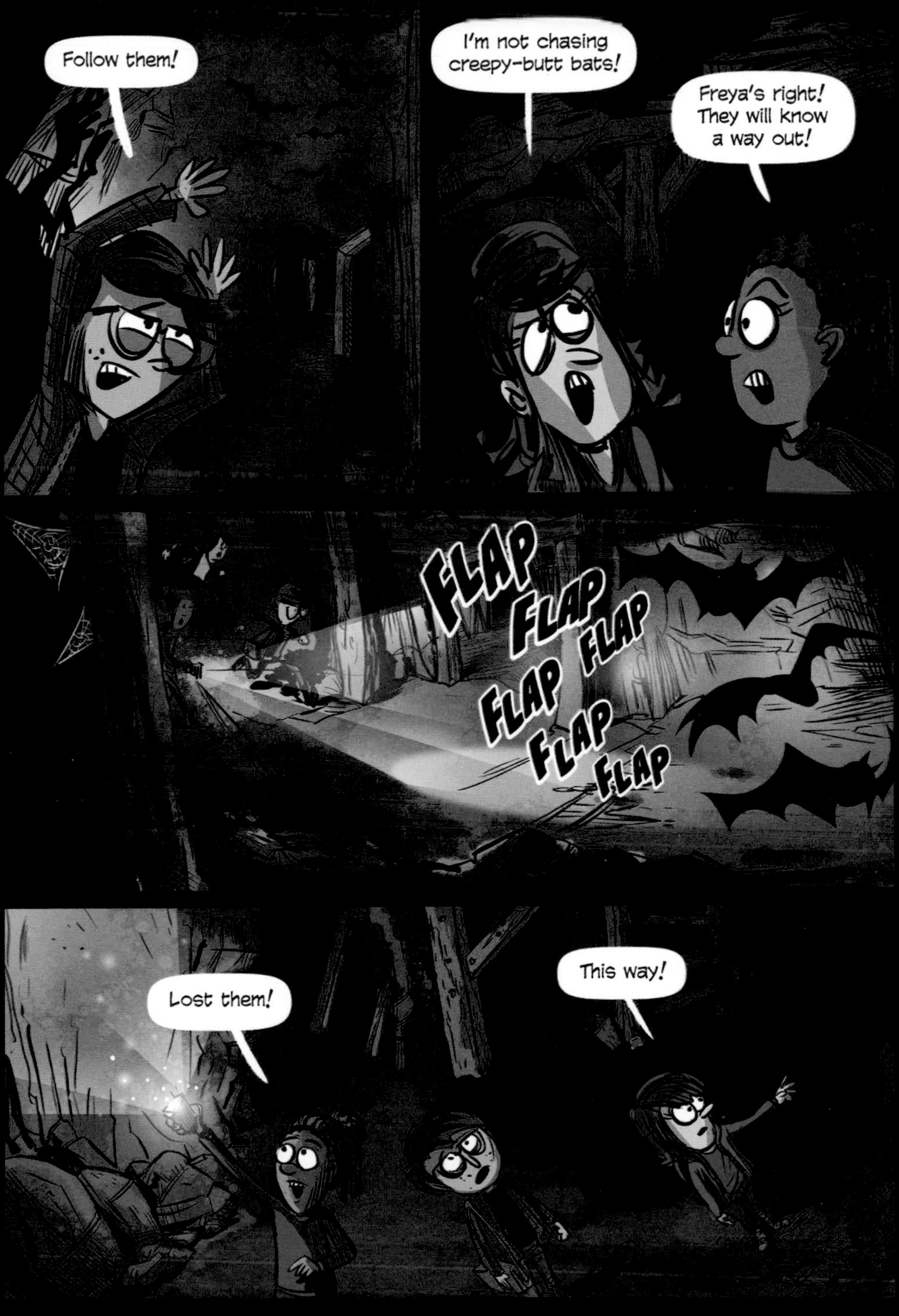
Follow them!
I'm not chasing creepy-butt bats!
Freya's right! They will know a way out!
FLAP FLAP FLAP FLAP FLAP FLAP
Lost them!
This way!

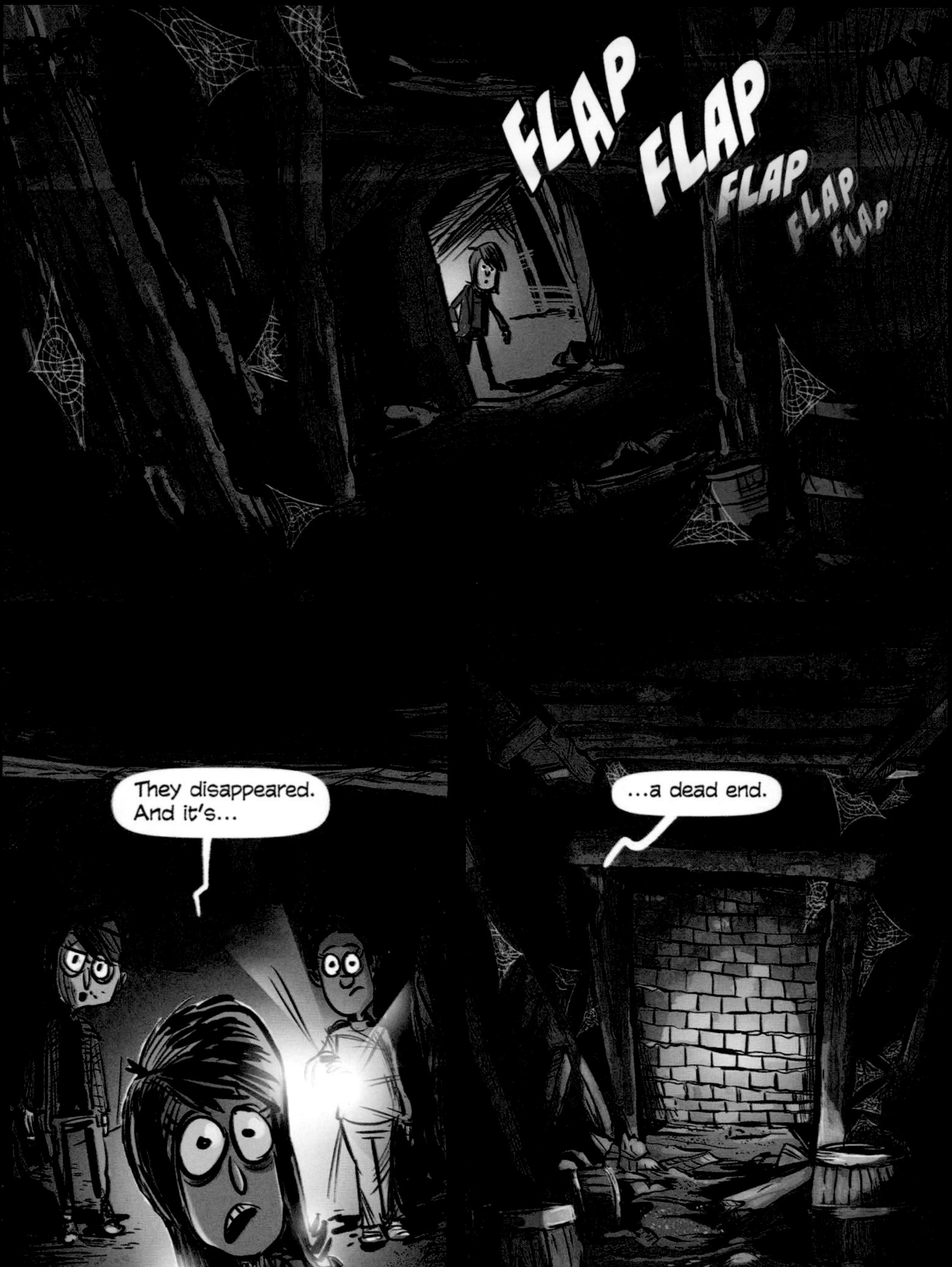
FLAP
FLAP
FLAP
FLAP
FLAP
They disappeared. And it's...
...a dead end.

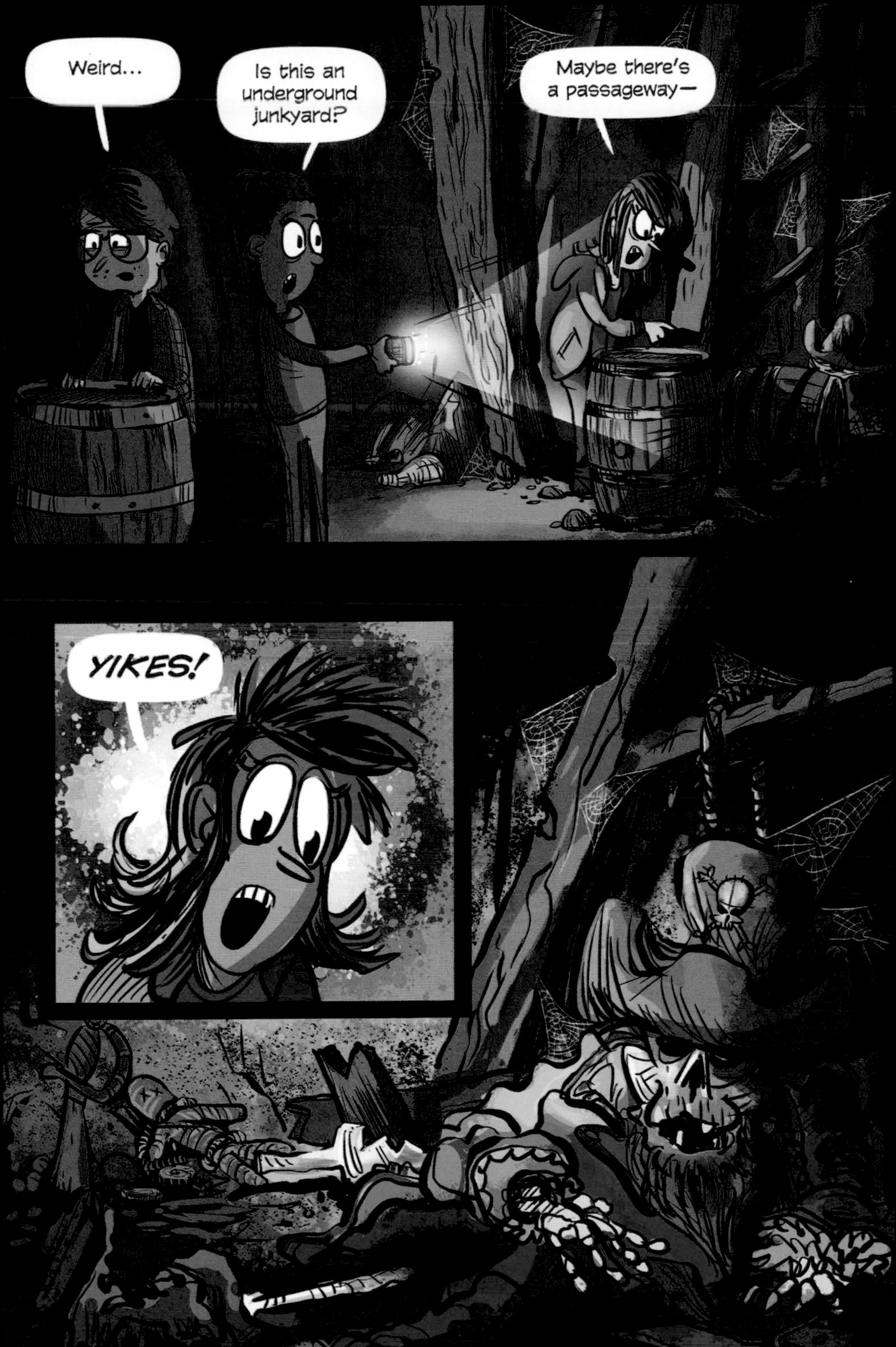
Weird...
Is this an underground junkyard?
Maybe there's a passageway—
YIKES!

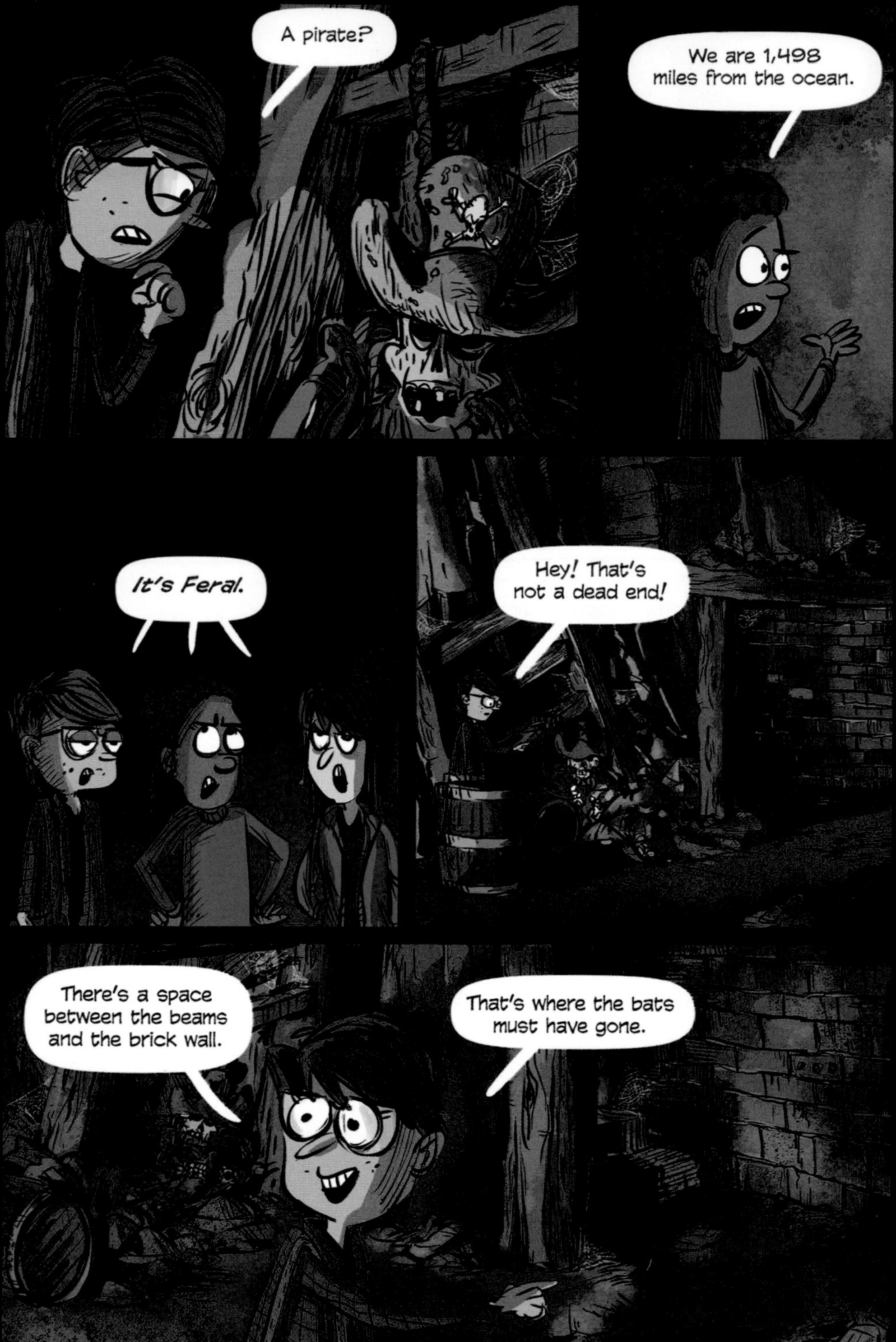
A pirate?
We are 1,498 miles from the ocean.
It's Feral.
Hey! That's not a dead end!
There's a space between the beams and the brick wall.
That's where the bats must have gone.

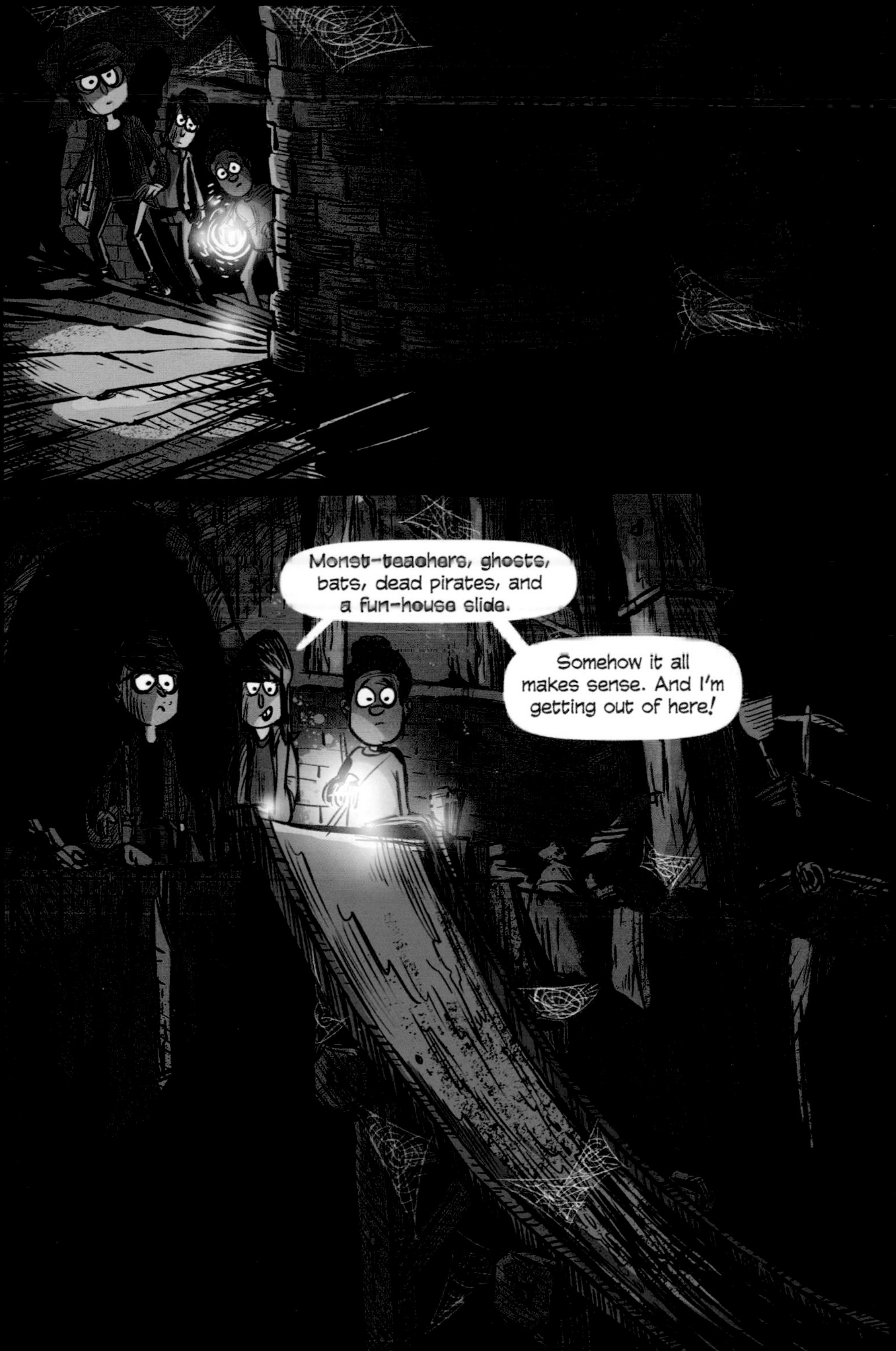
Monst-teachers, ghosts, bats, dead pirates, and a fun-house slide.
Somehow it all makes sense. And I'm getting out of here!

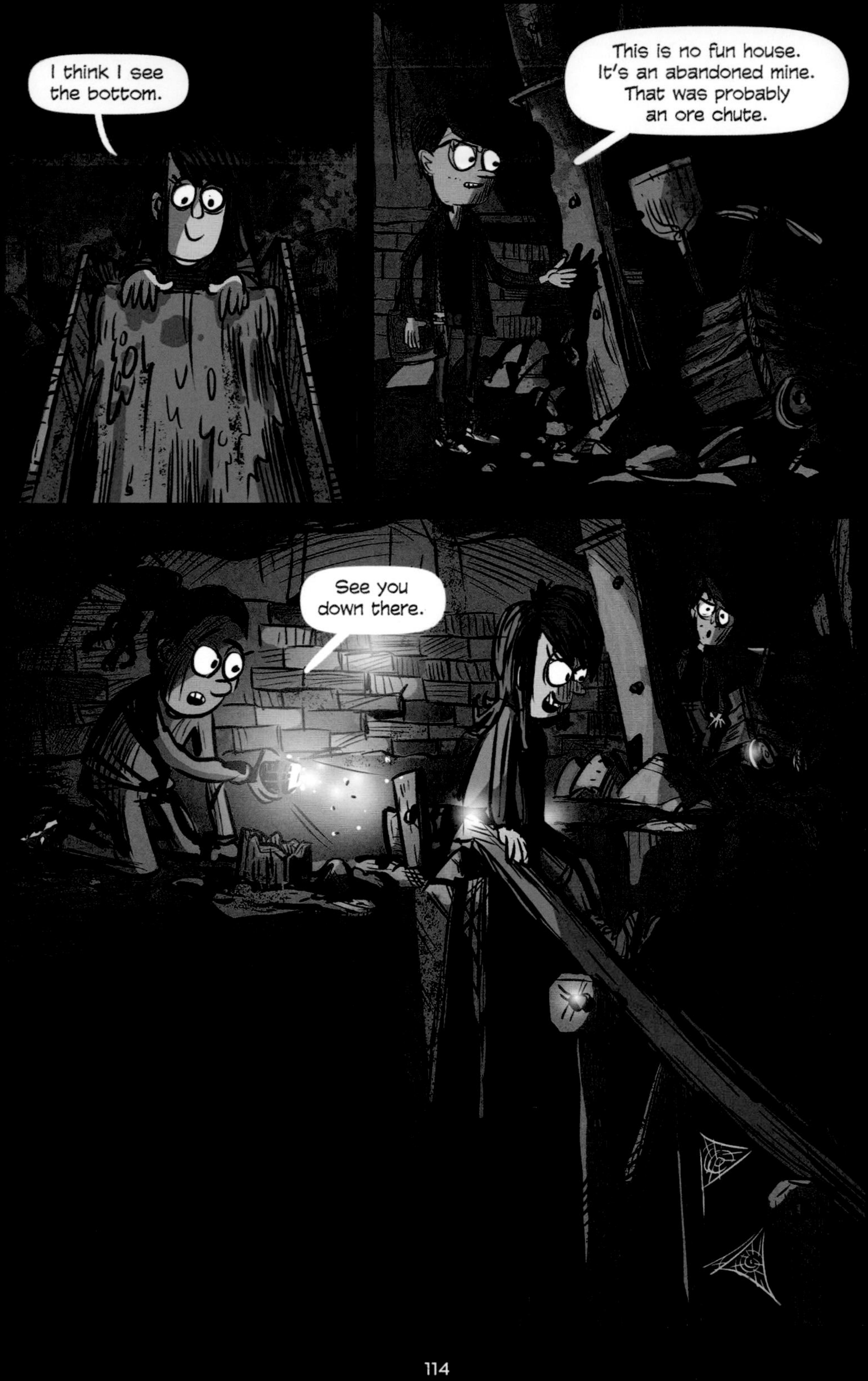
I think I see the bottom.
This is no fun house. It's an abandoned mine. That was probably an ore chute.
See you down there.

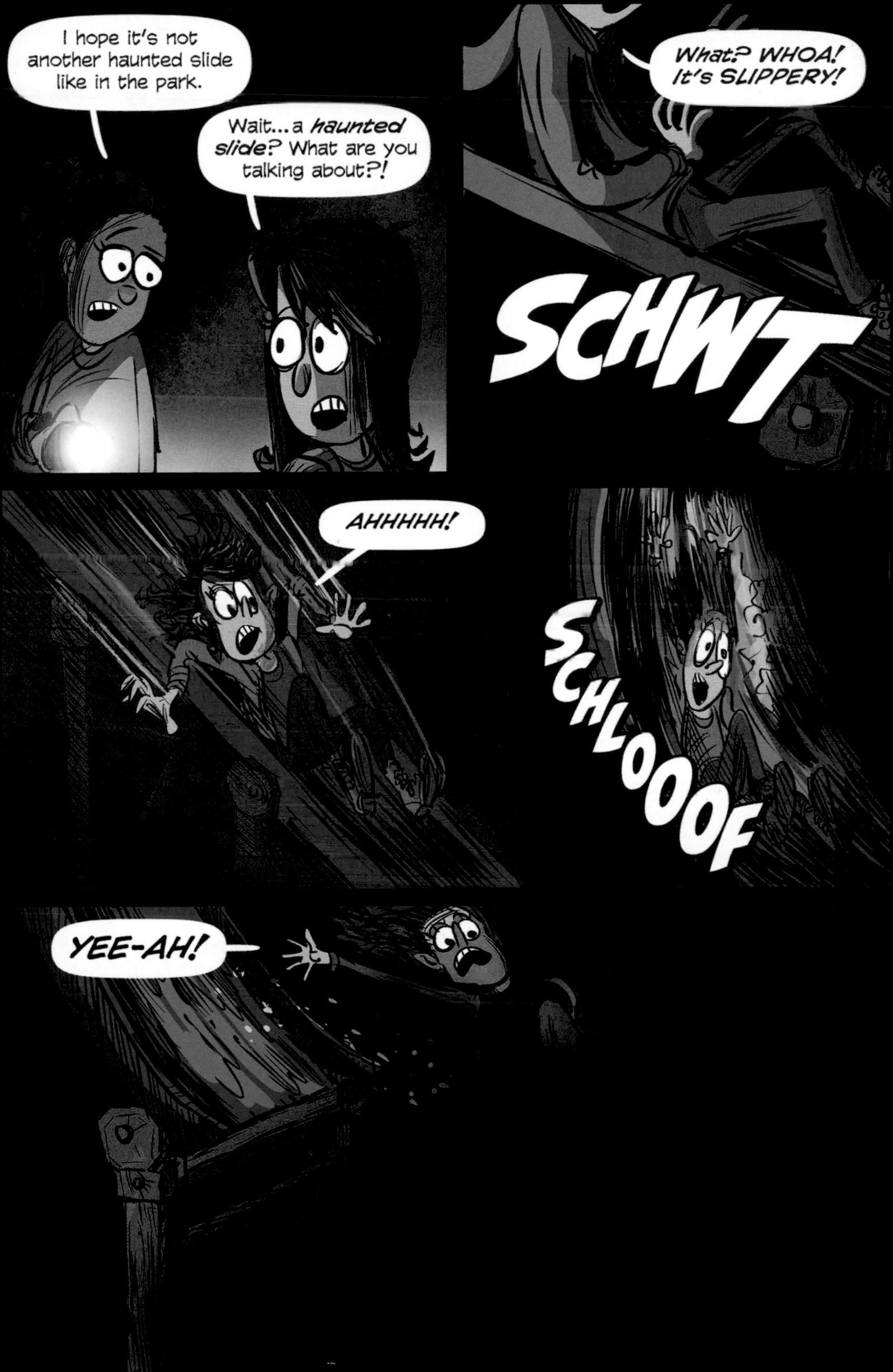
I hope it's not another haunted slide like in the park.
Wait... a *haunted slide*? What are you talking about?!
What? WHOA! It's SLIPPERY!
SCHWT
AHHHHH!
SCHLOOOF
YEE-AH!

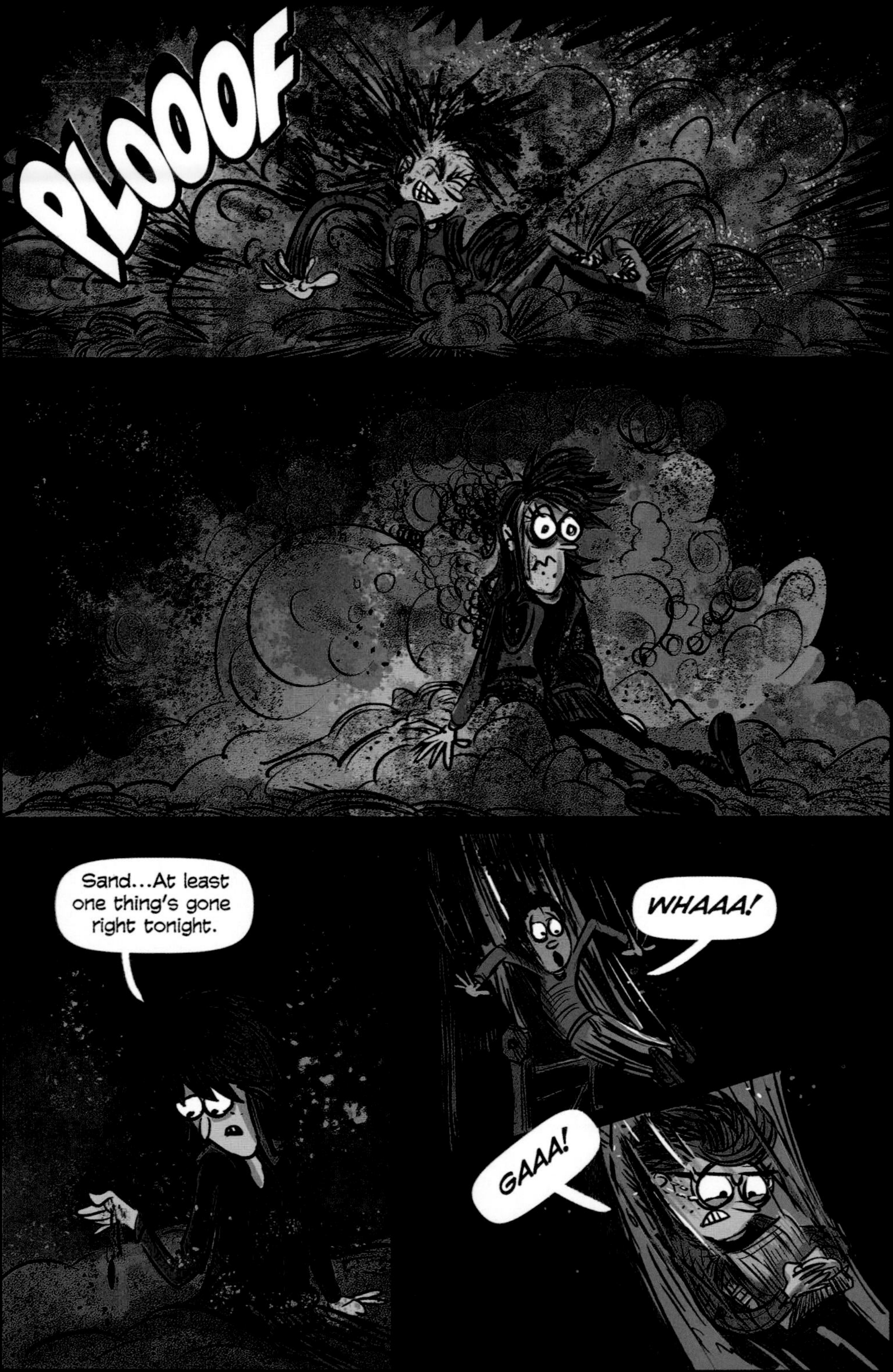
PLOOOF
Sand...At least one thing's gone right tonight.
WHAAA!
GAAA!

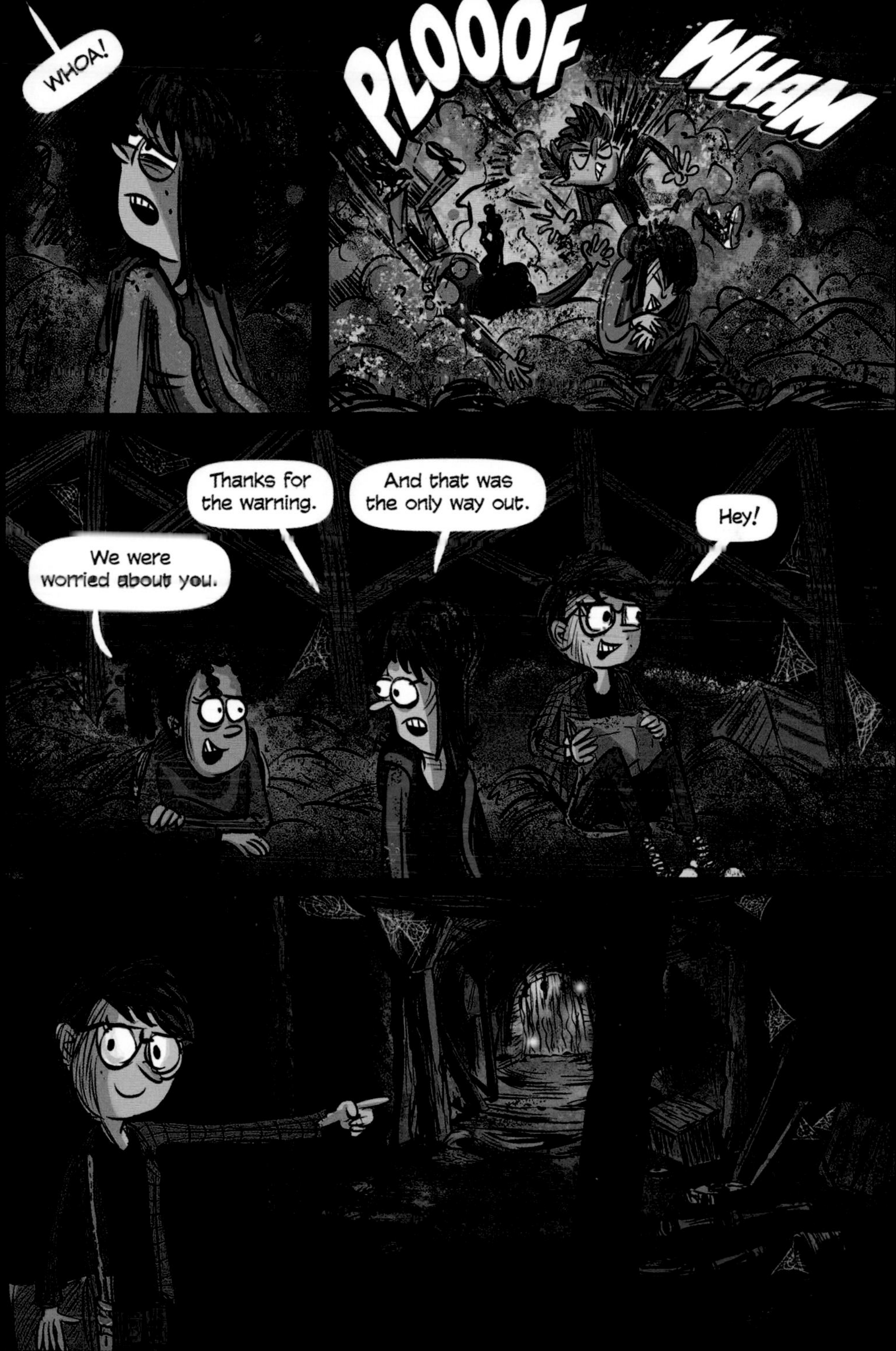
WHOA!
PLOOOF
WHAM
We were worried about you.
Thanks for the warning.
And that was the only way out.
Hey!

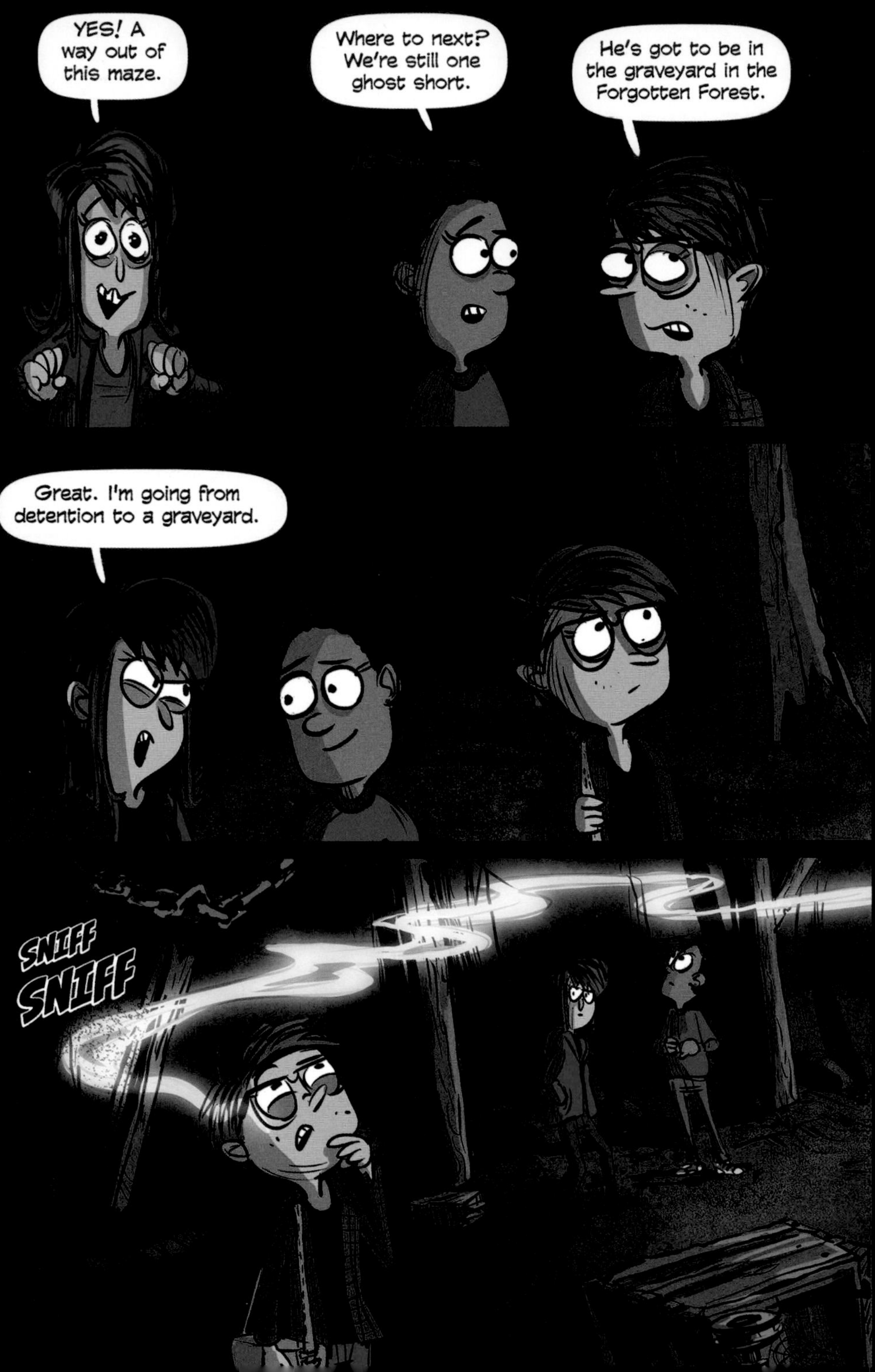
YES! A way out of this maze.
Where to next? We're still one ghost short.
He's got to be in the graveyard in the Forgotten Forest.
Great. I'm going from detention to a graveyard.
SNIFF
SNIFF

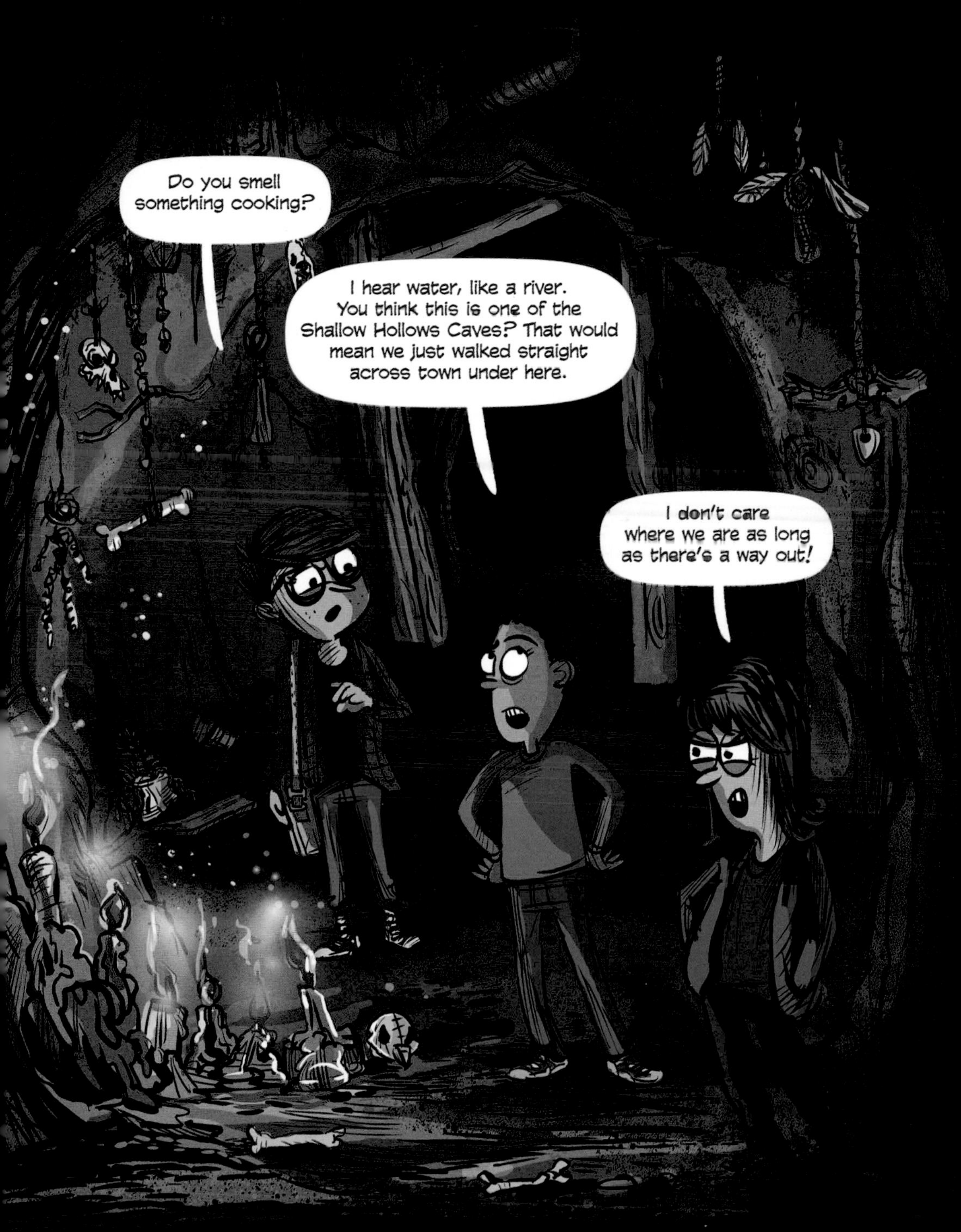
Do you smell something cooking?
I hear water, like a river. You think this is one of the Shallow Hollows Caves? That would mean we just walked straight across town under here.
I don't care where we are as long as there's a way out!

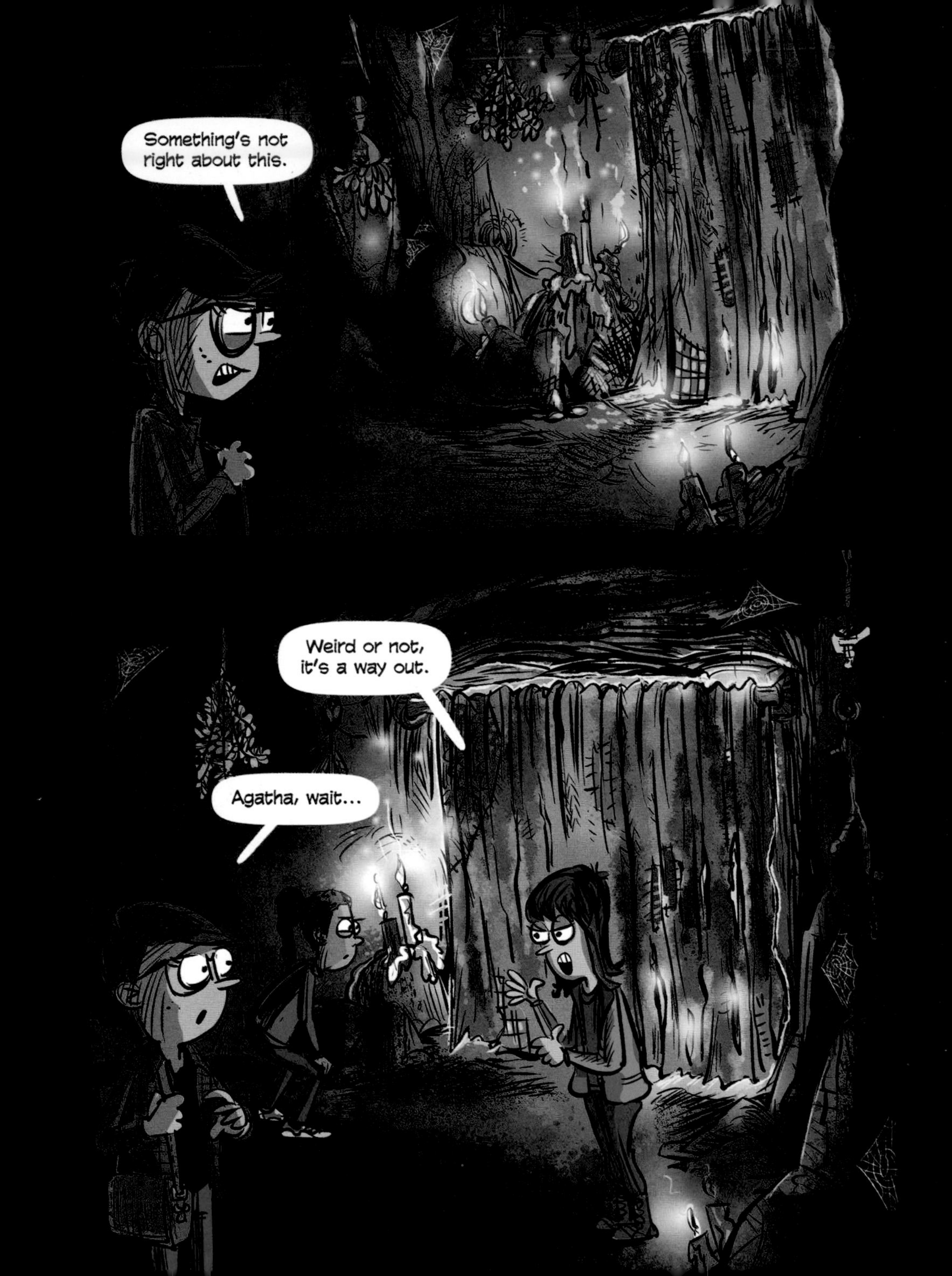
Something's not right about this.
Weird or not, it's a way out.
Agatha, wait...

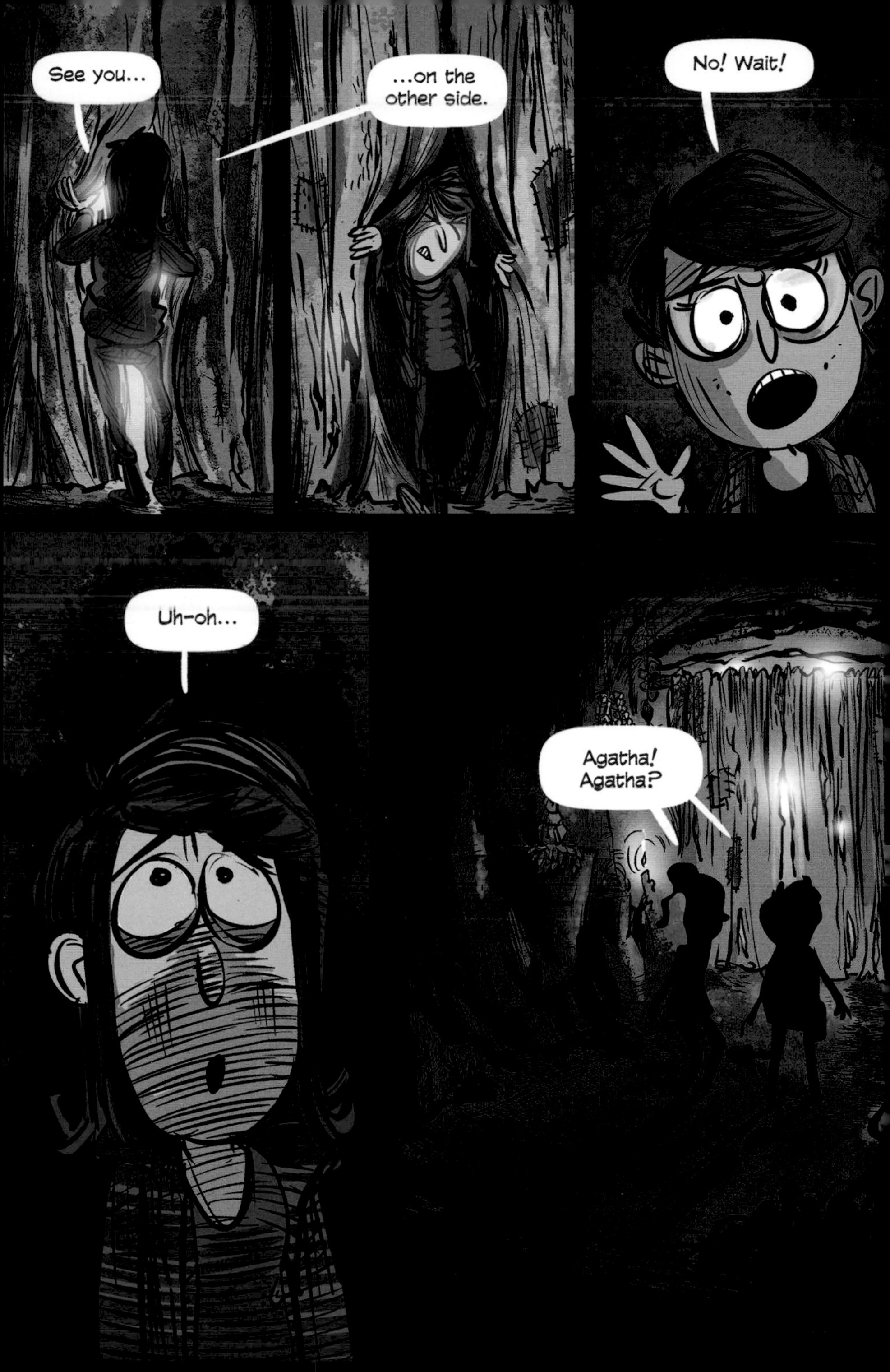
See you...
...on the other side.
No! Wait!
Uh-oh...
Agatha! Agatha?

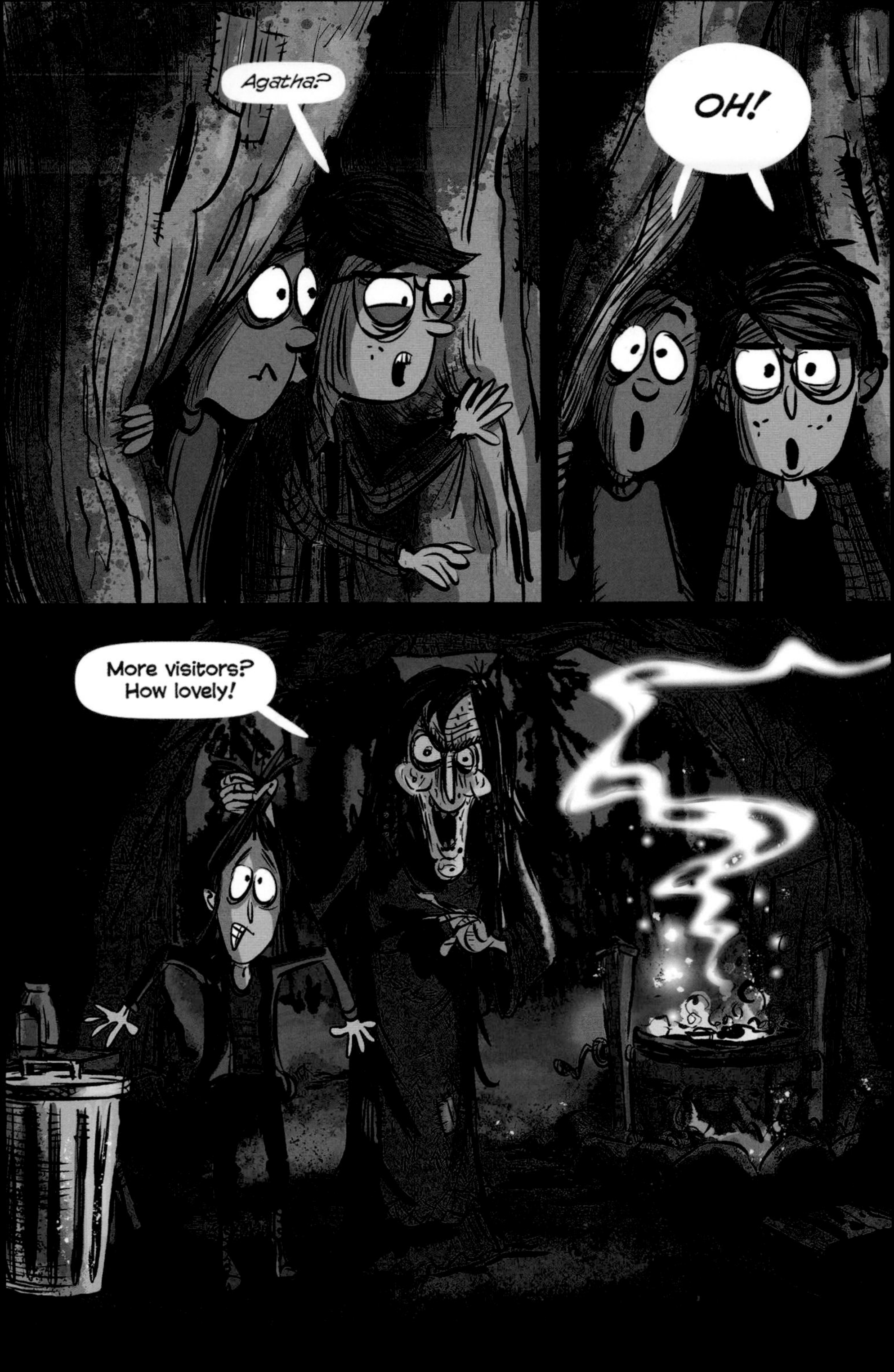
Agatha?
OH!
More visitors? How lovely!

CHAPTER 6

Picturesque
COUNTY ROAD 52 IN FERAL

Driving for days. Hope to be home soon, but this town has a way of not letting go.

Gret Vac Travel
7286 Oharsell Ave
Jencen WY 70470

10¢ Postage

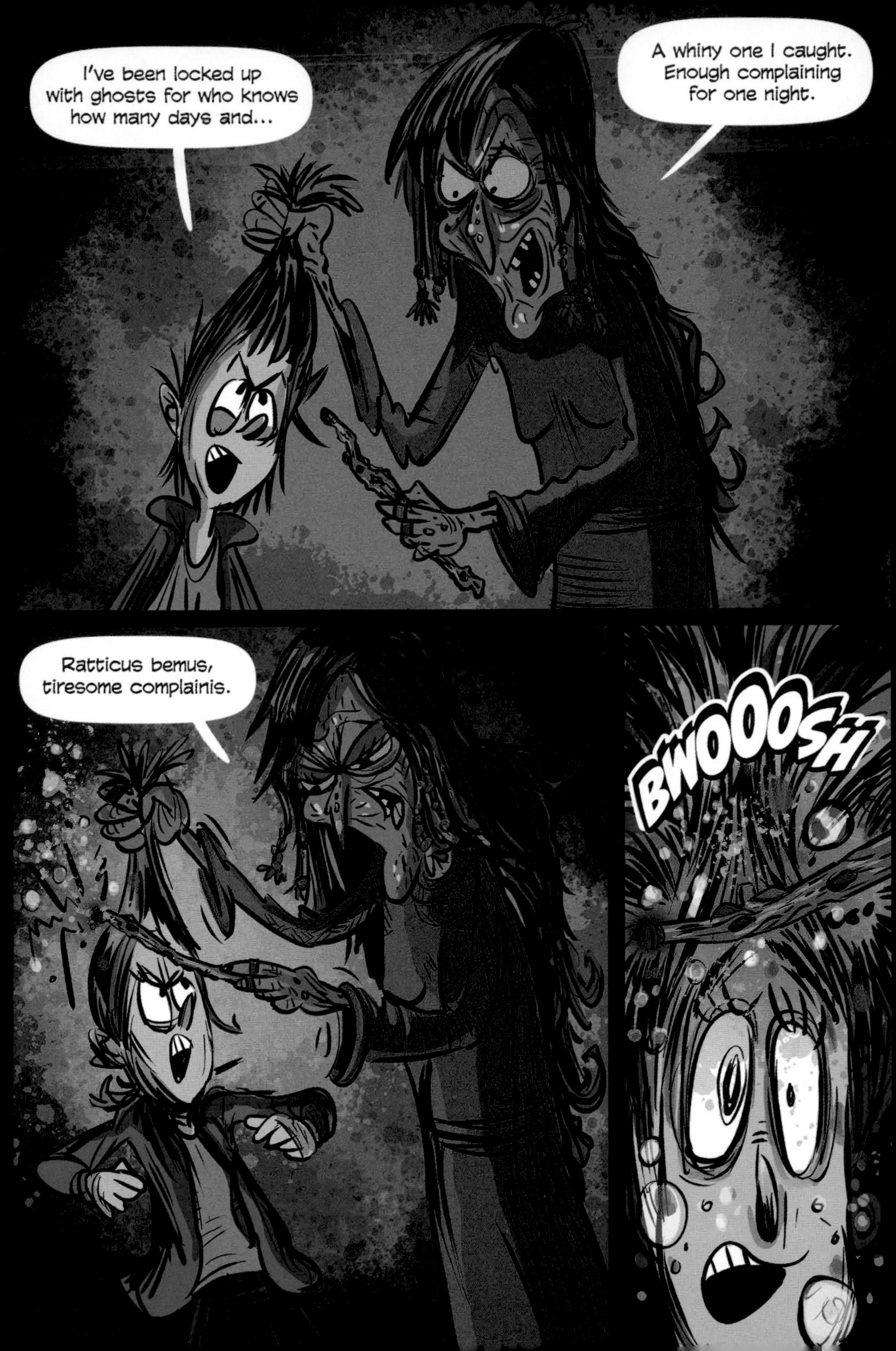
I've been locked up with ghosts for who knows how many days and...
A whiny one I caught. Enough complaining for one night.
Ratticus bemus, tiresome complainis.
BWOOOSH

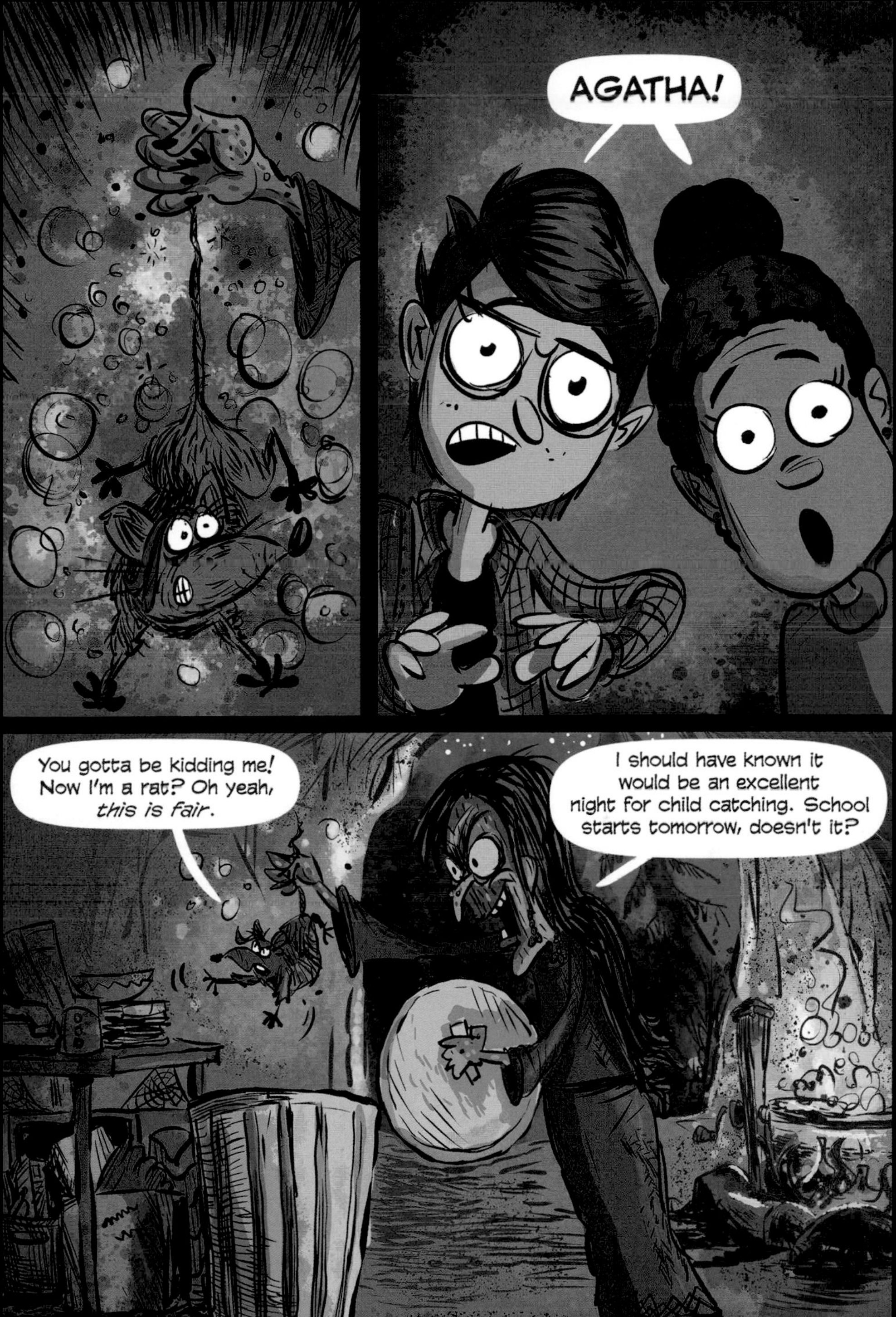
AGATHA!
You gotta be kidding me! Now I'm a rat? Oh yeah, *this is fair*.
I should have known it would be an excellent night for child catching. School starts tomorrow, doesn't it?

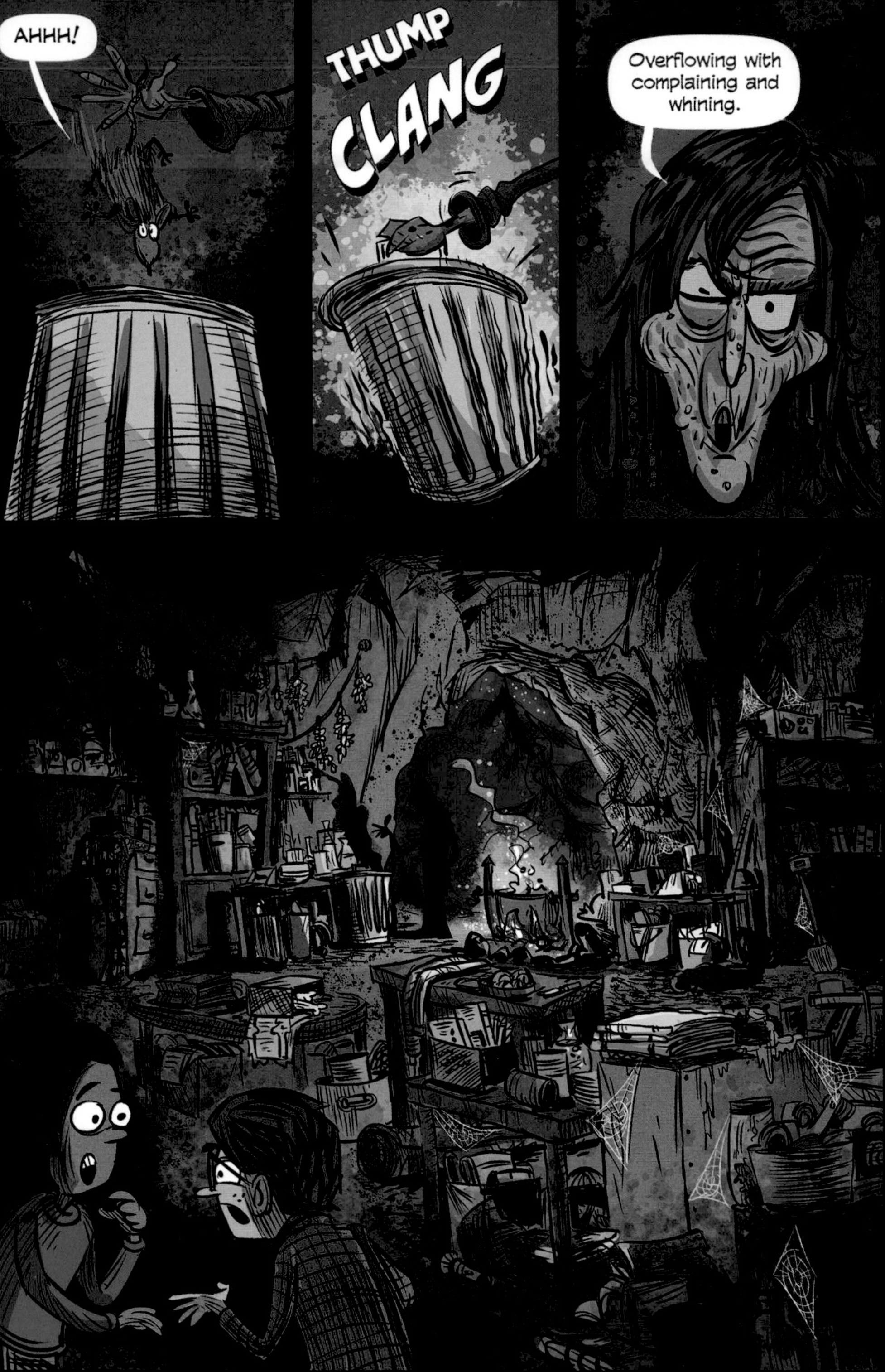
AHHH!
THUMP
CLANG
Overflowing with complaining and whining.

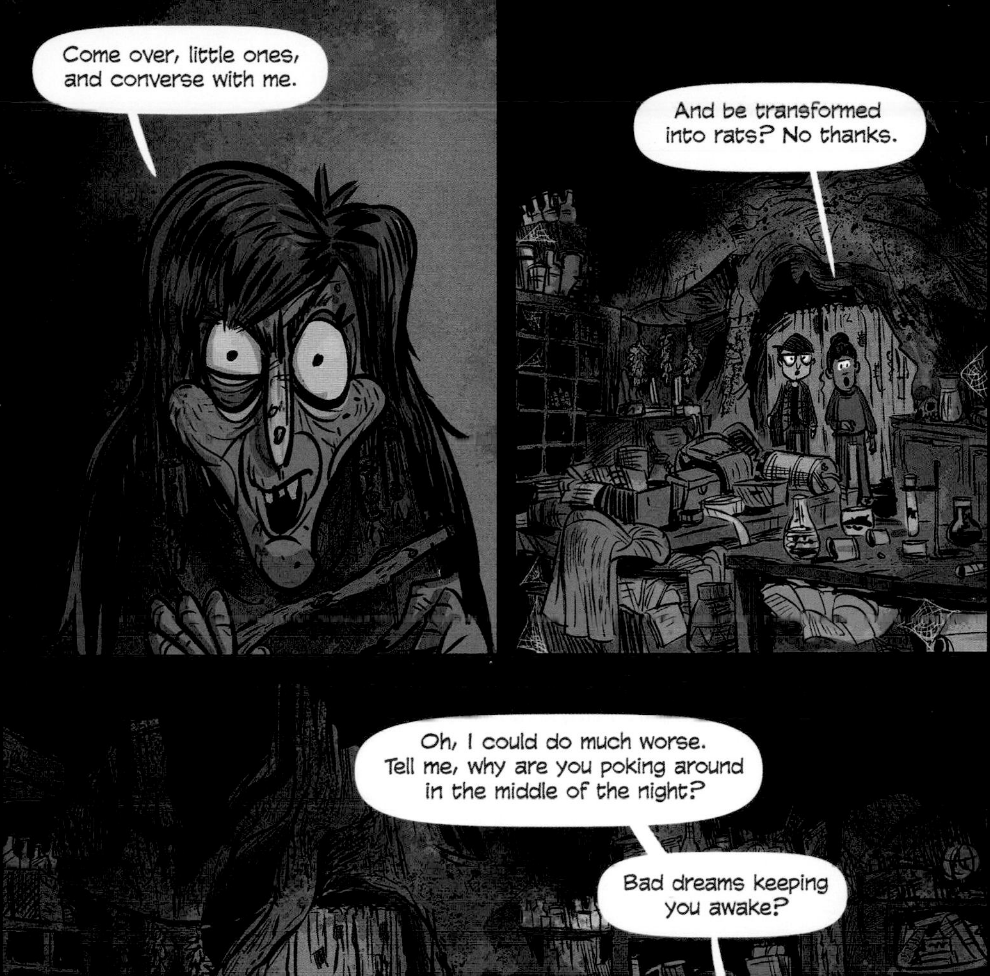
Come over, little ones, and converse with me.
And be transformed into rats? No thanks.
Oh, I could do much worse. Tell me, why are you poking around in the middle of the night?
Bad dreams keeping you awake?

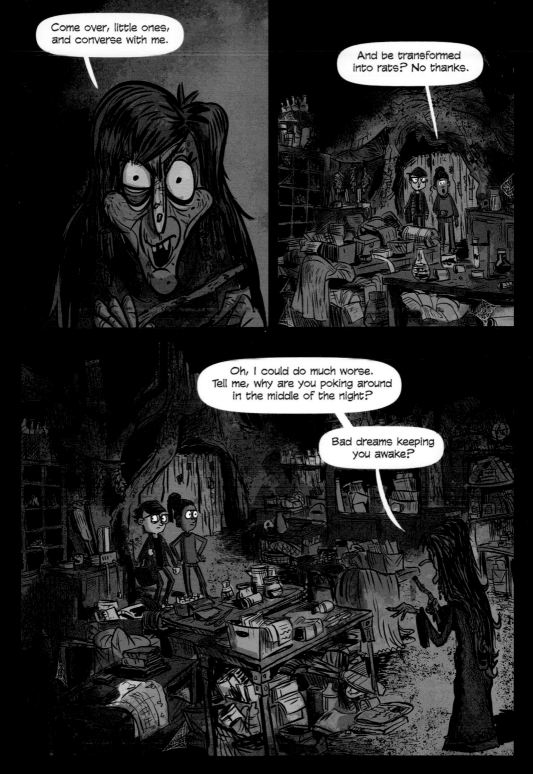

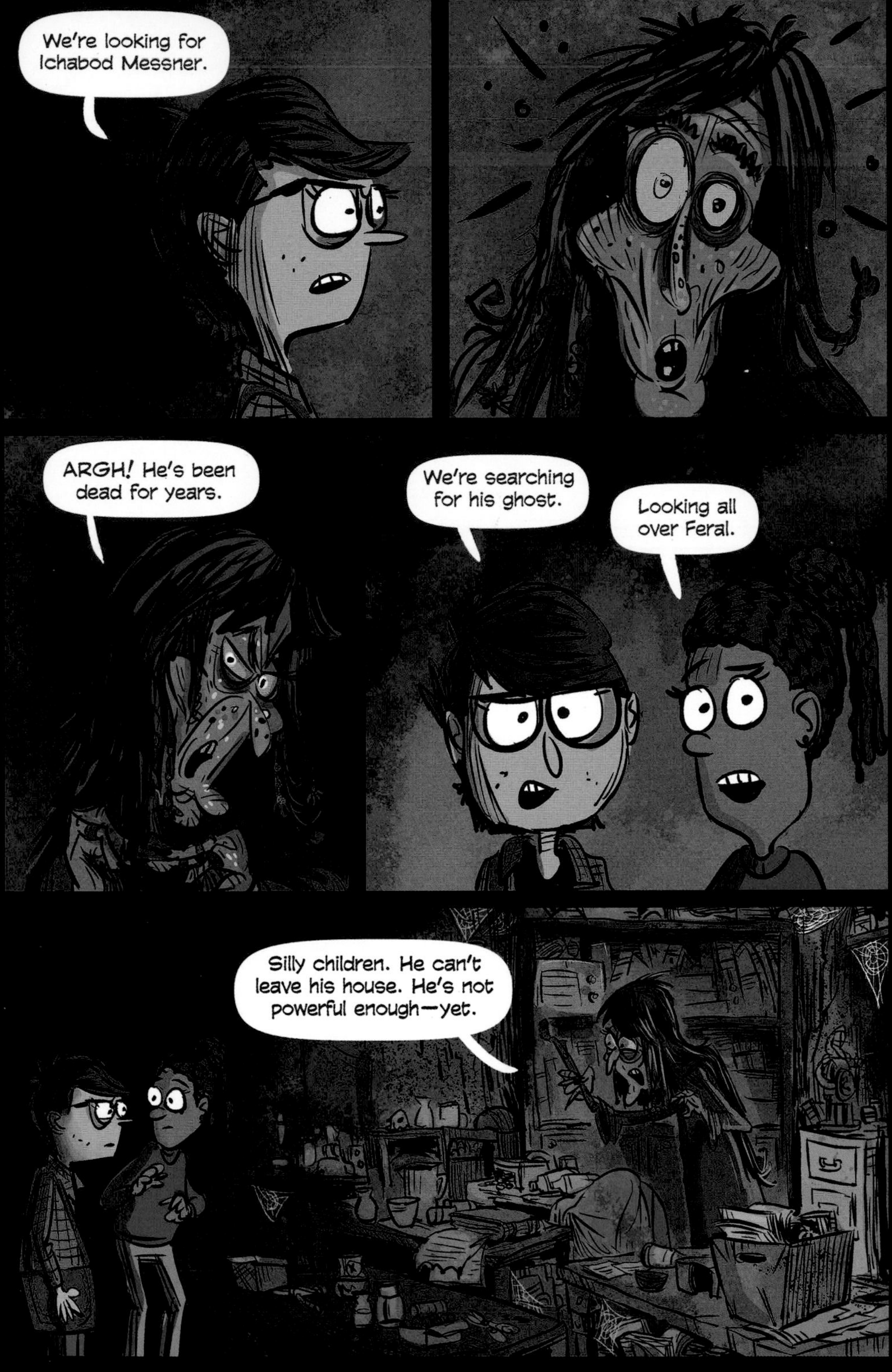
We're looking for Ichabod Messner.
ARGH! He's been dead for years.
We're searching for his ghost.
Looking all over Feral.
Silly children. He can't leave his house. He's not powerful enough—yet.

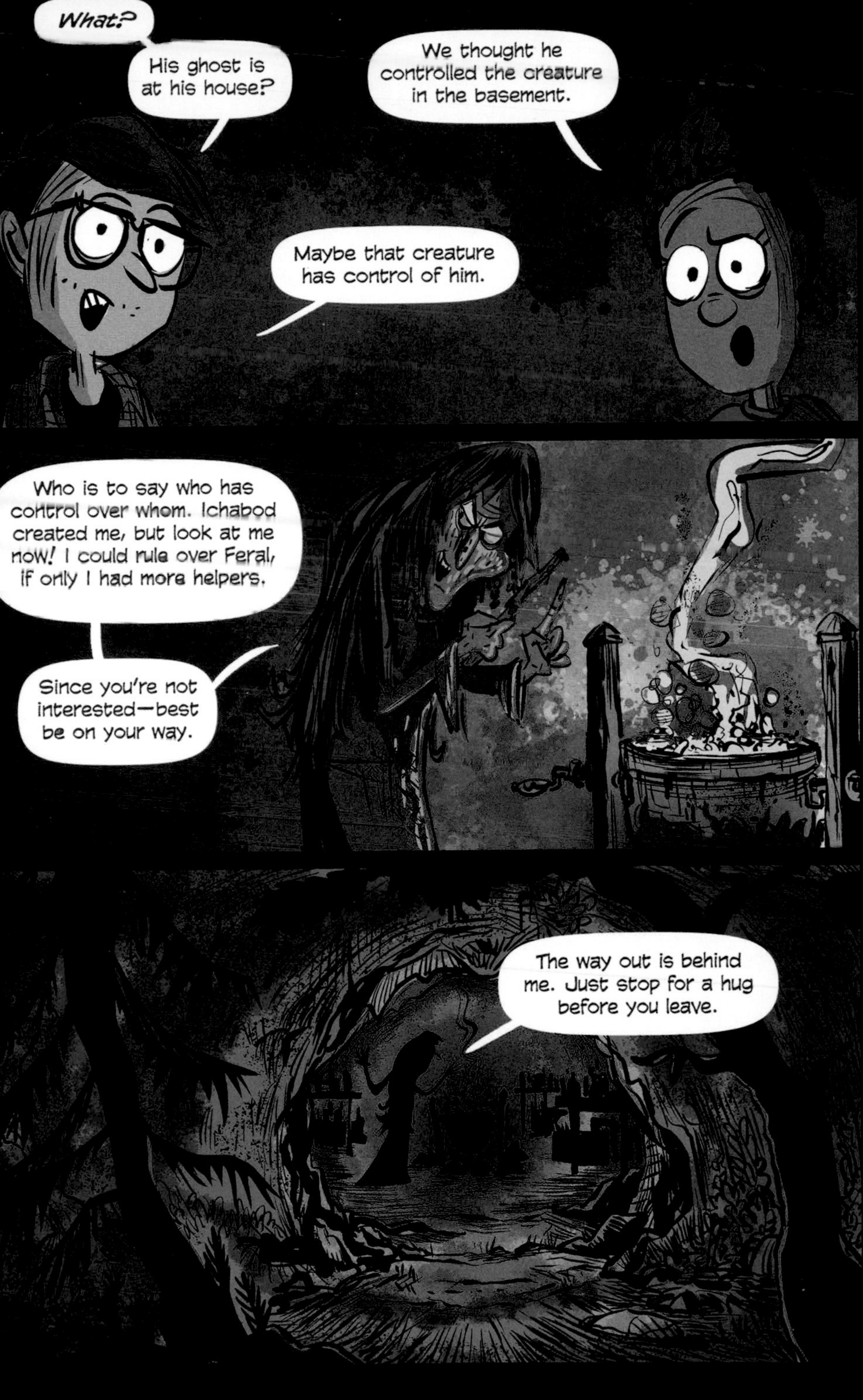
What?
His ghost is at his house?
We thought he controlled the creature in the basement.
Maybe that creature has control of him.
Who is to say who has control over whom. Ichabod created me, but look at me now! I could rule over Feral, if only I had more helpers.
Since you're not interested—best be on your way.
The way out is behind me. Just stop for a hug before you leave.

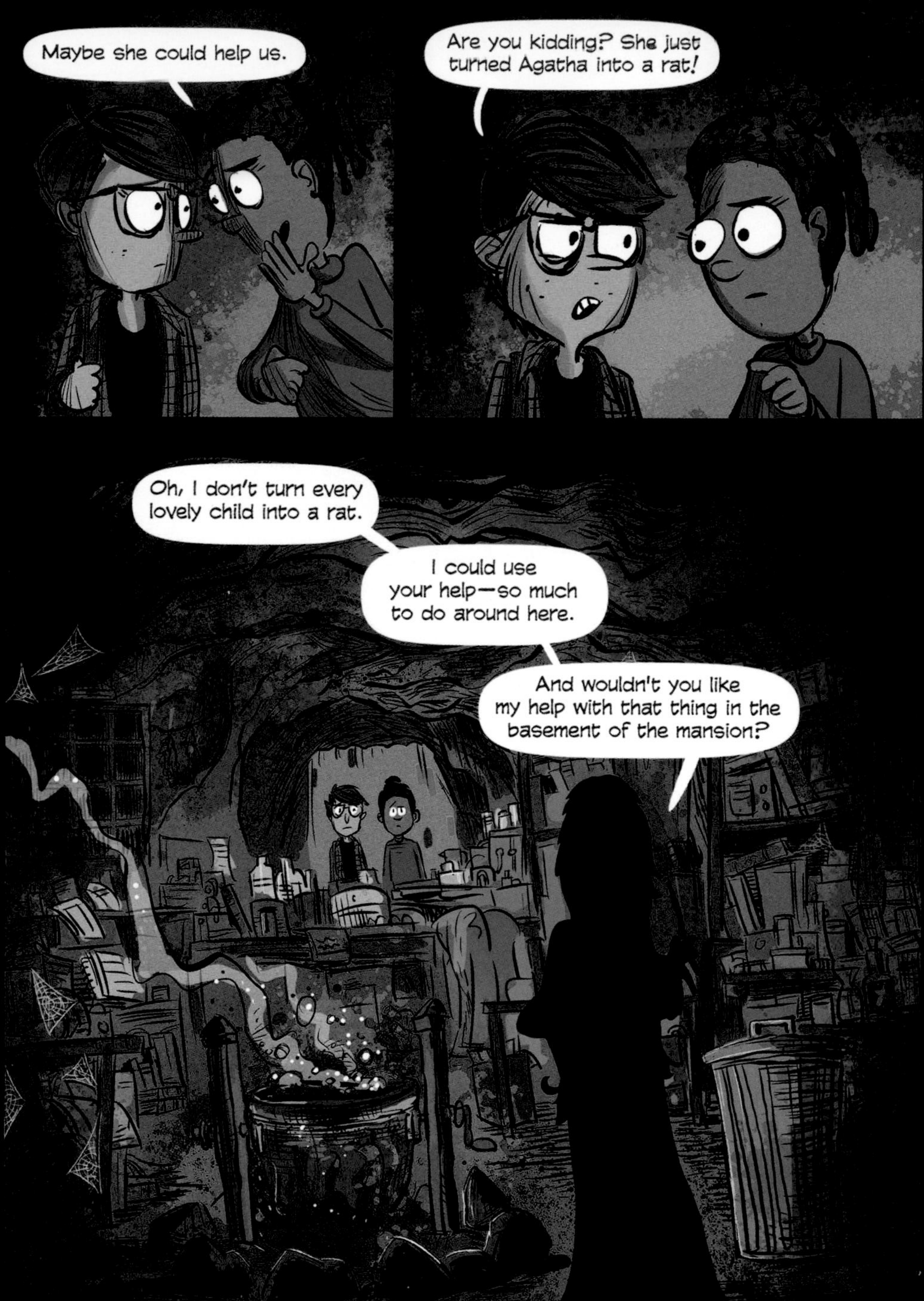
Maybe she could help us.
Are you kidding? She just turned Agatha into a rat!
Oh, I don't turn every lovely child into a rat.
I could use your help—so much to do around here.
And wouldn't you like my help with that thing in the basement of the mansion?

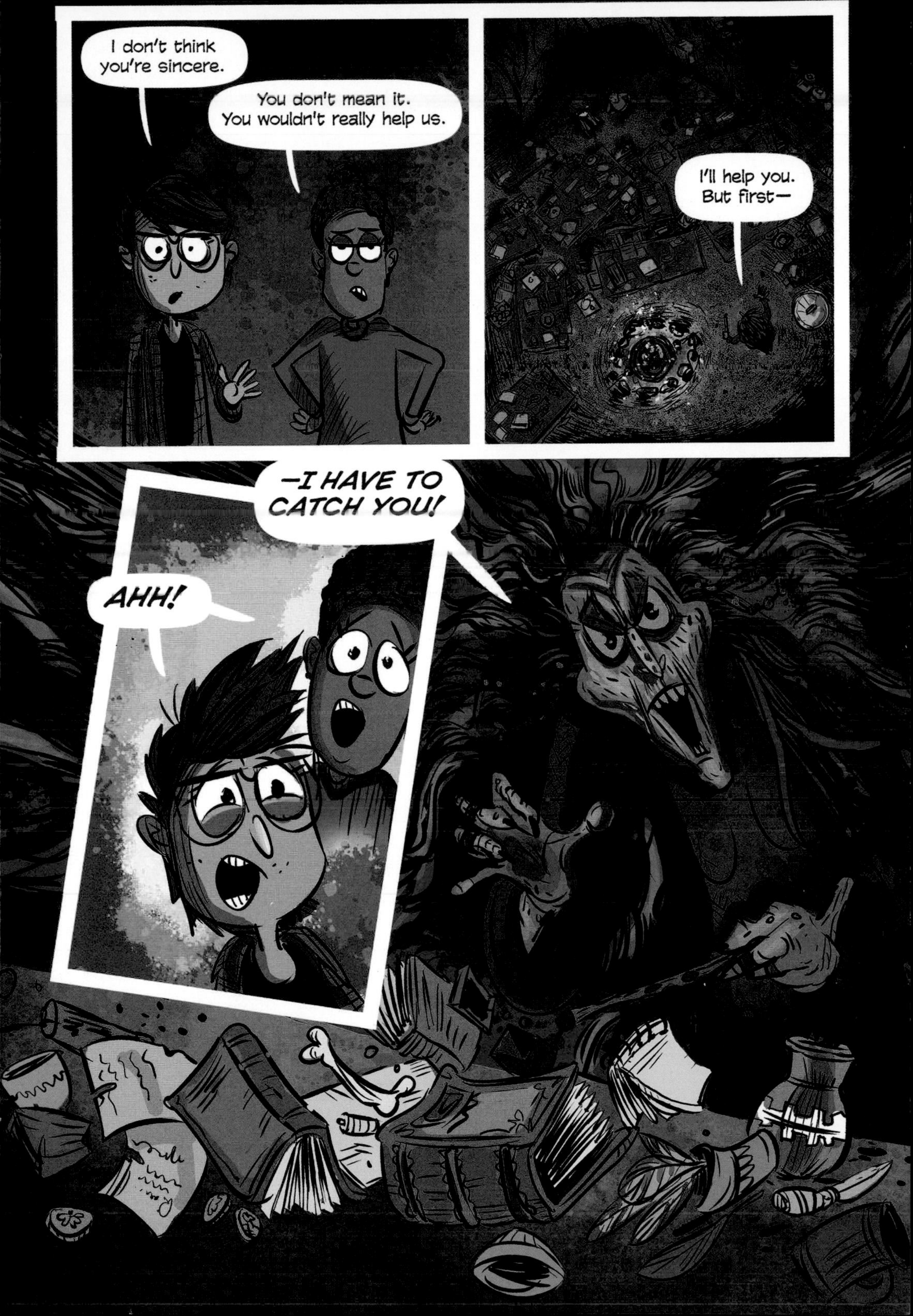
I don't think you're sincere.
You don't mean it. You wouldn't really help us.
I'll help you. But first—
—I HAVE TO CATCH YOU!
AHH!

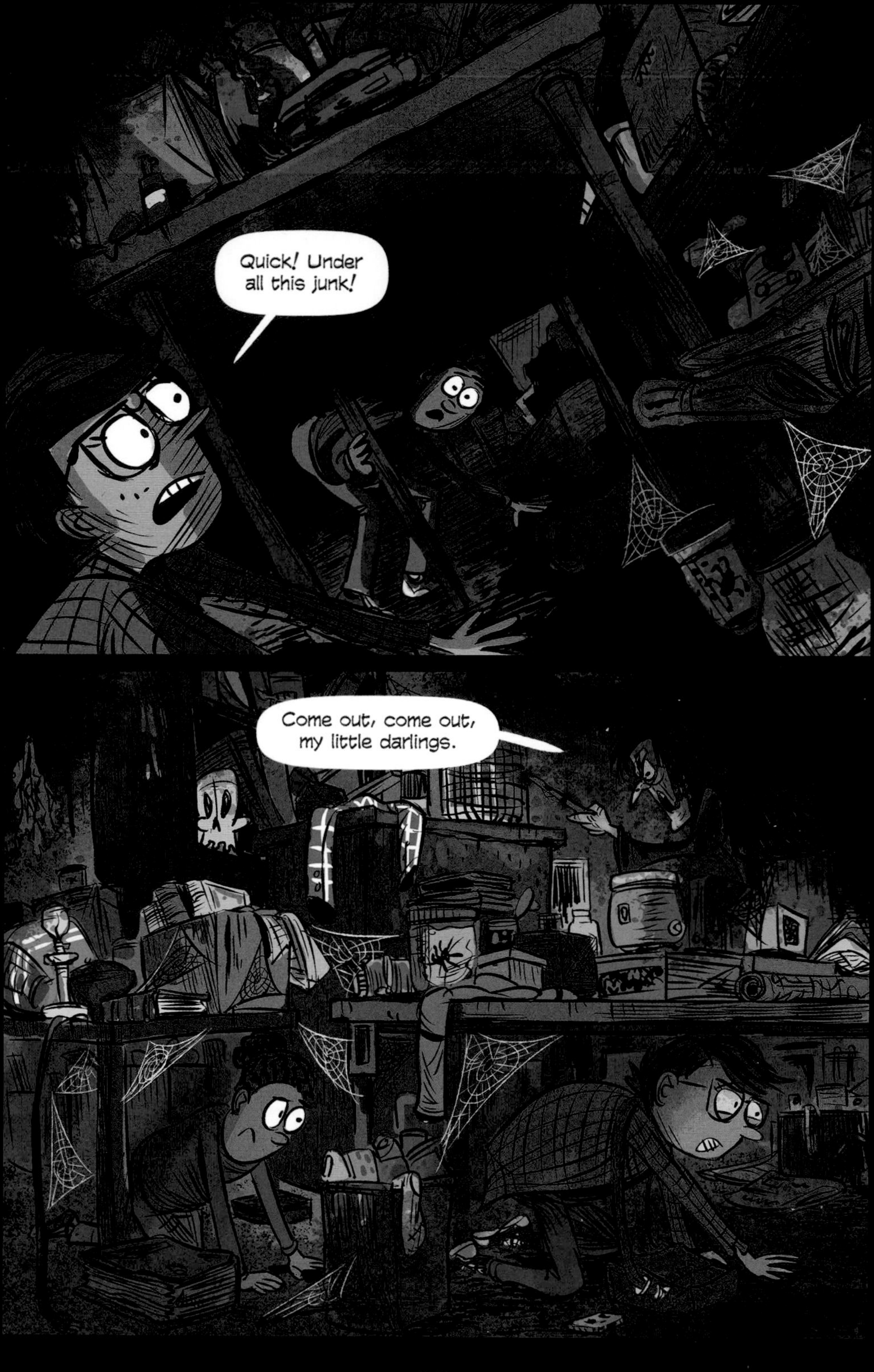
Quick! Under all this junk!
Come out, come out, my little darlings.

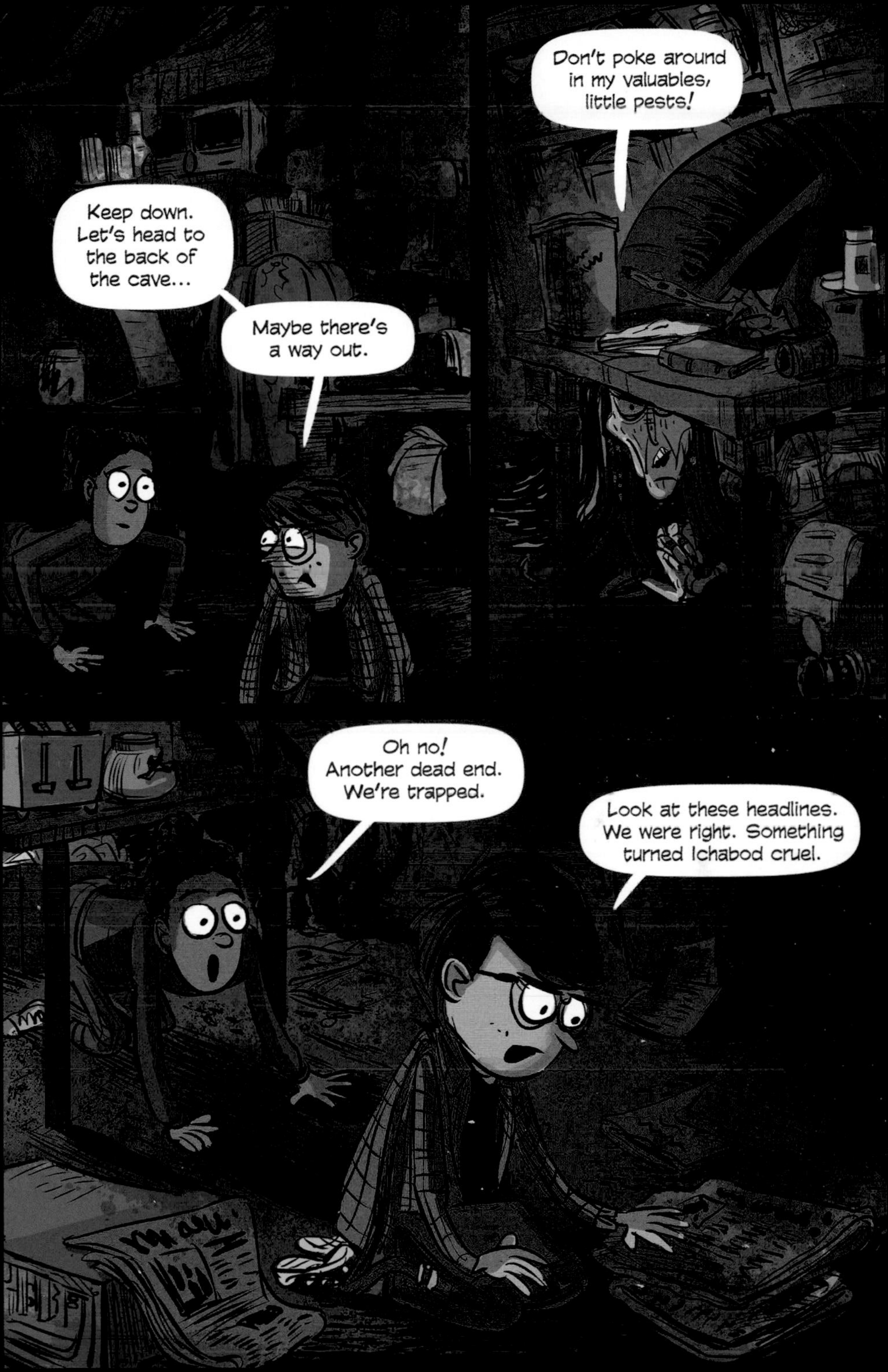
Keep down. Let's head to the back of the cave...
Maybe there's a way out.
Don't poke around in my valuables, little pests!
Oh no! Another dead end. We're trapped.
Look at these headlines. We were right. Something turned Ichabod cruel.

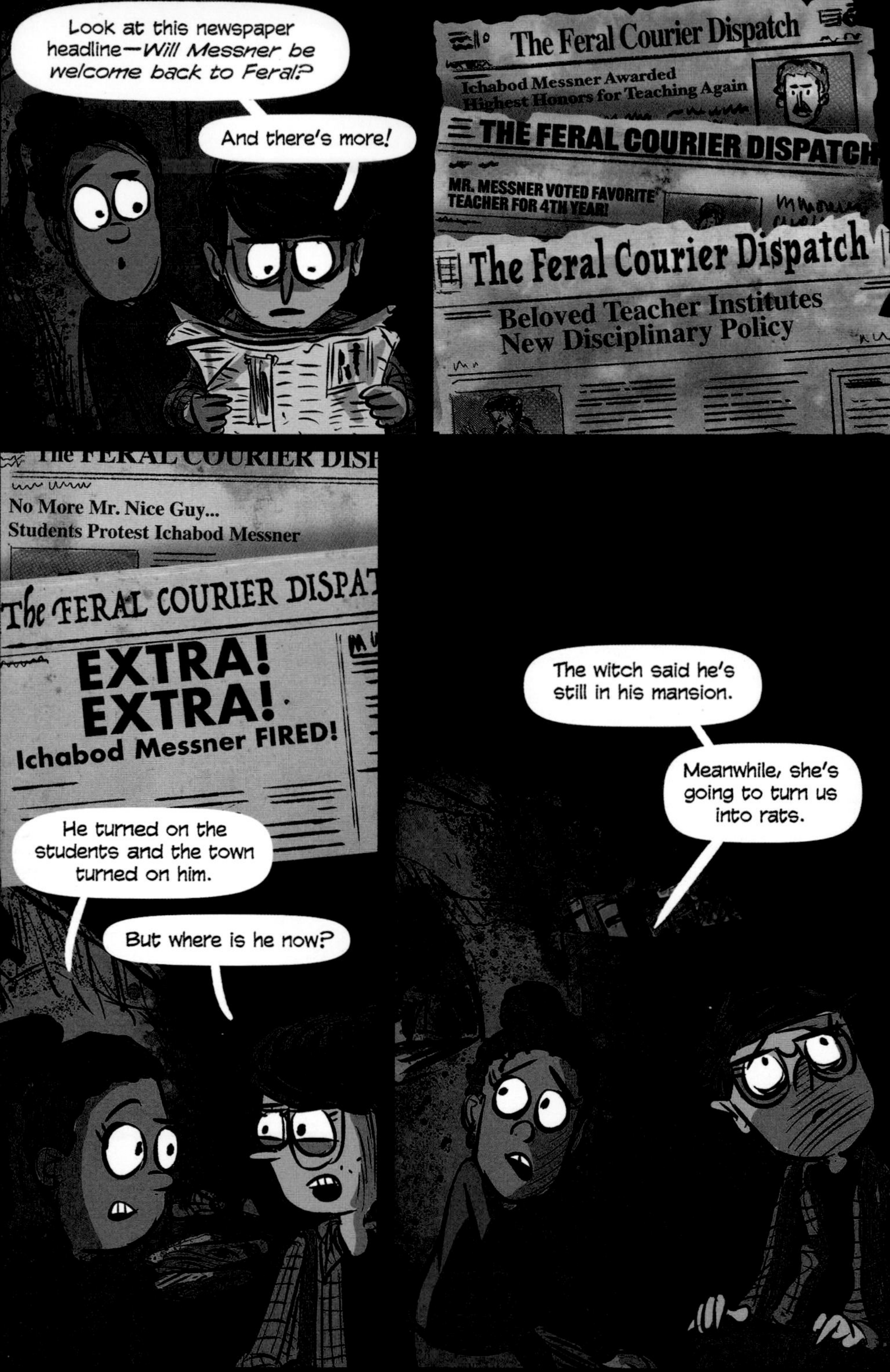
Look at this newspaper headline—*Will Messner be welcome back to Feral?*
And there's more!
The Feral Courier Dispatch
Ichabod Messner Awarded Highest Honors for Teaching Again
THE FERAL COURIER DISPATCH
MR. MESSNER VOTED FAVORITE TEACHER FOR 4TH YEAR!
The Feral Courier Dispatch
Beloved Teacher Institutes New Disciplinary Policy
No More Mr. Nice Guy... Students Protest Ichabod Messner
The FERAL COURIER DISPAT
EXTRA! EXTRA! Ichabod Messner FIRED!
He turned on the students and the town turned on him.
But where is he now?
The witch said he's still in his mansion.
Meanwhile, she's going to turn us into rats.

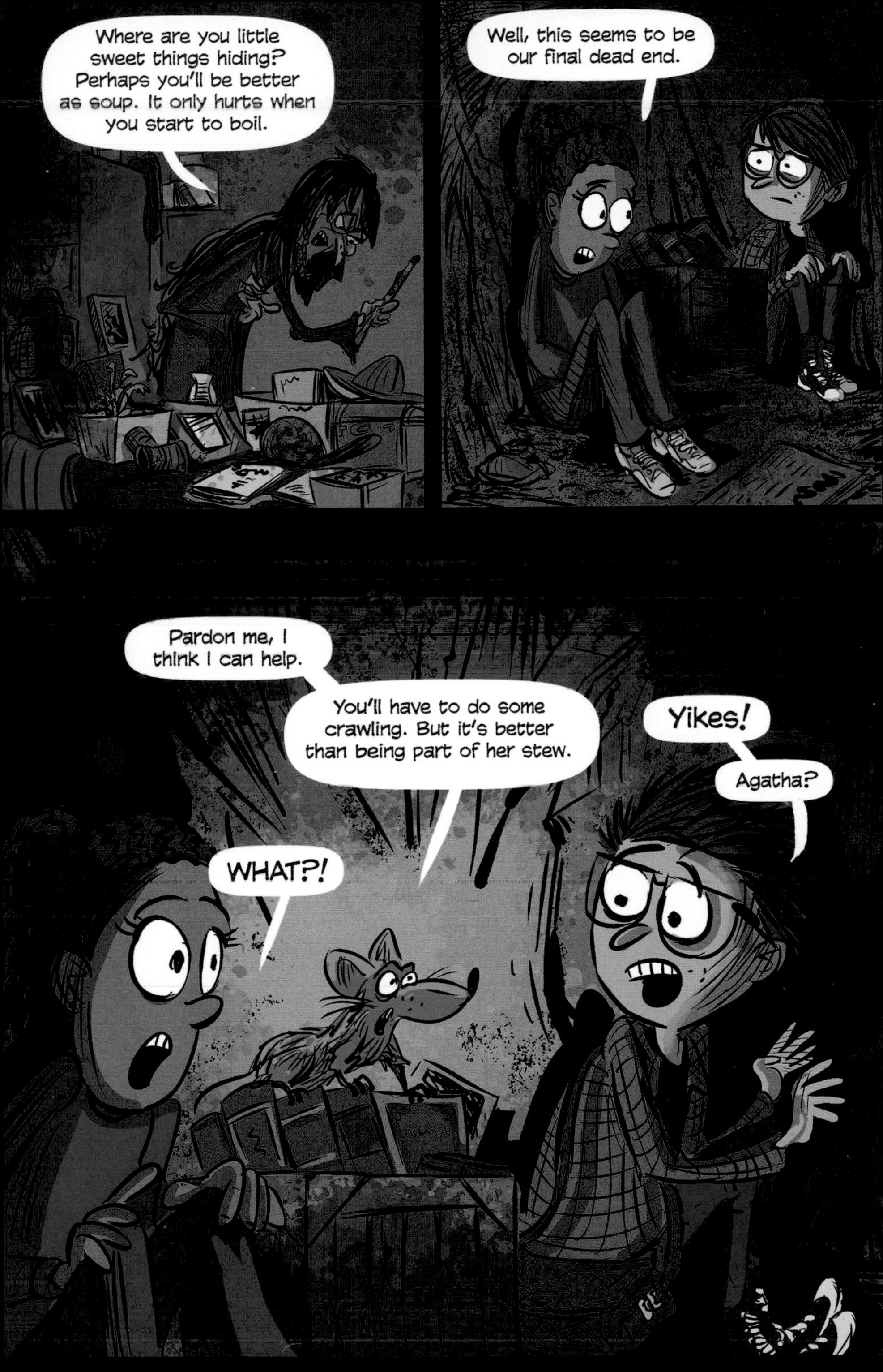
Where are you little sweet things hiding? Perhaps you'll be better as soup. It only hurts when you start to boil.
Well, this seems to be our final dead end.
Pardon me, I think I can help.
You'll have to do some crawling. But it's better than being part of her stew.
Yikes!
Agatha?
WHAT?!

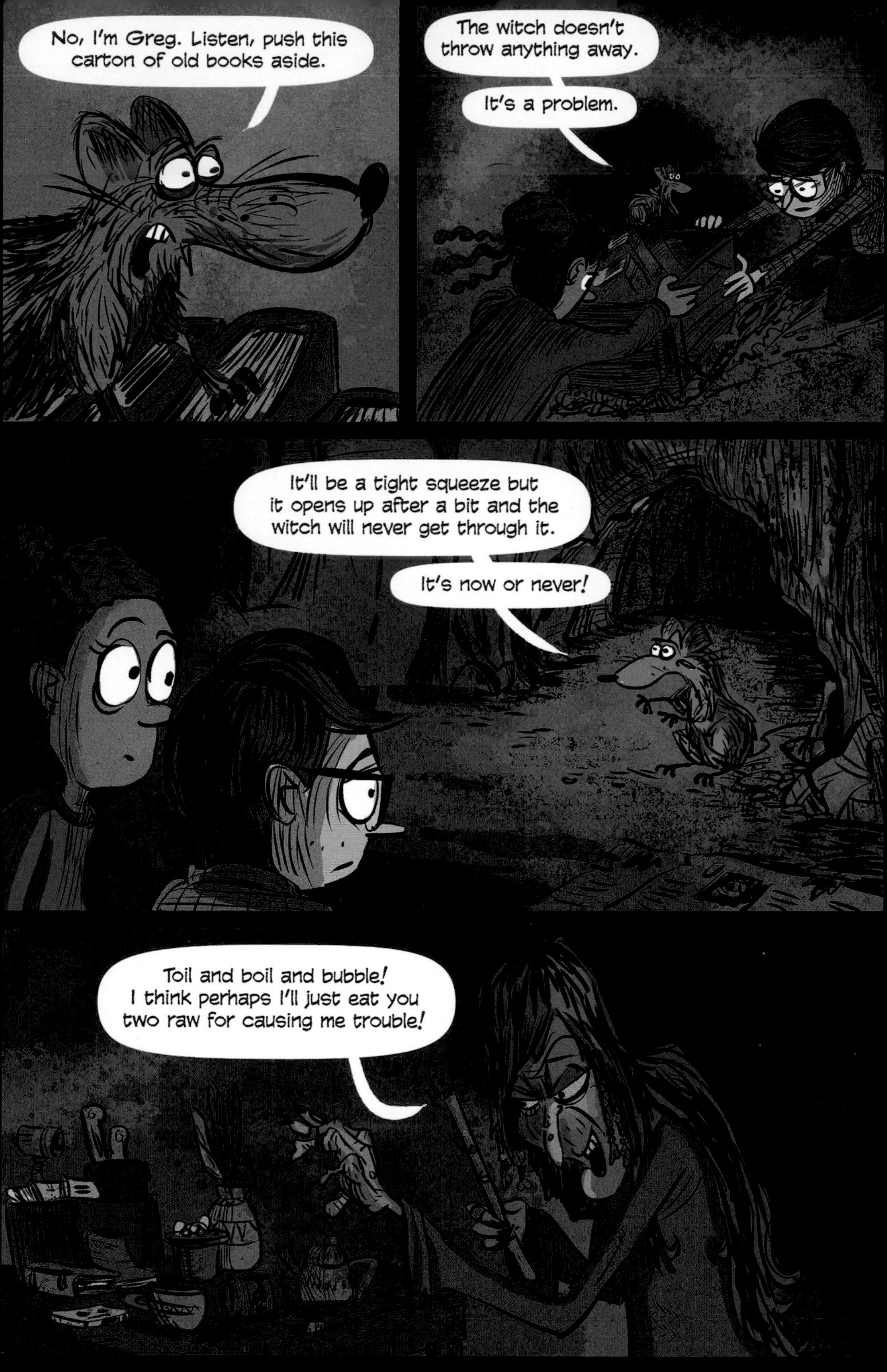
No, I'm Greg. Listen, push this carton of old books aside.
The witch doesn't throw anything away.
It's a problem.
It'll be a tight squeeze but it opens up after a bit and the witch will never get through it.
It's now or never!
Toil and boil and bubble! I think perhaps I'll just eat you two raw for causing me trouble!

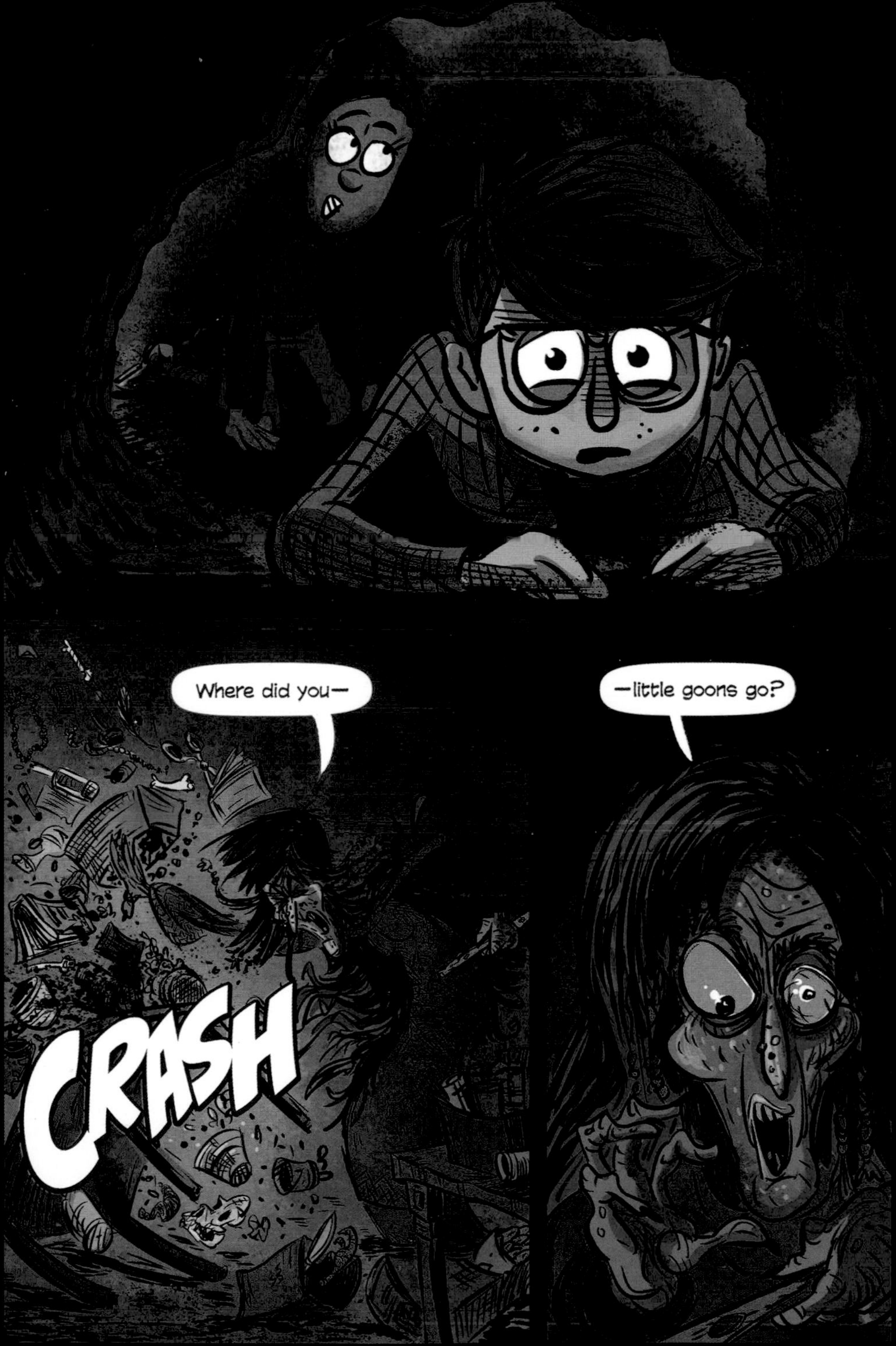
Where did you—
—little goons go?
CRASH

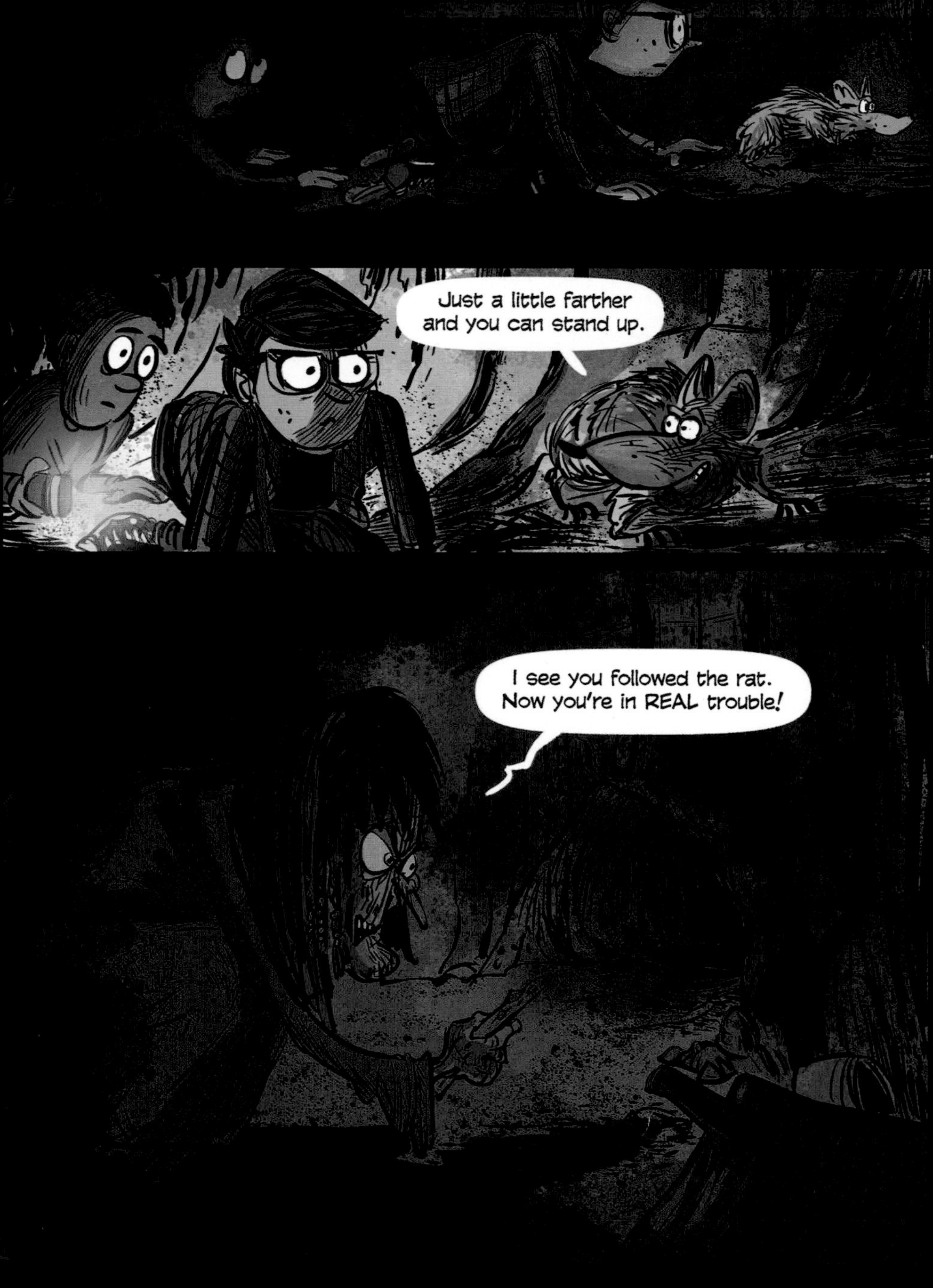
Just a little farther and you can stand up.
I see you followed the rat. Now you're in REAL trouble!

CHAPTER 7

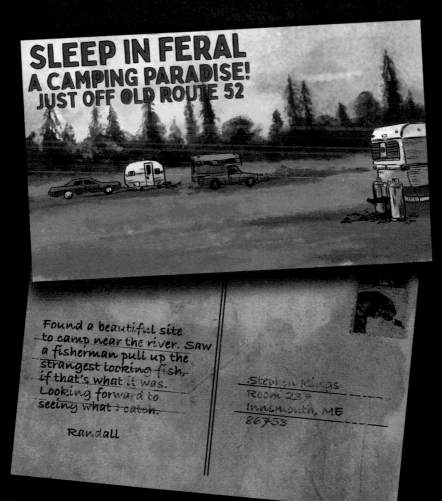

SLEEP IN FERAL
A CAMPING PARADISE!
JUST OFF OLD ROUTE 52

Found a beautiful site
to camp near the river. Saw
a fisherman pull up the
strangest looking fish,
if that's what it was.
Looking forward to
seeing what I catch.

Randall

Stephen Kings
Room 23
Innsmouth, ME
86753

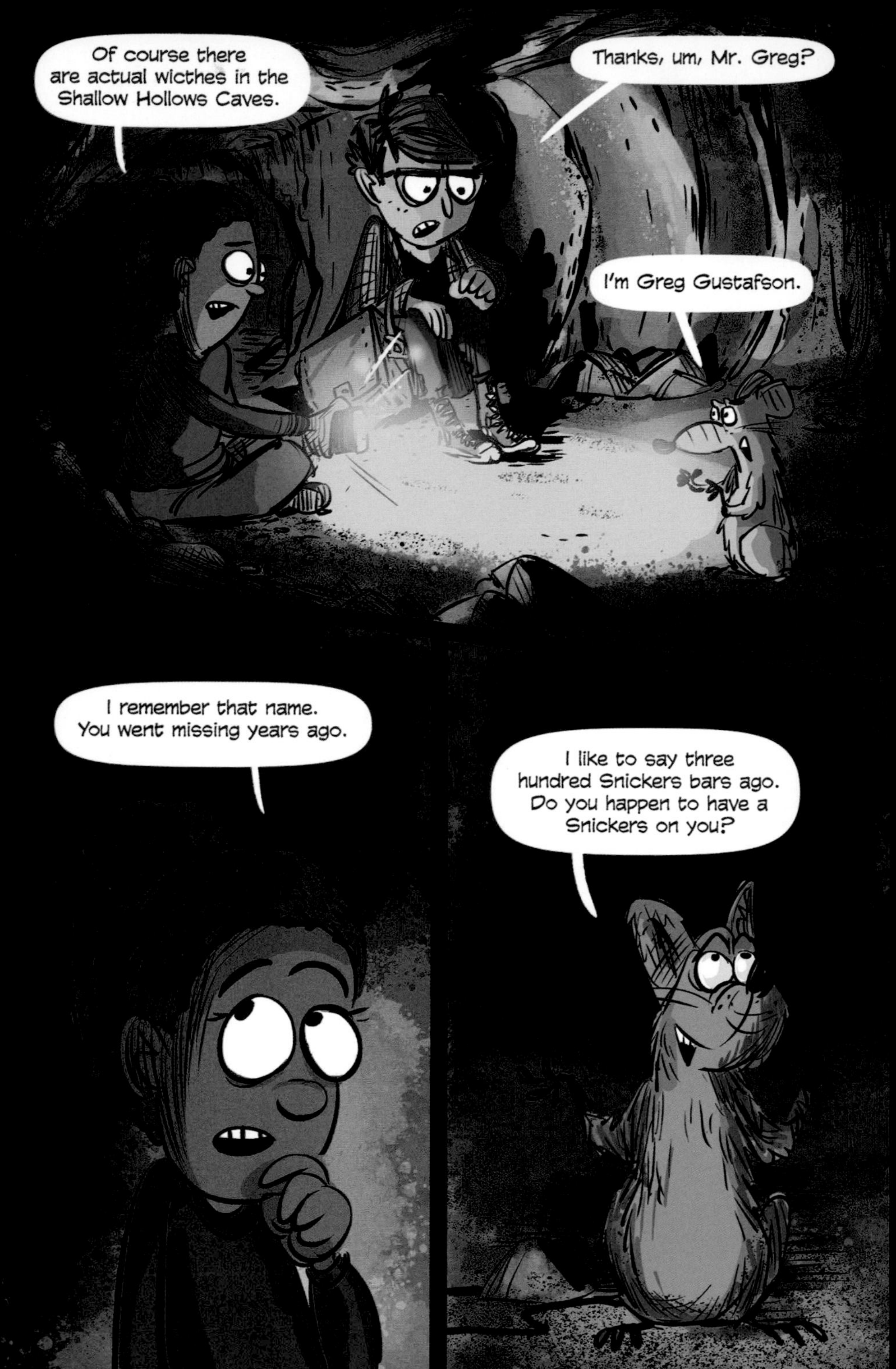
Of course there are actual wicthes in the Shallow Hollows Caves.
Thanks, um, Mr. Greg?
I'm Greg Gustafson.
I remember that name. You went missing years ago.
I like to say three hundred Snickers bars ago. Do you happen to have a Snickers on you?

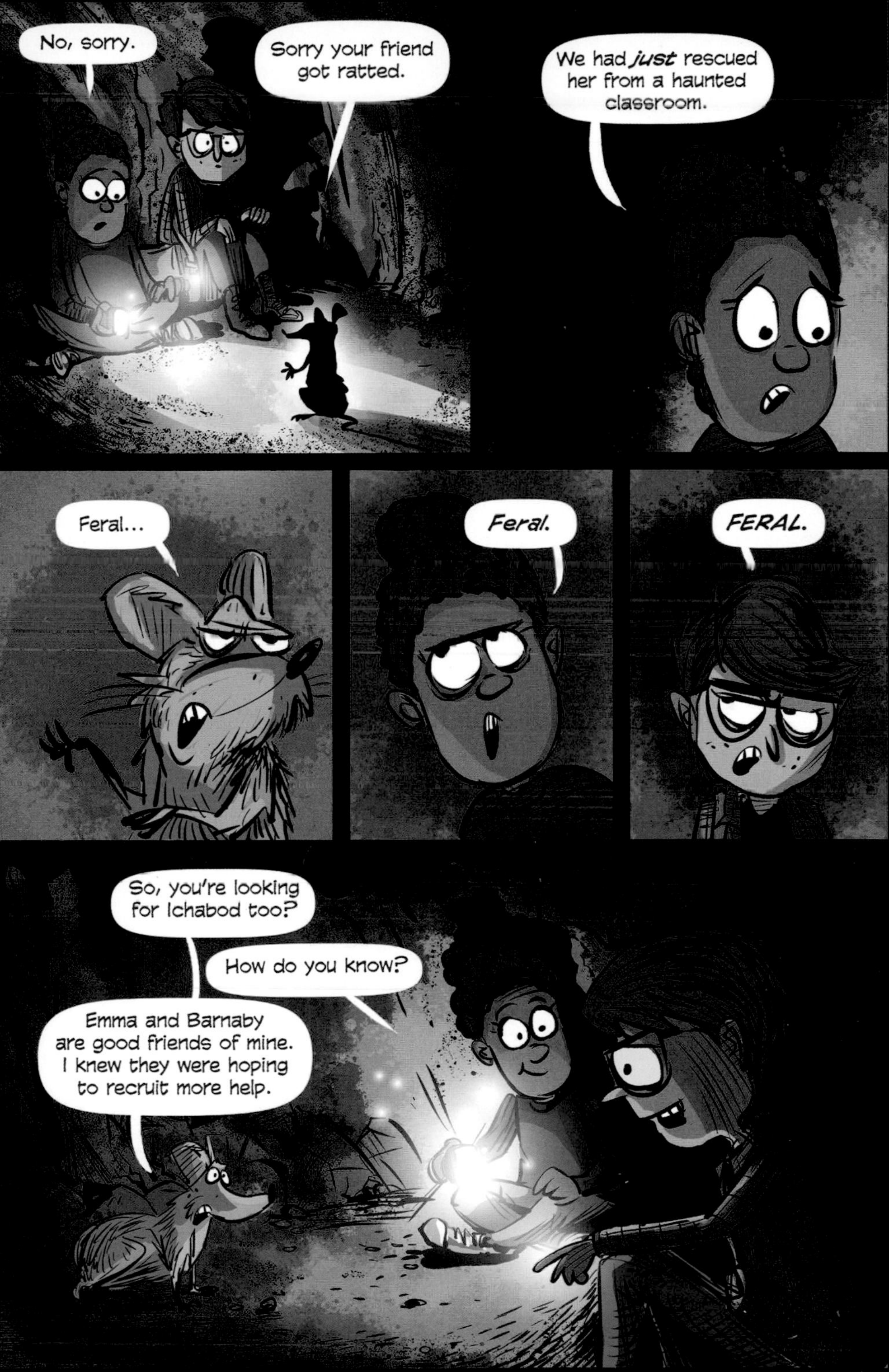
No, sorry.
Sorry your friend got ratted.
We had *just* rescued her from a haunted classroom.
Feral...
Feral.
FERAL.
So, you're looking for Ichabod too?
How do you know?
Emma and Barnaby are good friends of mine. I knew they were hoping to recruit more help.

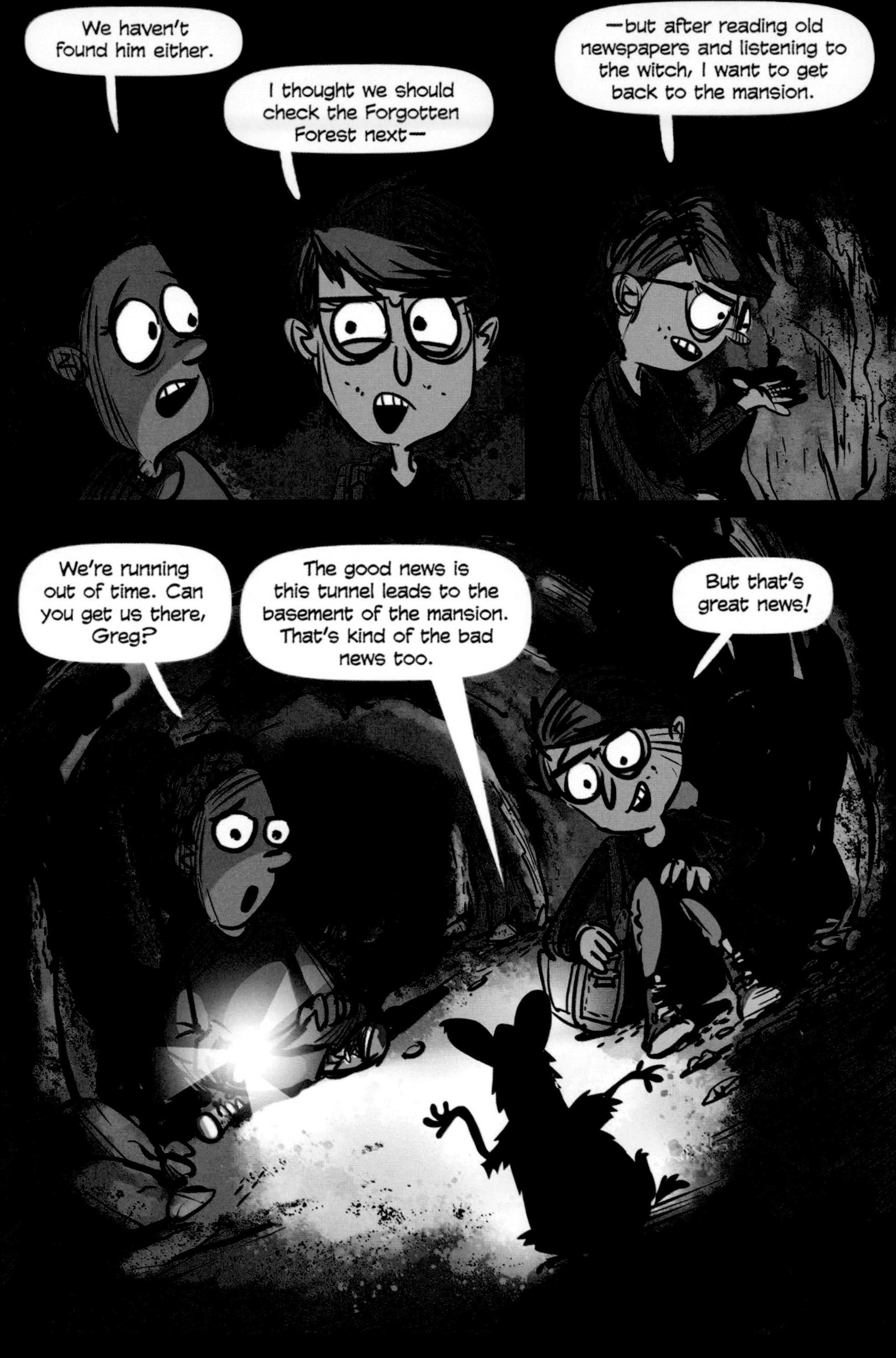
We haven't found him either.
I thought we should check the Forgotten Forest next—
—but after reading old newspapers and listening to the witch, I want to get back to the mansion.
We're running out of time. Can you get us there, Greg?
The good news is this tunnel leads to the basement of the mansion. That's kind of the bad news too.
But that's great news!

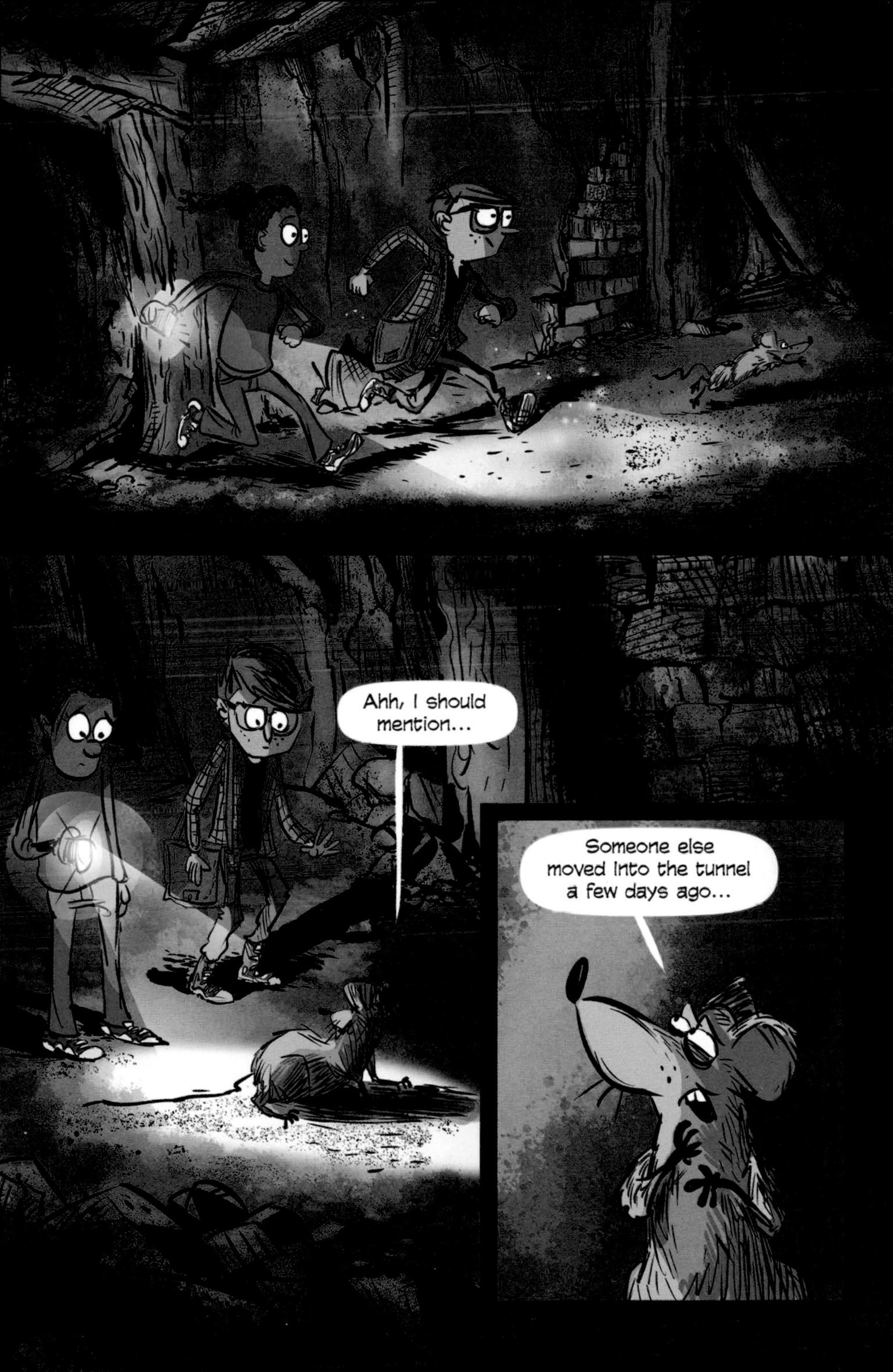
Ahh, I should mention...
Someone else moved into the tunnel a few days ago...

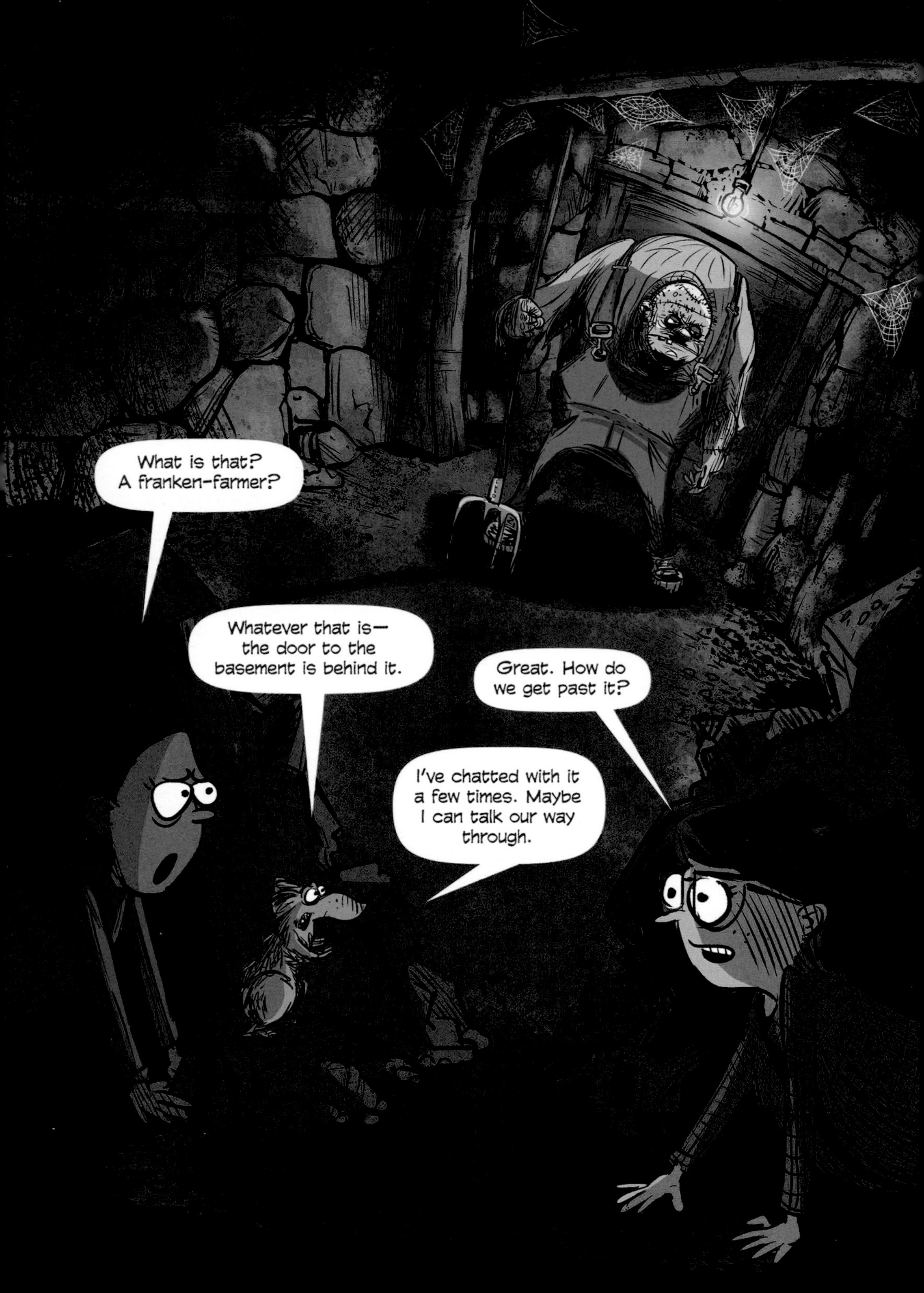
What is that? A franken-farmer?
Whatever that is— the door to the basement is behind it.
Great. How do we get past it?
I've chatted with it a few times. Maybe I can talk our way through.

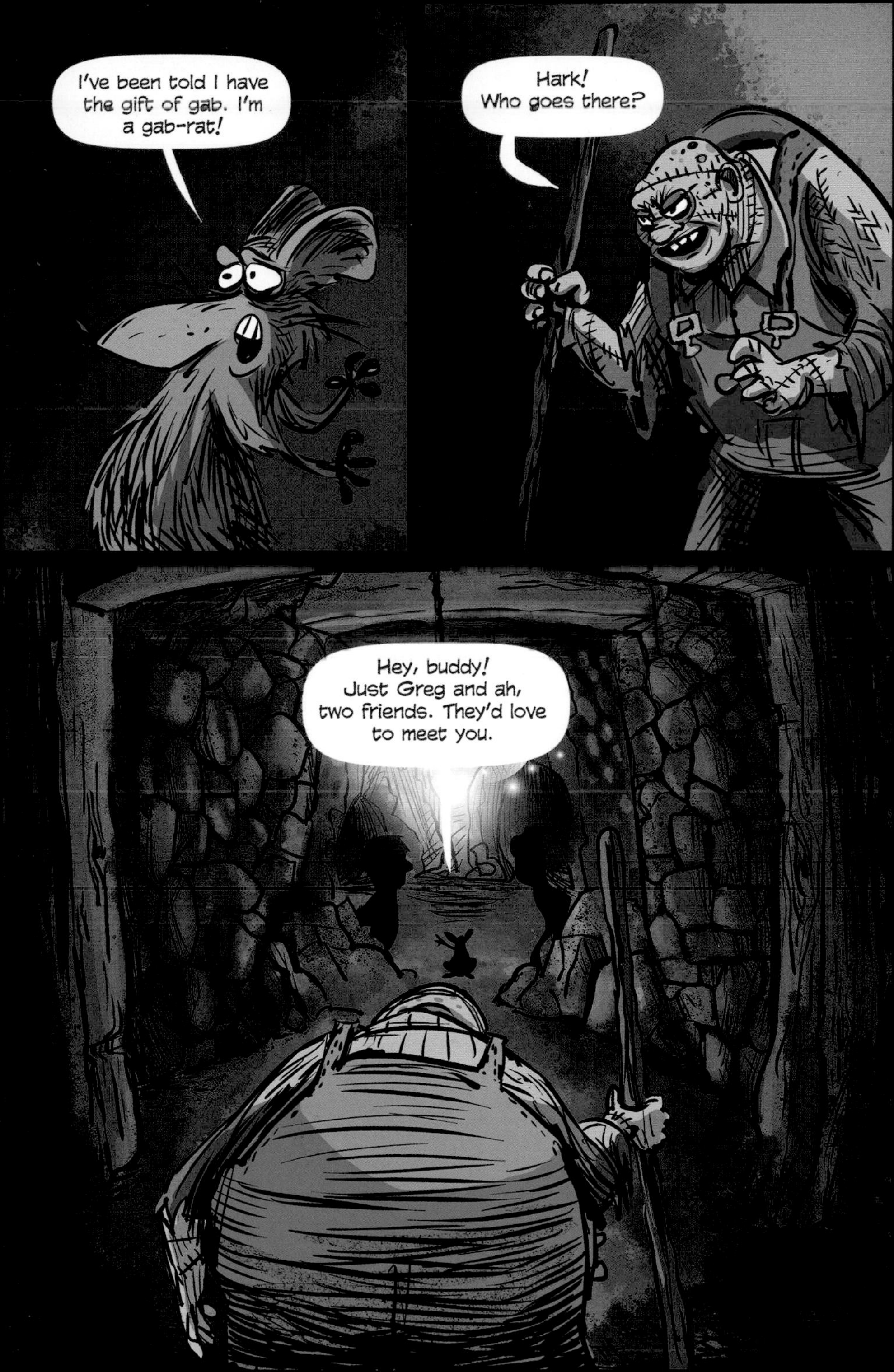
I've been told I have the gift of gab. I'm a gab-rat!
Hark! Who goes there?
Hey, buddy! Just Greg and ah, two friends. They'd love to meet you.

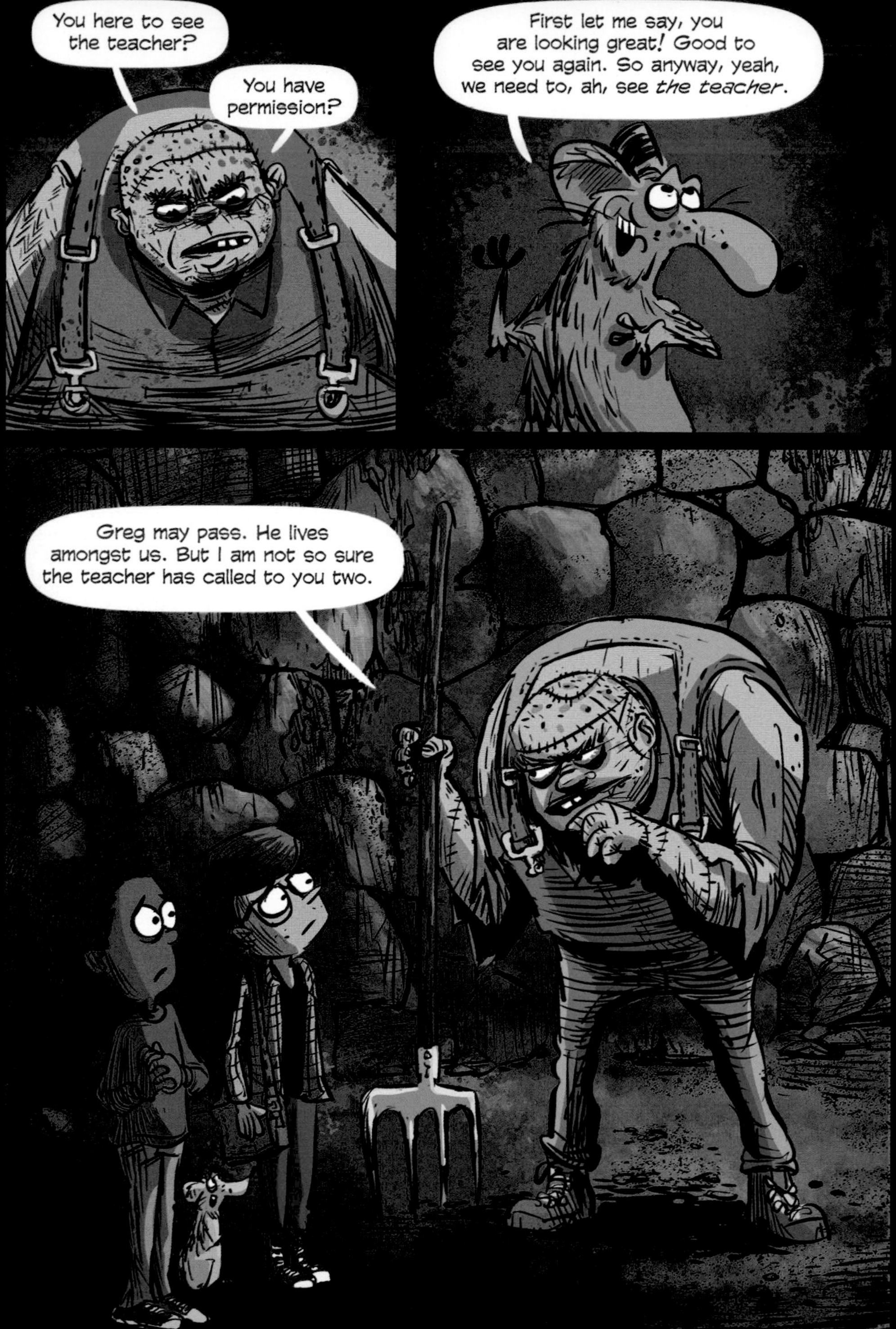
You here to see the teacher?
You have permission?
First let me say, you are looking great! Good to see you again. So anyway, yeah, we need to, ah, see *the teacher*.
Greg may pass. He lives amongst us. But I am not so sure the teacher has called to you two.

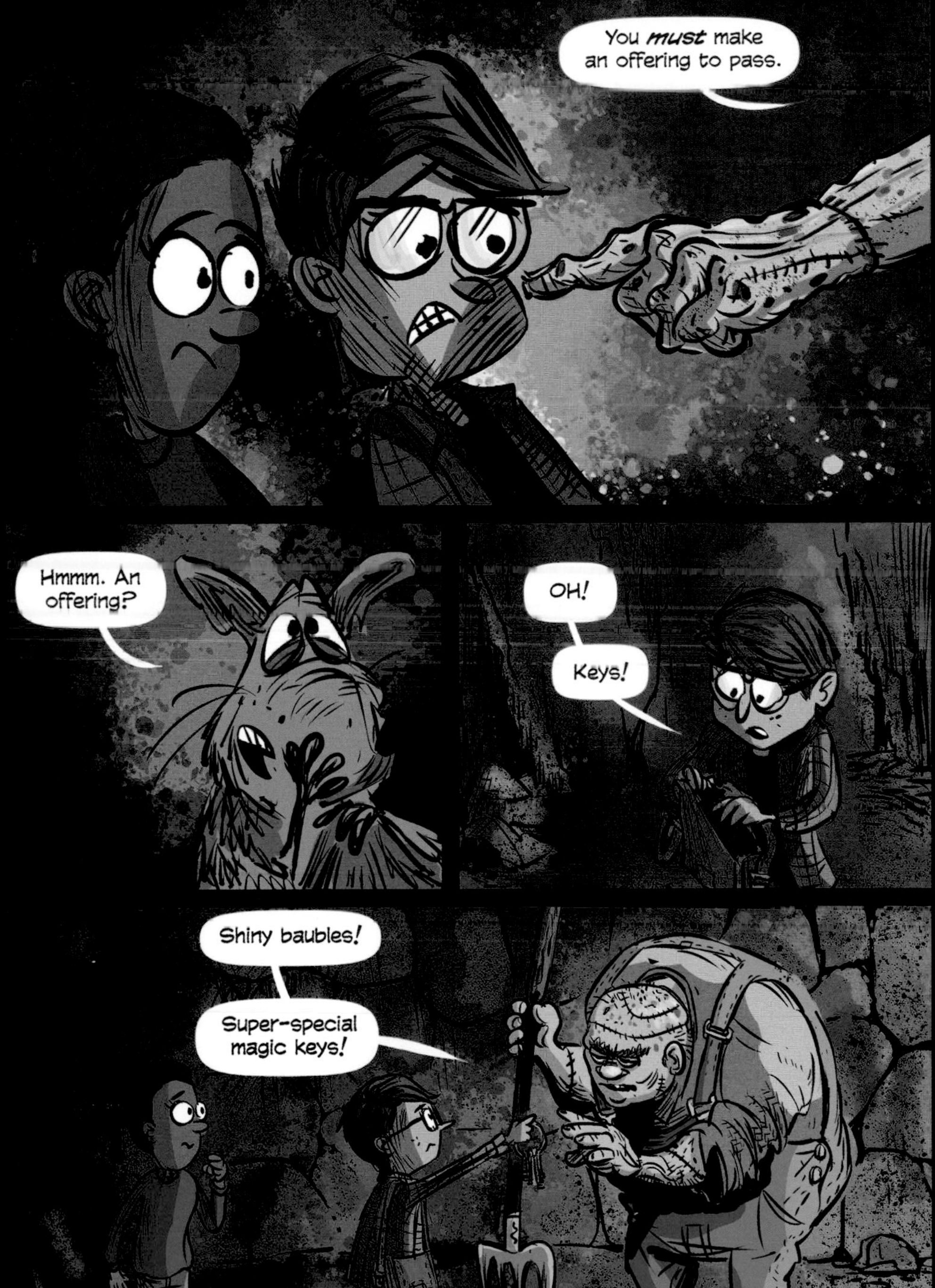
You *must* make an offering to pass.
Hmmm. An offering?
OH!
Keys!
Shiny baubles!
Super-special magic keys!

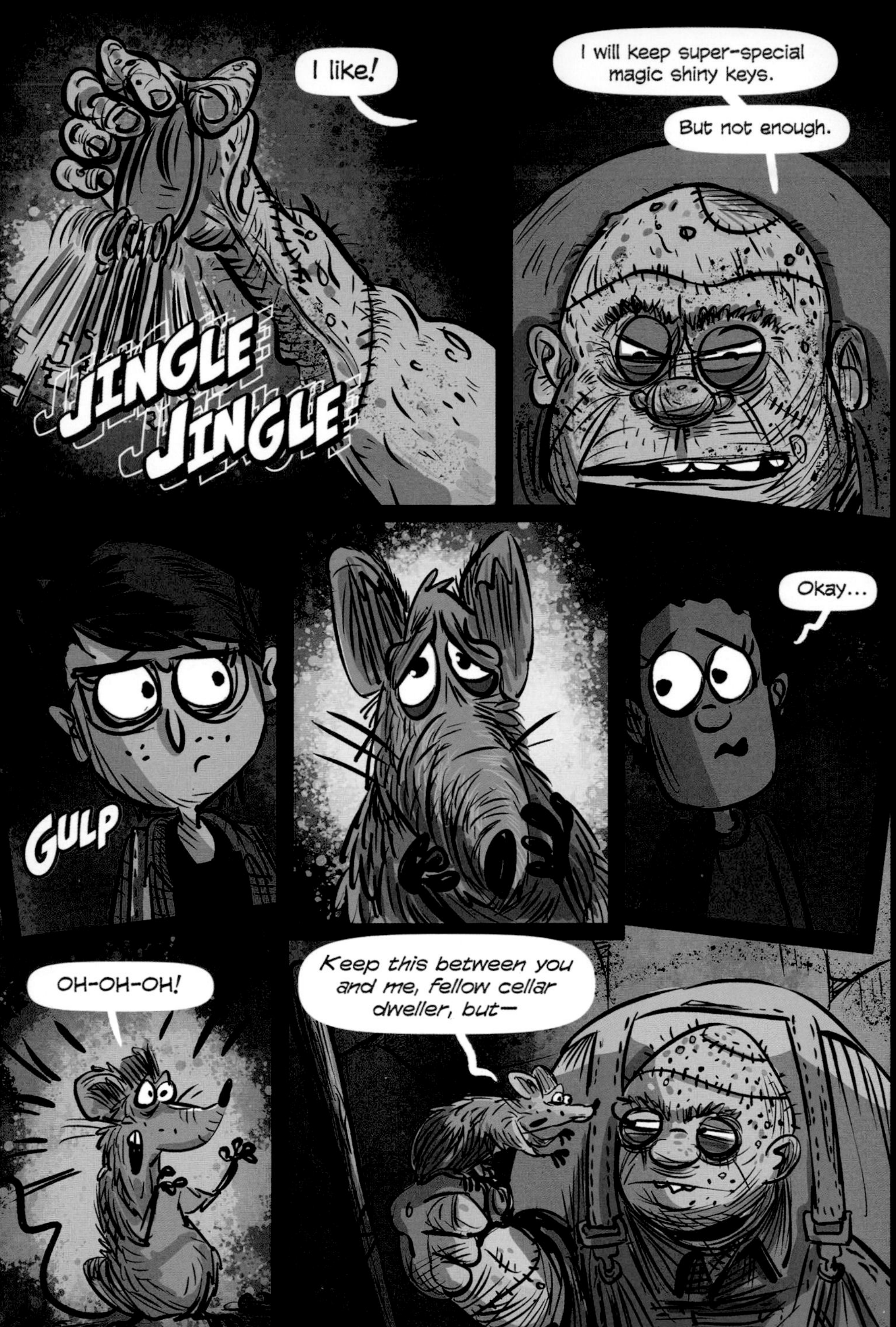
I like!
JINGLE
JINGLE
I will keep super-special magic shiny keys.
But not enough.
GULP
Okay...
OH-OH-OH!
Keep this between you and me, fellow cellar dweller, but—

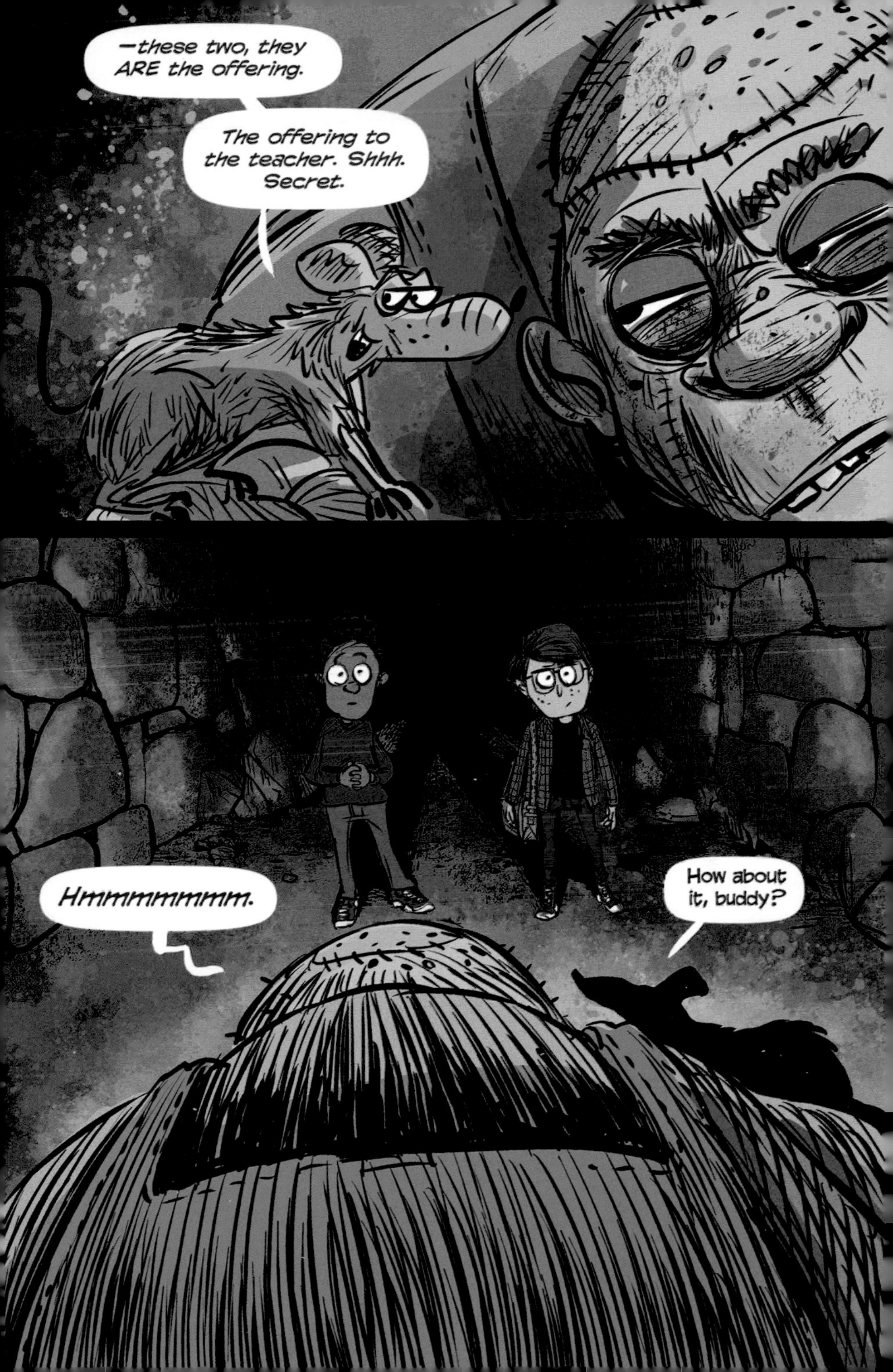
—these two, they ARE the offering.
The offering to the teacher. Shhh. Secret.
Hmmmmmmmm.
How about it, buddy?

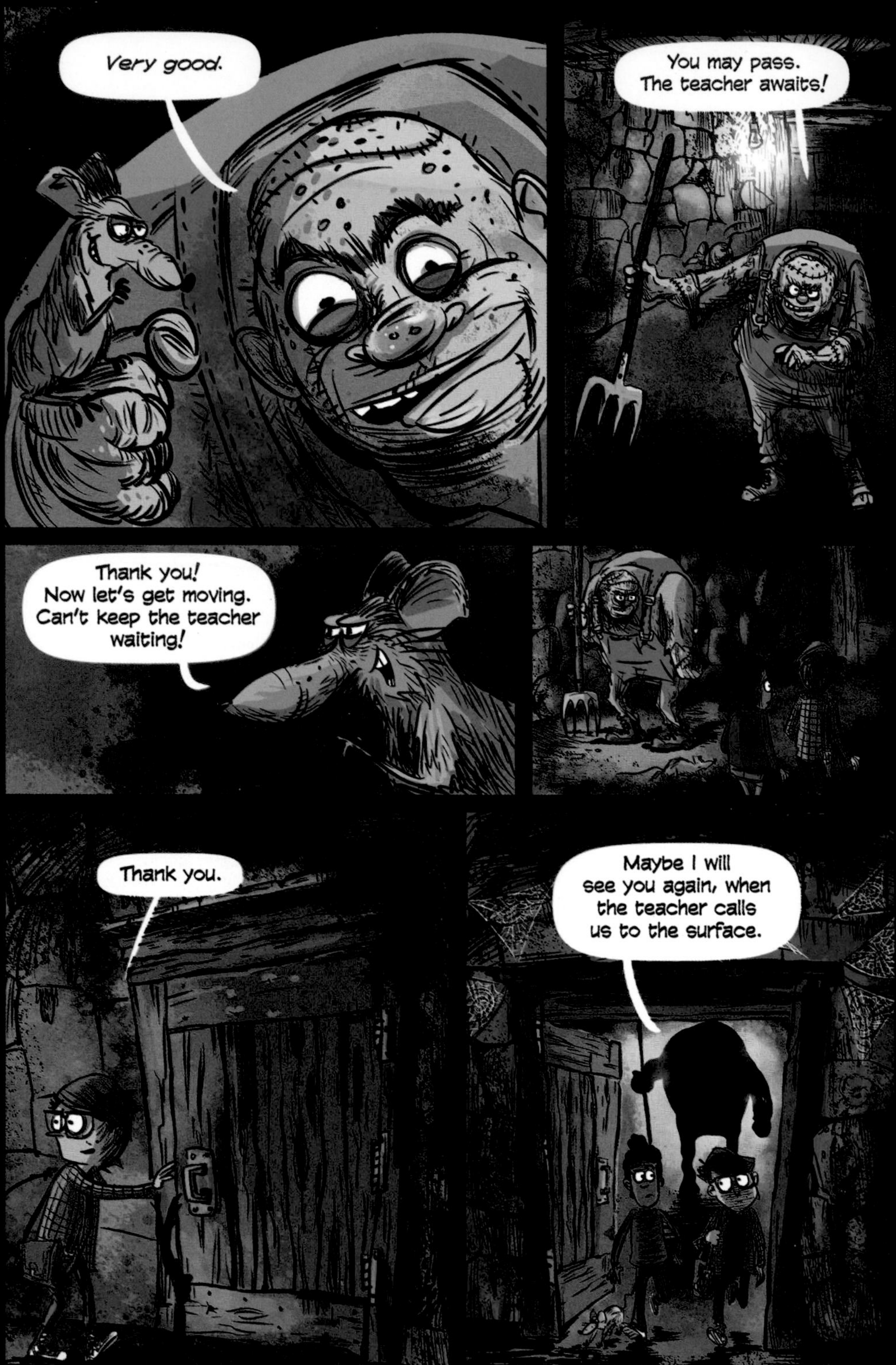
Very good.
You may pass. The teacher awaits!
Thank you! Now let's get moving. Can't keep the teacher waiting!
Thank you.
Maybe I will see you again, when the teacher calls us to the surface.

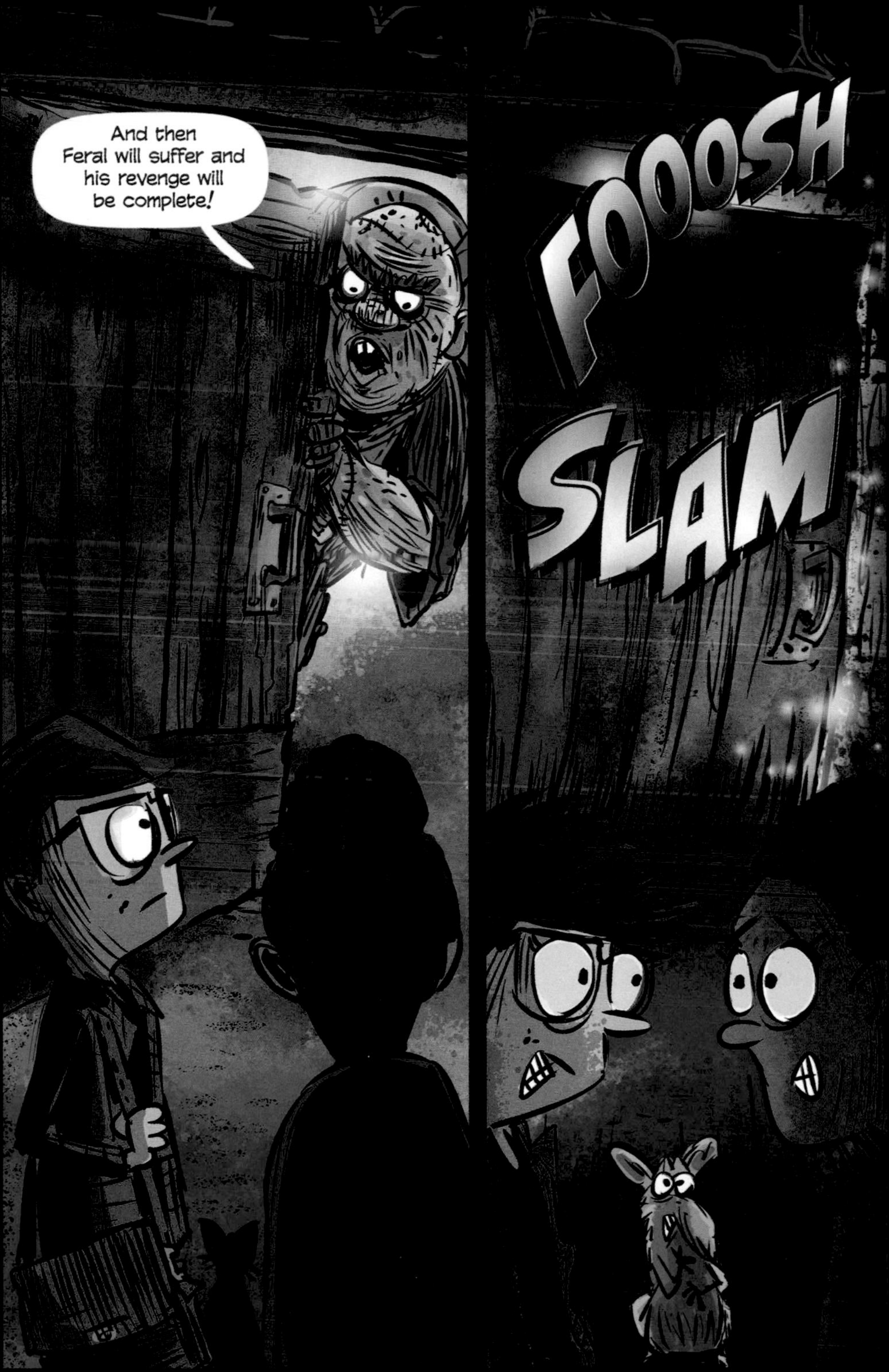
And then Feral will suffer and his revenge will be complete!
FOOOSH
SLAM

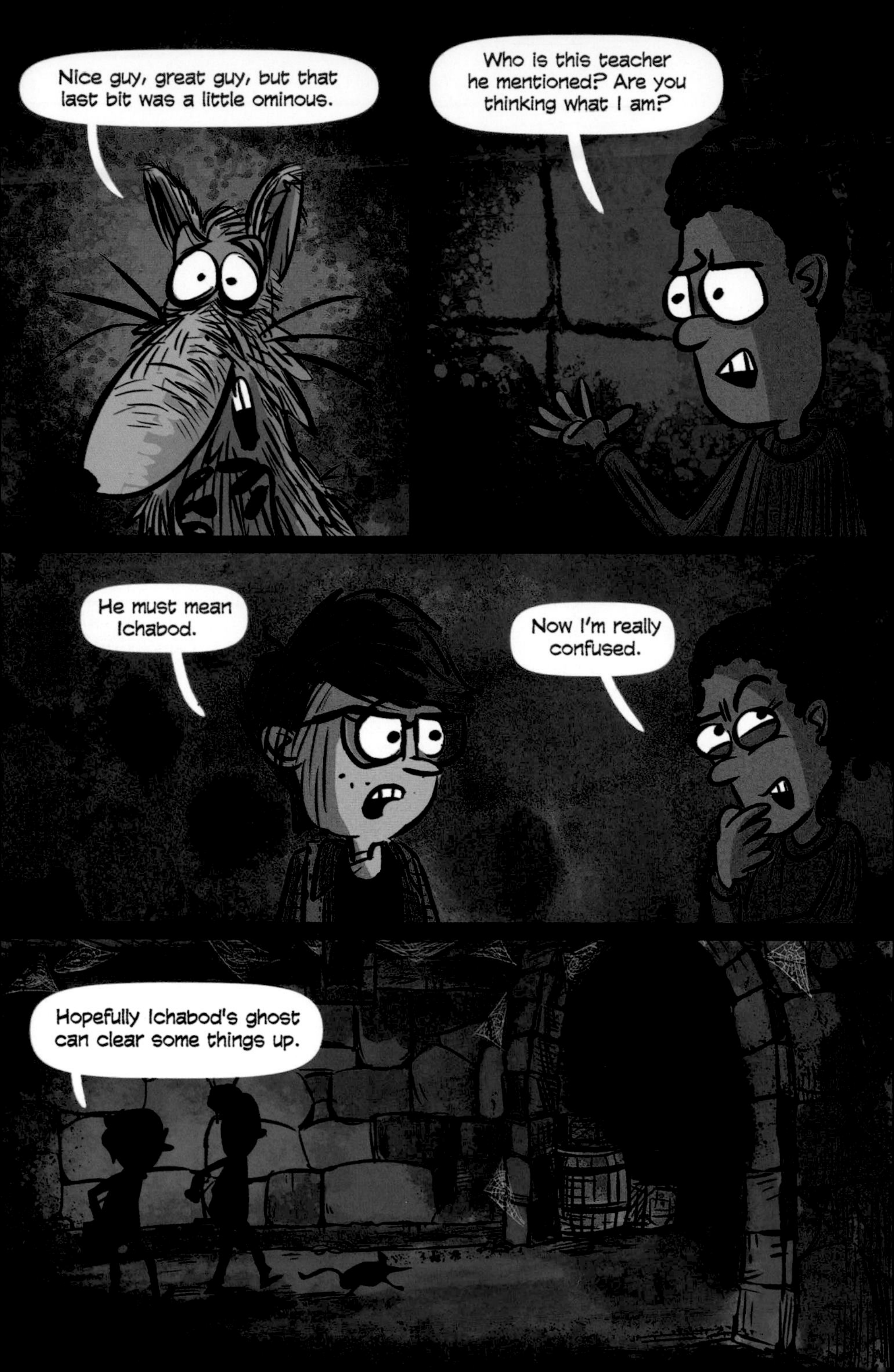
Nice guy, great guy, but that last bit was a little ominous.
Who is this teacher he mentioned? Are you thinking what I am?
He must mean Ichabod.
Now I'm really confused.
Hopefully Ichabod's ghost can clear some things up.

CHAPTER 8

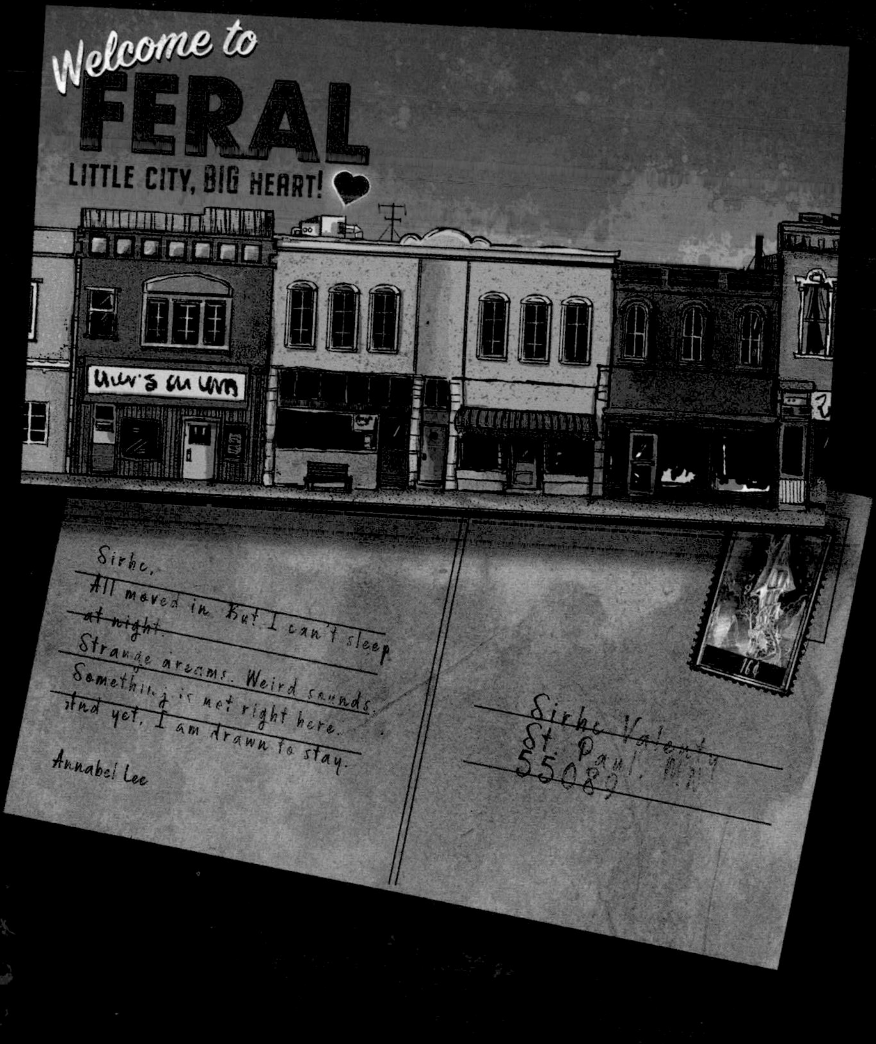
Welcome to
FERAL
LITTLE CITY, BIG HEART!
Sirhc,
All moved in. But I can't sleep at night.
Strange dreams. Weird sounds.
Something is not right here.
And yet, I am drawn to stay.
Annabel Lee

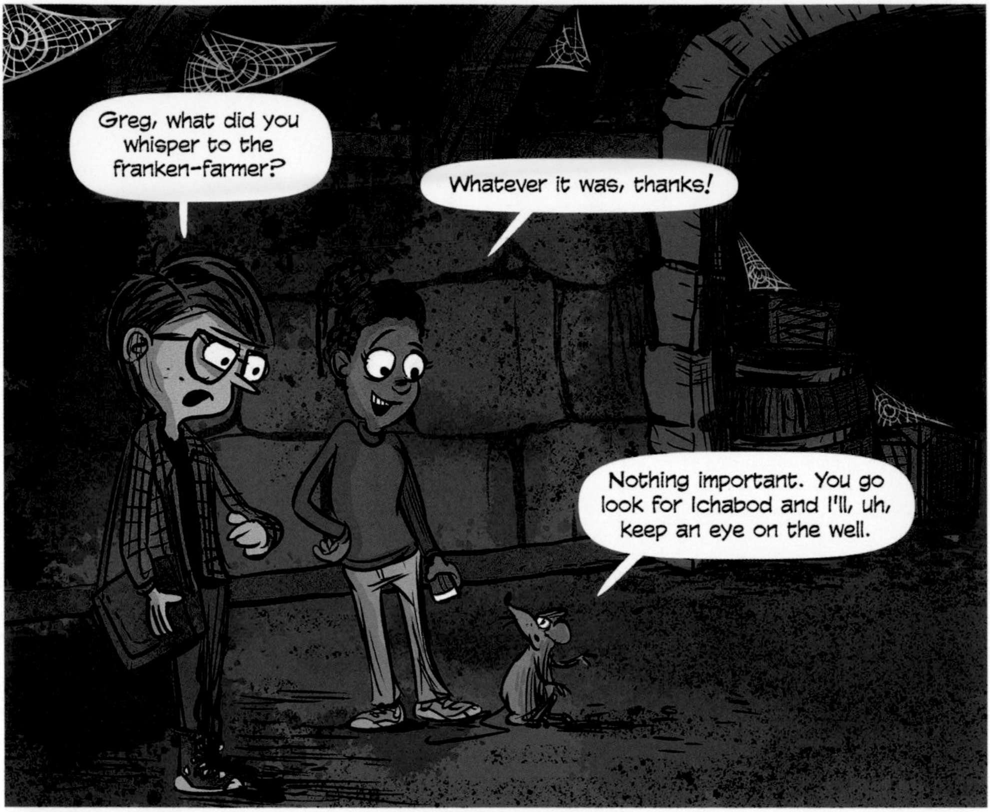
Greg, what did you whisper to the franken-farmer?
Whatever it was, thanks!
Nothing important. You go look for Ichabod and I'll, uh, keep an eye on the well.

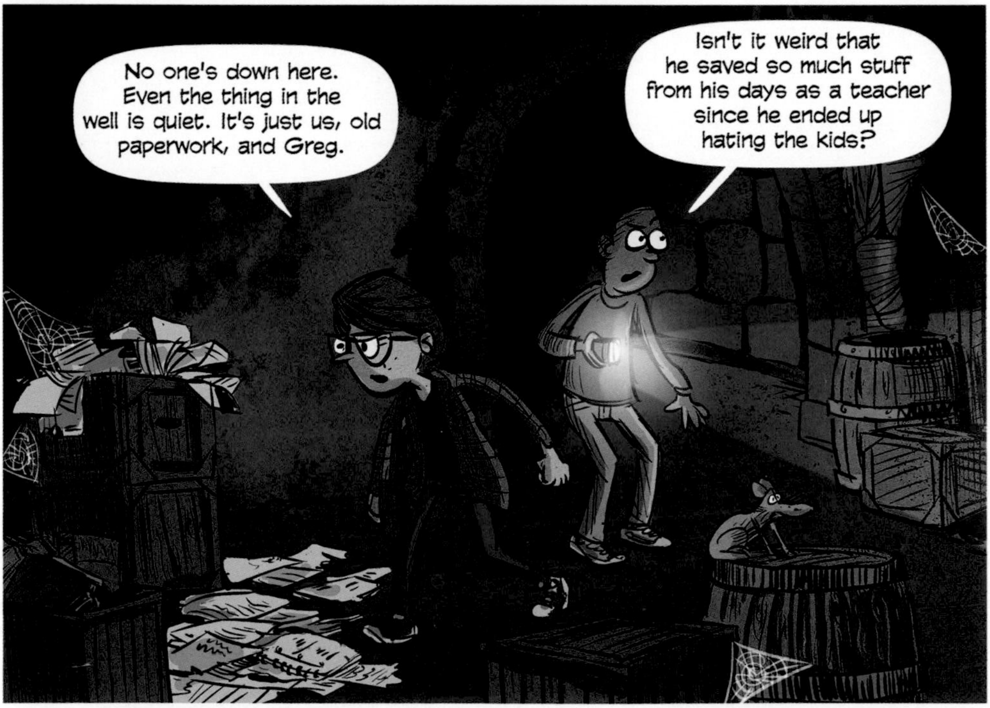
No one's down here. Even the thing in the well is quiet. It's just us, old paperwork, and Greg.
Isn't it weird that he saved so much stuff from his days as a teacher since he ended up hating the kids?

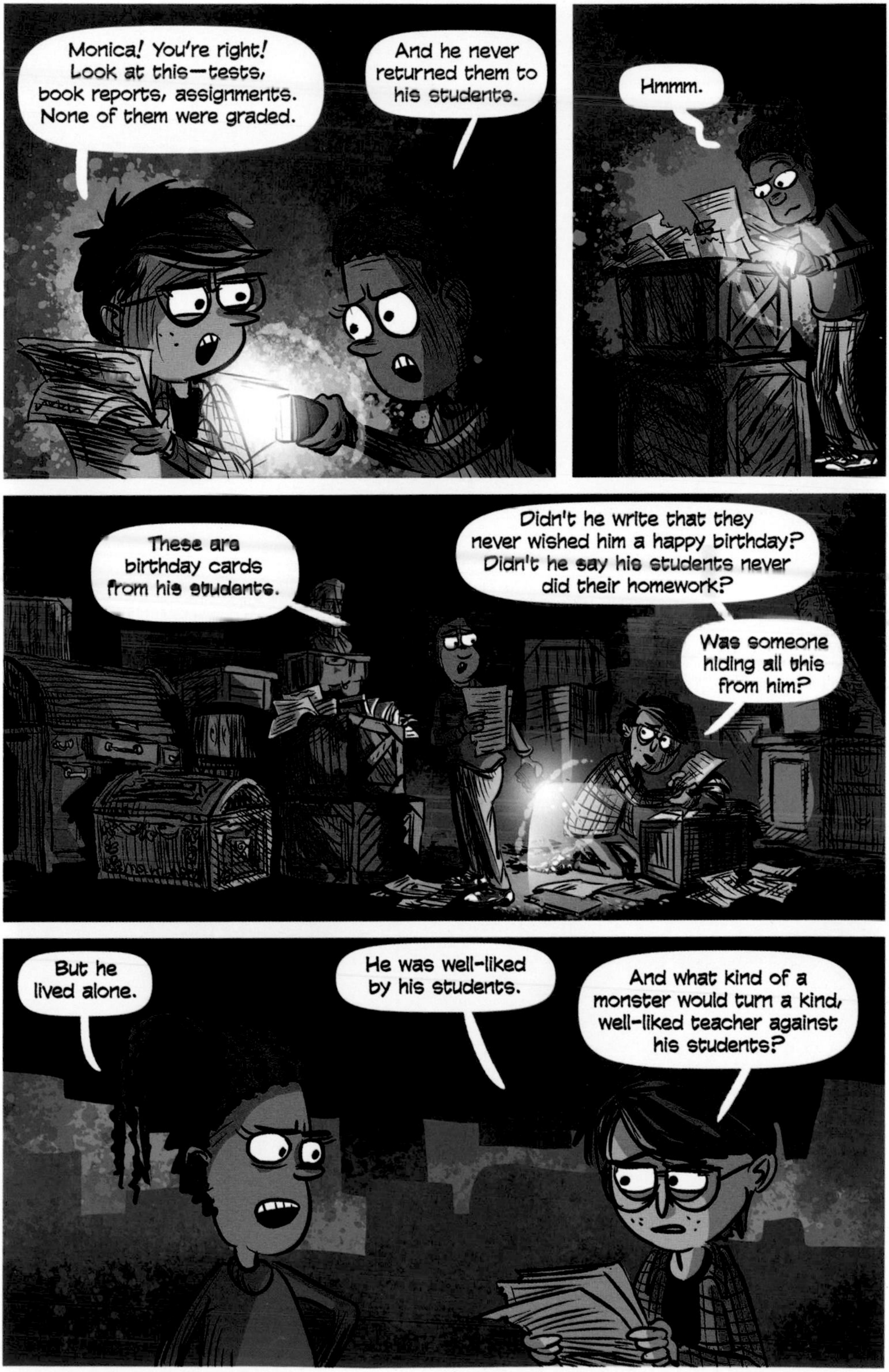
Monica! You're right! Look at this—tests, book reports, assignments. None of them were graded.
And he never returned them to his students.
Hmmm.
These are birthday cards from his students.
Didn't he write that they never wished him a happy birthday? Didn't he say his students never did their homework?
Was someone hiding all this from him?
But he lived alone.
He was well-liked by his students.
And what kind of a monster would turn a kind, well-liked teacher against his students?

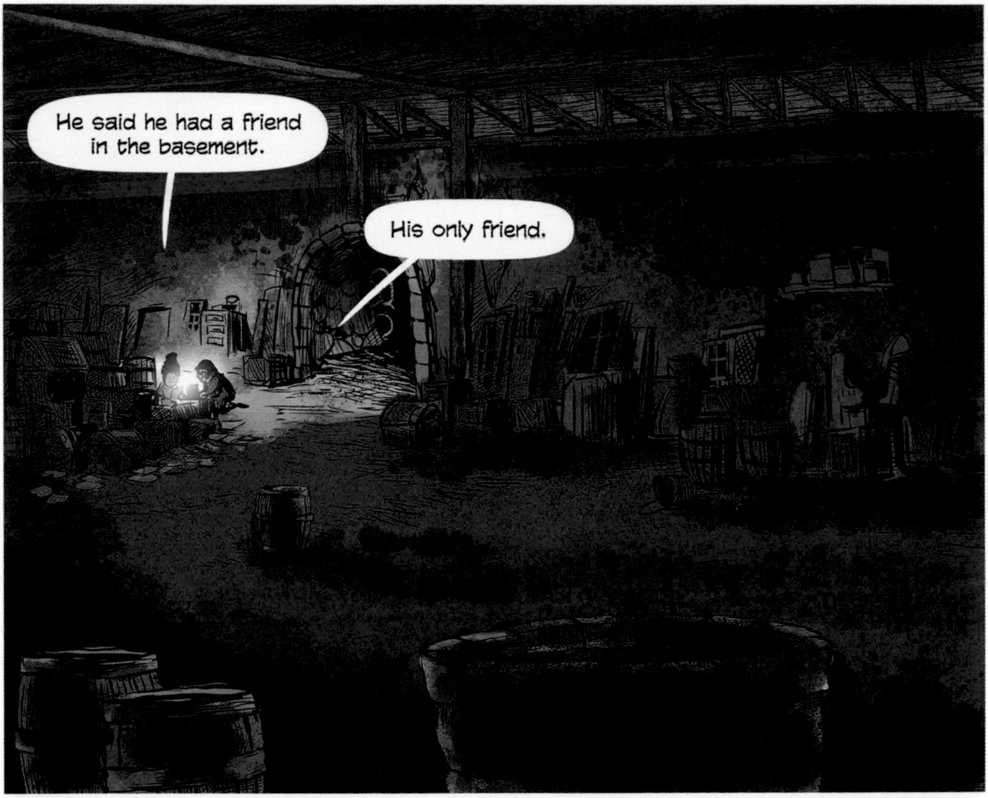
He said he had a friend in the basement.
His only friend.

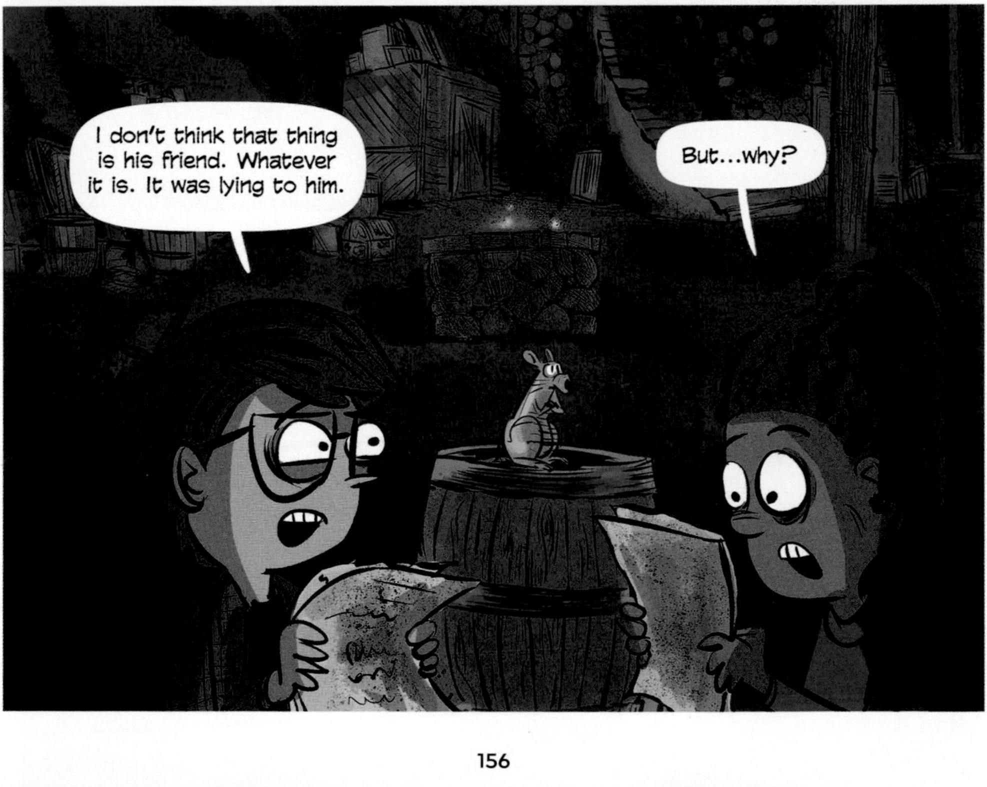
I don't think that thing is his friend. Whatever it is. It was lying to him.
But...why?

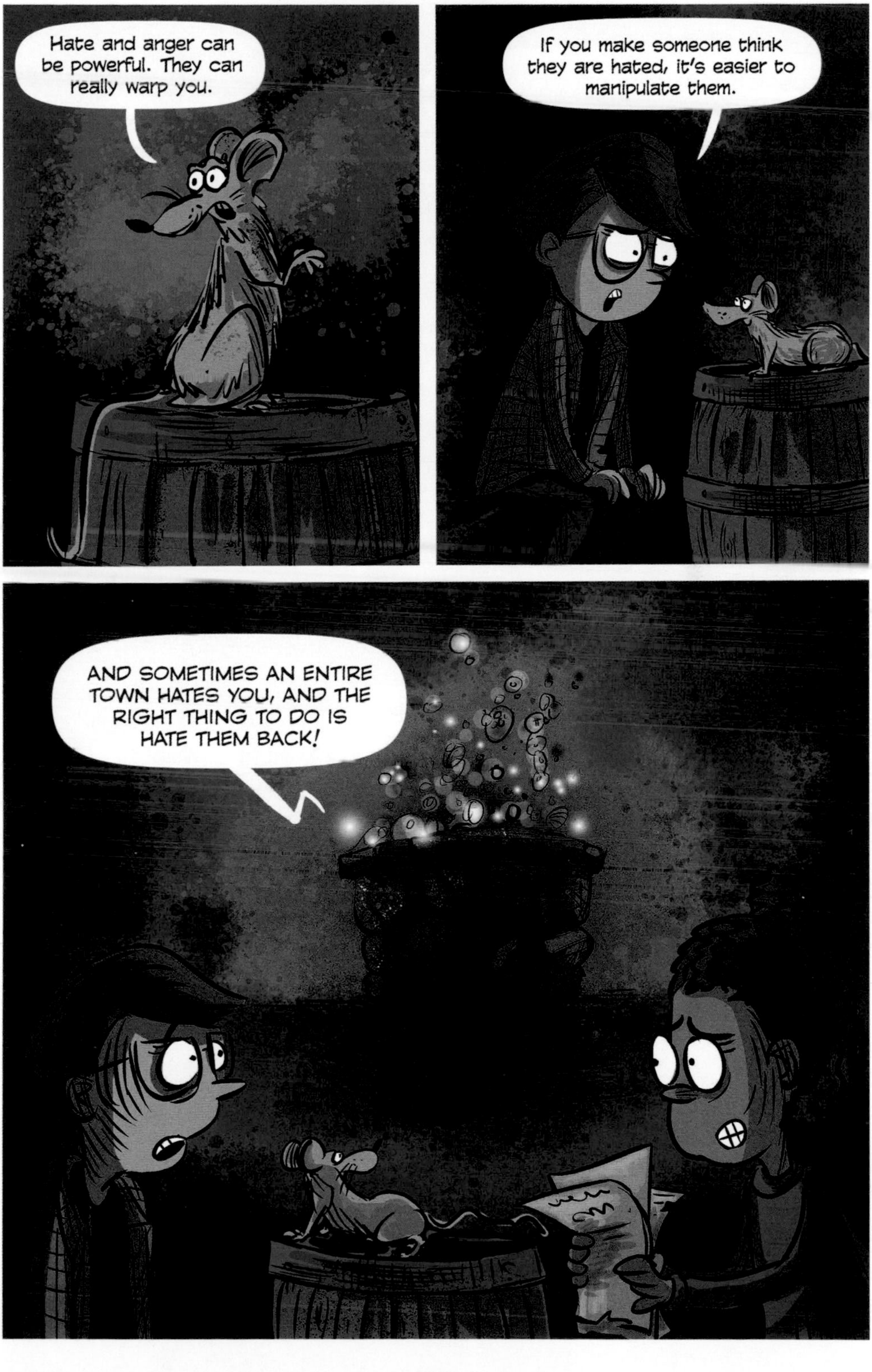
Hate and anger can be powerful. They can really warp you.
If you make someone think they are hated, it's easier to manipulate them.
AND SOMETIMES AN ENTIRE TOWN HATES YOU, AND THE RIGHT THING TO DO IS HATE THEM BACK!

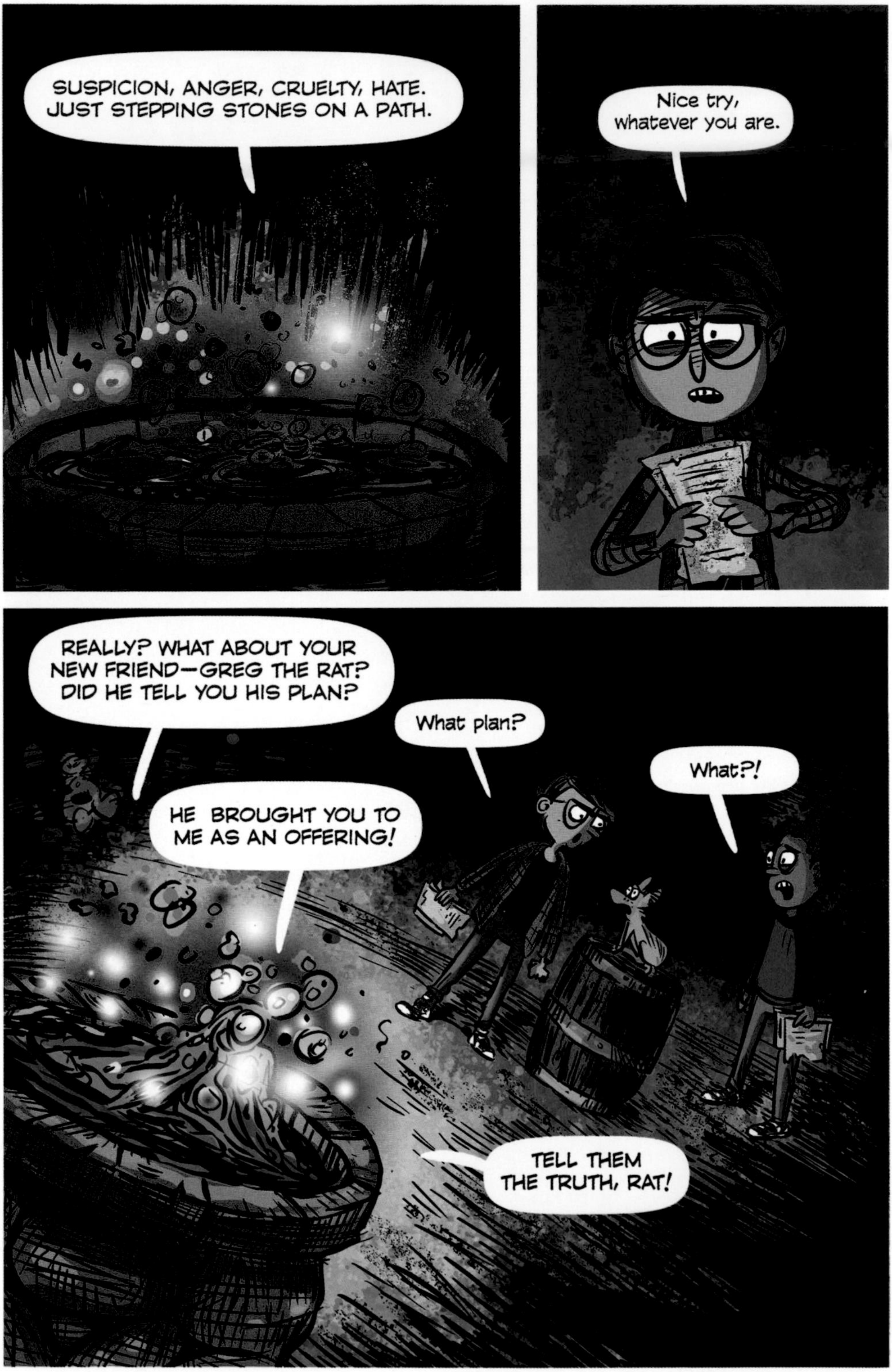
SUSPICION, ANGER, CRUELTY, HATE. JUST STEPPING STONES ON A PATH.
Nice try, whatever you are.
REALLY? WHAT ABOUT YOUR NEW FRIEND—GREG THE RAT? DID HE TELL YOU HIS PLAN?
What plan?
What?!
HE BROUGHT YOU TO ME AS AN OFFERING!
TELL THEM THE TRUTH, RAT!

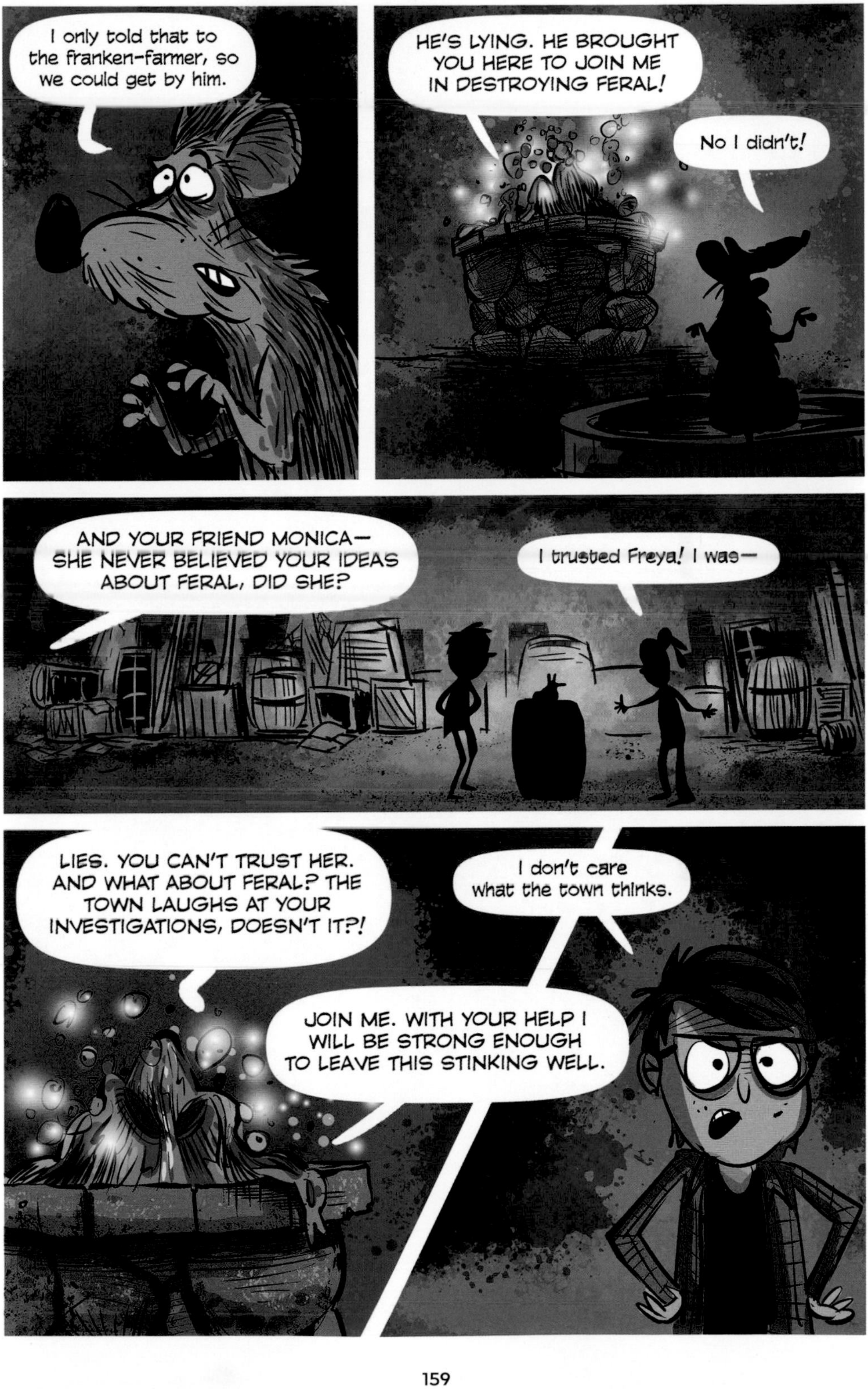
I only told that to the franken-farmer, so we could get by him.
HE'S LYING. HE BROUGHT YOU HERE TO JOIN ME IN DESTROYING FERAL!
No I didn't!
AND YOUR FRIEND MONICA— SHE NEVER BELIEVED YOUR IDEAS ABOUT FERAL, DID SHE?
I trusted Freya! I was—
LIES. YOU CAN'T TRUST HER. AND WHAT ABOUT FERAL? THE TOWN LAUGHS AT YOUR INVESTIGATIONS, DOESN'T IT?!
I don't care what the town thinks.
JOIN ME. WITH YOUR HELP I WILL BE STRONG ENOUGH TO LEAVE THIS STINKING WELL.

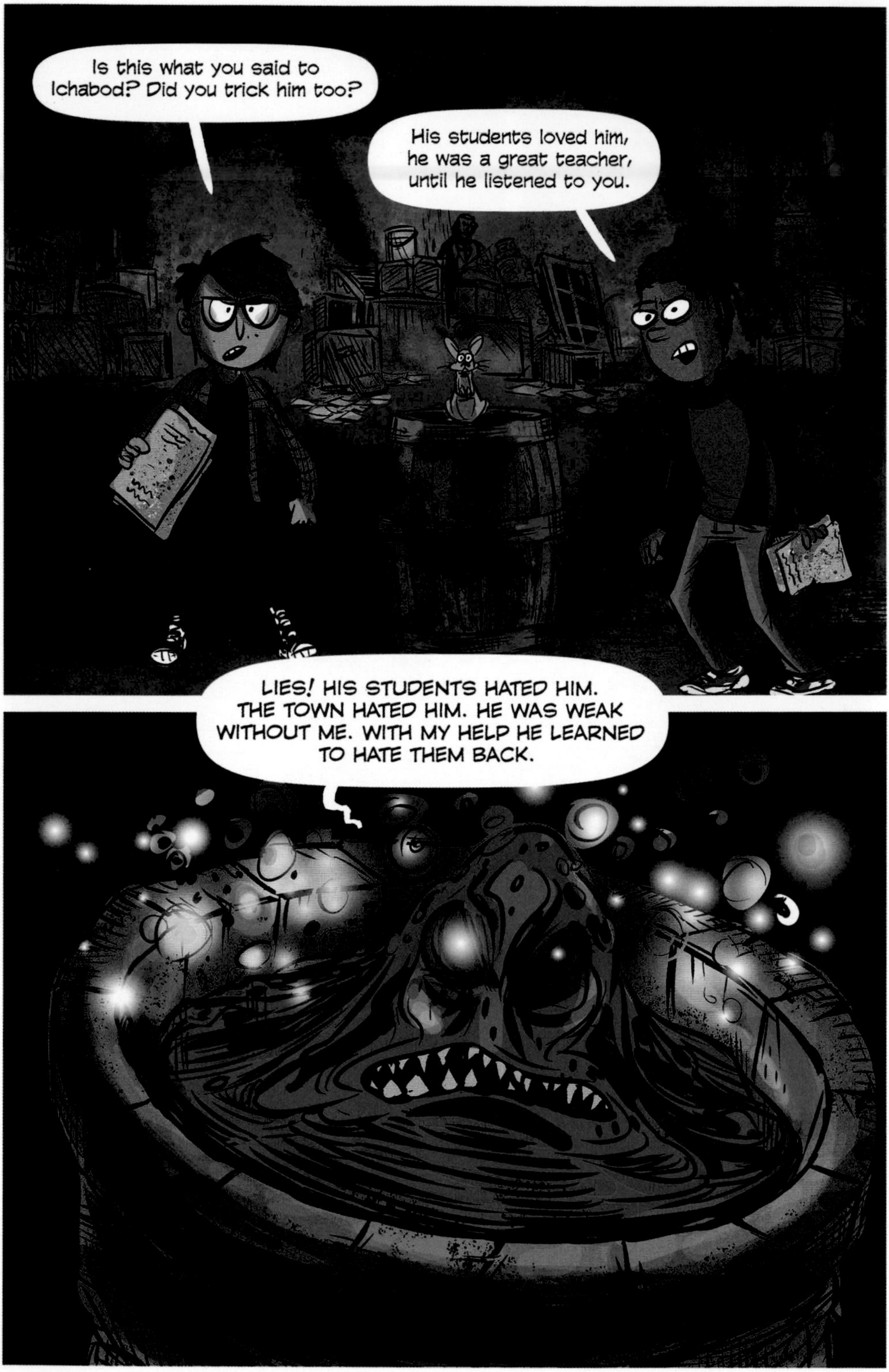
Is this what you said to Ichabod? Did you trick him too?
His students loved him, he was a great teacher, until he listened to you.
LIES! HIS STUDENTS HATED HIM. THE TOWN HATED HIM. HE WAS WEAK WITHOUT ME. WITH MY HELP HE LEARNED TO HATE THEM BACK.

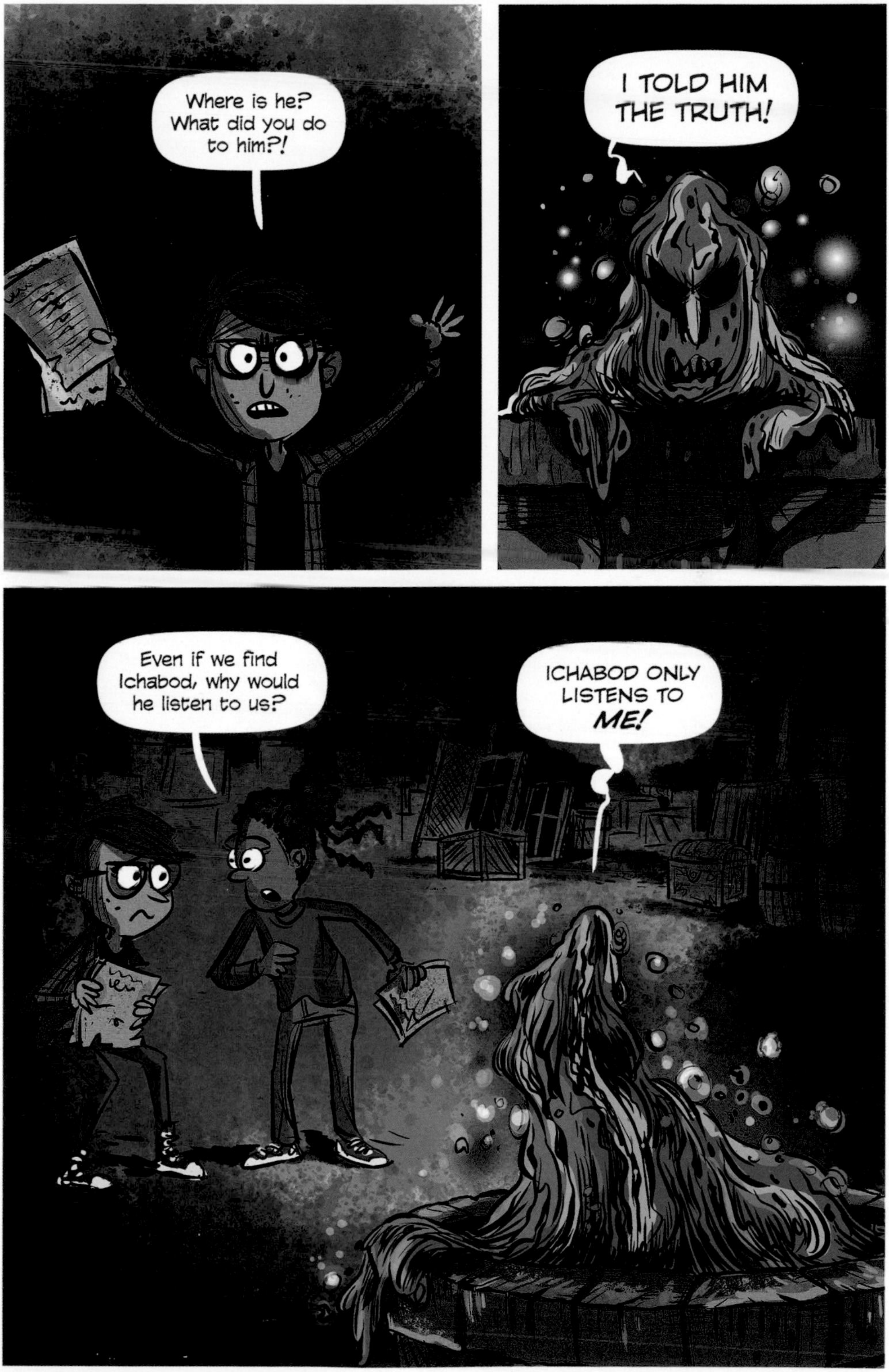
Where is he? What did you do to him?!
I TOLD HIM THE TRUTH!
Even if we find Ichabod, why would he listen to us?
ICHABOD ONLY LISTENS TO *ME!*

What did you do with Ichabod?
ICHABOD WAS WEAK, AND WEAK THINGS GET HURT! NOW I DO THE HURTING!
He needs to know his students loved him.
You need to stop whatever you have planned for Feral. Ichabod cared about the town.

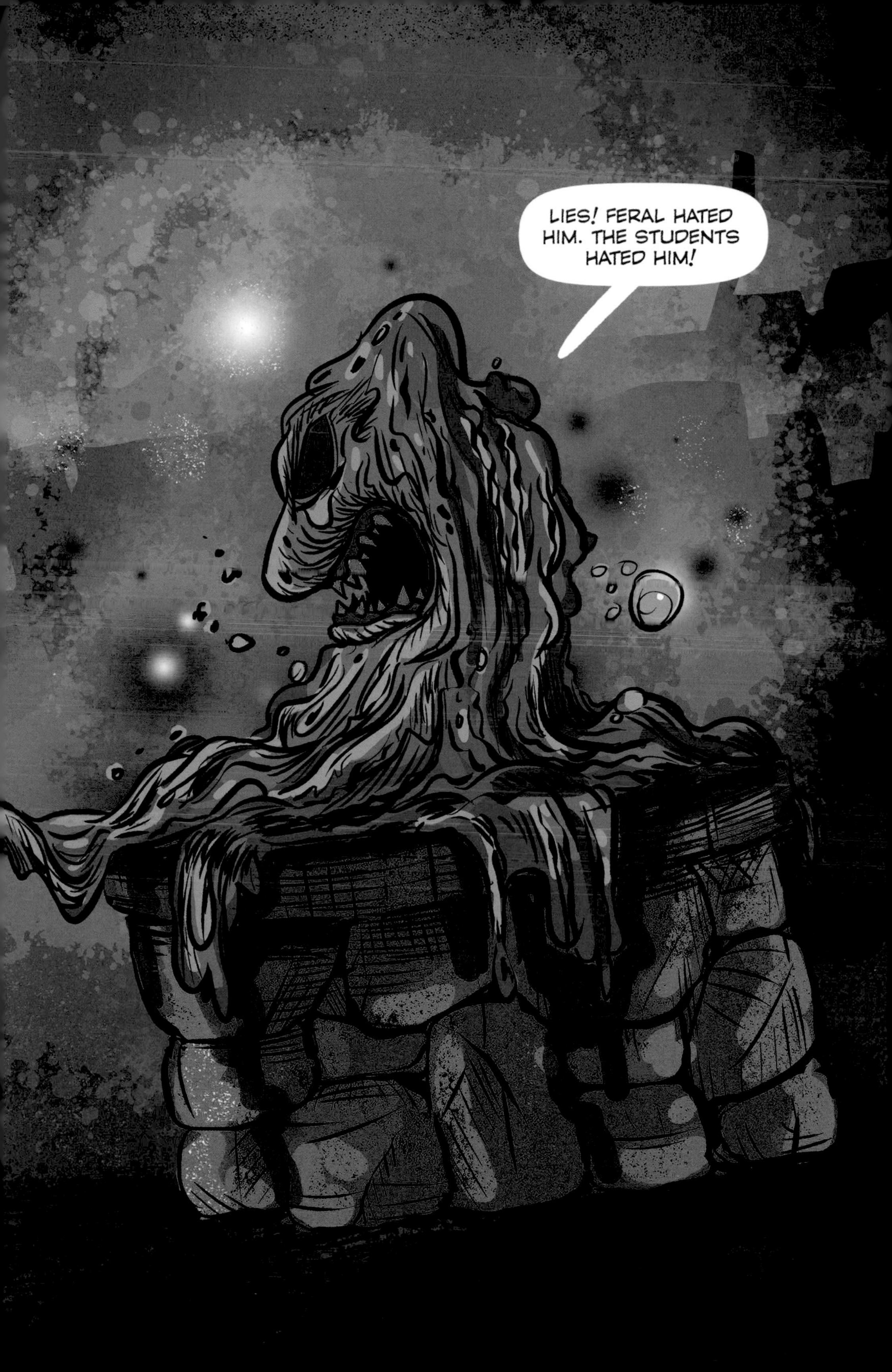
LIES! FERAL HATED HIM. THE STUDENTS HATED HIM!

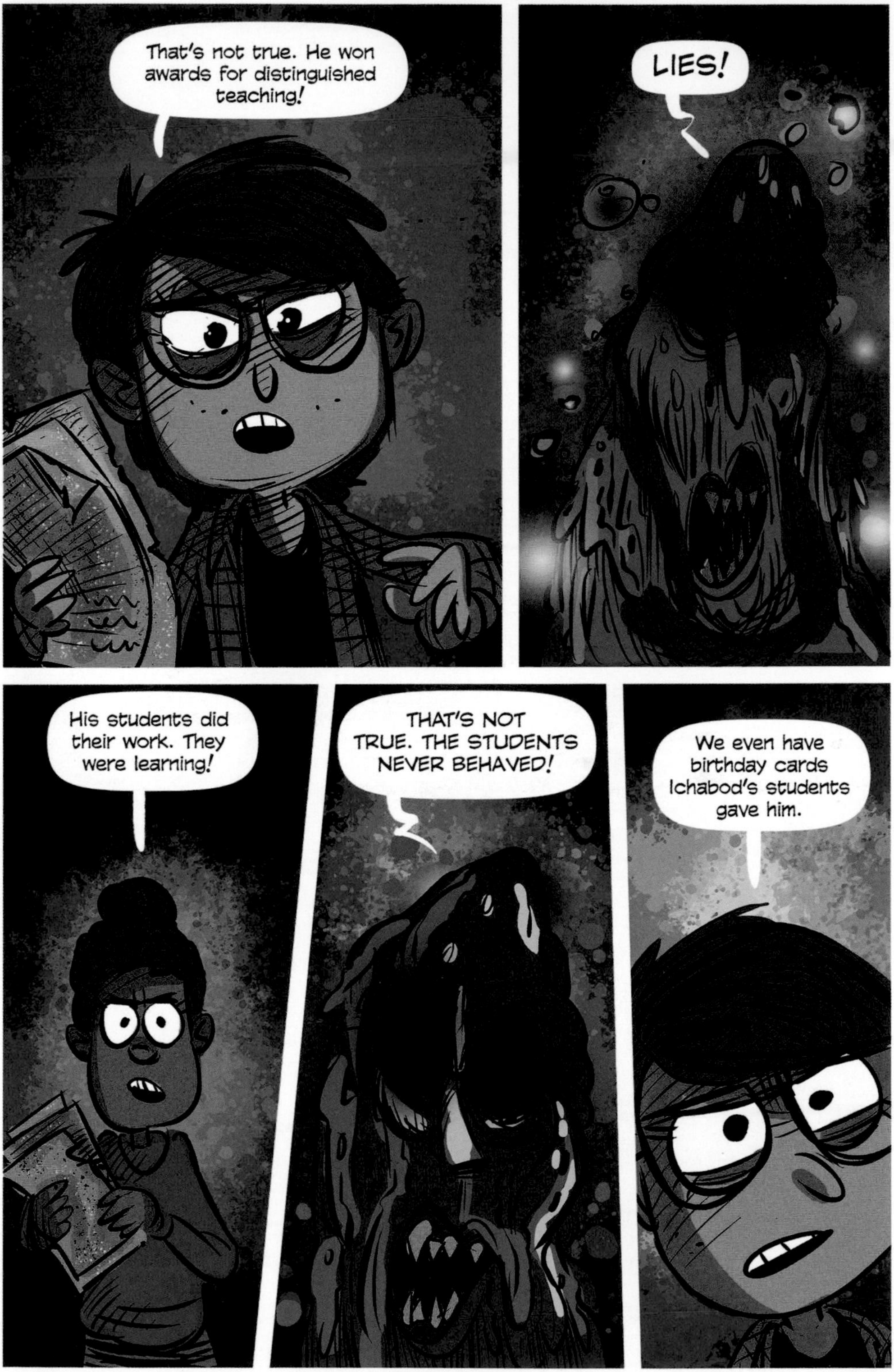
That's not true. He won awards for distinguished teaching!
LIES!
His students did their work. They were learning!
THAT'S NOT TRUE. THE STUDENTS NEVER BEHAVED!
We even have birthday cards Ichabod's students gave him.

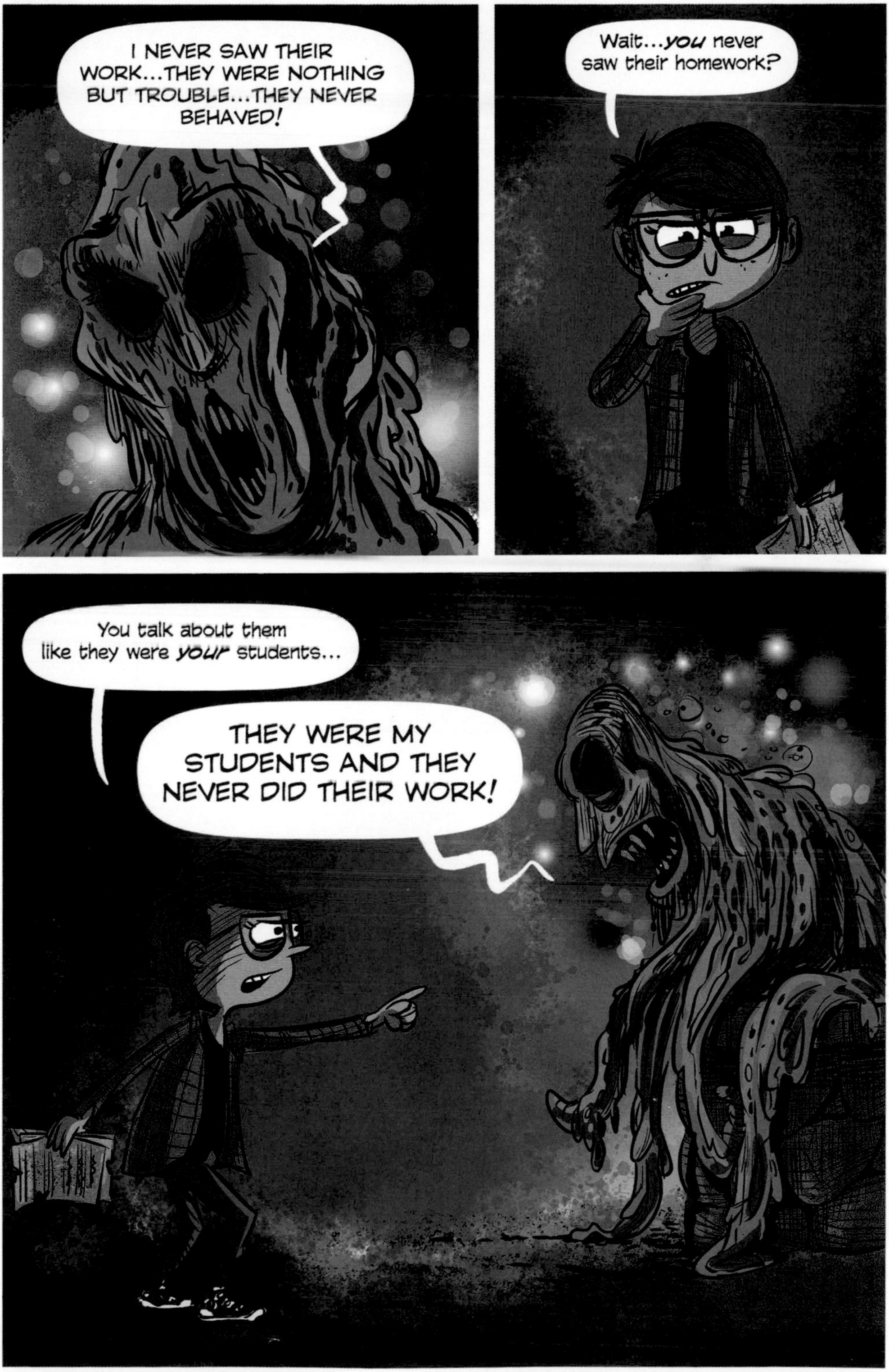
I NEVER SAW THEIR WORK...THEY WERE NOTHING BUT TROUBLE...THEY NEVER BEHAVED!
Wait...*you* never saw their homework?
You talk about them like they were *your* students...
THEY WERE MY STUDENTS AND THEY NEVER DID THEIR WORK!

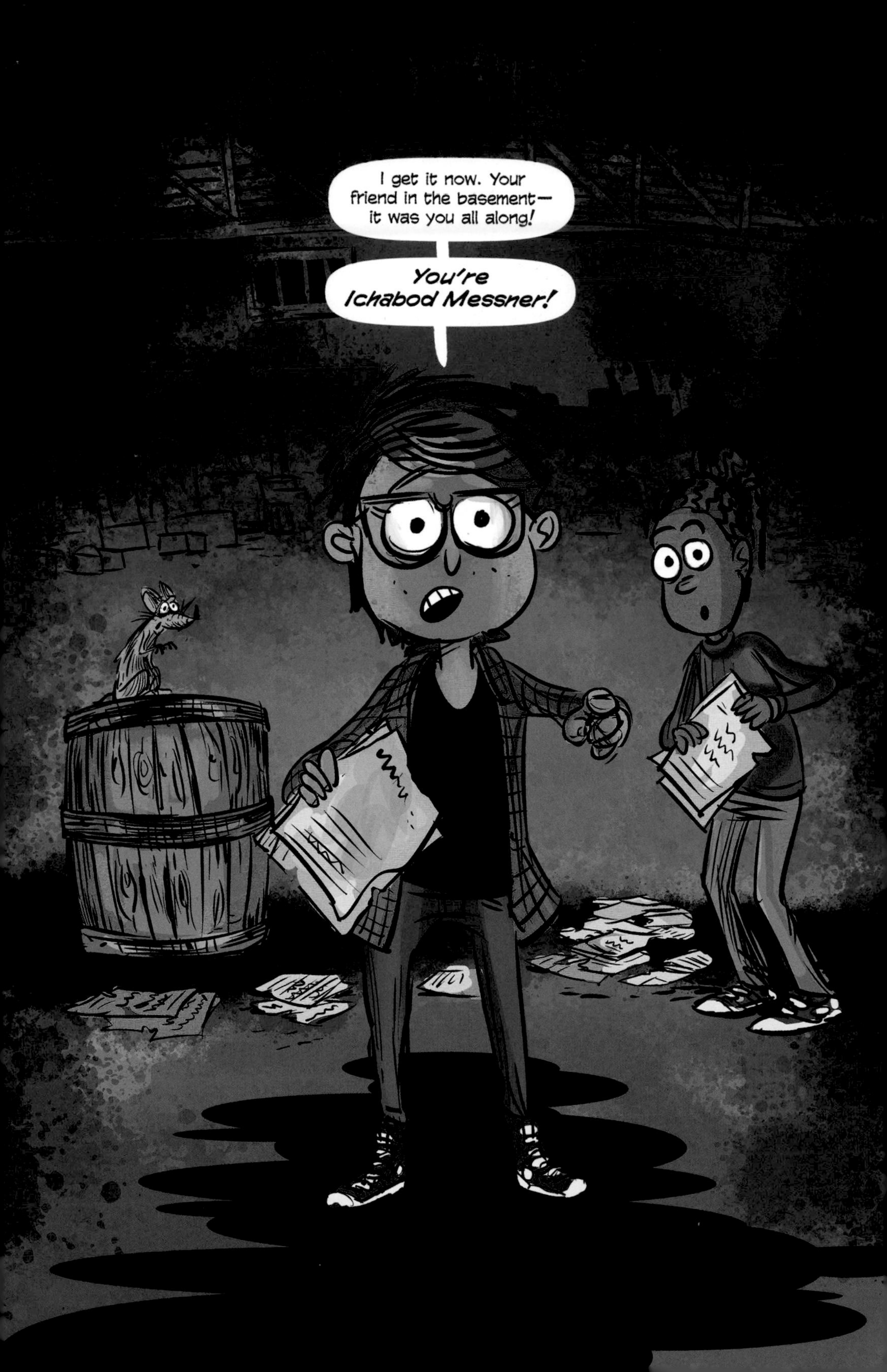
I get it now. Your friend in the basement— it was you all along!
You're Ichabod Messner!

CHAPTER 9

Car broke down just outside
this town. At least they have a
garage. The mechanic looks
a 100 years old. And the
only other car I've seen
is a hearse.

Home soon!

Karen

Brison Mc___berry
3215 State Street
Rockwel___

ARRRR!
The dark part of you grew and festered until it consumed you.
Your anger grew into irrational hate. That hate became a monster!
It IS Ichabod!

Yes, I am Ichabod. And Feral's students deserve everything that's about to happen to them!
What else can we do? How can we stop him?
I can't believe I'm saying this, but after everything I've seen tonight...
Being down here, surrounded by all his students' work...maybe they can help.
What?

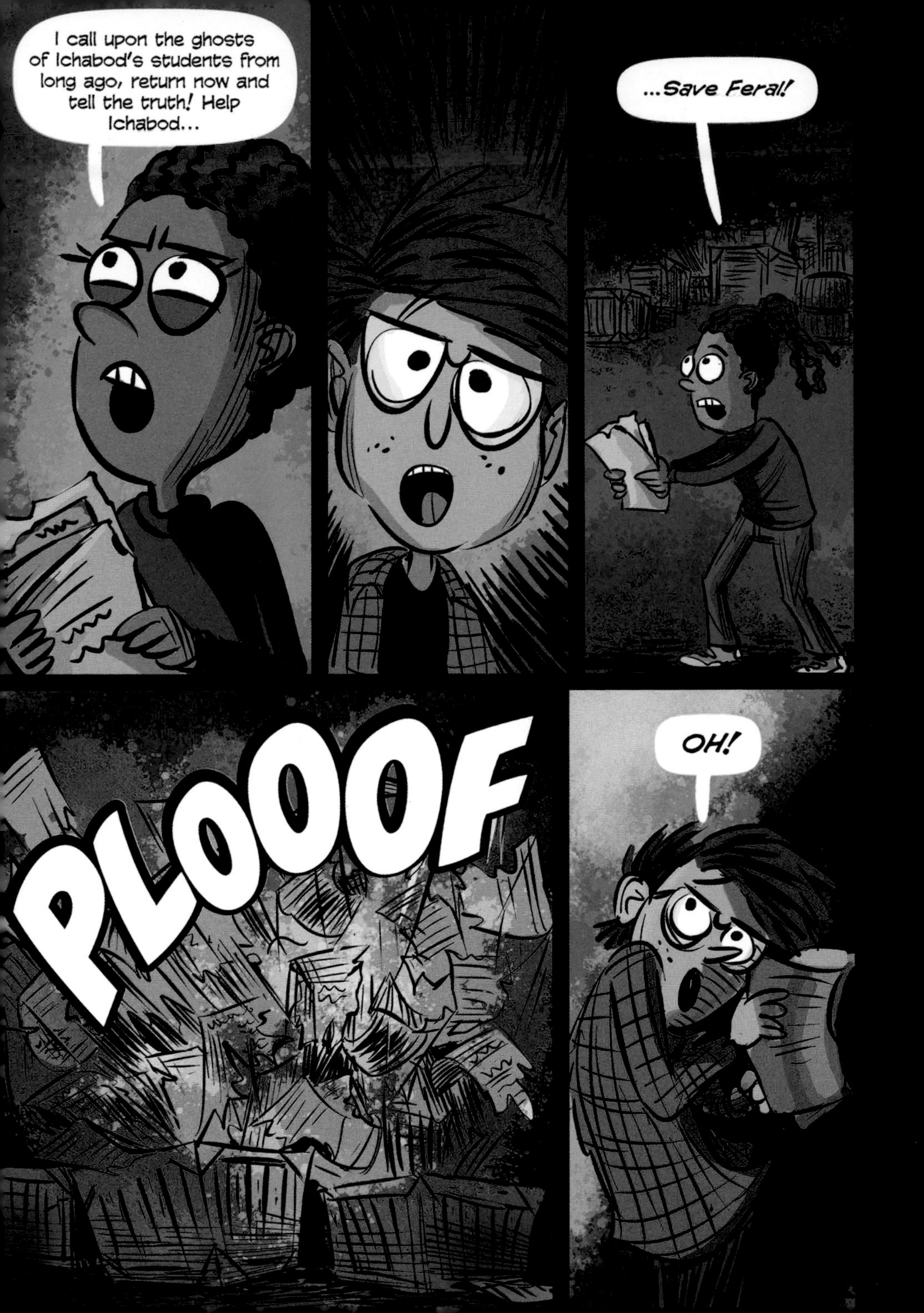
I call upon the ghosts of Ichabod's students from long ago, return now and tell the truth! Help Ichabod...
...Save Feral!
PLOOOF
OH!

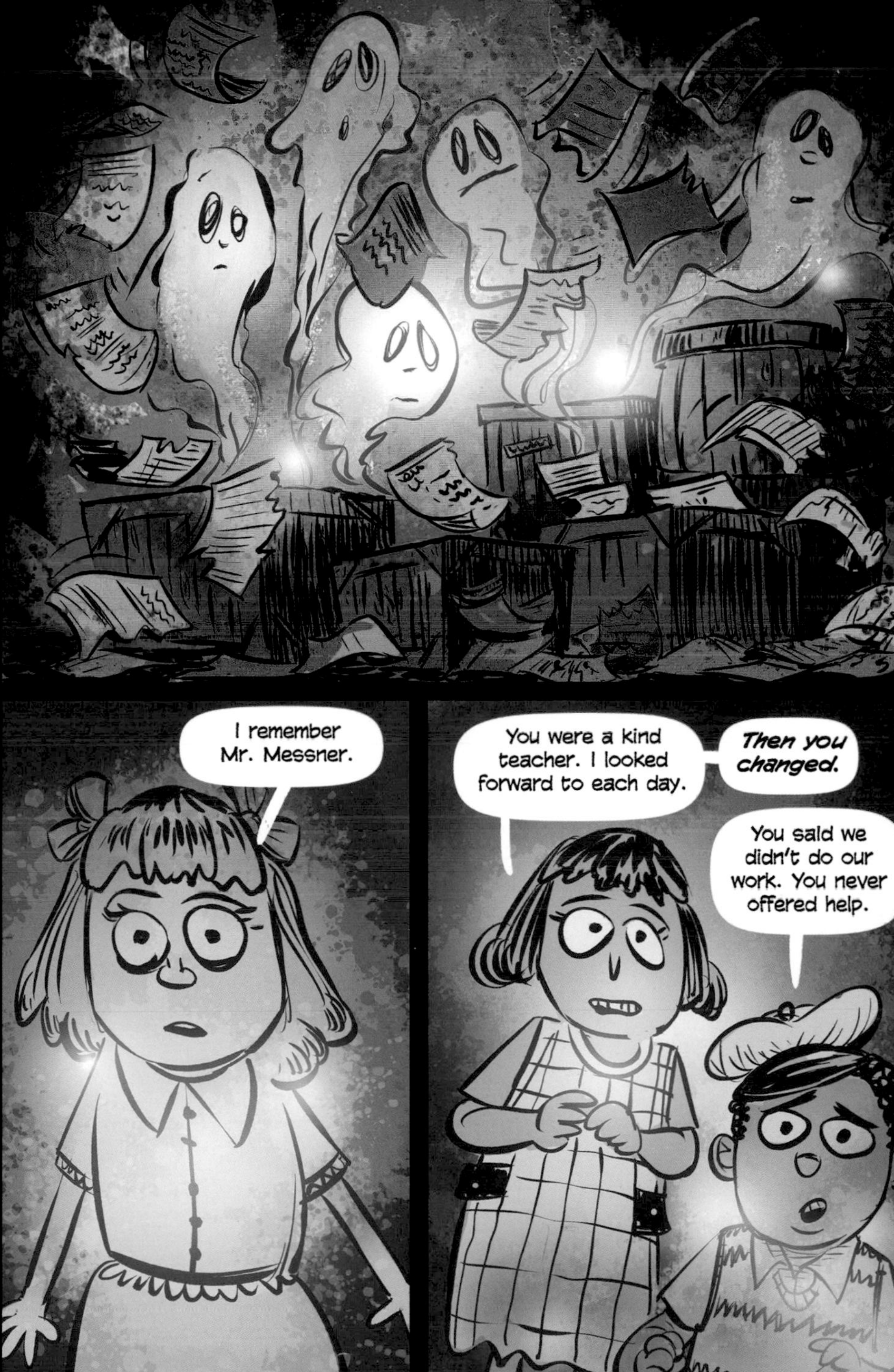
I remember Mr. Messner.
You were a kind teacher. I looked forward to each day.
Then you changed.
You said we didn't do our work. You never offered help.

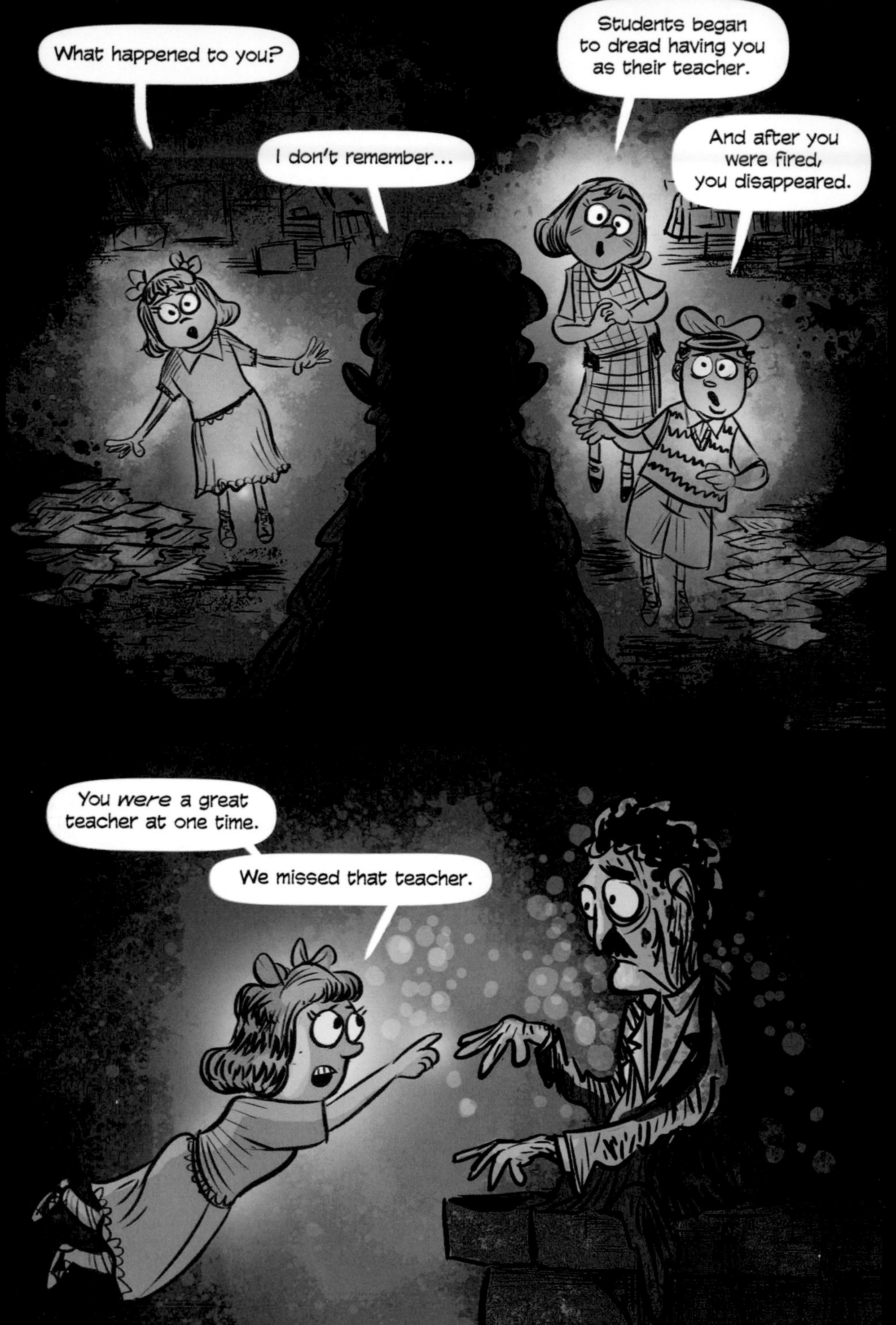
What happened to you?
I don't remember...
Students began to dread having you as their teacher.
And after you were fired, you disappeared.
You *were* a great teacher at one time.
We missed that teacher.

I remember now... Students were doing their work and I liked teaching. But the voice, the voice in the basement...
TOLD YOU THE TRUTH!
YOU ARE NOTHING WITHOUT ME!

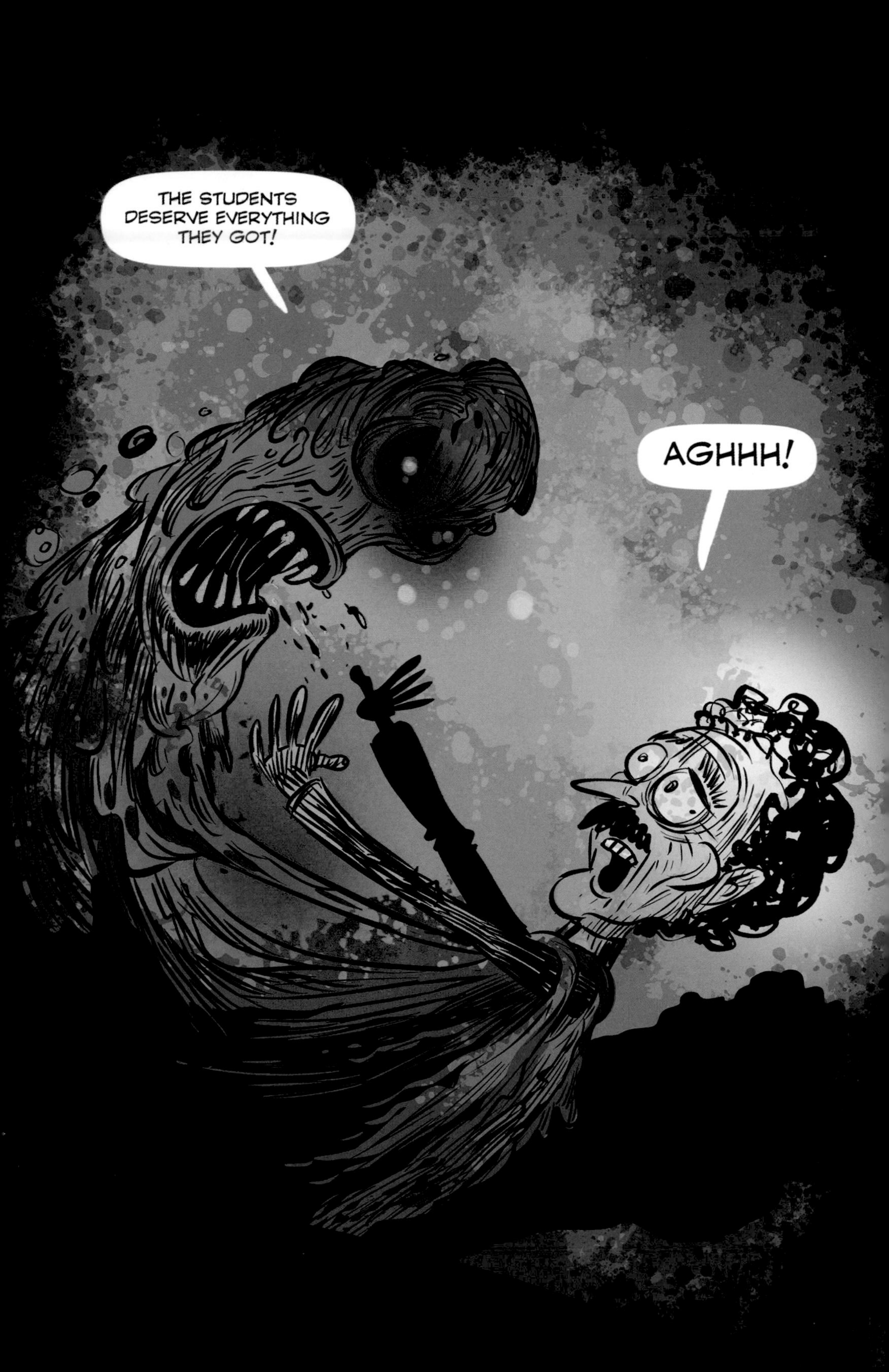
THE STUDENTS DESERVE EVERYTHING THEY GOT!
AGHHH!

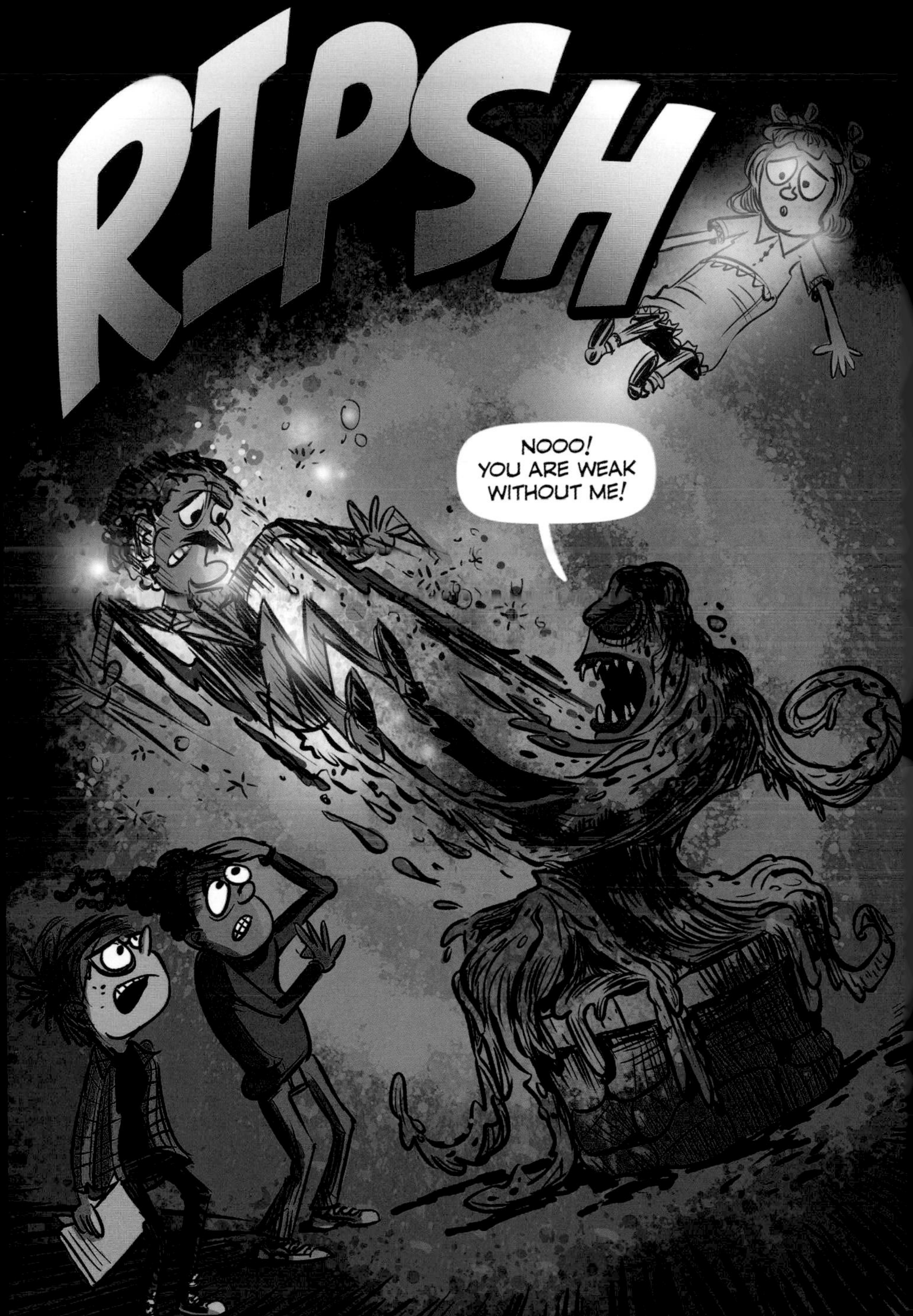
RIPSH
NOOO! YOU ARE WEAK WITHOUT ME!

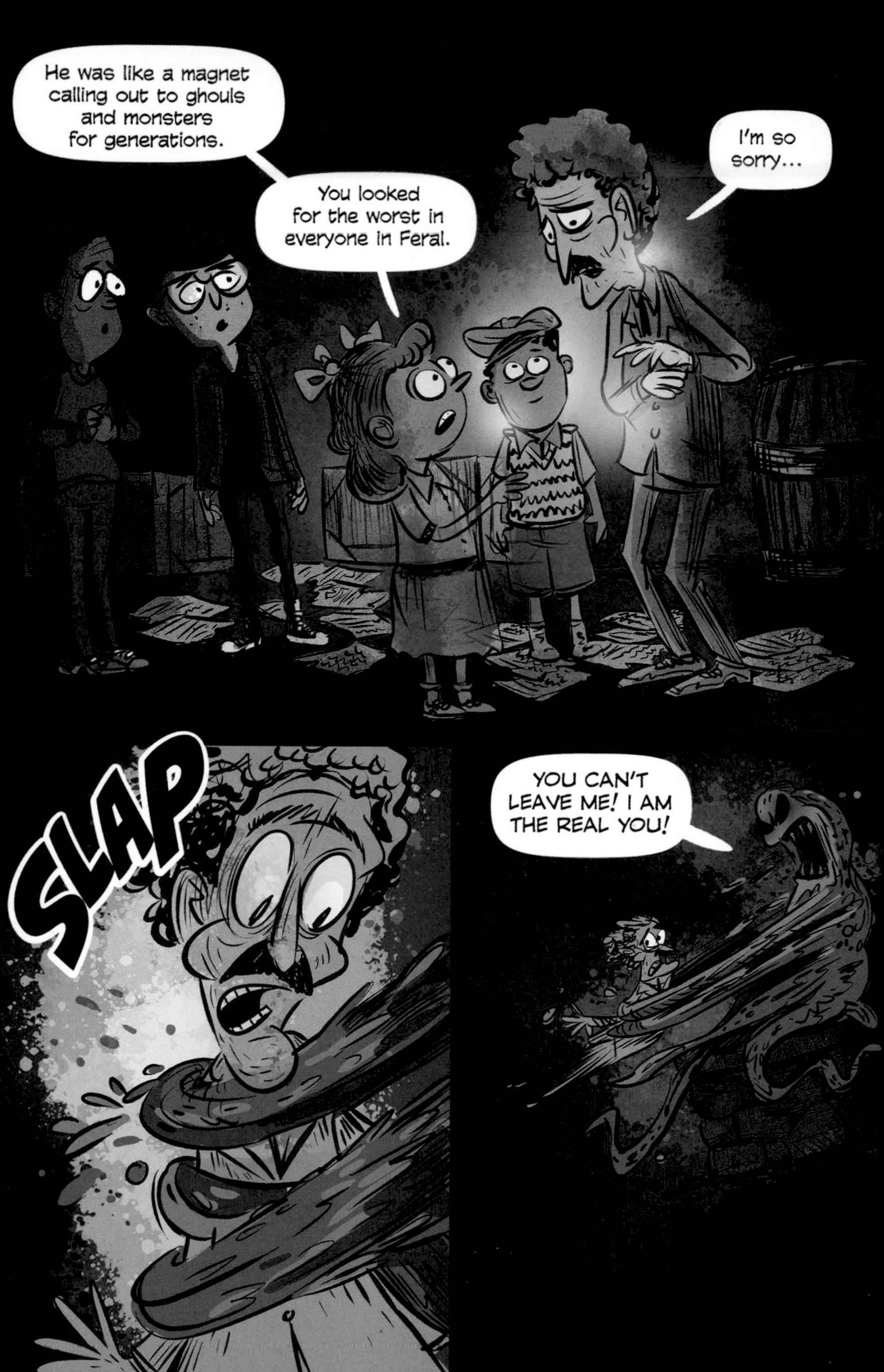
He was like a magnet calling out to ghouls and monsters for generations.
You looked for the worst in everyone in Feral.
I'm so sorry...
SLAP
YOU CAN'T LEAVE ME! I AM THE REAL YOU!

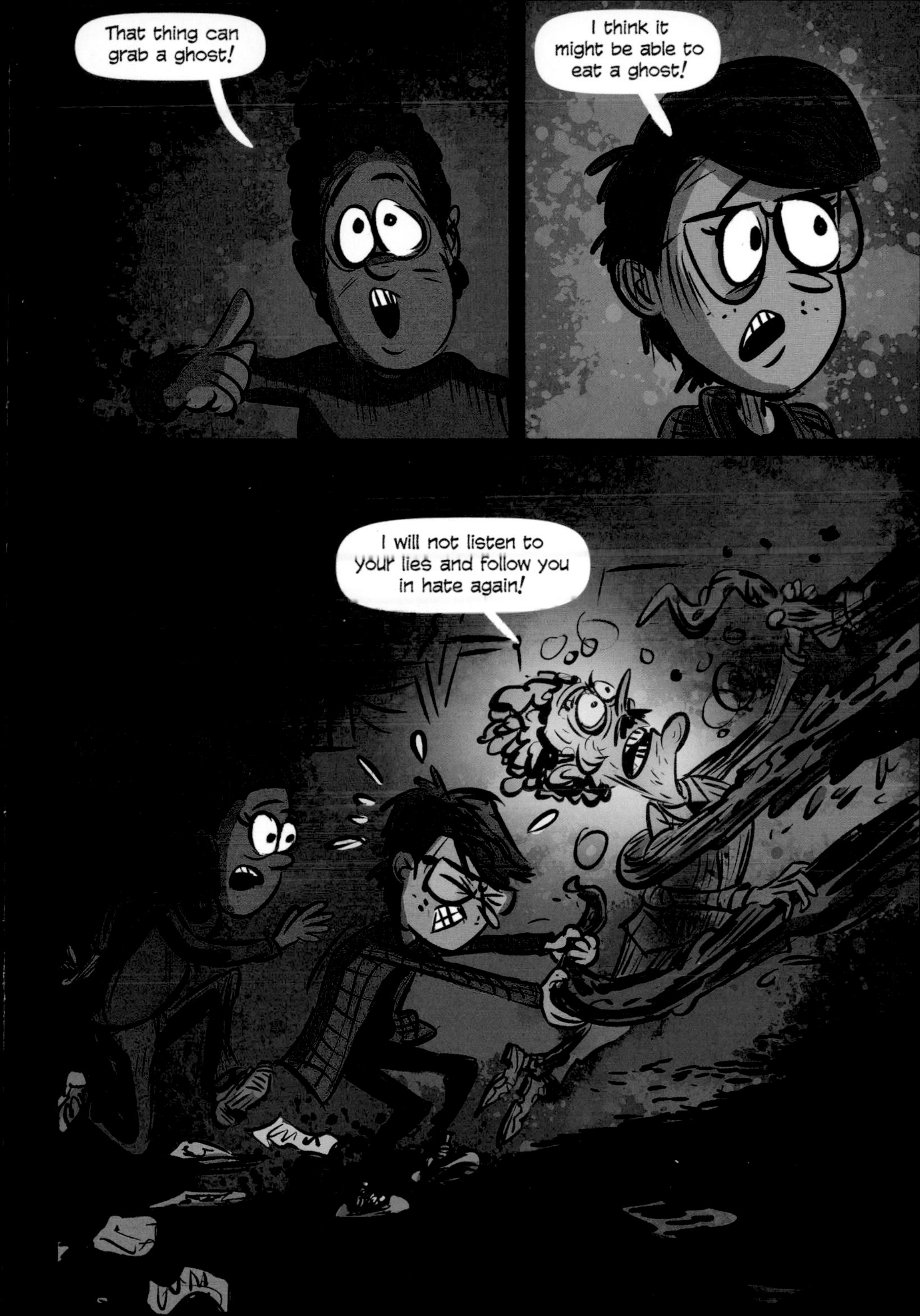
That thing can grab a ghost!
I think it might be able to eat a ghost!
I will not listen to your lies and follow you in hate again!

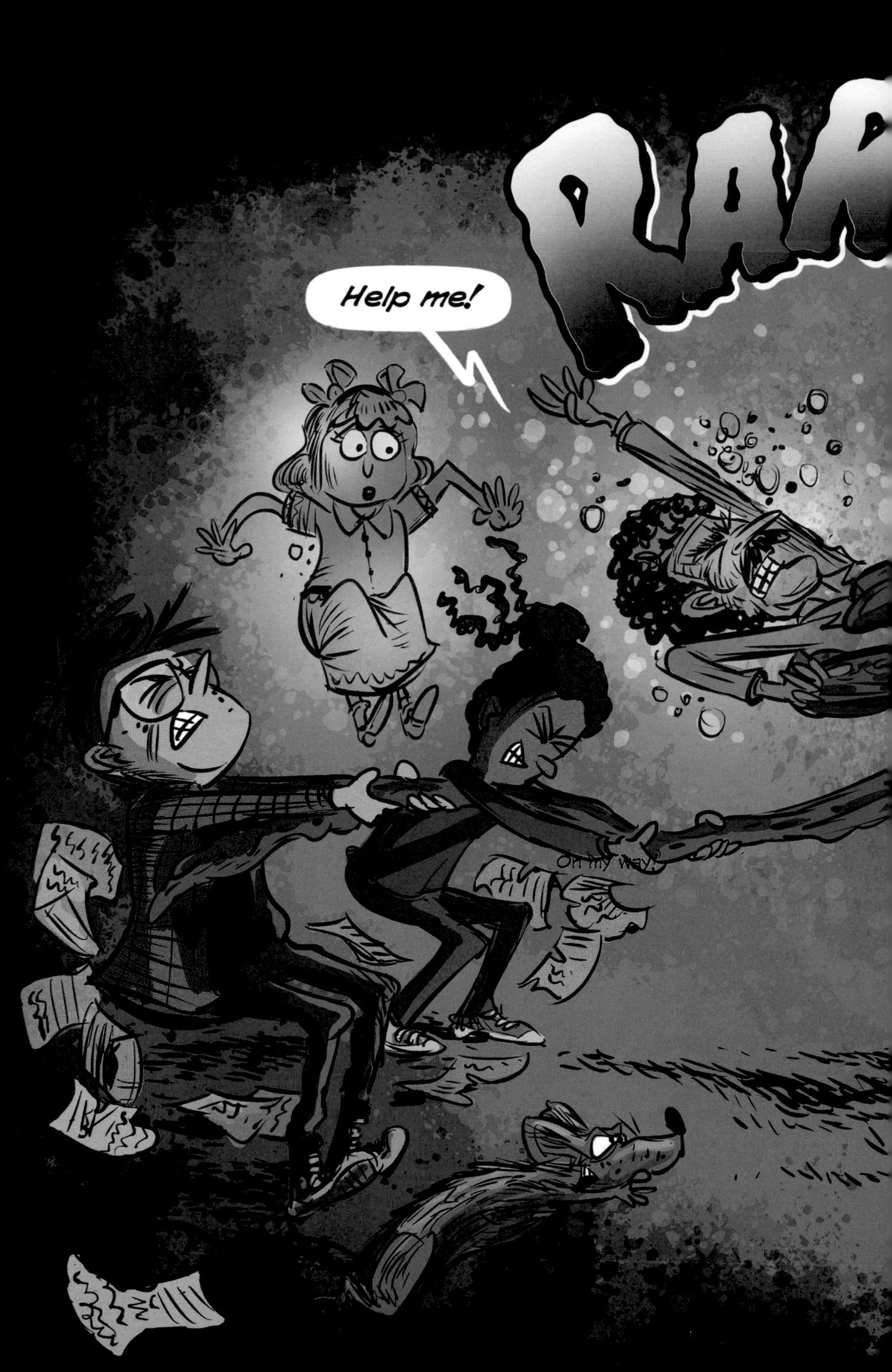
PLA
Help me!
On my way!

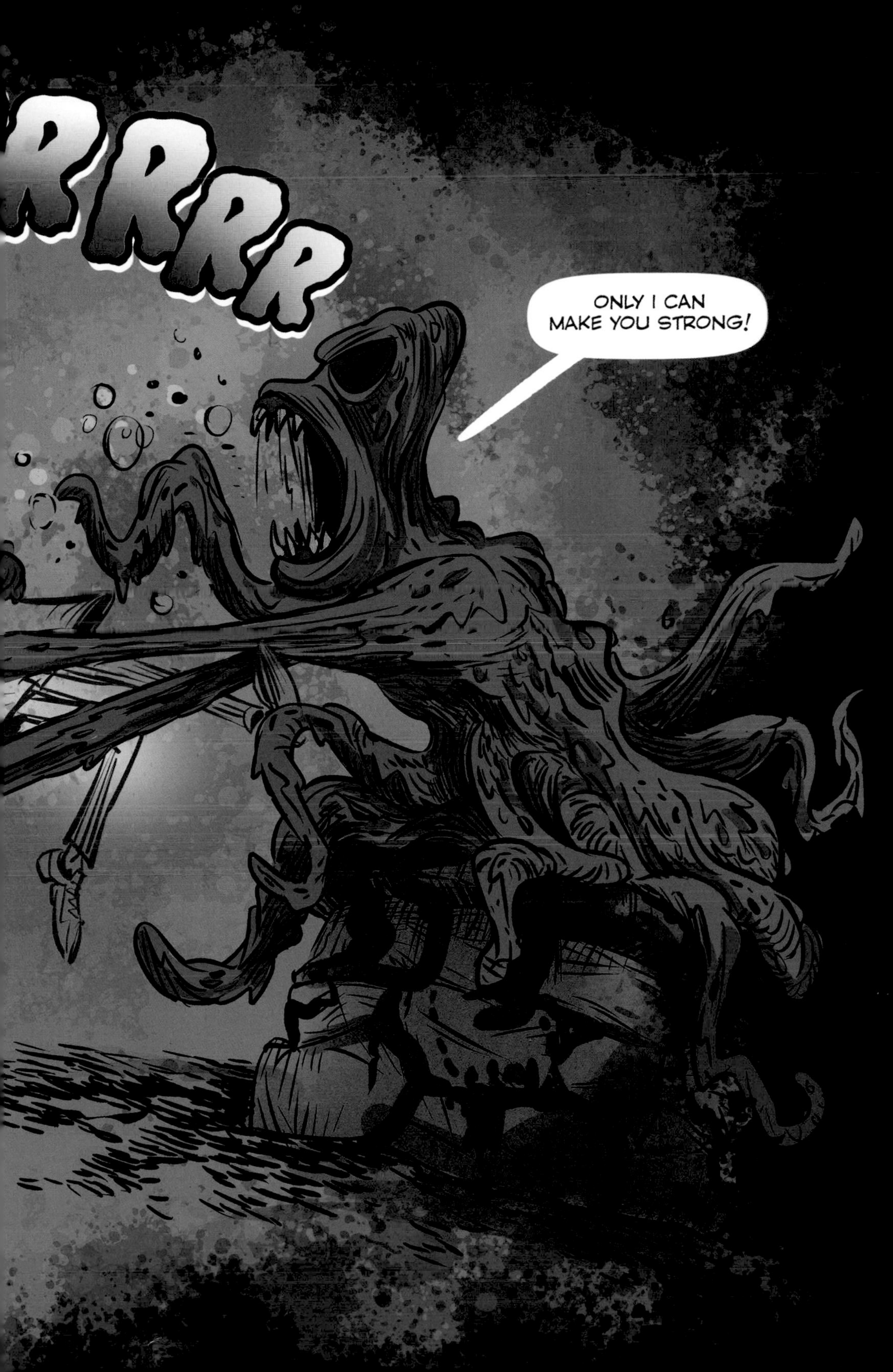
RRRR
ONLY I CAN MAKE YOU STRONG!

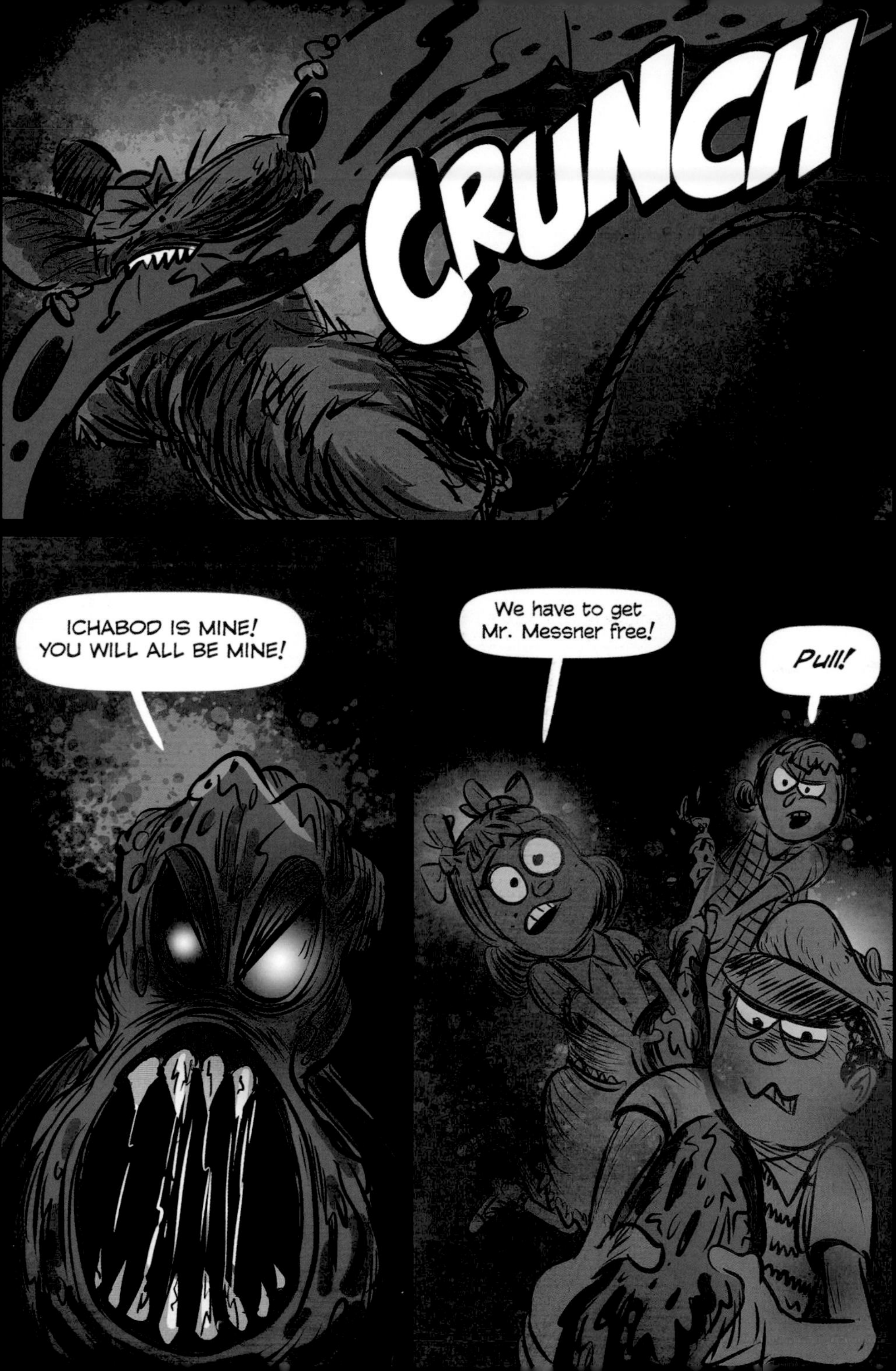
CRUNCH
ICHABOD IS MINE! YOU WILL ALL BE MINE!
We have to get Mr. Messner free!
Pull!

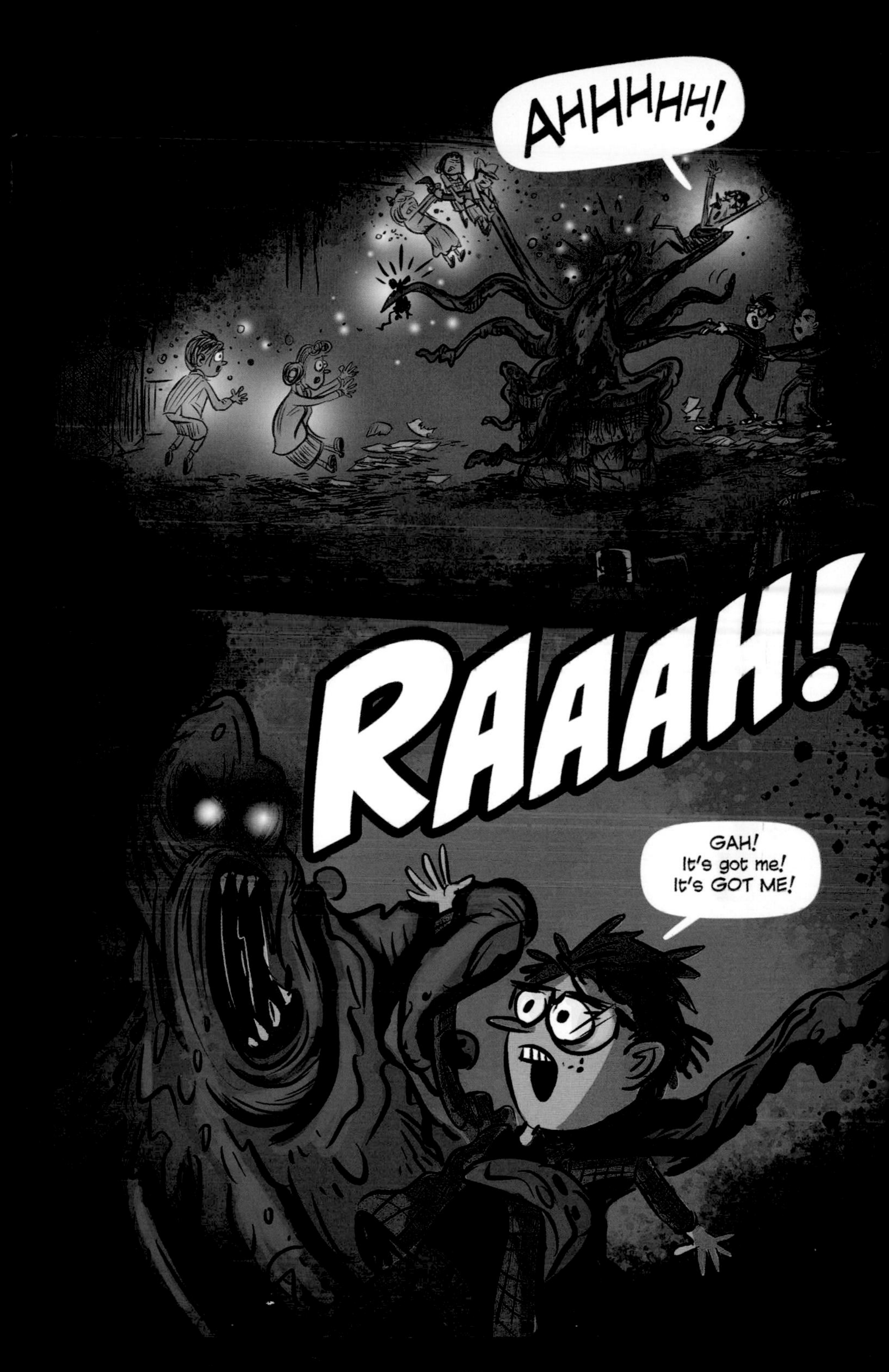
AHHHHH!
RAAAH!
GAH! It's got me! It's GOT ME!

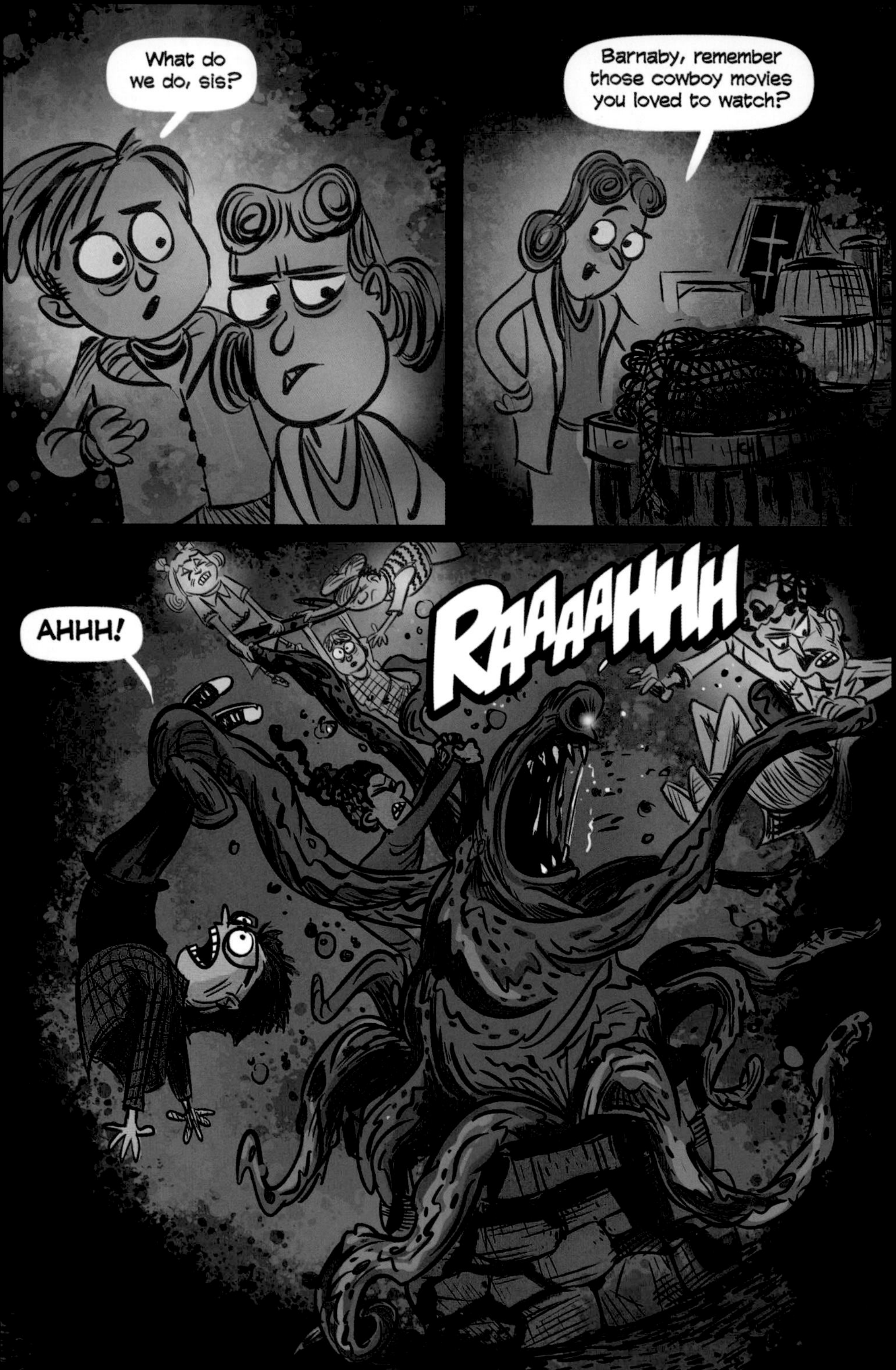
What do we do, sis?
Barnaby, remember those cowboy movies you loved to watch?
AHHH!
RAAAAHHH

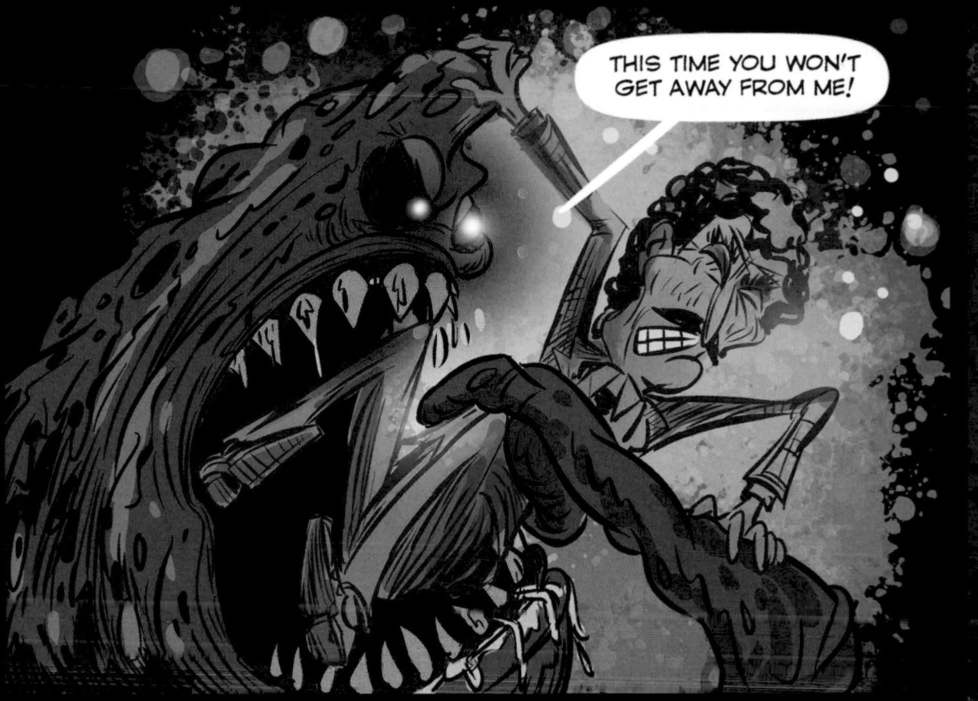
THIS TIME YOU WON'T GET AWAY FROM ME!

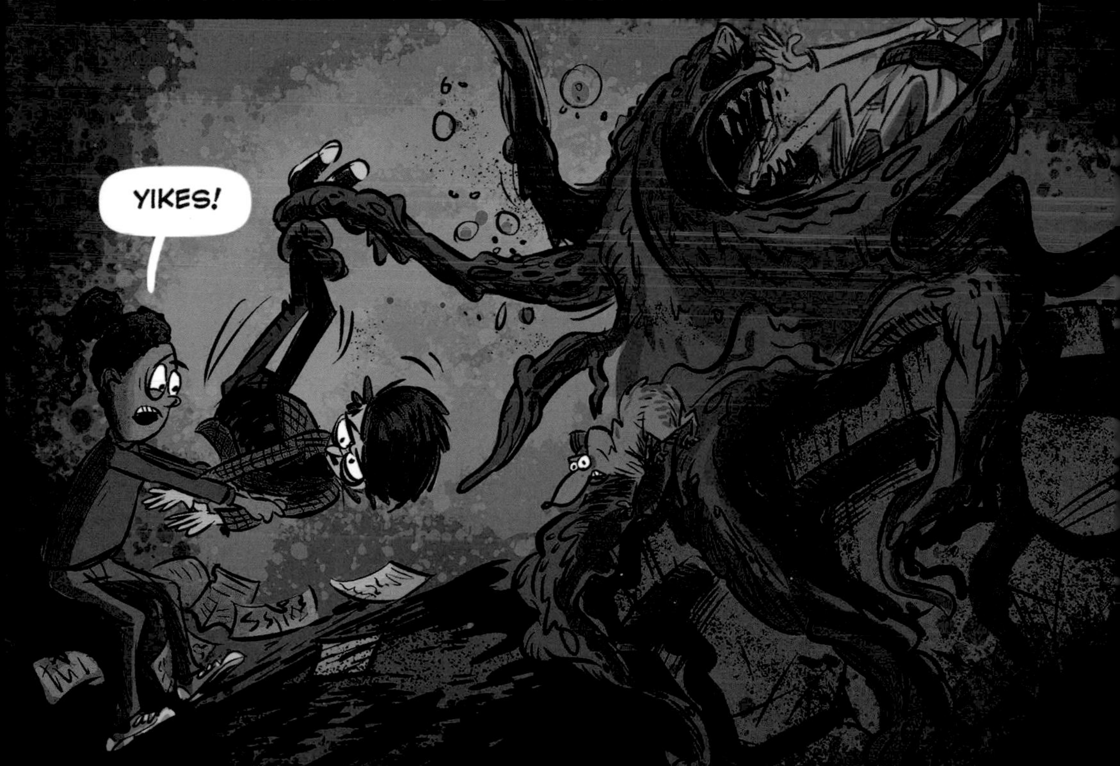
YIKES!

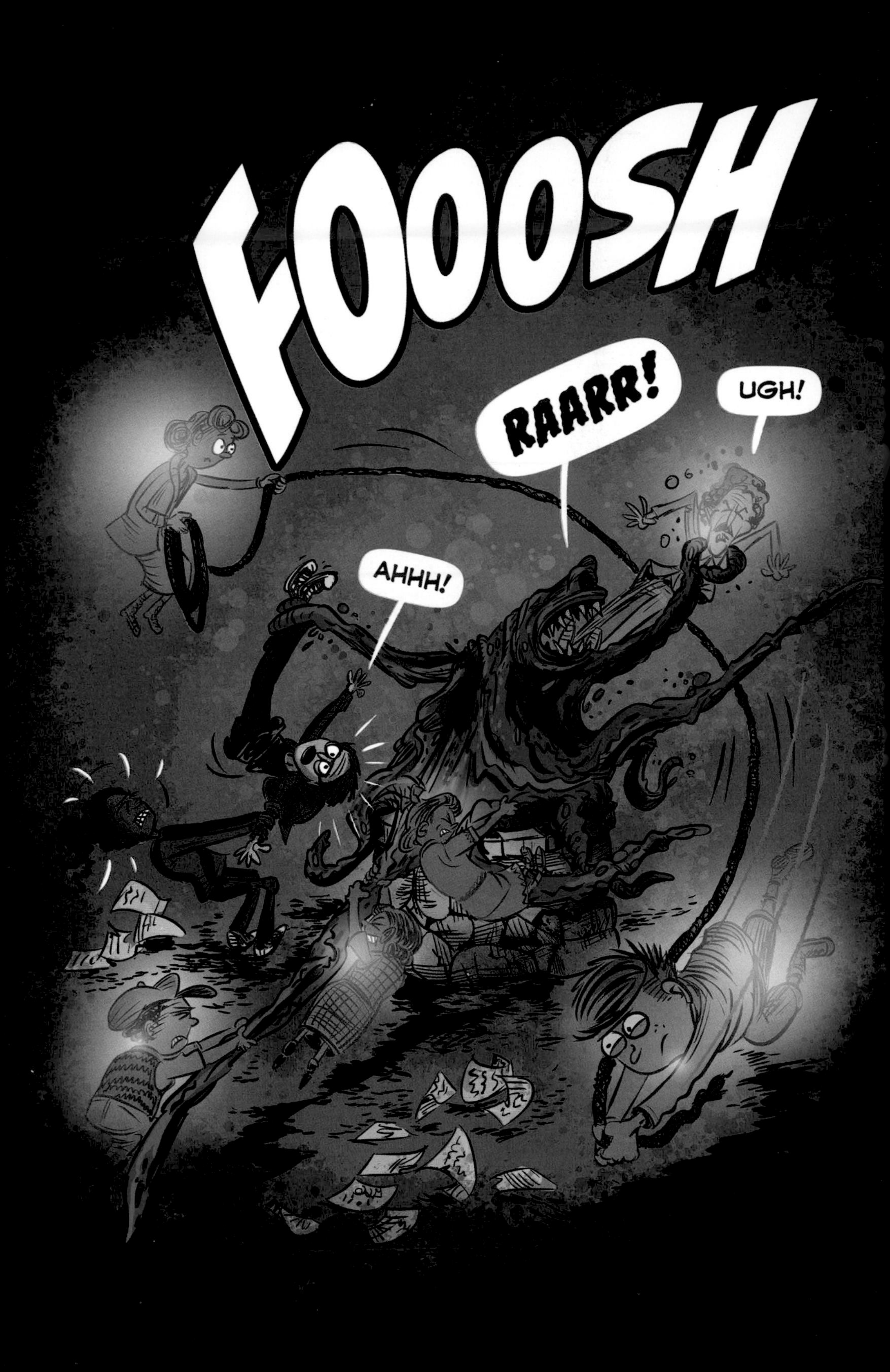
FOOOSH
RAARR!
UGH!
AHHH!

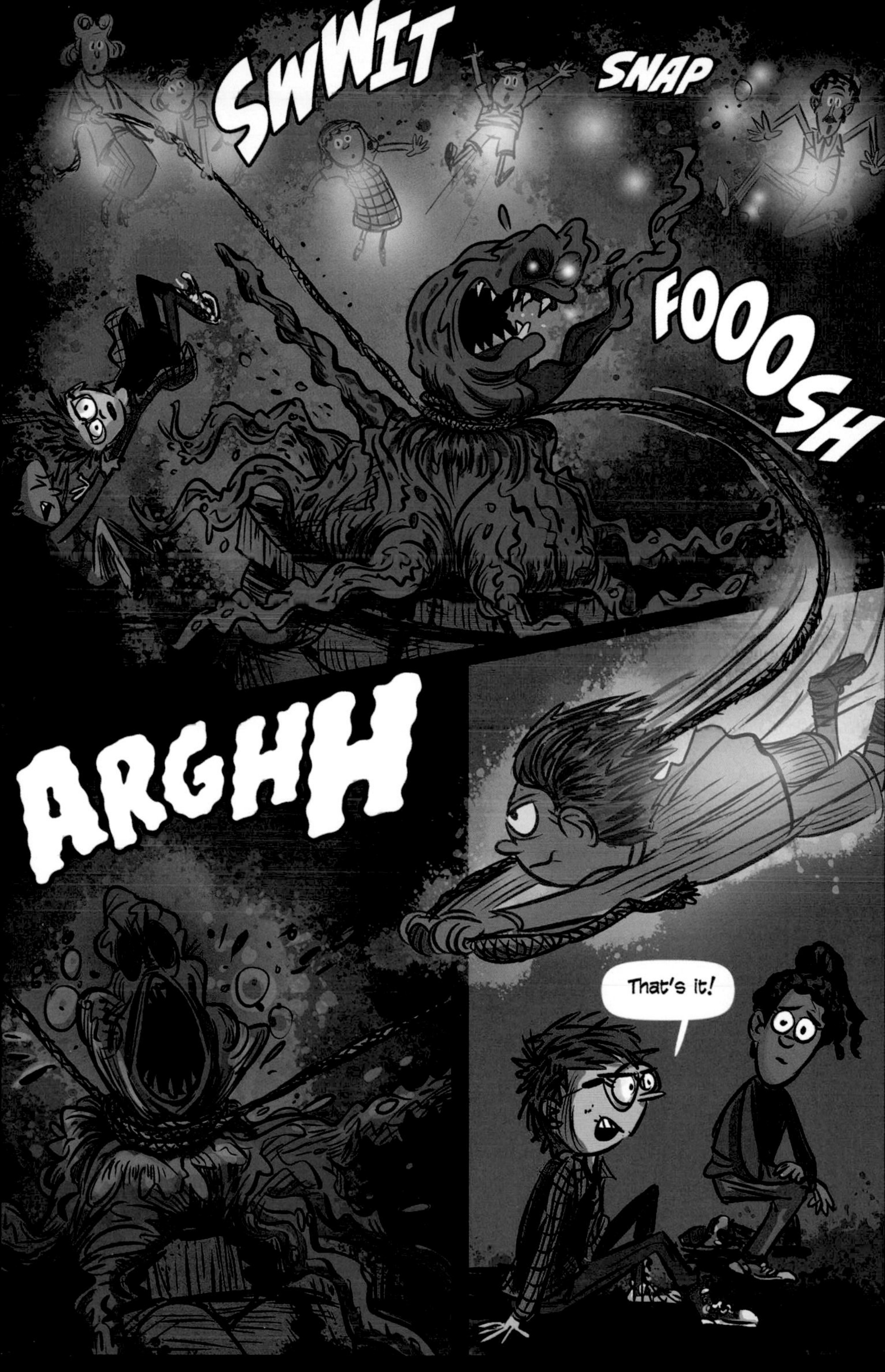
SWWIT
SNAP
FOOOSH
ARGHH
That's it!

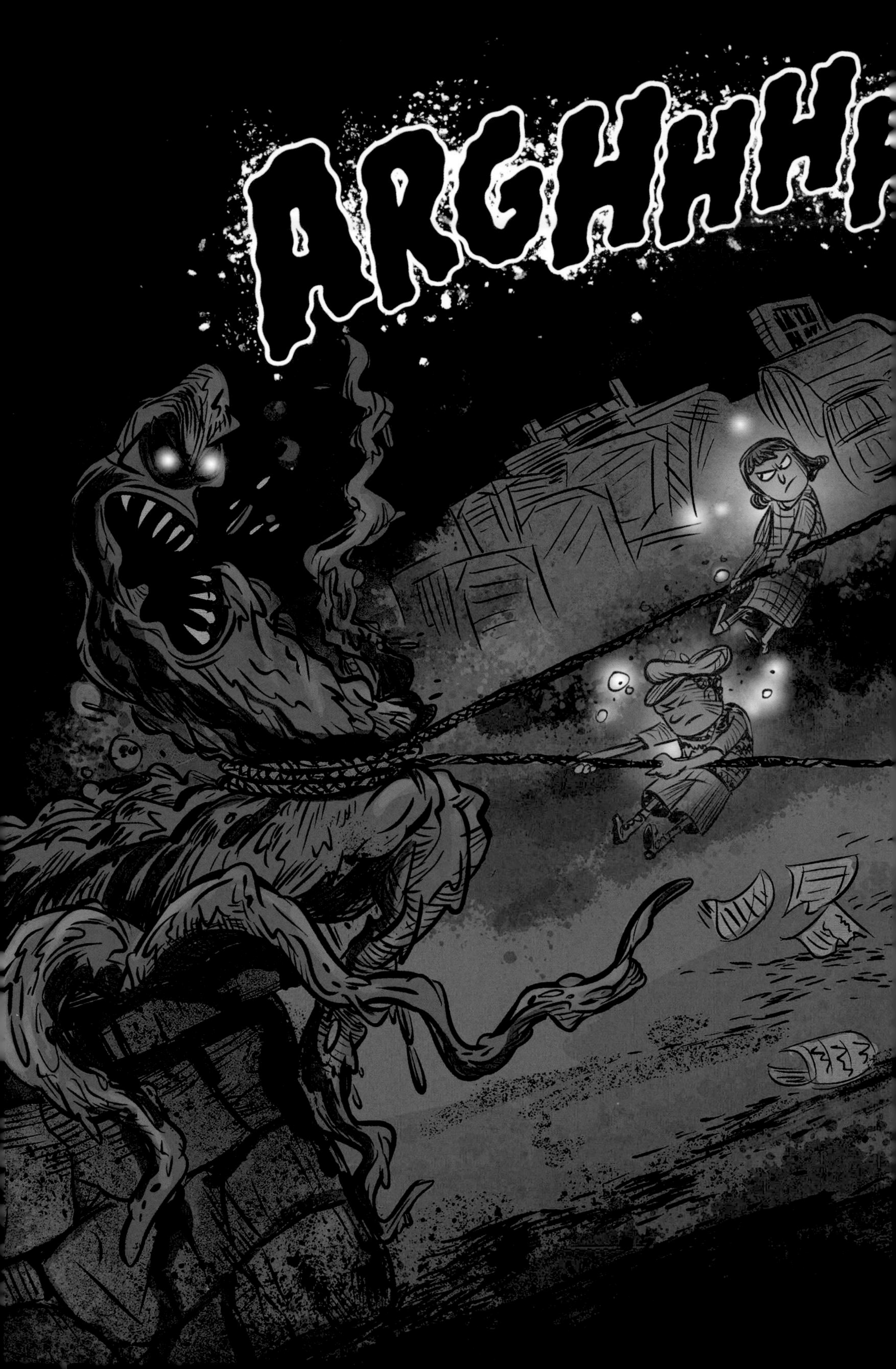
ARGHHH

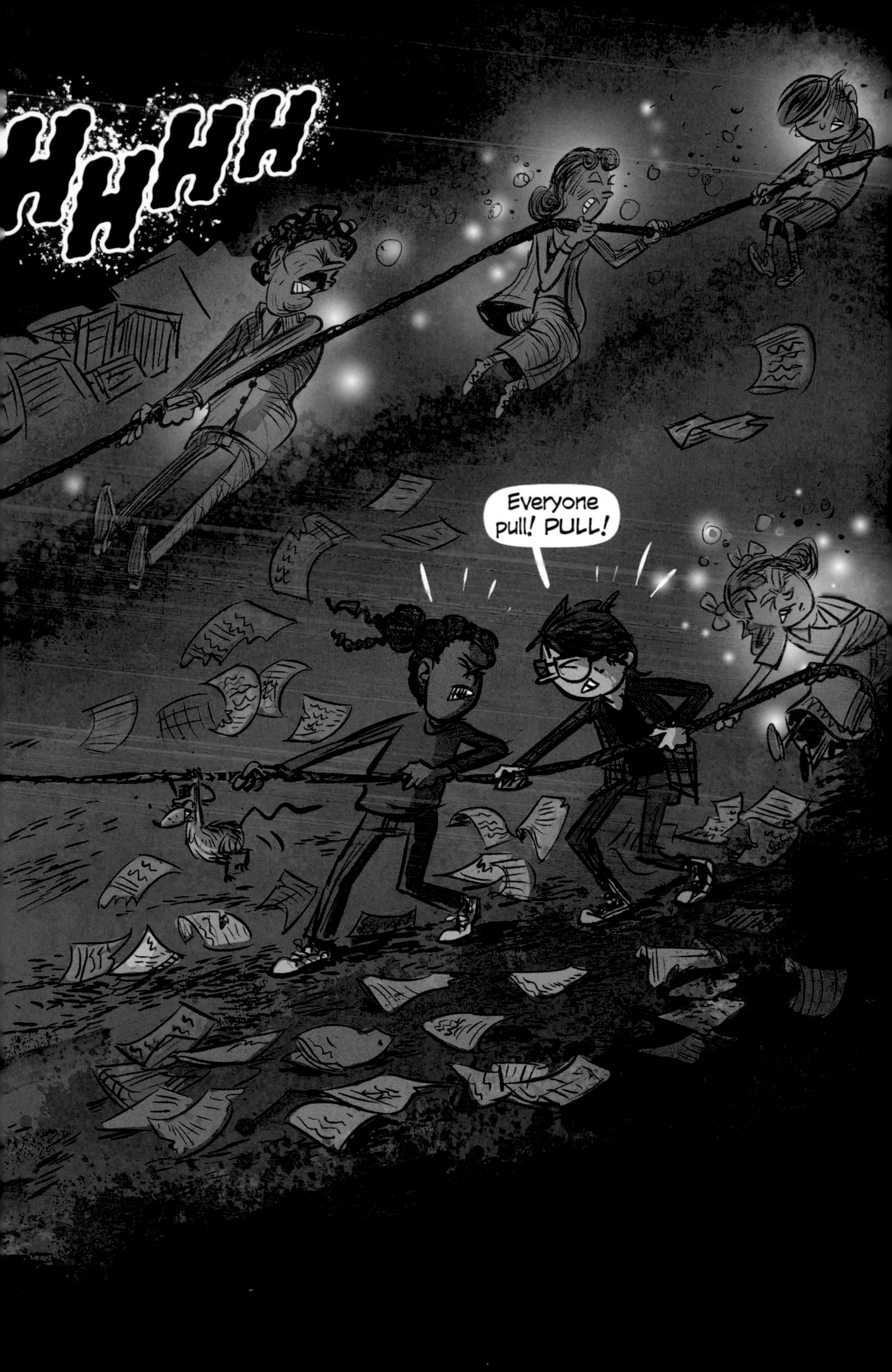
HHHHH
Everyone pull! PULL!

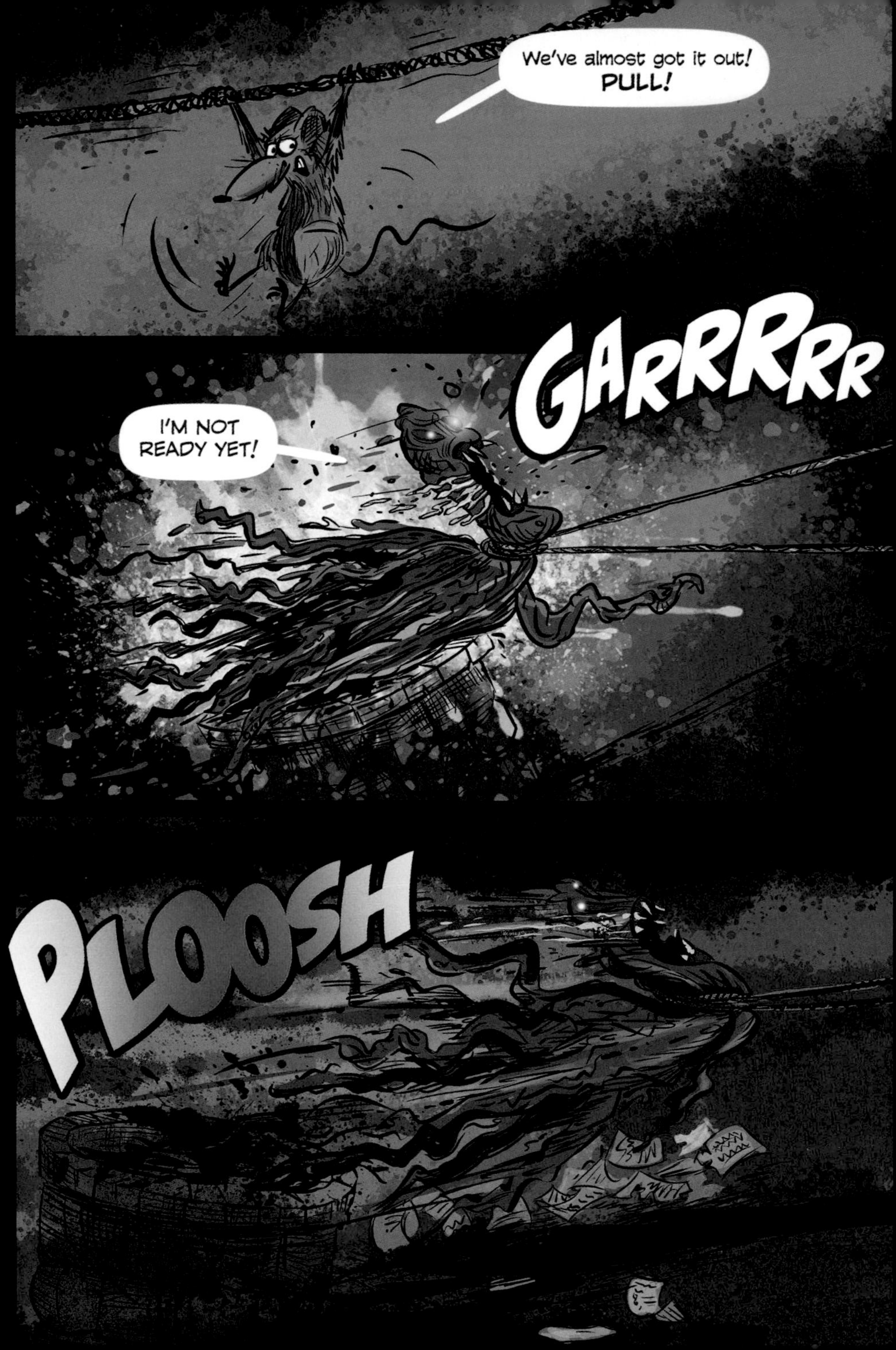
We've almost got it out! PULL!
GARRRRR
I'M NOT READY YET!
PLOOSH

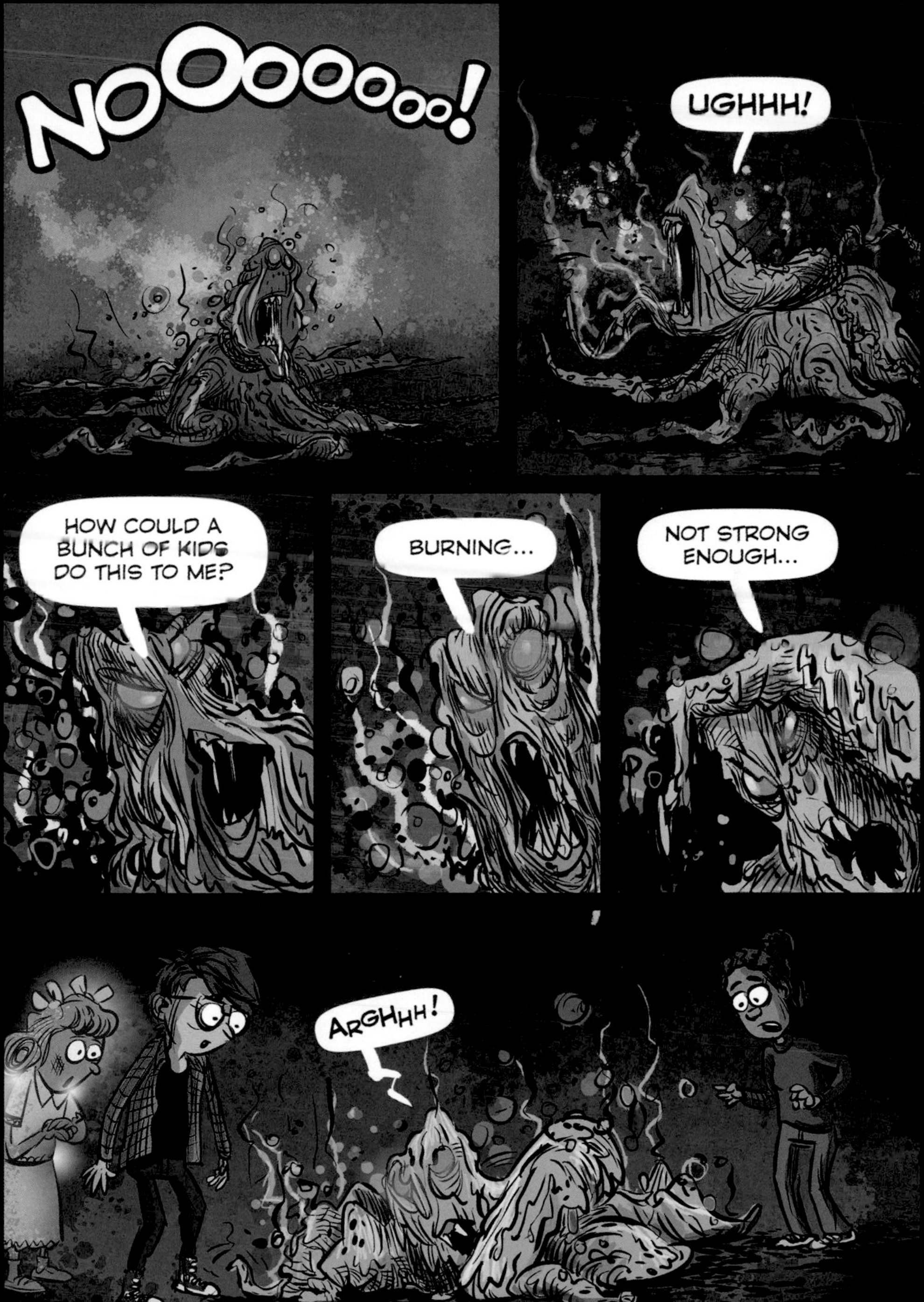
NOOOOOOO!
UGHHH!
HOW COULD A BUNCH OF KIDS DO THIS TO ME?
BURNING...
NOT STRONG ENOUGH...
ARGHHH!

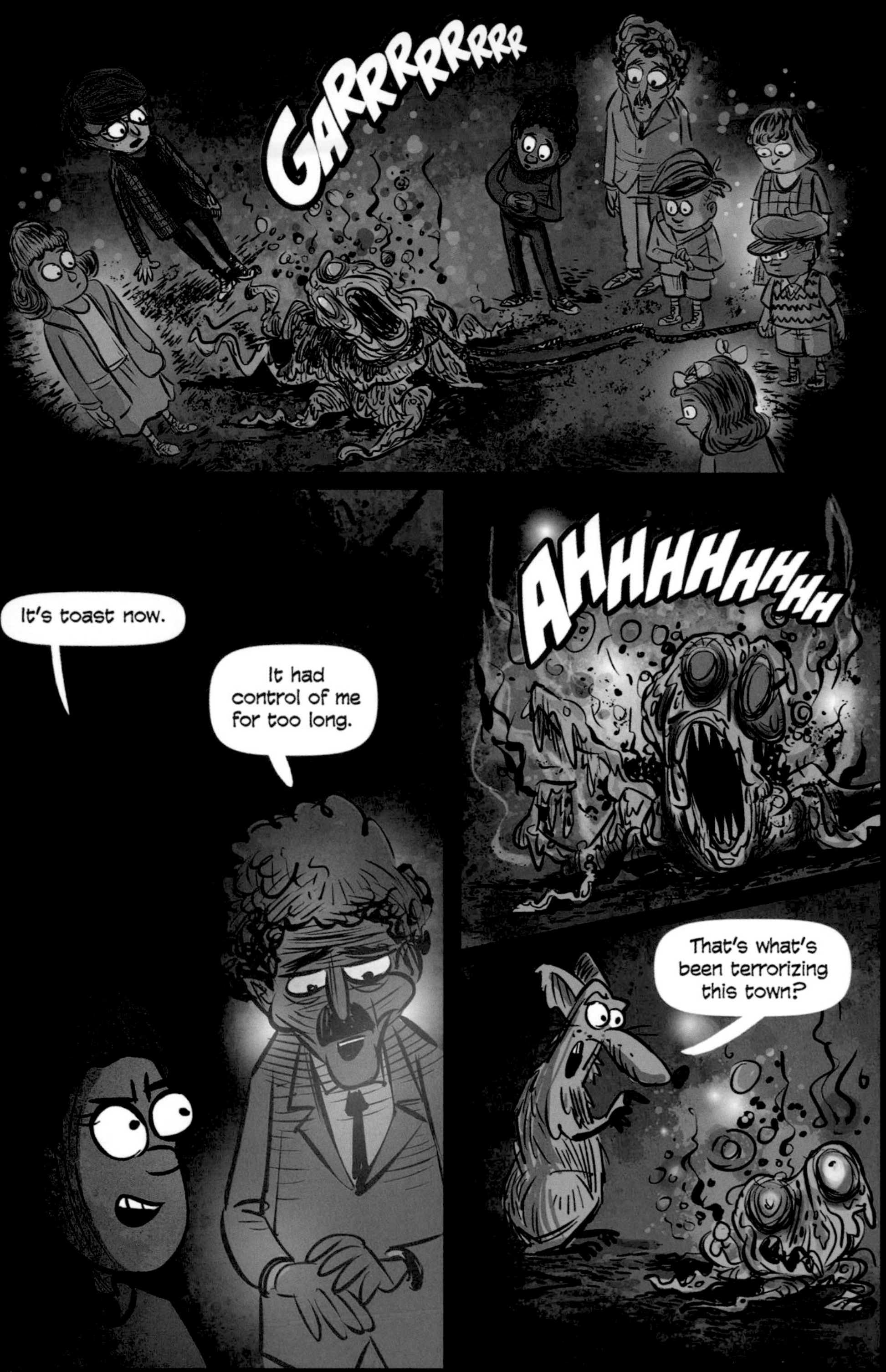
GARRRRRRR
It's toast now.
It had control of me for too long.
AHHHHHHHH
That's what's been terrorizing this town?

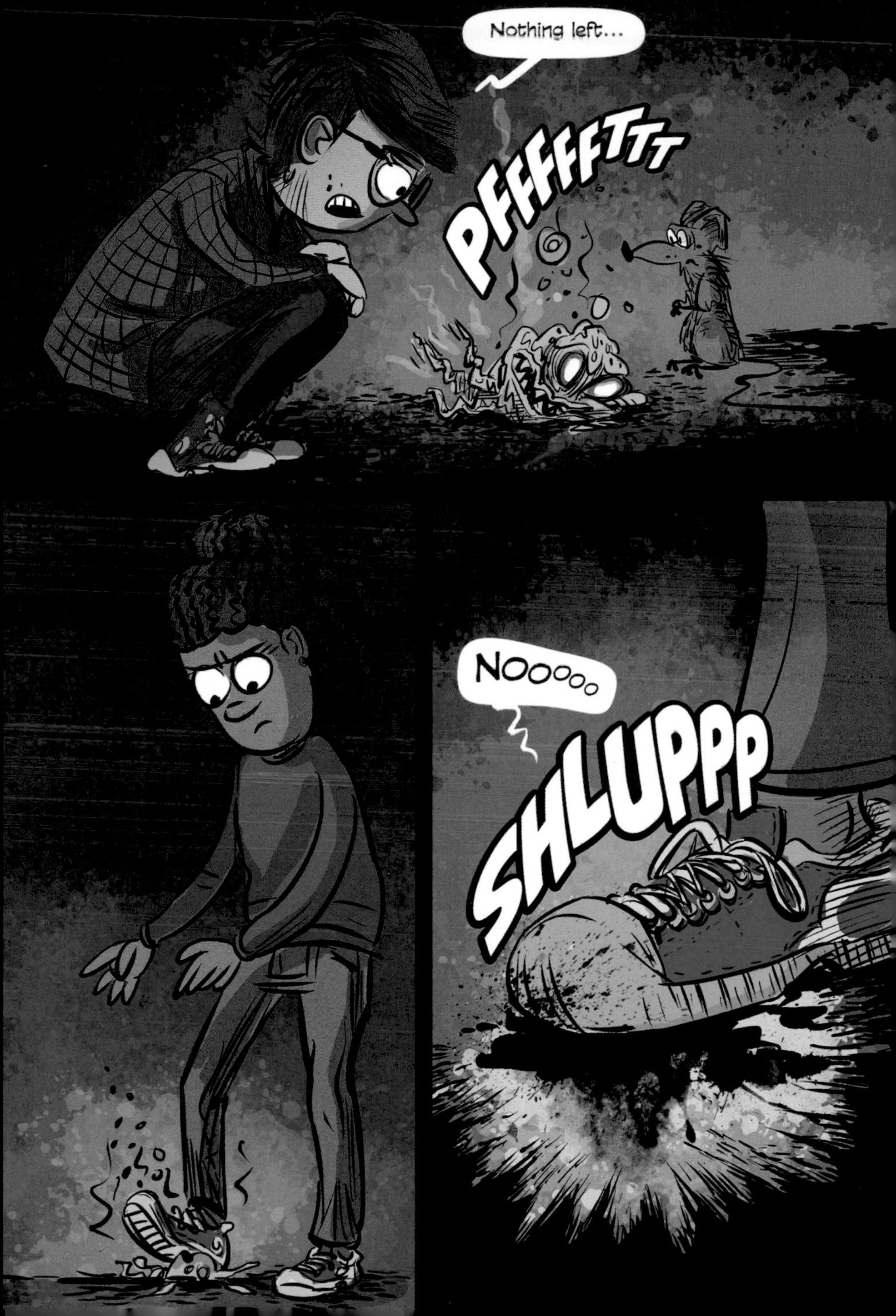
Nothing left...
PFFFFFTTTT
NOOOOO
SHLUPPP

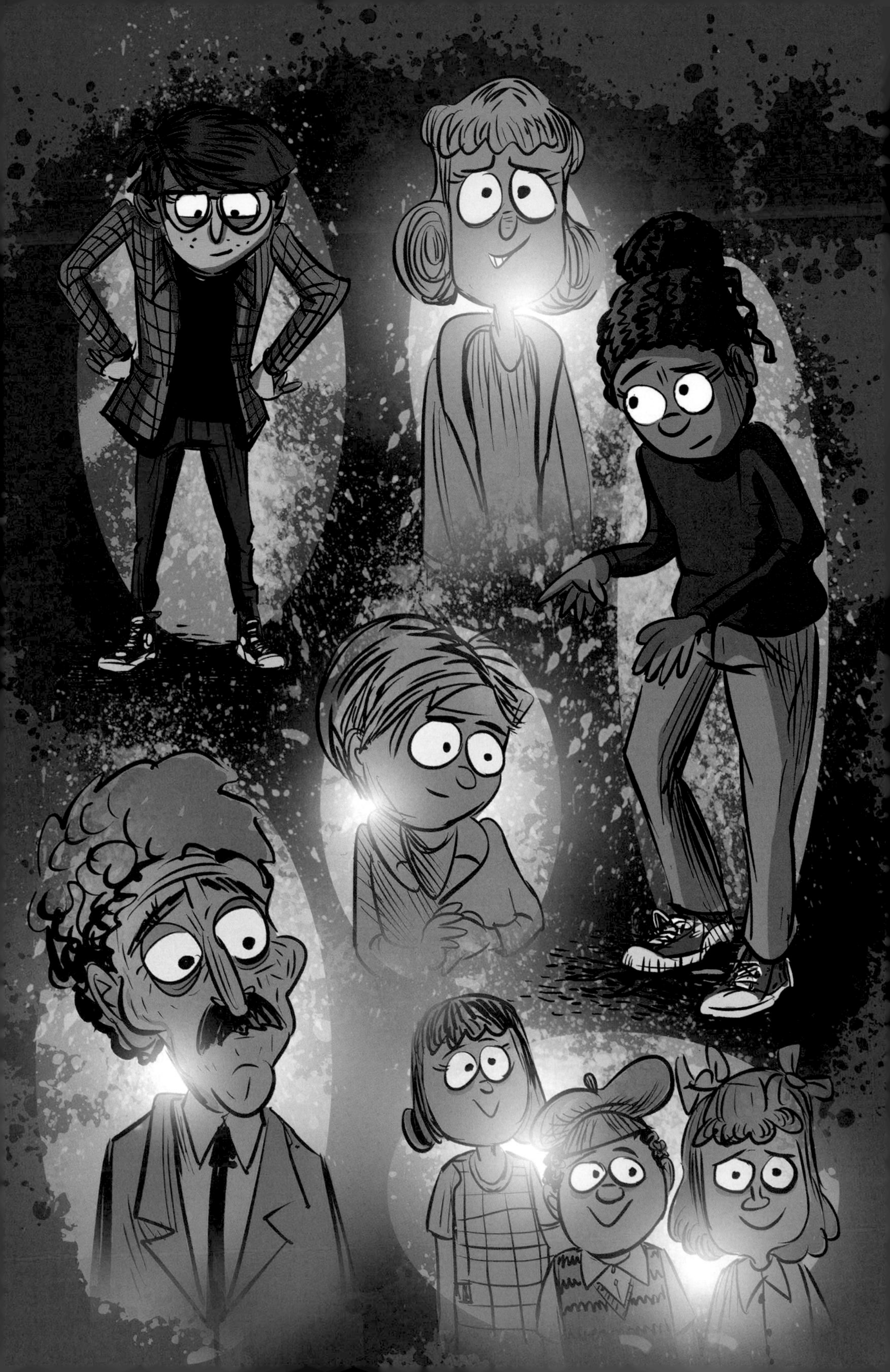

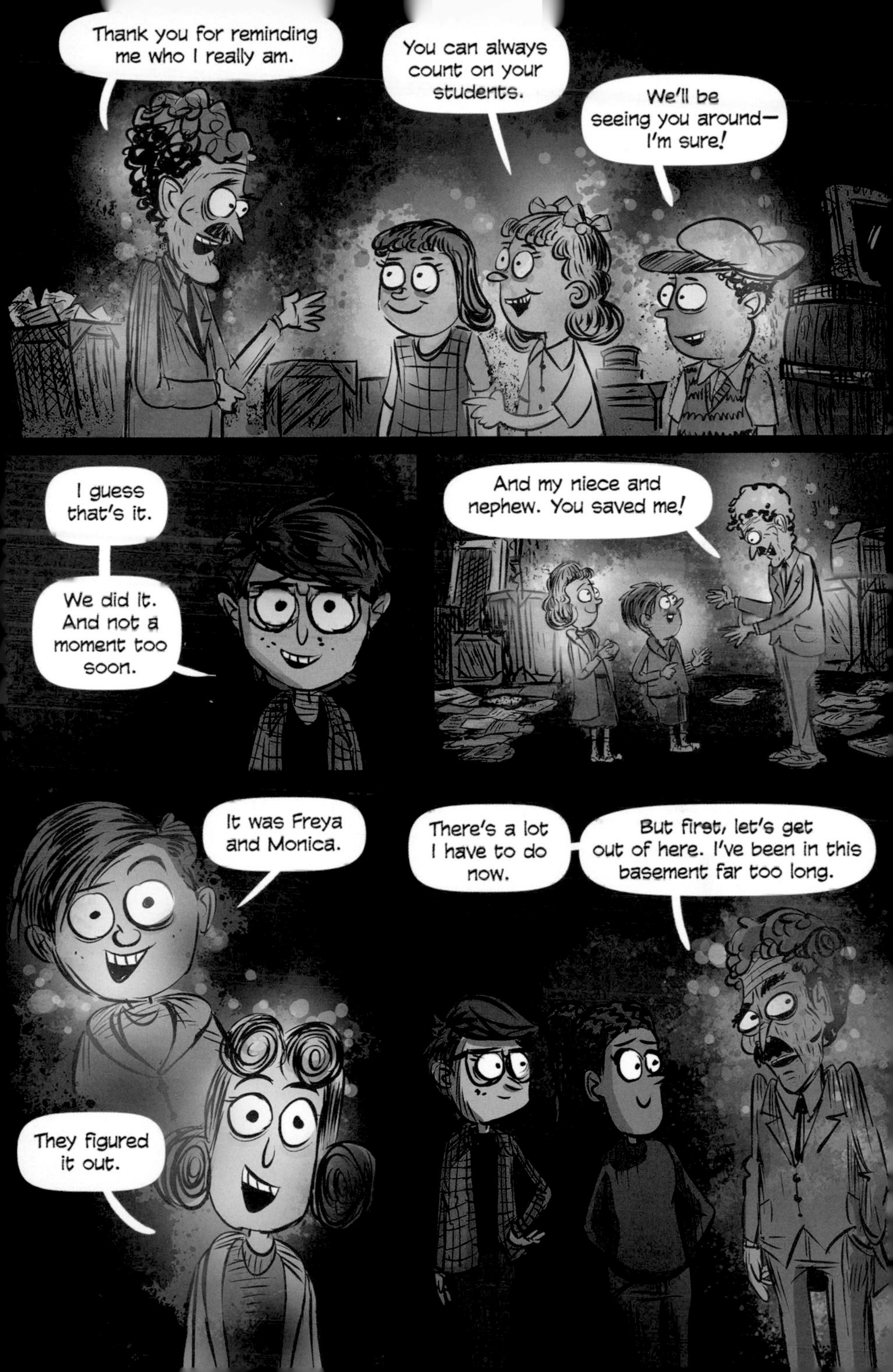
Thank you for reminding me who I really am.
You can always count on your students.
We'll be seeing you around— I'm sure!
I guess that's it.
We did it. And not a moment too soon.
And my niece and nephew. You saved me!
It was Freya and Monica.
They figured it out.
There's a lot I have to do now.
But first, let's get out of here. I've been in this basement far too long.

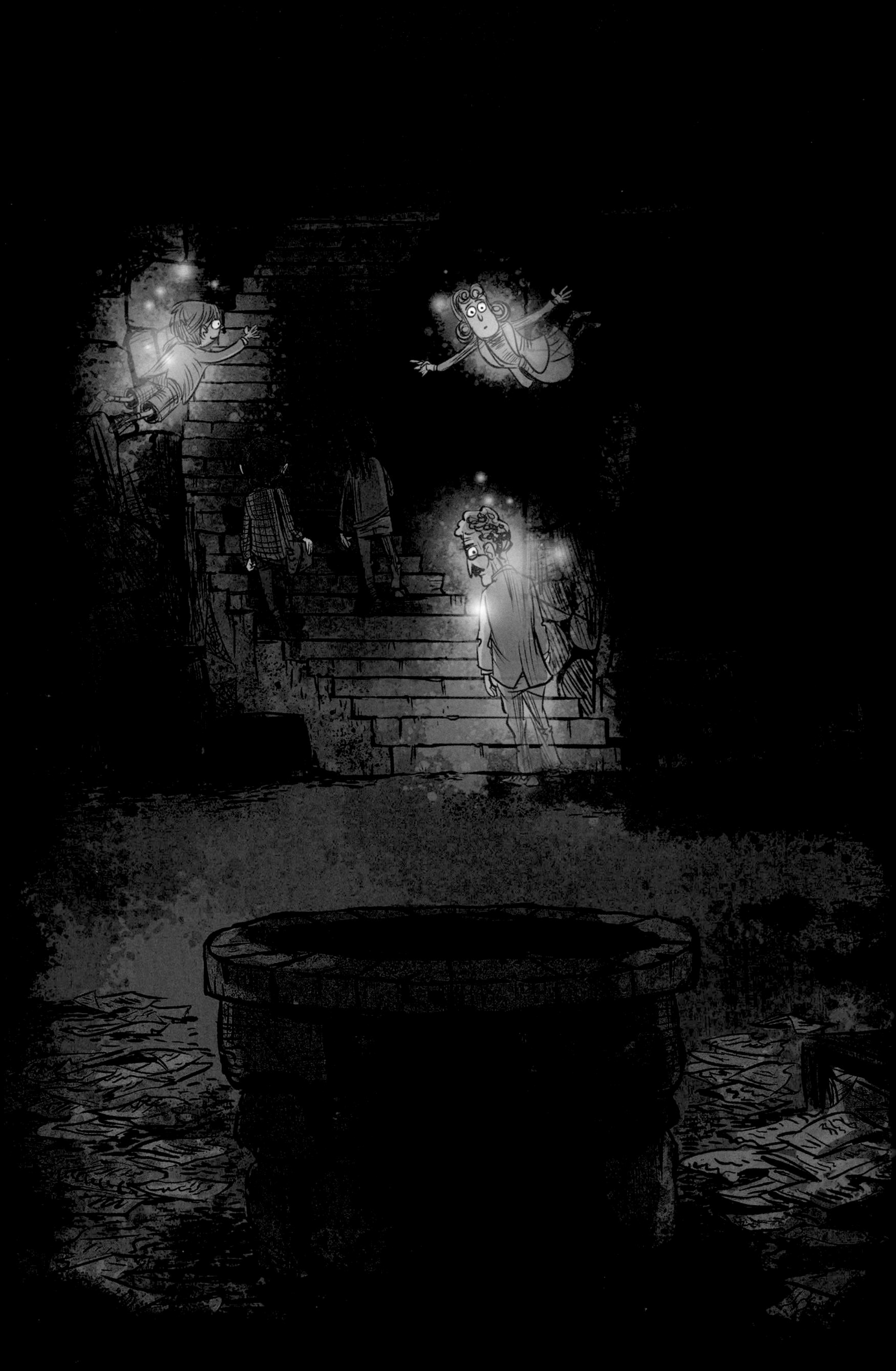

CHAPTER 10

Live the magic!
FERAL
ICE FISHING
So cold. It's just so cold here!
I don't know why anyone would
be out in this weather. Plus
I hear wolves howling at night,
but locals say there are no wolves.
Happy to get home.
- Kirk
Jonathan Hull
Seaside Ave
Torrance, CA

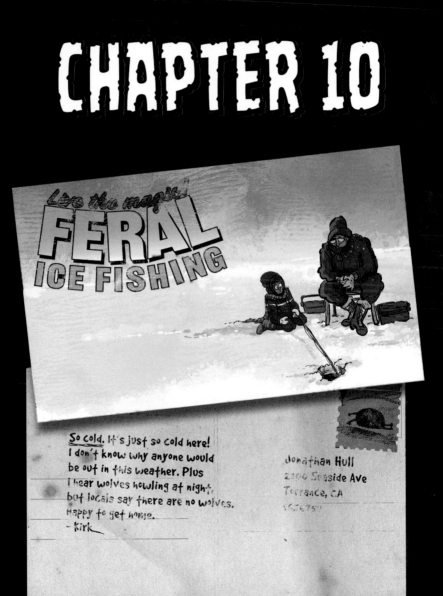

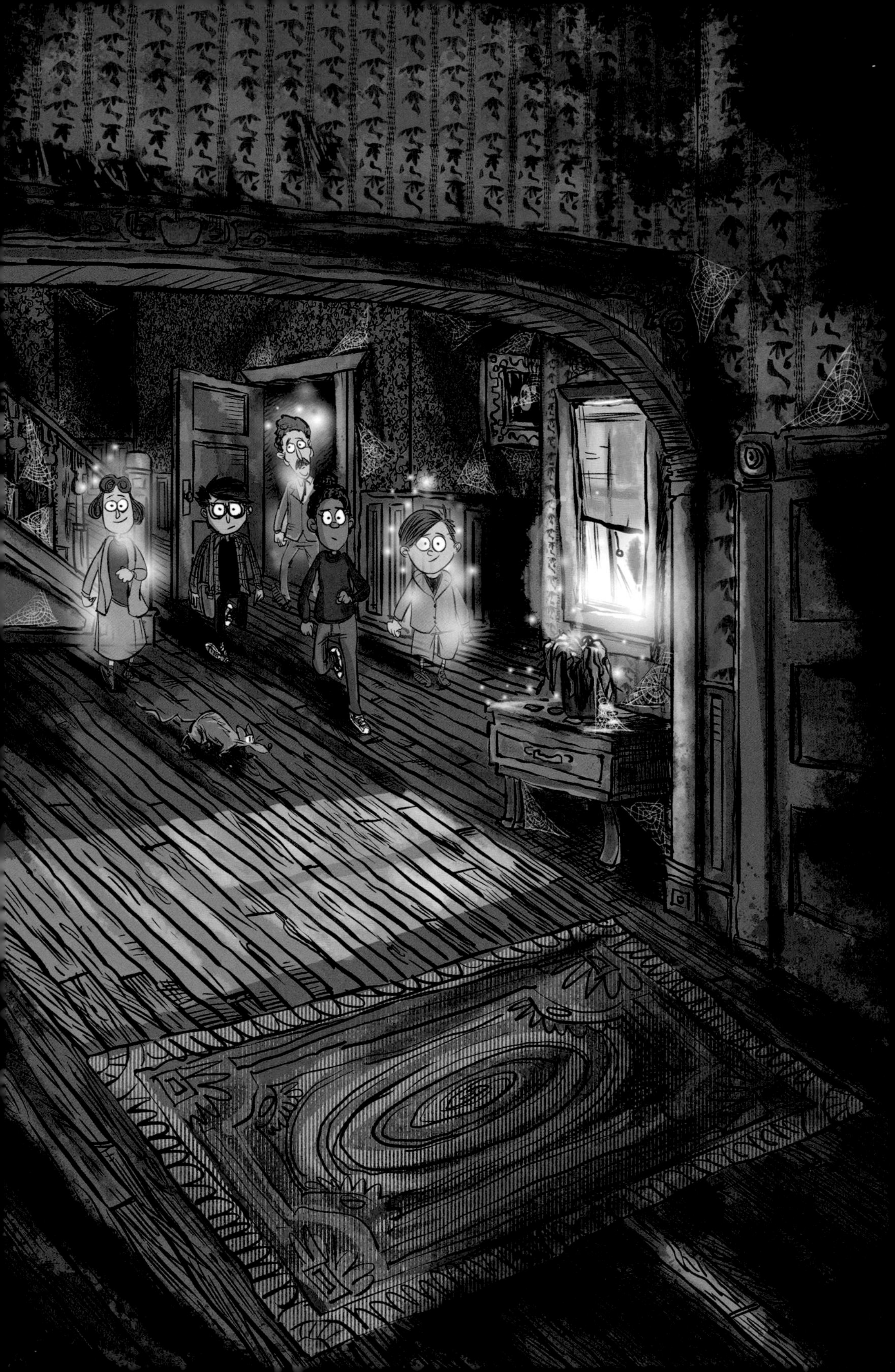

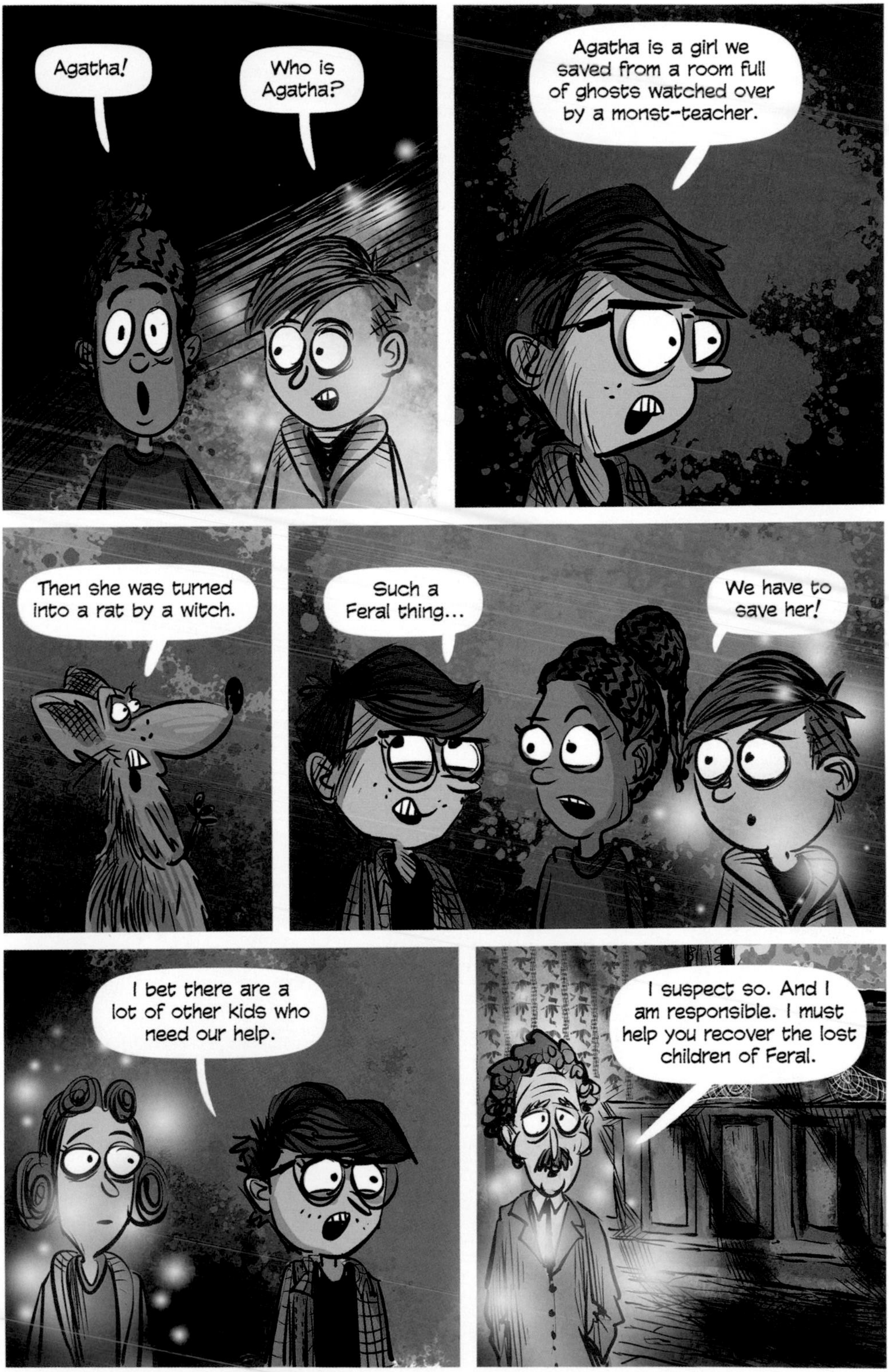
Agatha!
Who is Agatha?
Agatha is a girl we saved from a room full of ghosts watched over by a monst-teacher.
Then she was turned into a rat by a witch.
Such a Feral thing...
We have to save her!
I bet there are a lot of other kids who need our help.
I suspect so. And I am responsible. I must help you recover the lost children of Feral.

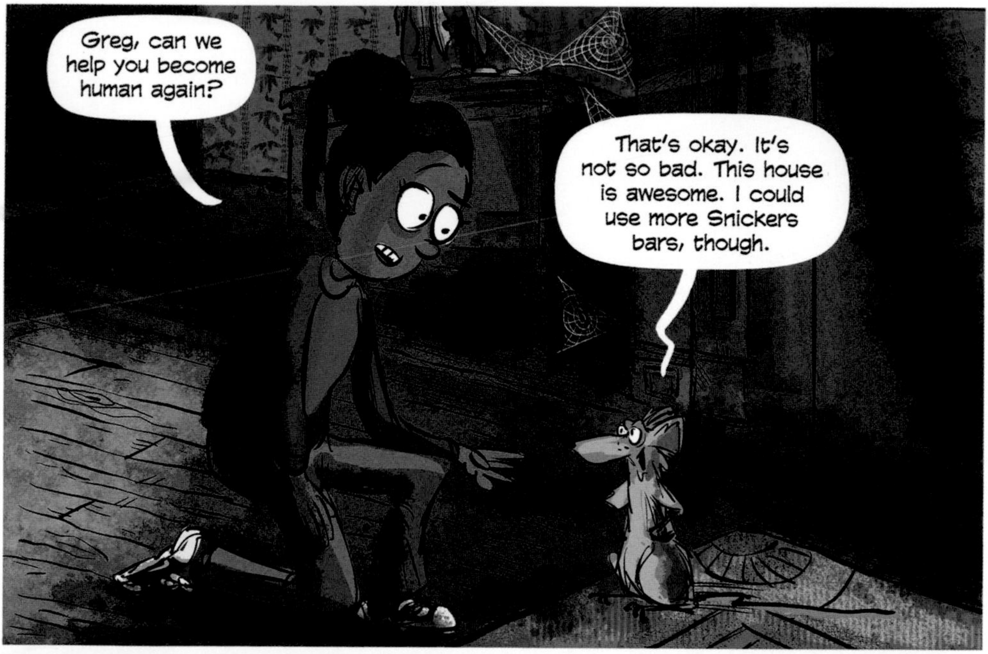
Greg, can we help you become human again?
That's okay. It's not so bad. This house is awesome. I could use more Snickers bars, though.

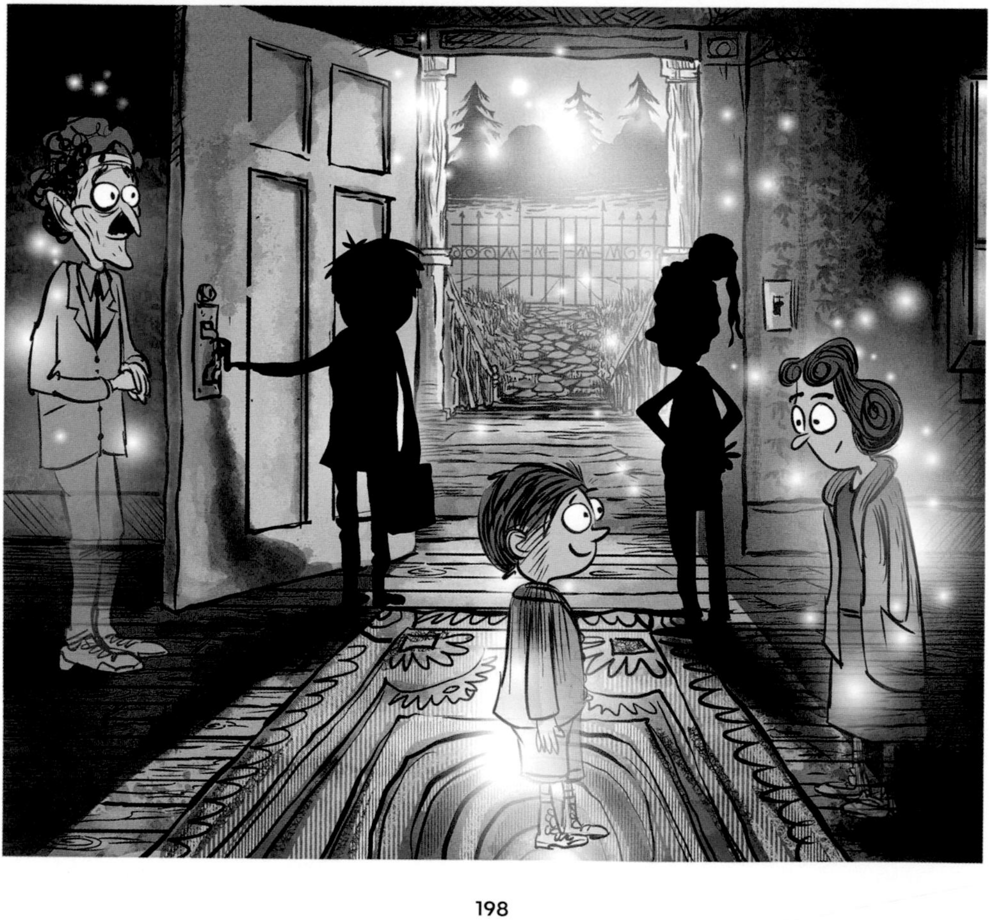

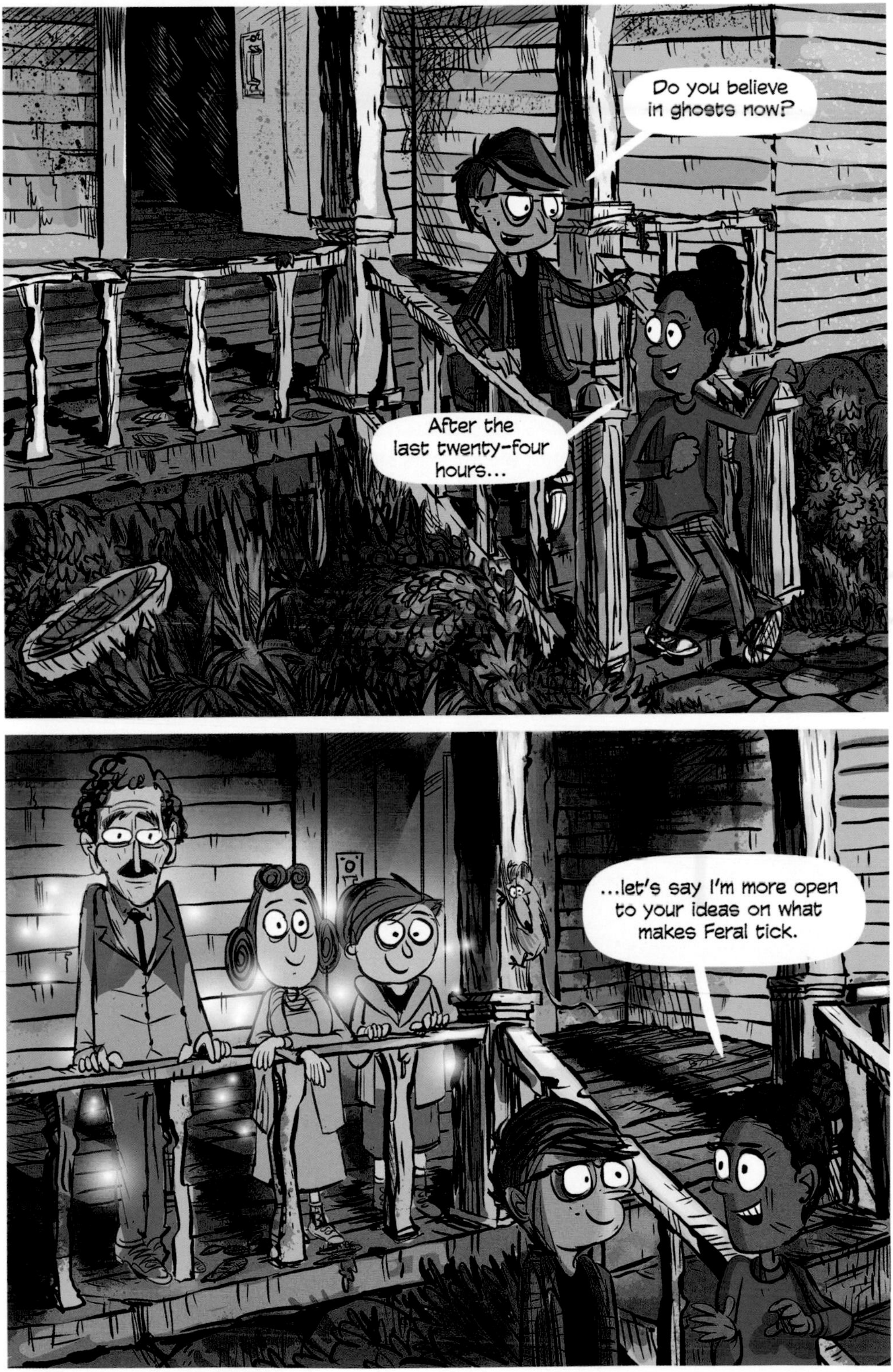
Do you believe in ghosts now?
After the last twenty-four hours...
...let's say I'm more open to your ideas on what makes Feral tick.

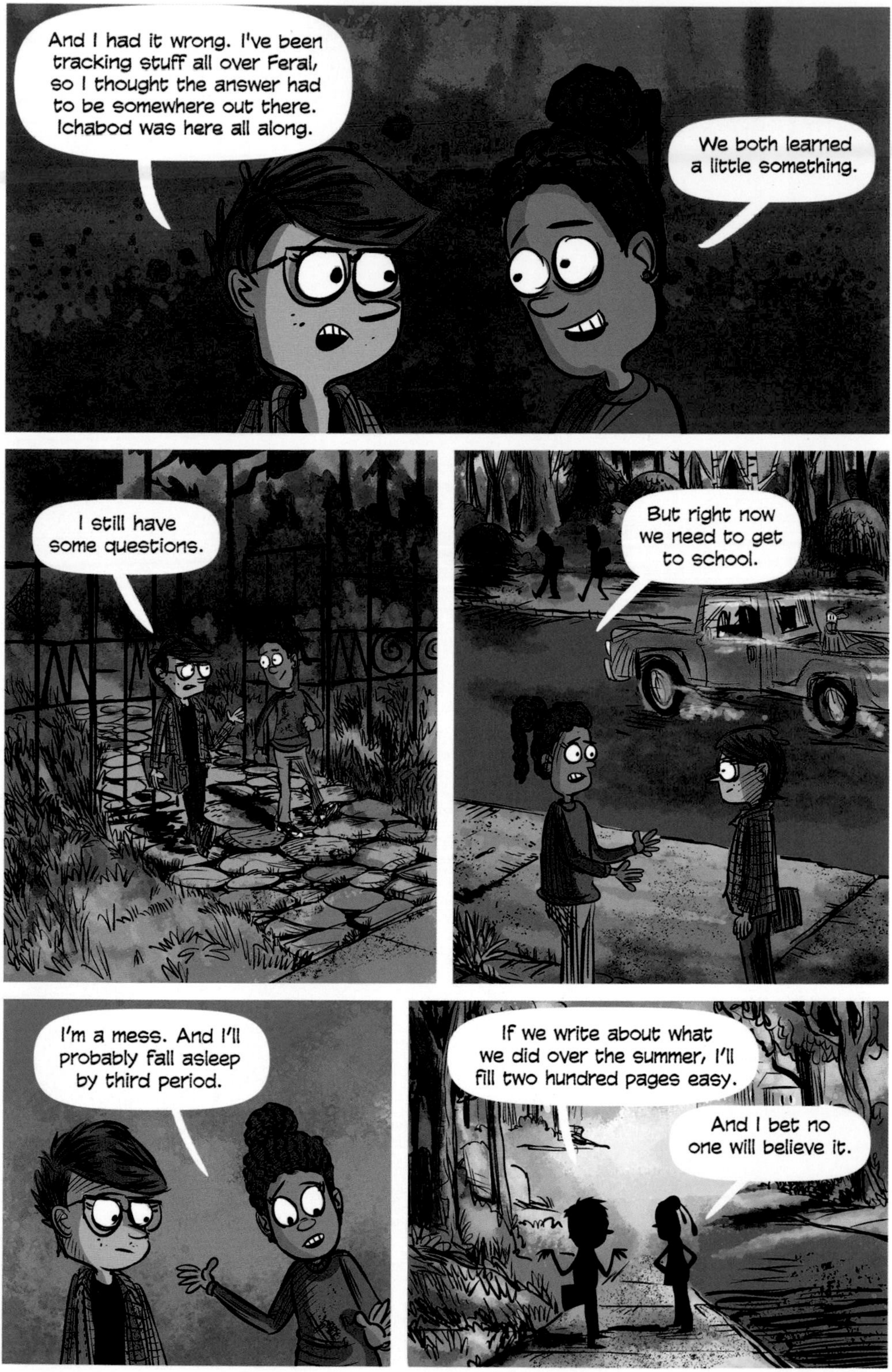
And I had it wrong. I've been tracking stuff all over Feral, so I thought the answer had to be somewhere out there. Ichabod was here all along.
We both learned a little something.
I still have some questions.
But right now we need to get to school.
I'm a mess. And I'll probably fall asleep by third period.
If we write about what we did over the summer, I'll fill two hundred pages easy.
And I bet no one will believe it.

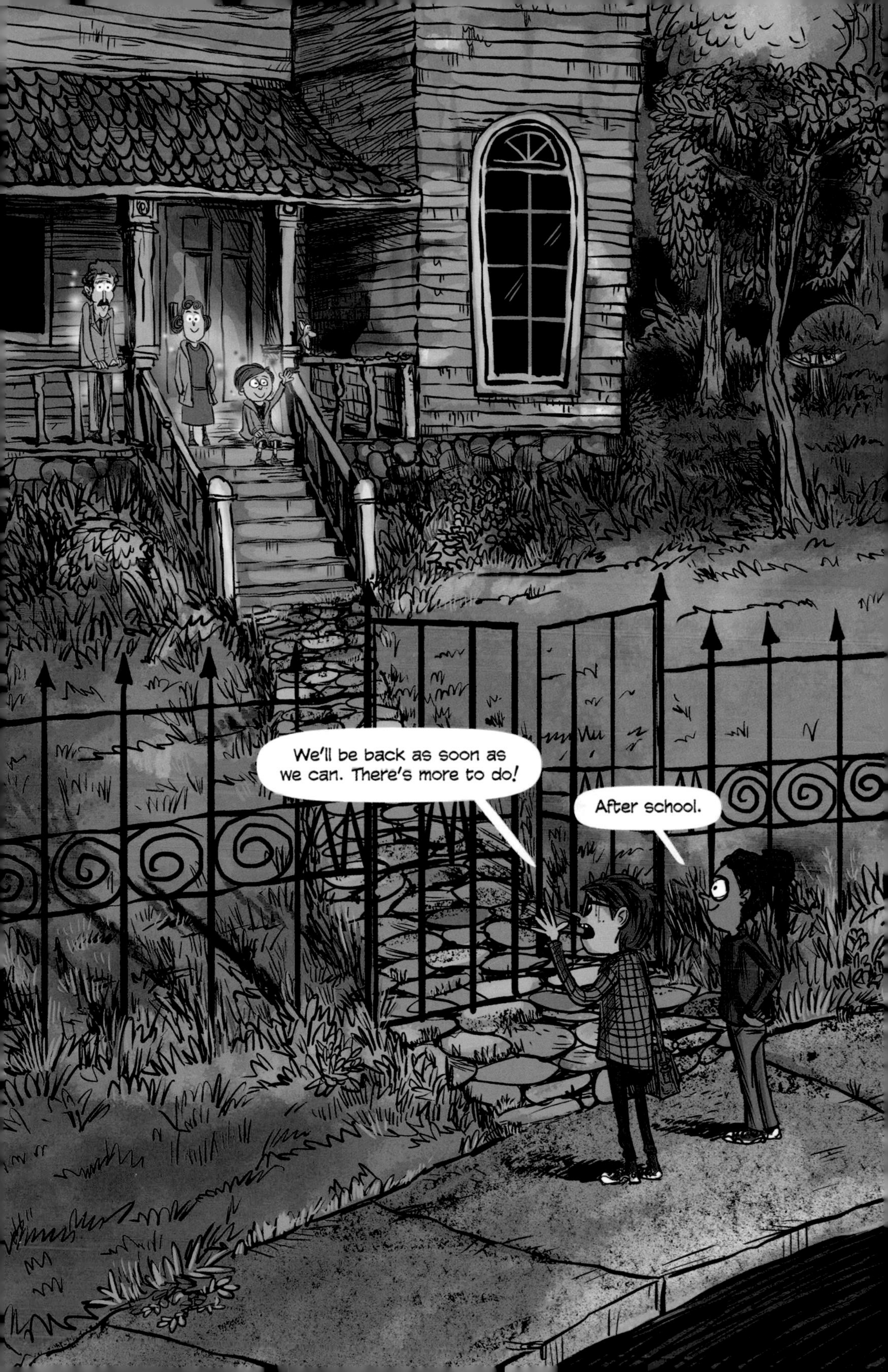
We'll be back as soon as we can. There's more to do!
After school.

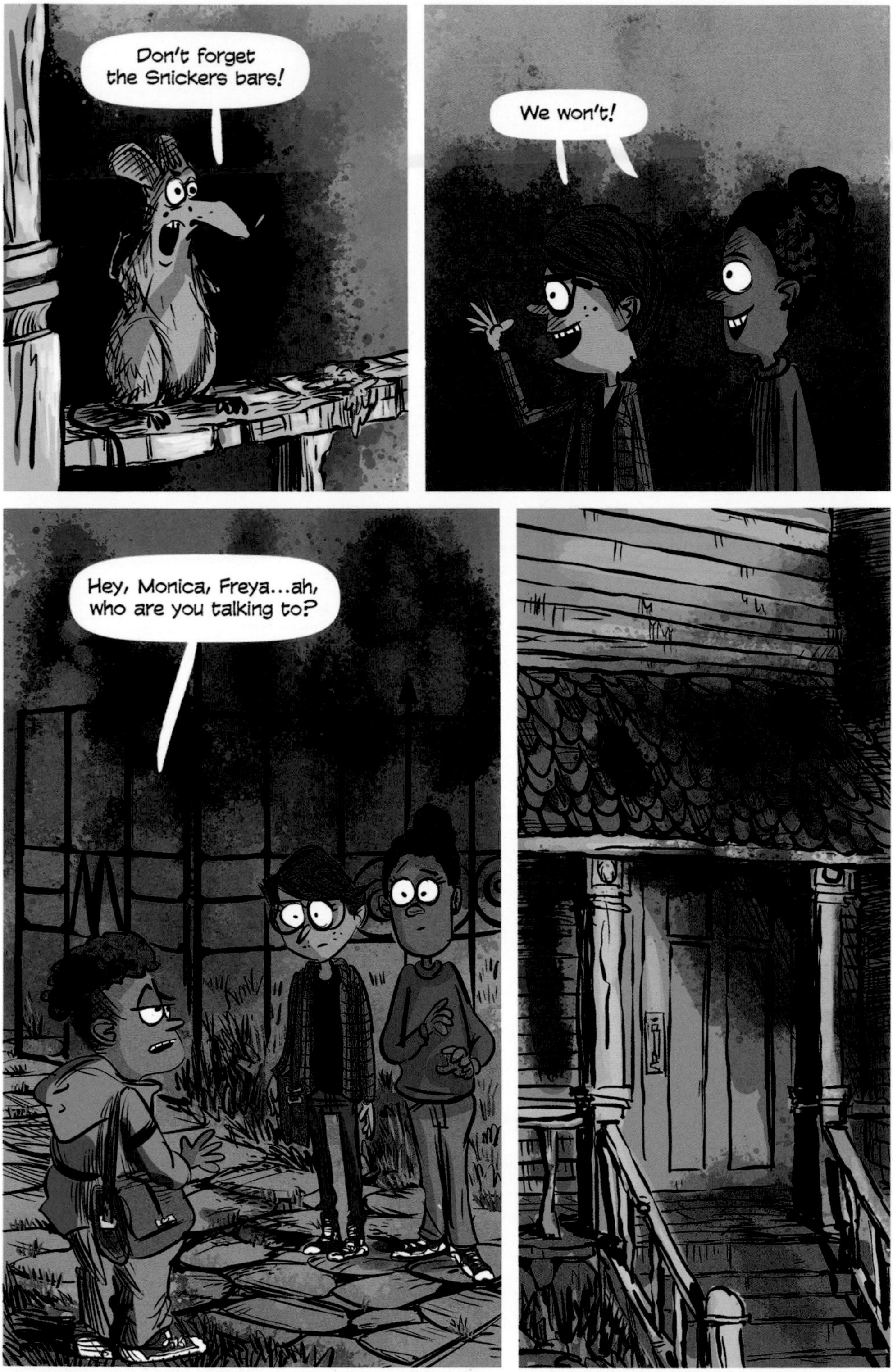
Don't forget the Snickers bars!
We won't!
Hey, Monica, Freya...ah, who are you talking to?

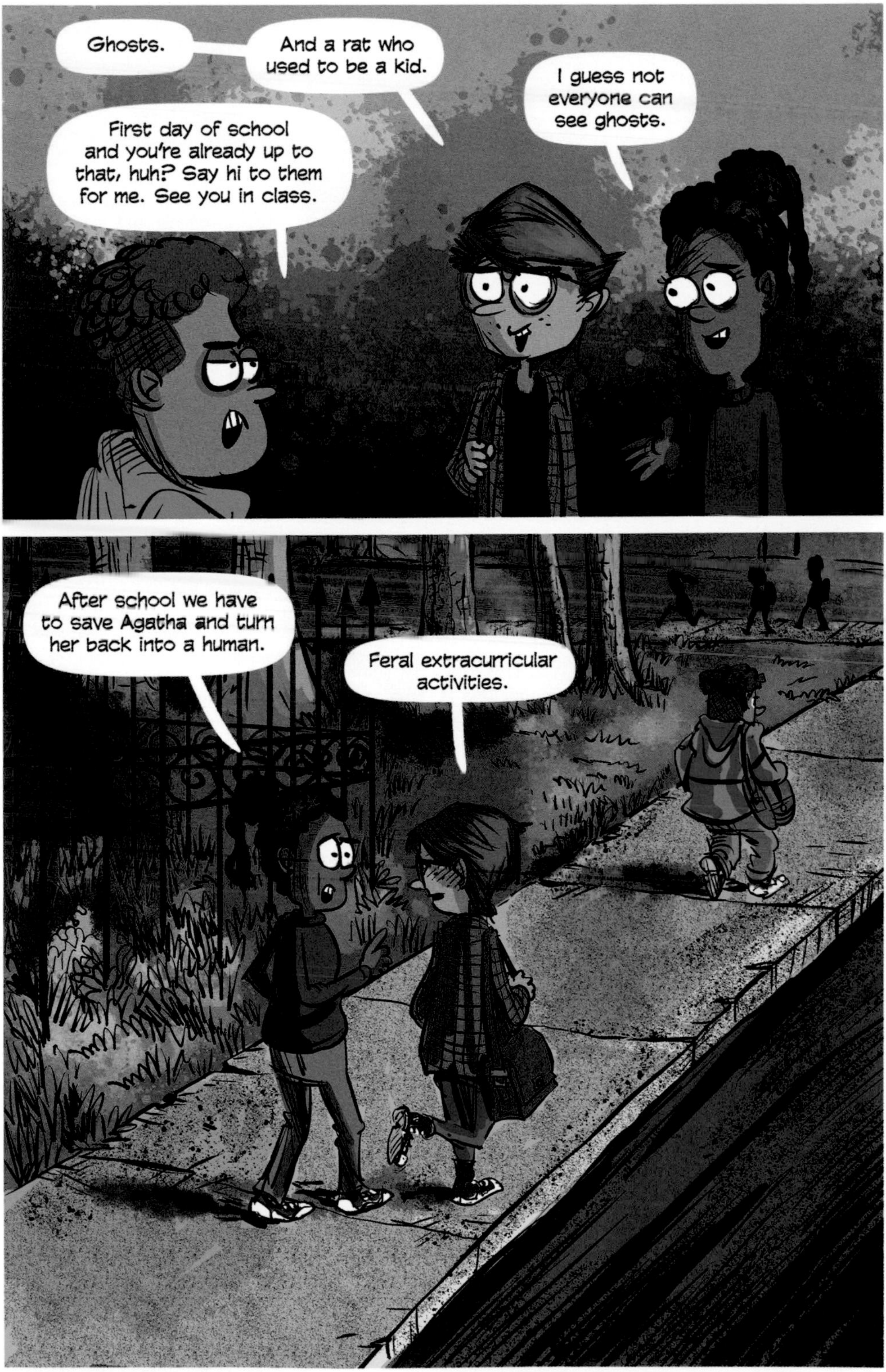
Ghosts.
And a rat who used to be a kid.
I guess not everyone can see ghosts.
First day of school and you're already up to that, huh? Say hi to them for me. See you in class.
After school we have to save Agatha and turn her back into a human.
Feral extracurricular activities.

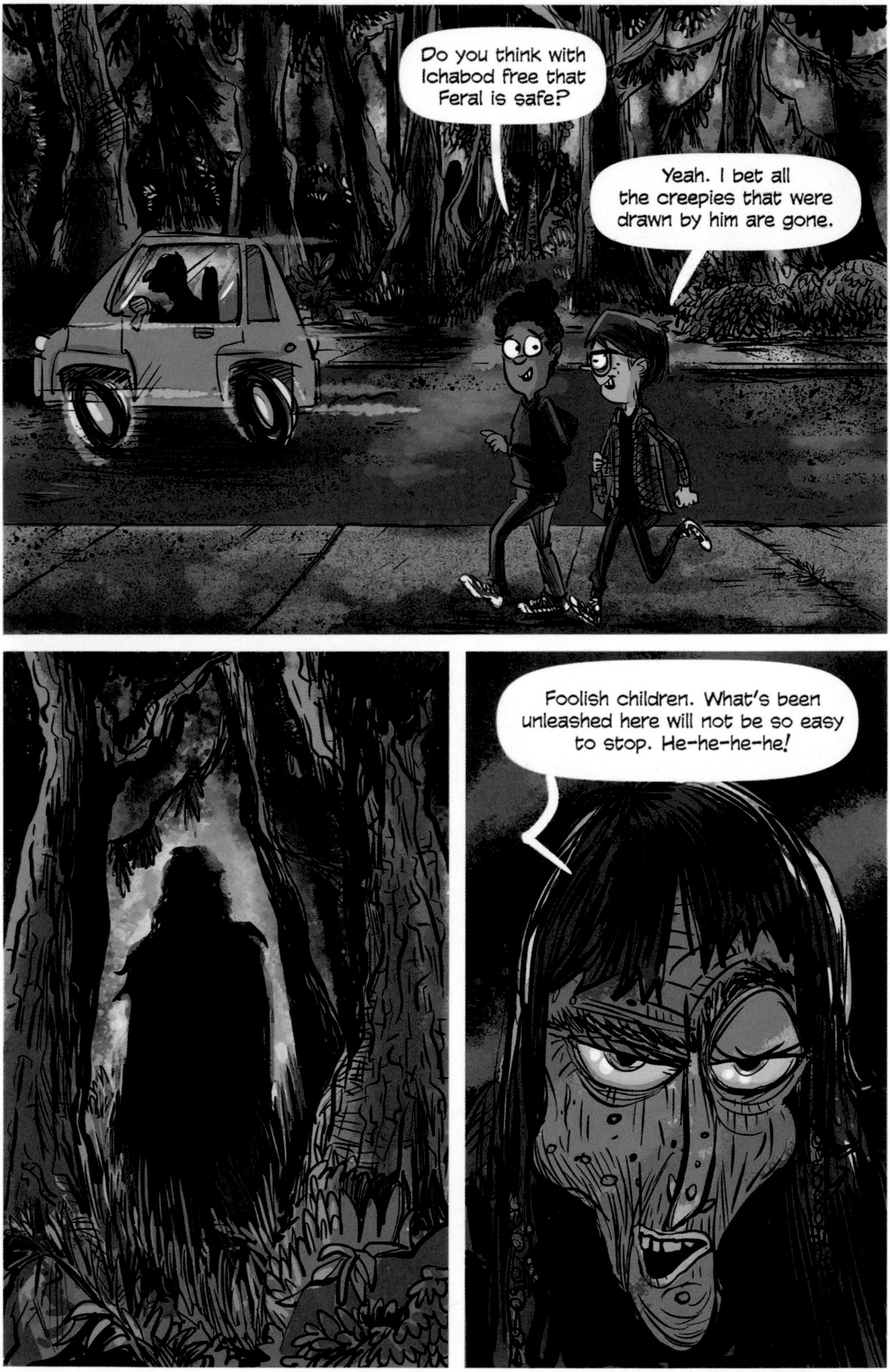
Do you think with Ichabod free that Feral is safe?
Yeah. I bet all the creepies that were drawn by him are gone.
Foolish children. What's been unleashed here will not be so easy to stop. He-he-he-he!

Being a rat rules! No book reports, no bedtime. I'm ready to get some revenge for myself.
Let's get busy, Agatha. Feral doesn't know what it has coming.

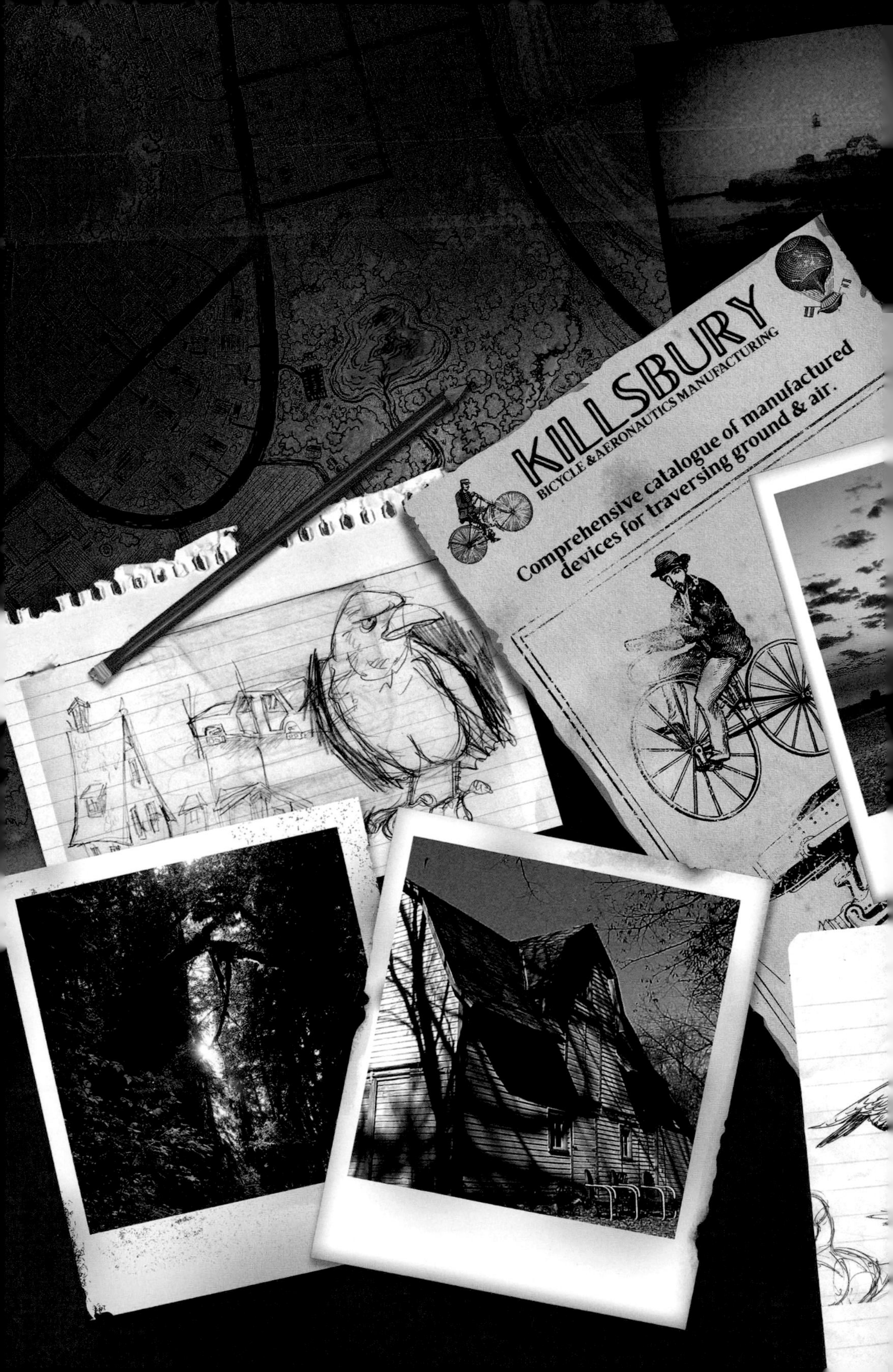
KILLSBURY
BICYCLE & AERONAUTICS MANUFACTURING
Comprehensive catalogue of manufactured devices for traversing ground & air.

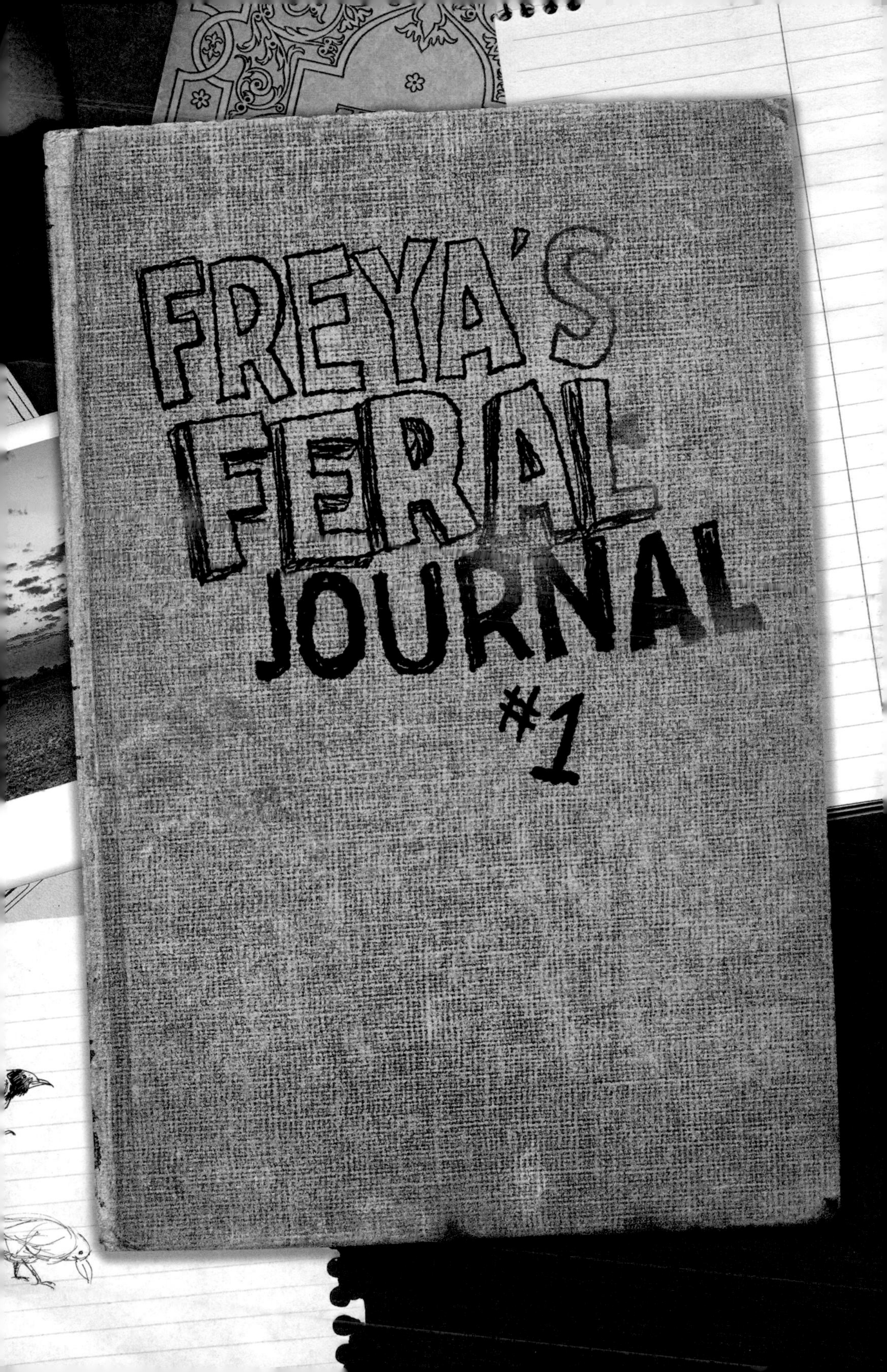
FREYA'S
FERAL
JOURNAL
#1

BABYSITTER NEEDED

Must be comfortable with dogs, cats, bats...other wild animals.

Can't be afraid of the dark.

Can't be afraid of anything...

Good with creatures and children that bite.

Won't fall asleep waiting up for us to return. It's not...safe.

On full moon nights, keep all doors and windows locked. Never go outside.

Take a number. Call after midnight.

986-663   985-663   984-663   983-663   983

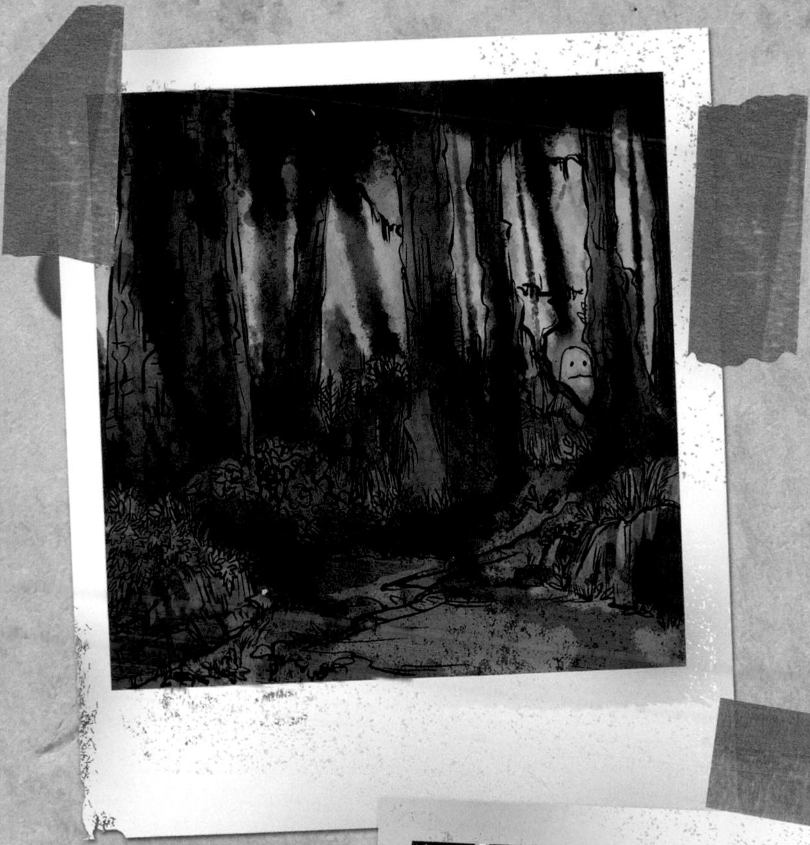

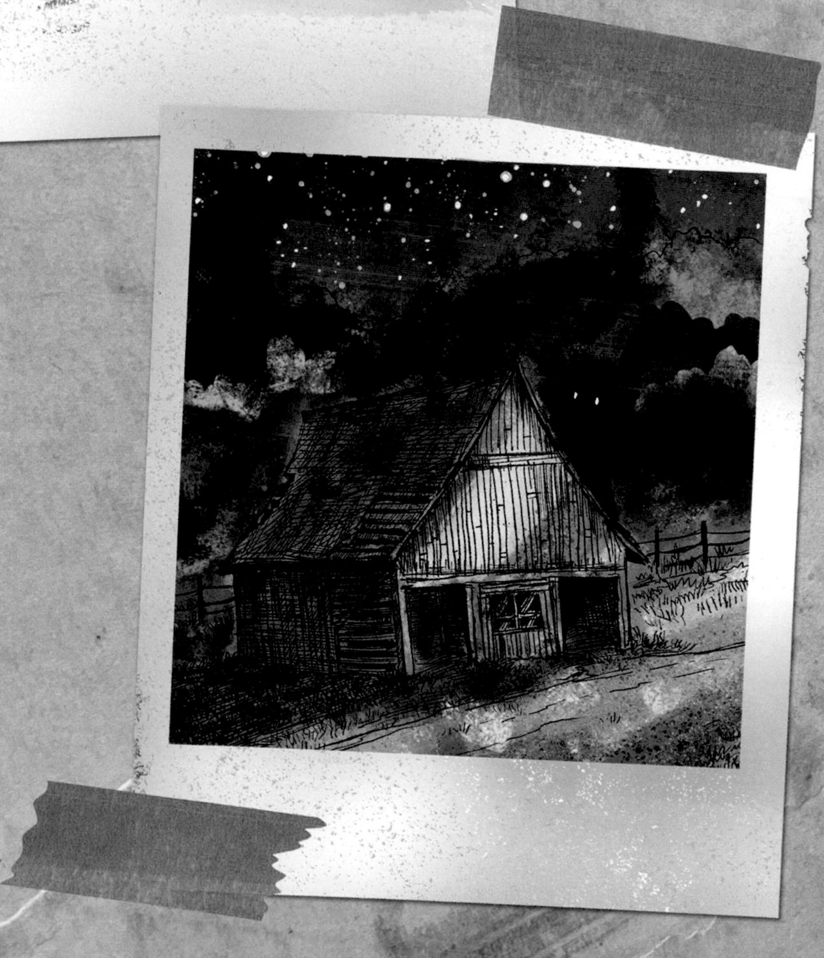

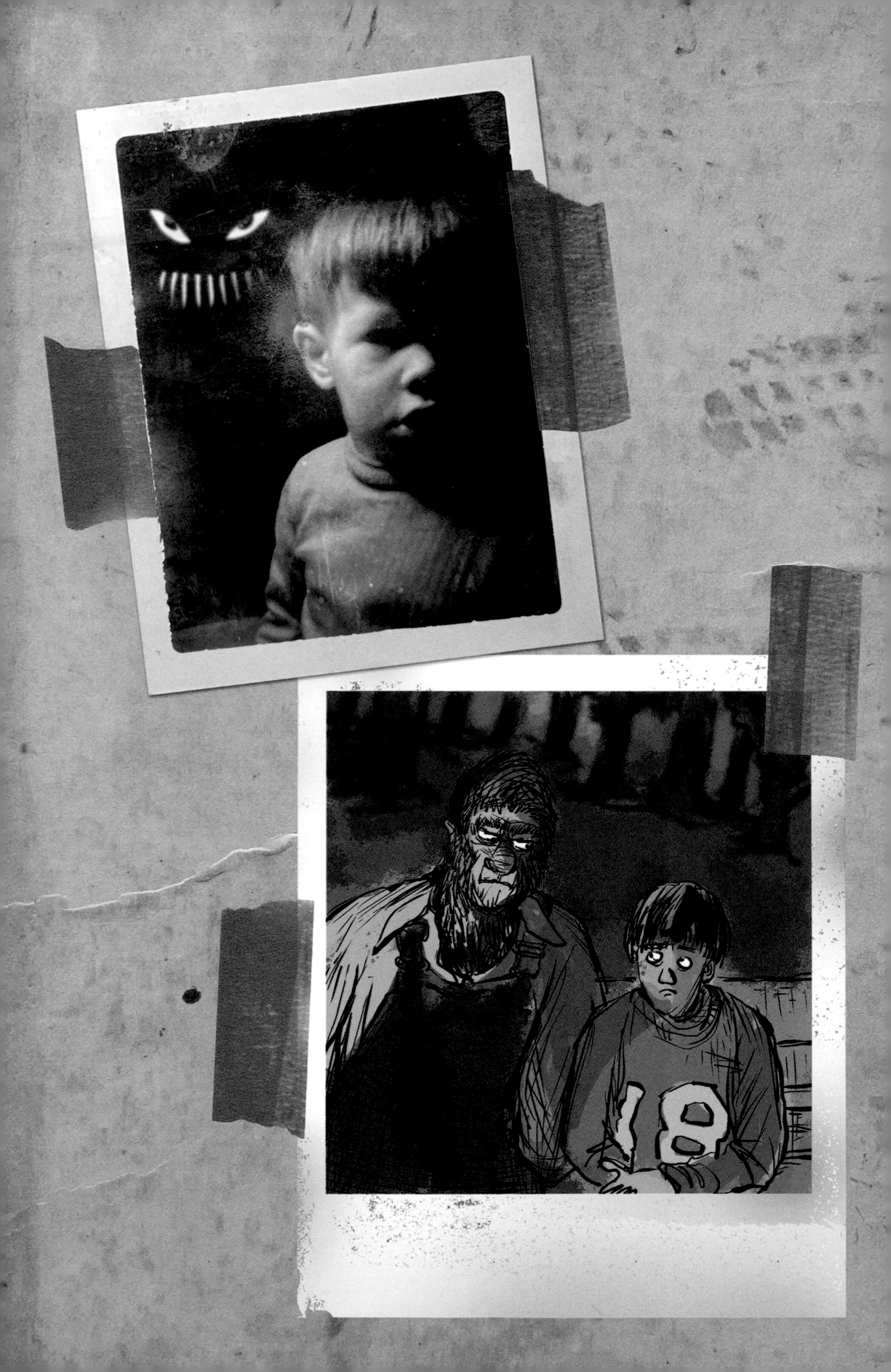
18

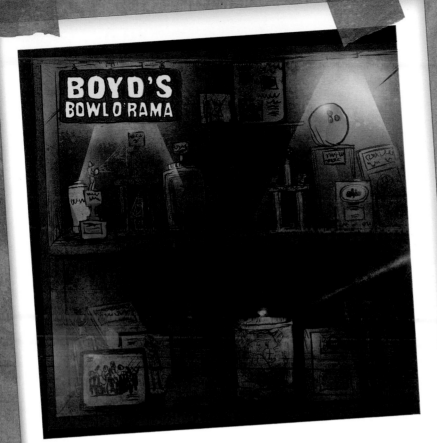

Feral
By Kaya Patel
FERAL COURIER DISPATCH STAFF WRITER

Boyd's Bowl O'Rama is in the news again. For many years, there were whispers in town that the trophy case at the popular bowling alley held more than just trophies and memorabilia. Many said that on certain nights, at specific times, strange things occurred at the bowling alley.

Now a photo by a local, who asked that their name not be used, has drawn attention to the family-friendly bowling alley once again.

The photo has since gone missing, but this reporter got a quick look, and I believe it was some sort of gag gone wrong.

For many years, tales have circulated about the recognizable sounds of bowling going on when the alley was closed.

Numerous times, the current owner was awoken from sleep by Constable Jahnson to open up the bowling alley well past closing because commotion was heard coming from inside. Never has anyone been found in the alley after hours.

Several students from the local middle school have claimed they saw a long line of people going into the bowling alley well past midnight. But again, this has never been proven.

I won't go into gruesome detail in a family publication, but the photo purported to show a human head in a jar. The head of none other than Boyd Brentson, the long-missing original owner of the bowling alley.

Is it just another Feral prank? This reporter thinks so. But with the photo missing, it looks to become just another odd tale for which Feral is well-known.

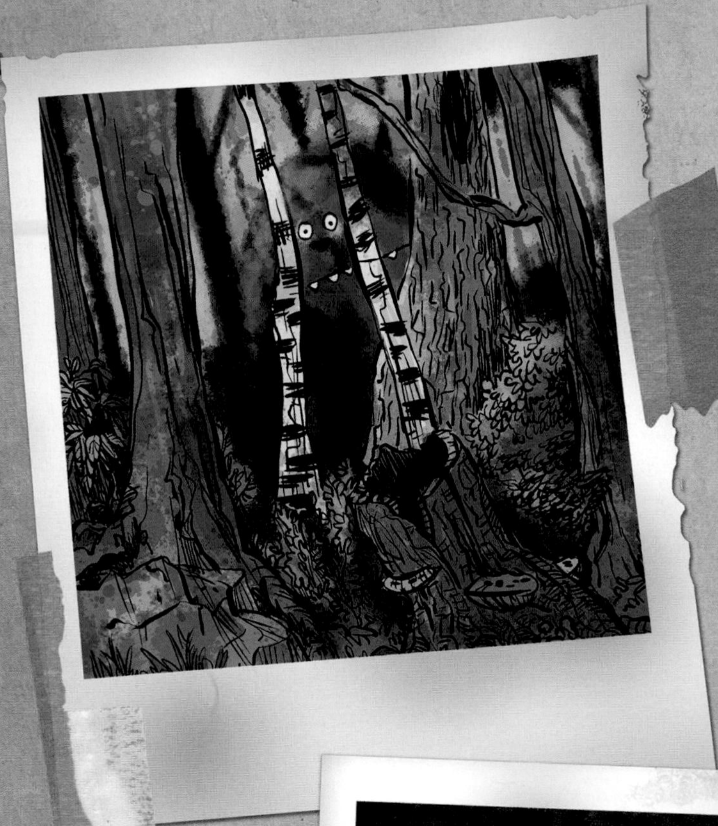

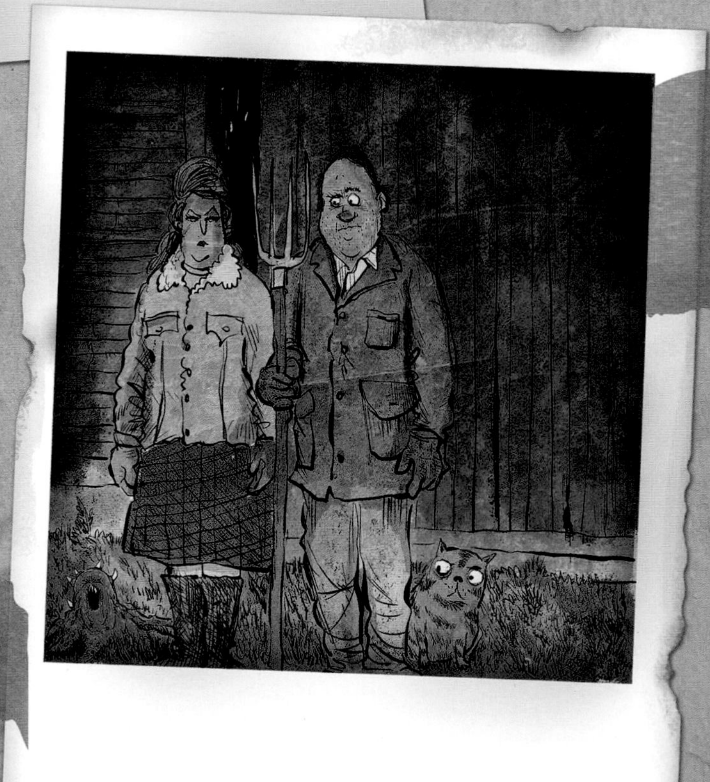

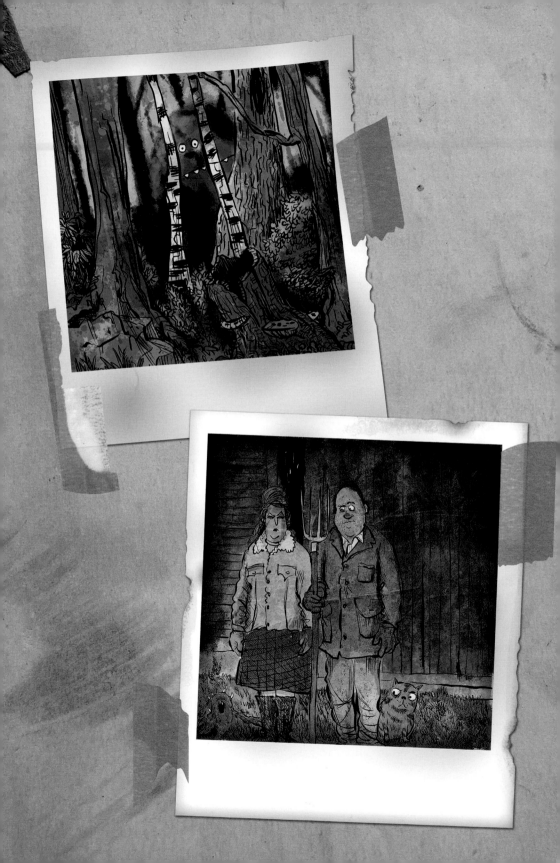